THE DROWNING

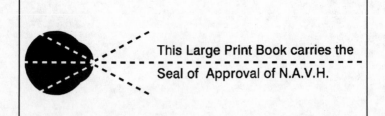

THE DROWNING

CAMILLA LÄCKBERG

Translated by Tiina Nunnally

THORNDIKE PRESS
A part of Gale, Cengage Learning

GALE
CENGAGE Learning·

Farmington Hills, Mich • San Francisco • New York • Waterville, Maine
Meriden, Conn • Mason, Ohio • Chicago

GALE
CENGAGE Learning

LIBRARY OF CONGRESS CATALOGING-IN-PUBLICATION DATA

Läckberg, Camilla, 1974-
 [Sjöjungfrun. English]
 The drowning / by Camilla Läckberg ; translated by Tiina Nunnally. — Large print edition.
  pages cm. — (Thorndike Press large print thriller)
  ISBN 978-1-4104-8469-7 (hardcover) — ISBN 1-4104-8469-6 (hardcover)
  1. Large type books. I. Nunnally, Tiina, 1952- II. Title.
PT9877.22.A34S5813 2015
839.73'8—dc23   2015029734

Published in 2015 by arrangement with Pegasus Books LLC

Printed in Mexico
1 2 3 4 5 6 7 19 18 17 16 15

THE DROWNING

He had known that sooner or later it would come to light again. Something like that was impossible to hide. Every word had led him closer to what was unnameable and appalling. What he had been trying for so many years to repress.

Now escape was no longer an option. He felt the morning air fill his lungs as he walked as fast as he could. His heart was pounding in his chest. He didn't want to go there, but he had to. So he had chosen to let fate decide. If someone was there, he would have to speak. If nobody was there, he would continue on his way to work as if nothing had happened.

But the door opened when he knocked. He stepped inside and squinted in the dim light. The person standing in front of him was not the one he had expected to see. It was somebody else.

Her long hair swung rhythmically from

side to side as he followed her into the next room. He started talking, asking questions. His thoughts were whirling around and around in his head. Nothing was what it appeared to be. This was all wrong, and yet it seemed right.

Suddenly he fell silent. Something had struck him in the solar plexus with a force that stopped his words in mid-sentence. He looked down and saw blood starting to seep out as the knife was pulled from the wound. Then a new stab, more pain, and the sharp blade twisting inside his body.

He knew it was over. It would all end here, even though there was still so much he had left to do and see and experience. At the same time, there was a kind of justice in what was happening. He hadn't deserved the good life he'd enjoyed, or all the love he'd been given. Not after what he had done.

After the pain had numbed his senses and the knife stopped moving, the water came. The rocking motion of a boat. And when he was enveloped by the cold sea, all other sensations ceased.

The last thing he remembered was her hair. Long, and dark.

1

"But it's been three months! Why haven't you found him?"

Patrik Hedström gazed at the woman in front of him. She looked more exhausted every time he saw her. And she came into the police station in Tanumshede once a week. Every Wednesday. She'd been doing this ever since her husband disappeared in early November.

"We're doing everything we can, Cia. You know that."

She nodded without saying a word. Her hands were trembling as she held them clasped in her lap. Then she looked at him, her eyes filled with tears. It wasn't the first time Patrik had seen this happen.

"He's not coming back, is he?"

Now her voice was trembling as well as her hands, and Patrik had to resist the urge to go around his desk and give the fragile woman a comforting hug. Somehow, even though it went against all his protective instincts, he remained cool and professional, considering how to respond. Finally he took a deep breath and said:

"No, I don't think he is."

She didn't ask any more questions, but he could see that his words had only reinforced what Cia Kjellner already knew. Her husband was never coming home. On the third of November, Magnus had gotten up at six thirty, showered, dressed, waved good-bye first to his two children and then to his wife as they left for the day. Just after eight o'clock, Magnus was seen leaving the house on the way to Tanum Windows, his place of work. After that, nobody knew where he had gone. He had never showed up at the house of his colleague, who was supposed to give him a ride to the office. Somewhere between his own home in the neighborhood near the sports pitch and his colleague's house by the Fjällbacka miniature golf course, Magnus Kjellner had vanished.

The police had examined every aspect of his life. They had put out an APB and spoken with more than fifty people, including co-workers, family members, and friends. They had searched for debts that might have compelled him to flee, and for secret lovers. They investigated the possibility that he might have embezzled money from his employer — anything that might explain why a respectable man of forty with a wife and two teenaged kids would suddenly just leave the house and disappear. But the police hadn't found a single lead. There was nothing to indicate that he had traveled abroad, nor had any money been withdrawn from the couple's joint bank account. Magnus Kjellner had simply vanished without a trace.

After Patrik had shown Cia out, he knocked cautiously on Paula Morales's door. "Come in," she said at once. He stepped inside, closing the door behind him.

"Was it his wife again?"

"Yes," said Patrik with a sigh, sitting down on the visitor's chair. He put his feet up on the desk, but after a fierce look from Paula he quickly took them down.

"Do you think he's dead?"

"I'm afraid so," said Patrik, for the first time voicing the suspicion he had felt ever since Magnus went missing. "We've checked out everything, and the guy had none of the usual reasons for disappearing. It seems he just left home one day and then . . . he was gone."

"But no body has been found."

"No, there's no body," said Patrik. "And

where are we supposed to look? We can't drag the whole sea or search all the woods around Fjällbacka. All we can do is twiddle our thumbs and hope that someone finds him. Either dead or alive. Because I have no idea what else to do. And I don't know what to say when Cia shows up here each week, expecting us to have made some sort of progress in the case."

"That's just her way of dealing with the situation. It makes her feel like she's doing something instead of simply sitting at home waiting for news. I know that would drive me crazy." Paula glanced at the photograph she kept next to her computer.

"I understand that," said Patrik. "But it doesn't make things any easier."

"No, of course not."

For a few moments silence descended over the cramped office. At last Patrik stood up. "We'll just have to hope that he turns up. One way or another."

"I suppose you're right," said Paula. But she sounded just as dejected as Patrik.

2

"What a fatty."

"You should talk!" Anna pointed at Erica's belly as she stared at her sister in the mirror.

Erica Falck turned so that she stood in profile, just like Anna, and she had to agree. Good God, she was huge. She looked like a gigantic belly with a tiny Erica stuck onto it, just for the sake of appearances. And that was exactly how she felt. By comparison, her body had been a miracle of suppleness when she was pregnant with Maja. But this time she was carrying two babies.

"I'm really not the least bit envious of you," Anna said with the brutal honesty of a younger sister.

"Thanks a lot," said Erica, bumping her with her belly. Anna bumped her in return, and both of them almost lost their balance. For a moment they stood flailing their arms in the air in an effort to stay on their feet, but then they started laughing so hard that they had to sit down on the floor.

"What a joke!" said Erica, wiping tears from her eyes. "Nobody should look like this. I'm a cross between Barbapapa and the man in the Monty Python film who explodes when he eats a wafer-thin mint."

"Well, I'm eternally grateful that you're having twins. Thanks to you, I feel like a slender nymph in comparison."

"You're welcome," replied Erica, making a move to get up. But nothing came of her efforts.

"Wait, I'll help you," said Anna, but she too lost the battle with gravity and ended up on her backside again. They both had the same thought as they looked at each other. And then they yelled in unison: "Dan!"

"What is it?" they heard from downstairs.

"We can't get up!" Anna called.

"What'd you say?"

They heard him coming up the stairs toward the bedroom where they were sitting on the floor.

"What on earth are you two doing?" Dan said with amusement when he caught sight of his fiancée Anna and her sister sitting on the floor in front of the full-length mirror.

"We can't get up," said Erica with as much

14

dignity as she could muster, reaching out her hand.

"Hold on; I'll go get the forklift," said Dan, pretending to head back downstairs.

"Cut that out," said Erica, as Anna laughed so hard she had to lie down.

"Okay, I'll give it a try." Dan took hold of Erica's hand and began to pull her up. "Erggggg!" he groaned.

"Skip the sound effects, if you don't mind," Erica told him as she slowly got to her feet.

"Damn, you're huge," exclaimed Dan, and Erica punched him in the arm.

"You've said that at least a hundred times, and you're not the only one. Why don't you stop staring at me and focus on your own little chub-ette instead?"

"Okay. Sure." Dan now pulled Anna to her feet, and then gave her a big kiss on the lips.

"You guys should get a room if you're going to do that," said Erica, poking Dan in the side.

"This *is* our room," said Dan, kissing Anna again.

"Okay. Then let's concentrate on the reason I'm here," said Erica, going over to her sister's wardrobe.

"I don't know why you think I can help

you," said Anna, waddling after Erica. "I can't imagine that I have anything that'll fit you."

"So what am I supposed to do, then?" Erica was looking through the clothes on the hangers. "Christian's book launch is tonight, and the only thing I can fit into is Maja's wigwam."

"Okay, we'll work something out. The trousers you have on look fine, and I think I have a shirt that might fit you. It's a little too big for me, at any rate."

Anna reached for an embroidered lavender tunic hanging in the wardrobe. Erica took off her T-shirt and pulled the tunic over her head with Anna's help. Getting it down over her belly was like stuffing a Christmas sausage, but she managed it. Then she turned toward the mirror and stared at herself with a critical expression.

"You look fantastic," Anna said, and Erica grunted in response. With her present figure, "fantastic" sounded way beyond reach, but at least she looked decent and as if she'd made an effort.

"It'll do," she said. She tried to take the tunic off by herself, but had to give up and let Anna help her.

"Where's the party?" Anna asked as she smoothed out the tunic and put it back on the hanger.

"At the Grand Hotel."

"Nice of the publisher to throw a launch party for a first-time author," said Anna, heading for the stairs.

"The company is really enthusiastic about the book. And the advance orders are incredibly good for a first novel, so they're more than happy to host a party. There seems to be plenty of support from the press as well, according to what I've heard from the publisher."

"So what do you think of the book? I assume you like it, or else you wouldn't have recommended it to your publisher. But how good is it?"

"It's. . . ." Erica pondered what to say about the book as she cautiously made her way down the stairs, following her sister. "It's magical. Dark and beautiful, disturbing and powerful and . . . well, magical is the best word I can think of to describe it."

"Christian must be over the moon."

"Yes, I suppose he is." Erica sounded a bit doubtful as she went into the kitchen. Knowing where everything was, she went straight for the coffee-maker. "At the same time, he seems. . . ." She stopped talking so she wouldn't lose count as she spooned coffee into the filter. "He was ecstatic when his

17

book was accepted for publication, but I get the feeling the writing process has stirred up something for him. It's hard to say, because I don't really know him that well. I'm not sure why he asked me for advice, but I was happy to help. And I do have a lot of experience when it comes to editing manuscripts, even though I don't write novels. At first everything went smoothly, and Christian seemed open to all my suggestions. But toward the end he would sometimes withdraw when I wanted to discuss certain issues. I can't really explain it. But he *is* a bit eccentric. Maybe that's all there is to it."

"Then I suppose he found the right profession," said Anna solemnly.

Erica turned to face her. "So now I'm not only fat but eccentric too?"

"And don't forget absent-minded." Anna nodded toward the coffee-maker that Erica had just turned on. "It helps if you put water in it first."

The coffee-maker puffed in agreement, and with a stern look at her sister Erica shut it off.

Moving as if on automatic, she took care of all the usual household chores. She put the dishes in the dishwasher after rinsing off the plates and cutlery. She cleaned the food scraps out of the drain with her hand and scrubbed the sink with the dish brush and soap. Then she wet the dishcloth, wrung it out, and wiped the kitchen table to remove any remaining crumbs and sticky spots.

"Mama, can I go over to Sandra's?" Elin asked as she came into the kitchen. The defiant look on the fifteen-year-old's face showed that she was resigned in advance to hearing a negative response.

"You know you can't do that. Grandpa and Grandma are coming over tonight."

"But they come over so often. Why do I have to be here every time?" Elin's voice rose, taking on the whiny tone that Cia couldn't stand.

"You and Ludvig are who they want to see. You know they'd be disappointed if you weren't here."

"But it's so boring! And Grandma always starts crying, and then Grandpa tells her to stop. I want to go over to Sandra's house. All my friends are going to be there."

"Now you're exaggerating," said Cia, rinsing out the dishcloth and hanging it over the tap. "I doubt they'll 'all' be there. You can go to Sandra's some other night, when Grandma and Grandpa aren't coming to visit."

"Papa would've let me go."

Cia's lungs seemed to constrict. She couldn't do this. She couldn't handle the anger and defiance right now. Magnus would have known how to deal with things. He would have handled the situation with Elin. But she couldn't do it. Not by herself.

"Papa isn't here now."

"So where is he?" Elin shrieked, and the tears began to flow. "Where did he go? He probably just got tired of you and your nagging. You . . . you . . . bitch!"

Utter silence settled over Cia's mind. It was as if all sound vanished and everything around her was transformed into a gray fog.

"He's dead." Cia's voice sounded like it was coming from somewhere else, as if a stranger were speaking.

Elin stared at her.

"He's dead," Cia said again. She felt strangely calm, as if she were hovering above herself and her daughter, peacefully observing the scene.

"You're lying," Elin said, her chest heaving as if she had run several miles.

"I'm not lying. That's what the police think. And I know it's true." When she heard herself say the words, she realized how true the statement was. She had refused to believe it, clinging to a faint hope. But the truth was that Magnus was dead.

"How do you know that? How do the police know?"

"He wouldn't just leave us."

Elin shook her head as if to prevent the idea from taking hold. But Cia saw that her daughter knew it too. Magnus would never simply up and leave them.

She took a few steps across the kitchen floor and put her arms around her daughter. Elin stiffened, but then relaxed and allowed herself to be embraced, as if she were a little child. Cia stroked Elin's hair as the girl sobbed harder.

"Hush now," Cia whispered, feeling her own strength grow as her daughter surrendered to grief. "You can go to Sandra's this evening. I'll explain to Grandma and Grandpa."

Christian Thydell looked at himself in the mirror. Sometimes he really didn't know how to relate to his own appearance. He was forty years old. Somehow the years had raced by, and he found himself gazing at a man who was not only grown up but who had even begun to go gray at the temples.

"How distinguished you look."

Christian jumped as Sanna appeared

behind him and put her arms around his waist.

"You scared me. Don't sneak up on me like that." He extricated himself from her embrace and caught a glimpse of her disappointed expression in the mirror before he turned around.

"Sorry." She sat down on the bed.

"You look lovely too," he said, and felt even guiltier when he saw how the compliment made her eyes light up. But he also felt annoyed. He hated it when she acted like a little puppy wagging its tail at the slightest attention from its master. His wife was ten years younger, but sometimes it felt as if there were at least twenty years between them.

"Could you help me with my tie?" He went over to Sanna, who got up and knotted it expertly. It was perfect on the first try, and she took a step back to inspect her work.

"You're going to be a big hit tonight."

"Mmm. . . ." he said, mostly because he didn't know what she expected him to say.

"Mama! Nils hit me!" Melker dashed into the room as if a pack of wolves were after him. Looking for refuge, he wrapped his sticky fingers around the first things within reach: Christian's legs.

"Damn!" Christian brusquely shook off his five-year-old son, but it was too late. Both trouser legs now had bright splotches of ketchup around the knees. He struggled to keep his temper — something that was proving more and more difficult lately.

"Can't you keep the kids in line?" he snapped, demonstratively unbuttoning his suit trousers so he could change.

"I'm sure I can clean that off," said Sanna as she grabbed for Melker, who was on his way toward the bed with his sticky fingers.

"And how do you expect to do that, when I have to be there in an hour? I'll just have to change."

"But I think I can. . . ." Sanna sounded on the verge of tears.

"Look after the kids instead."

Sanna flinched at every word, as if he had struck her. Without replying, she took Melker by the arm and hustled him out of the room.

After she left, Christian sat down heavily on the bed. He glanced at himself in the mirror. A tight-lipped man. Dressed in a suit jacket, shirt, tie, and underwear. Hunched over as if all the troubles of the world were resting on his shoulders. He tried straightening up and puffing out his chest. He looked better already.

This was his night. And nobody could take it away from him.

"Anything new?" asked Gösta Flygare as he held up the coffeepot toward Patrik, who had just stepped into the police station's little kitchen.

Patrik nodded that he'd like some coffee and sank down onto a chair at the table. Ernst the dog, hearing that they were taking a break, came plodding into the room and lay down under the table in the hope that some morsel would be dropped on the floor for him to lick up.

"Here you go." Gösta placed a cup of black coffee in front of Patrik and then sat down across from him.

"You're looking a bit pale around the gills," said Gösta, studying his younger colleague.

Patrik shrugged. "Just a bit tired. Maja isn't sleeping well, and that makes her cranky. And Erica is totally worn out. Understandably so. Which means things haven't exactly been easy on the home front."

"And it's only going to get worse," said Gösta.

Patrik laughed. "Wow, that's encouraging. But you're right, it probably will."

"So you haven't come up with anything new on Magnus Kjellner?" Gösta discreetly sneaked a cookie under the table, and Ernst happily thumped his tail against Patrik's feet.

"No, not a thing," said Patrik, taking a sip of coffee.

"I saw that Cia was here again."

"Yes, it's like some sort of obsessive ritual — but I suppose that's not surprising. How is a woman supposed to act when her husband suddenly vanishes?"

"Maybe we should interview some more people," said Gösta, sneaking another cookie under the table for Ernst.

"Who do you have in mind?" Patrik could hear how annoyed he sounded. "We've talked to his family and his friends. We've knocked on doors throughout the neighborhood, and we've put up notices and appealed for information via the local paper. What else can we do?"

"It's not like you to give up so easily."

"Well, if you've got any suggestions, I'd like to hear them." Patrik immediately regretted his brusque tone of voice, even though Gösta didn't seem to take offense. "It sounds terrible to hope that the man will turn up dead," he added in a calmer manner. "But I'm convinced that only then

25

will we work out what happened to him. I'll bet you he didn't disappear voluntarily, and if we had a body then at least there'd be something to go on."

"I think you're right. It's horrible to think that his body will float ashore somewhere or be discovered in the woods. But I have the same feeling you do. And it must be awful. . . ."

"Not to know, you mean?" said Patrik, shifting his feet, which were getting hot underneath the heavy weight of the dog.

"Well, just imagine not knowing where the person you love has gone. It's the same thing for parents when a child goes missing. There's an American website devoted to kids who have disappeared. Page after page of pictures of missing kids. All I can say is Jesus H. Christ."

"Something like that would kill me," said Patrik. He pictured his whirlwind of a daughter. The thought of her being taken from him was unbearable.

"What on earth are you guys talking about? The atmosphere in here is positively funereal." Annika's cheerful voice broke the dismal mood as she joined them at the table. The station's youngest member, Martin Molin, came in right behind her, lured by all the voices coming from the kitchen and the smell of coffee. He was working only part-time now, since he was on paternity leave, and he seized every possible opportunity to hang out with his colleagues and take part in adult conversations.

"We were discussing Magnus Kjellner," said Patrik, his tone of voice making it clear that the conversation was over. To make sure the others understood, he changed the subject.

"How's it going with the little girl?"

"Oh, we got new pictures yesterday," said Annika, taking some photos out of the pocket of her tunic.

"Look how big she's getting." She put the pictures on the table, and Patrik and Gösta took turns looking at them. Martin had already been given a preview when he arrived that morning.

"Ah, she's so pretty," said Patrik.

Annika nodded in agreement. "She's ten months old now."

"When do you two get to go there to collect her?" Gösta asked with genuine interest. He was fully aware that he had played a part in persuading Annika and Lennart to seriously consider adoption, so he took a slightly proprietary interest in the little girl in the photographs.

"Well, we're getting some mixed messages," Annika told him. She gathered up the pictures and put them carefully back in her pocket. "But in a couple of months, I should think."

"It must seem like a long wait." Patrik got up and put his cup in the dishwasher.

"Yes, it does. But at the same time . . . at least the process has been started. And we know that she'll be ours."

"Yes, she certainly will," said Gösta. On impulse he put his hand on Annika's and then snatched it away. "Right, back to work. Haven't got time to sit around here chatting," he muttered in embarrassment, getting to his feet.

His three colleagues looked at him in amusement as he slouched out of the kitchen.

"Christian!" The publishing director, reeking of perfume, came over to give him a big hug.

Christian held his breath so he wouldn't have to inhale the cloying scent. Gaby von Rosen was not known for subtlety. Everything was always excessive when it came to Gaby: too much hair, too much makeup, too much perfume, all combined with a fashion sense that, putting it politely, could best be described as startling. This evening,

28

in honor of the occasion, she wore a shocking pink ensemble with a green cloth rose
on the lapel, and teetered on dangerously
high stilettos. But despite her slightly
ridiculous appearance, as the head of Sweden's hot new publishing house was a force
to be reckoned with. She had over thirty
years' experience in the field and an intel-
lect as acute as her tongue was sharp. Those
who underestimated her as a competitor
never made the same mistake twice.

"This is going to be such fun!" Gaby held
Christian at arm's length as she beamed at
him.

Christian, still struggling to breathe in the
cloud of perfume, could only nod.

"Lars-Erik and Ulla-Lena here at the
hotel have been simply fantastic," she went
on. "What delightful people! And the buffet
looks wonderful. This feels like the perfect
venue to launch your brilliant book. So how
does it feel?"

Christian finally managed to extricate
himself and took a step back.

"Well, a little unreal, I have to admit. I've
been working on this novel for so long, and
now . . . well, now here it is." He glanced at
the stacks of books on the table by the exit.
He could read his own name on the spine
of each copy, along with the title: *The Mer-*

maid. He felt his stomach flip. It was really happening.

"So this is what we have in mind," Gaby said, tugging at his sleeve and pulling him along. Christian followed, offering no resistance. "We'll start by meeting with the journalists who are here, so they can talk to you in peace and quiet. We're very pleased with the media response. Journalists from *Göteborgs Posten, Göteborgs Tidningen, Bohusläningen,* and *Strömstads Tidning* — they're all here. None from the national newspapers, but that's all right, considering today's rave review in *Svenska Dagbladet.*"

"A review?" asked Christian as he was escorted to a small dais next to the stage where he would talk to the press.

"I'll tell you later," said Gaby, pushing him down onto a chair next to the wall.

He tried to regain some control of the situation, but he felt as if he'd been sucked into a tumble-dryer with no possibility of escape. The sight of Gaby already on her way out, leaving him behind, merely reinforced that feeling. Assistants were dashing about, setting the tables. Nobody paid any attention to him. He permitted himself to close his eyes for a moment. He thought about his book, *The Mermaid,* and all the hours he'd spent sitting at the computer.

Hundreds, thousands of hours. He thought about her, about the Mermaid.

"Christian Thydell?"

A voice roused him from his reverie, and he looked up. The man standing before him was holding his hand out and seemed to be waiting for him to respond. So he stood up and shook hands.

"Birger Jansson, *Strömstads Tidning.*" The man set a big camera bag on the floor.

"Oh, er, welcome. Please have a seat," said Christian, not sure how to act. He looked around for Gaby but caught only a glimpse of her shocking pink outfit, fluttering about near the entrance.

"They're really putting a lot of PR behind your book," said Jansson, looking around.

"Yes, it seems so," said Christian. Then both of them fell silent and fidgeted a bit.

"Shall we get started? Or should we wait for the others?"

Christian gave the reporter a blank look. How should he know? He'd never done anything like this before. But Jansson seemed to take the whole situation in his stride as he placed a tape recorder on the table and switched it on.

"So," he said, fixing Christian with a penetrating gaze. "This is your first novel, right?"

Christian wondered whether he was supposed to do more than confirm this statement. "Yes, it is," he said, clearing his throat.

"I liked it a lot," said Jansson in a gruff tone of voice that belied the compliment.

"Thank you," said Christian.

"What did you intend to say with this novel?" Jansson checked the tape recorder to make sure it was recording properly.

"What did I intend to say? I don't really know. It's a novel, a story that I've had in the back of my mind and that needed to come out."

"It's an awfully dark story. I'd almost call it bleak," said Jansson, studying Christian as if trying to peer inside the deepest recesses of his soul. "Is this how you view society?"

"I don't know if it's my view of society that I was trying to communicate through the book," said Christian, searching frantically for something intelligent to say. He'd never thought of his writing in this way before. The story had been part of him for so long, inside his head, and finally he'd felt compelled to put it down on paper. But did it have anything to do with what he wanted to say about society? The thought had never even occurred to him.

Finally Gaby came to his rescue, arriving

with the other reporters in tow, and Jansson turned off his tape recorder as they all greeted one another and sat down around the table. The whole process took several minutes, and Christian used the opportunity to gather his thoughts.

Gaby then motioned for everyone's attention.

"Welcome to this gathering in honor of the new superstar in the literary firmament, Christian Thydell. All of us at the publishing company are incredibly proud of producing his first novel, *The Mermaid*. And we think this marks the beginning of a long and amazing writing career. Christian hasn't yet seen any of the reviews. So it's with great joy that I can tell you, Christian, that today there were fantastic reviews in *Svenska Dagbladet*, *Dagens Nyheter*, and *Arbetarbladet*, just to name a few. Let me read a few quotes to all of you."

She put on her reading glasses and reached for a stack of papers lying in front of her on the table. A pink highlighter had been used to mark phrases against the white newsprint.

" 'A linguistically virtuoso performance depicting the plight of ordinary people without losing sight of the larger perspective.' That was from *Svenska Dag-*

bladet," Gaby explained with a nod to Christian. Then she turned to the next review. " 'It's both pleasant and painful to read Christian Thydell's book, since his pared-down prose shines light on society's false promises of security and democracy. His words cut like a knife through flesh, muscle, and conscience, which kept me reading with feverish urgency and seeking, like a fakir, more of the torturous but wonderfully cleansing pain.' That's from *Dagens Nyheter,*" said Gaby, taking off her glasses as she handed the small stack of reviews to Christian.

In stunned disbelief, he took the reviews. He'd heard the words, and it felt good to be showered with praise, but he honestly didn't understand what the critics were talking about. All he'd done was write about her, told her story. Let out the words and everything about her in an outpouring that had occasionally left him completely drained. It wasn't his intention to say anything about society. He just wanted to say something about her.

But he bit back the protests. No one would understand, and maybe it was better just to let things be. He'd never be able to explain.

"How marvelous," he said, hearing how

the words fell meaninglessly from his lips.

Then came more questions. More praise and comments about his book. And he realized that he couldn't give a sensible answer to a single question. How could he describe something that had filled the smallest corners of his life? Something that wasn't merely a story — it was also about survival. About pain. He did the best he could, trying to speak clearly and thoughtfully. Apparently he succeeded, because Gaby kept nodding her approval.

When the interview session was finally over, all Christian wanted to do was go home. He felt totally drained. But he was forced to linger on in the beautiful dining room of the Grand Hotel. He took a deep breath and prepared himself to meet the guests who had started to stream in. He smiled, but it was a smile that cost him more effort than anyone would ever know.

"Could you manage to stay sober tonight?" Erik Lind quietly snapped at his wife so that the others waiting in the queue to get into the party wouldn't hear him.

"Could you manage to keep your hands to yourself tonight?" Louise replied, not bothering to whisper.

"I don't know what you're talking about,"

said Erik. "And lower your voice, please."

Louise eyed her husband coldly. He was an elegant man — that much she couldn't deny. And once upon a time, that had attracted her. They'd met at the university, and plenty of girls had looked at her with envy because she'd nabbed Erik Lind. Since then, he had slowly but surely fucked away any love, respect, or trust she'd ever felt for him. Not with her. God, no. On the other hand, he didn't seem to have any problem finding willing lovers outside of the marriage bed.

"Hi, there! You're here too? How nice!" Cecilia Jansdotter made her way over to them and gave them both the obligatory kiss on the cheek. She was Louise's hairdresser, and she and Erik had also been lovers for the past year. But of course they didn't think Louise knew about that.

"Hi, Cecilia," said Louise with a smile. She was a sweet girl, and if Louise had held a grudge against everyone who had slept with her husband, she wouldn't have been able to carry on living in Fjällbacka. Besides, she'd stopped caring years ago. She had the girls. And that wonderful invention: wine in a box. What did she need Erik for?

"It's so exciting that we have another author here in Fjällbacka! First Erica Falck, and now Christian." Cecilia was practically jumping up and down. "Have either of you read his book?"

"I only read business journals," said Erik.

Louise rolled her eyes. How typical of Erik to flirt by saying that he never read books.

"I'm hoping that we'll get to take a copy home with us," she said, drawing her coat tighter around her. She hoped the queue would move a little faster so they could get inside where it was warm.

"Yes, Louise is the big reader in the family. But then, what else is there to do when you don't have to work? Right, sweetheart?"

Louise shrugged, letting the spiteful remark roll right off her. It wouldn't do any good to point out that it was Erik who had insisted that she stay home while the girls were young. Or that she slaved from morning to night to make sure that everything ran smoothly in the well-ordered home that he took for granted.

The small talk continued as they slowly moved forward. At last they were able to enter the lobby and hang up their coats before descending the stairs to the dining hall.

With Erik's eyes burning into her back, Louise headed straight for the bar.

■ ■ ■ ■

"Now, don't wear yourself out," Patrik told Erica, giving her a kiss before she swept out the door, her belly leading the way.

Maja whimpered a bit when she saw her mother disappear, but she stopped fussing as soon as Patrik set her down in front of the TV to watch *Bolibompa.* The show with the green dragon had just started. Maja had been much more fretful and difficult to handle during the past few months, and the fits of temper that followed whenever she was told "no" were enough to make any diva envious. Patrik could partly understand. She must feel the excited anticipation, combined with apprehension, regarding the arrival of her two siblings. Good lord. Twins. Even though they'd known from the very first ultrasound, done in Erica's eighteenth week, he still hadn't really been able to take in the news. Sometimes he wondered how they were going to manage. It had been hard enough with one baby; how were they going to cope with two? How would they handle the breastfeeding and trying to get some sleep, and everything else? And they needed to buy a new car that was big enough for three kids and their strollers. And that was just one of many matters to consider.

Patrik sat down on the sofa next to Maja and stared into space. He'd been so tired lately. It felt as though his energy was just ebbing away, and some mornings it was all he could do to haul himself out of bed. But maybe that wasn't so strange. In addition to everything going on at home, with Erica so worn out and Maja transformed into a tiny defiant monster, he was having a hard time at work. In the years since he'd met Erica, he and his colleagues had handled several difficult murder investigations; the grim nature of his work and the constant battle with his boss, Bertil Mellberg, was beginning to take its toll on Patrik.

And now they were dealing with Magnus Kjellner's disappearance. Patrik didn't know whether it was experience or instinct, but he was convinced that something had happened to the man. Whether he was the victim of an accident or foul play, it was impossible to say, but Patrik would bet his police badge that Kjellner was no longer alive. The fact that every Wednesday he had to meet with the man's wife, who looked smaller and shabbier each time, had really begun to wear on him. The police had done absolutely everything they could, but he still couldn't get the sight of Cia Kjellner's face out of his mind.

"Papa!" Maja roused him from his reveries, using vocal powers that were far stronger than she knew. She was pointing her finger at the TV, and he saw at once what had caused the crisis. He must have been lost in thought much longer than he realized, because *Bolibompa* was over, replaced by a show for grownups that didn't interest Maja in the least.

"Papa will fix it," he said, holding up his hands. "How about Pippi Longstocking?"

Since Pippi was currently the big favorite, Patrik knew what his daughter's answer would be. He got out the DVD, and when *Pippi in the South Seas* began to play, he sat down next to Maja again, putting his arm around her. Like a warm little animal, she snuggled happily into his armpit. Five minutes later, Patrik was asleep.

Christian was sweating profusely. Gaby had just told him that it would soon be time for him to go up on stage. The dining hall wasn't exactly packed, but about sixty guests with expectant expressions on their faces were seated at the tables, with plates of food and glasses of beer or wine in front of them. Christian himself hadn't been able to eat a thing, but he was drinking red wine.

He was now on his third glass, even though he knew that he shouldn't be drinking so much. It wouldn't be good if he ended up slurring his words into the microphone when he was interviewed. But without the wine, he wouldn't be able to function at all.

He was surveying the room when he felt a hand on his arm.

"Hi. How's it going? You look a little tense." Erica was peering at him with concern.

"I guess I'm just nervous," he admitted, finding consolation in telling someone about it.

"I know exactly how you feel," said Erica. "I made my first public appearance at an event for first-time authors in Stockholm, and they practically had to scrape me off the floor afterwards. And I can't remember a single thing I said when I was on stage."

"I have a feeling they're going to have to scrape me off the floor too," said Christian, touching his hand to his throat. For a second he thought about the letters, and then he was overwhelmed by panic. His knees buckled, and it was only thanks to the fact that Erica was holding on to him that he didn't fall on his face.

"Upsy-daisy," said Erica. "Looks like you've had a few stiff drinks. You probably shouldn't have any more before your appearance." She carefully removed the glass of red wine from Christian's hand and set it on the nearest table. "I promise you that everything will go just fine. Gaby will start off by introducing you and your novel. Then I'll ask you a few questions — and you and I have already discussed what they'll be. Trust me. The only problem is going to be hauling this body of mine up on stage."

She laughed, and Christian joined in. Not wholeheartedly, and he sounded a bit shrill, but the joke worked. Some of the tension eased out of him, and he could feel himself breathing again. He pushed all thought of the letters far away. He wasn't going to let that affect him tonight. The Mermaid had been given a voice through his book, and now he was done with her.

"Hi, honey." Sanna came over to join them, her eyes sparkling as she looked around the hall. Christian knew that this was a big moment for her. Maybe even bigger than for him.

"How lovely you look," he said, and she basked in the praise. She really did look lovely. He knew that he'd been lucky to meet her. She put up with a great deal from him, more than most people would have been willing to endure. It wasn't her fault that she couldn't fill the empty space inside of him. Probably nobody could. He put his arm around her and kissed her hair.

"How sweet you two are!" Gaby came striding over to them, her high heels clacking. "Someone has sent you flowers, Christian."

He stared at the bouquet she was holding. It was beautiful but simple, composed solely of white lilies.

With fingers that trembled uncontrollably, he reached for the white envelope fastened to the bouquet. He was shaking so much that he could hardly open it, and he was barely aware of the surprised glances from the women standing around him.

The card was also very simple. A plain white card of heavy stock, the message written in black ink, with the same elegant handwriting used in the letters. He stared at the words. And then everything went black before his eyes.

She was the most beautiful person he'd ever seen. She smelled so good, and her long hair was tied back with a white ribbon. It shone so brightly that he almost felt the need to squint. He took a tentative step toward her, uncertain whether he would be allowed to partake of all this beauty. She held out her arms to give him permission, and with quick steps he leaped into her embrace. Away from the blackness, away from the evil. Instead he was enveloped in whiteness, in light, in a floral scent and with silky soft hair against his cheek.

"Are you my mother now?" he asked at last, reluctantly taking a step back. She nodded. "Really?" He was waiting for someone to come in and, with some brusque remark, smash everything to pieces, telling him that he'd only been dreaming. And that someone this wonderful couldn't possibly be the mother of somebody like him.

But no voice spoke. Instead, she simply

44

nodded, and he couldn't help himself. He threw himself into her arms again and never, ever wanted to leave. Somewhere inside his head there were other pictures, other scents and sounds that wanted to surface, but they were drowned out by the floral perfume and the rustling of her dress. He pushed those images away. Forced them to disappear, to be replaced by all that was new and amazing. All that was unbelievable.

He looked up at his new mother, and his heart beat twice as fast with joy. When she took his hand and led him away from there, he went with her quite willingly.

3

"I heard that things took a rather dramatic turn last night. What was Christian thinking, getting drunk at an event like that?" Kenneth Bengtsson was late arriving at the office after a rough morning at home. He tossed his jacket on the sofa, but a disapproving glance from Erik made him pick it up again and hang it on a hook in the hall.

"You're right. It was undeniably a lamentable end to the evening," Erik replied. "On the other hand, Louise seemed determined to escape into an alcoholic haze, so at least I was spared that experience."

"Are things really that bad?" asked Kenneth, looking at Erik. It was rare for Erik to confide anything personal to him. That was how he'd always been. Both when they were kids, playing together, and now that they were adults. Erik treated Kenneth as if he barely tolerated him, as if he was doing the man a favor by deigning to spend time with him. If it hadn't been for the fact that Kenneth actually had something to offer Erik, their friendship would have been over long ago. That was exactly what had happened while Erik was studying at the university and working in Göteborg, while Kenneth had stayed in Fjällbacka and started up his small accounting firm, a company that, over the years, had become a very successful business.

Because Kenneth was, in fact, quite talented. He was aware that he wasn't particularly good-looking or charming, and he had no illusions about having more than average intelligence. But he did have a remarkable ability to work wonders when it came to numbers. He could juggle the sums in a profit-and-loss report or balance sheet as if he were the David Beckham of the accounting world. Combined with his ability to persuade the tax authorities to see his side of things, Kenneth had suddenly, and for the first time ever, become a highly valuable person for Erik. He was the natural choice when Erik needed an associate as he entered the construction market, which had lately become such a lucrative enterprise on the west coast of Sweden. Erik had, of course, made it very clear that Kenneth needed to know his place, since he owned only a third of the company and not half — although he really should have owned half, considering what he contributed to the firm. But that didn't matter. Kenneth wasn't interested in amassing wealth or power. He was content to work with the things he was good at, and to be Erik's associate.

"I really have no idea what to do about Louise," said Erik, getting up from behind his desk. "If it weren't for the children. . . ." He shook his head as he put on his coat.

Kenneth nodded sympathetically. He knew full well what the situation was. And it had nothing to do with the children. What was stopping Erik from divorcing Louise was the fact that she would then be entitled to half of their money and other assets.

"I'm going out for lunch, and I'll be gone for a while. A long lunch today."

"Okay," said Kenneth. A long lunch. Oh, right.

"Is he home?" Erica was standing on the porch of the Thydell home.

Sanna seemed to hesitate for a few seconds before stepping aside to let her in.

"He's upstairs. In his workroom. He's just sitting in front of the computer, staring."

"Is it all right if I go up to talk to him?"

Sanna nodded. "Sure. Nothing I say

seems to do any good. Maybe you'll have better luck."

There was a bitter tone to Sanna's voice, and Erica paused for a moment to study her. She looked tired. But there was something else that Erica couldn't quite put her finger on.

"Let me see what I can do." Slowly Erica made her way up the stairs, supporting her oversized belly with one hand. Lately, even such a simple task sapped her of all energy.

"Hi." She knocked gently on the open door, and Christian turned around. He was sitting in his desk chair, but the computer screen was blank. "You really gave us a scare last night," said Erica, sinking onto an armchair in the corner.

"Just a bit overworked, I guess," said Christian. But there were dark shadows under his eyes, and his hands were shaking. "Plus I've been worried about Magnus disappearing."

"Are you sure there's not some other reason?" Her voice sounded sharper than she'd intended. "I picked this up last night and brought it along." She reached into her jacket pocket and pulled out the note that had come with the bouquet of white lilies. "You must have dropped it."

Christian stared at the card.

"Put that away."

"What does the message mean?" Erica looked with concern at this man she had started to regard as a friend.

He didn't answer.

Erica repeated her question, this time a bit more gently: "Christian, what does it mean? Your reaction was awfully strong last night. So don't try to make me believe that you were just feeling overworked."

Still he said nothing. Suddenly the silence was broken by Sanna's voice from the doorway.

"Tell Erica about the letters," she said.

Sanna stayed where she was, waiting for her husband to respond. A few more minutes of silence ensued before Christian sighed, pulled out the bottom drawer of his desk, and took out a small bundle of letters.

"I've had these for a while."

Erica picked up the letters and cautiously leafed through the pages. White sheets of paper with black ink. And there was no doubt that the handwriting was the same as on the card she'd brought along. Some of the words were familiar too. The sentences were different, but the theme was the same. She began reading aloud from the letter on top:

"She walks at your side, she follows along

with you. You have no right to your life. It belongs to her."

Erica looked up in astonishment. "What's this all about? Do you understand any of this?"

"No." Christian's reply was swift and firm. "No, I have no clue. I don't know of anyone who would want to harm me. At least, I don't think so. And I have no idea who 'she' is. I should have thrown out those letters," he said, reaching for them. But Erica had no intention of relinquishing them.

"You should tell the police about this."

Christian shook his head. "No, it's probably just someone having fun at my expense."

"This doesn't sound like a joke to me. And I can see that you don't think it's especially funny, either."

"That's exactly what I said," Sanna interjected. "I think it's really creepy, especially since we have children and everything. What if there's some mentally disturbed person who. . . ." She stared at Christian, and Erica could tell that it wasn't the first time they'd had this conversation. But he stubbornly shook his head again.

"I don't want to make a big deal out of it."

"When exactly did this whole thing begin?"

"When you started writing the book," said Sanna, receiving a look of annoyance from her husband.

"I guess that's about right," he admitted. "A year and a half ago."

"Could there be some sort of connection? Did you put any real person or event in your book? Someone who might feel threatened because you wrote about them?" Erica kept her eyes fixed steadily on Christian, who was looking extremely uncomfortable. It was obvious that he had no desire to discuss this topic.

"No, it's a work of fiction," he said, grimacing. "No one should be able to recognize themselves in my story. You've read the manuscript. Does it seem autobiographical to you?"

"That's not something that I would be able to tell," said Erica with a shrug. "But I know from my own experience that writers weave parts of their own lives into their manuscripts, whether consciously or not."

"Well, I didn't!" exclaimed Christian, pushing back his chair and standing up.

Realizing that it was time for her to leave, Erica tried to get up from the armchair. But her heavy body resisted her efforts, and all she could manage were a few grunts. Christian's stern expression softened, and he reached out a helping hand.

"It's probably just some lunatic who heard that I was writing a book and started getting strange ideas about it. That's all," he said, sounding calmer.

Erica doubted that was the whole truth, but her opinion was based more on a gut feeling than any concrete evidence. As she walked toward her car, she hoped Christian hadn't noticed that there were now only five letters in his desk drawer instead of six. She didn't know what had made her take such a bold step, but if Christian wasn't going to tell her the truth, then she was just going to have to find out more on her own. The tone of the letters was clearly threatening, and she was worried that her friend might be in danger.

"Did you have to cancel any appointments?" Erik nibbled on Cecilia's nipple. She gasped as she stretched out on the bed in her apartment. The beauty salon that she owned was within easy reach on the ground floor of the building.

"You'd like that, wouldn't you? To hear that I had to cancel clients in order to make room for you in my calendar. What makes you think you're so important?"

"What could be more important than this?" He ran his tongue over her breast, and she pulled him down on top of her, unable to wait any longer.

Afterward, she lay next to him, her head resting on his arm. A few rough hairs tickled her cheek.

"It was a bit strange, running into Louise last night. And you."

"Mmmm," replied Erik, dozing. He had no wish to discuss his wife or his marriage with his mistress.

"I like Louise, you know," said Cecilia, playing with the hairs on his chest. "And if she knew. . . ."

"But she doesn't," Erik snapped, propping himself up on his elbows. "And she's never going to find out."

Cecilia looked up at him, and he knew from experience exactly how this discussion was going to proceed.

"Sooner or later she'll have to know."

Erik sighed to himself. Why did they always have to talk about the past and the future? He swung his legs over the side of the bed and began getting dressed.

"Do you have to leave already?" asked Cecilia. The hurt expression on her face annoyed him even more.

"I've got a lot of work to do," he said curtly, buttoning his shirt. He had the smell of sex in his nostrils, but he would take a shower at the office. He always kept a change of clothes there, for just such occasions.

"So this is the way it's going to be?" Cecilia was still lying on the bed, and Erik couldn't help staring at her naked body. Her breasts were pointing upward with big, dark nipples that were stiff from the cool temperature in the room. He made a quick calculation. He really didn't need to hurry back to the office, and he wouldn't mind having another go-around. It would take a bit of persuasion, so to speak, but the excitement that was already starting to build inside his body told him that it would be worth the effort. He sat down on the edge of the bed and softened his voice and expression as he caressed her cheek.

"Cecilia," he said, and then he went on to speak words that rolled as easily from his lips as they had so many times before. When she pressed her body against his, he could feel her breasts through his shirt. He reached up and began unfastening the buttons.

After a late lunch at Källaren restaurant,

Patrik parked his car in front of the low, white building, which would never win any sort of architectural prize, and entered the reception area of the Tanumshede police station.

"You've got a visitor," Annika told him, peering over her reading glasses.

"Who is it?"

"I can't say, but she's a real looker. Maybe a bit on the plump side, but I think you're going to like her."

"What on earth are you talking about?" said Patrik, bewildered. He wondered why Annika suddenly seemed to have taken on the role of pimp for happily married colleagues.

"You'll just have to go and see for yourself. She's waiting in your office," said Annika, giving him a wink.

Patrik went to his office and came to a halt in the doorway.

"Hi, sweetheart," he said. "What are you doing here?"

Erica was sitting in the visitor's chair in front of his desk, paging absentmindedly through an issue of the journal *Police.*

"You're certainly late getting back from lunch," she said, ignoring his question. "Is this what a busy day at police headquarters is like?"

Patrik merely snorted. He knew that Erica loved to tease him.

"So, what are you doing here?" he asked, sitting down in his desk chair. He leaned forward to study his wife more closely. Again he saw how beautiful she was. He thought about the first time she had visited him at the police station six years earlier, in connection with the murder of her friend Alexandra Wijkner, and it seemed to him that she'd grown even lovelier since then. It was something that he occasionally forgot, caught up as he was in daily routines. One day followed another, filled with work, dropping Maja off at the day-care center and then picking her up again, grocery shopping, and weary evenings spent on the sofa watching TV. But occasionally he was struck by how far from ordinary his love for Erica was. And now that she was sitting right here in front of him, with the winter sun shining through the window and lighting up her blond hair, and with those two babies inside her belly, the love he felt for her was so strong that it was enough to last an entire lifetime.

Patrik suddenly realized that he hadn't heard what Erica said, so he asked her to repeat it.

"I was just saying that I went over to see

Christian this morning and have a talk with him."

"How's he doing?"

"He seemed okay, just a little shaky. But. . . ." She bit her lip.

"But what? I thought he simply had a little too much to drink, on top of being nervous."

"Hmmm. Well, I don't think that's all of it." Erica took a plastic bag out of her purse and handed it to Patrik. "Last night, that card was attached to a bouquet of flowers that was sent to him. And the letter is one of six that he's received, starting about a year and a half ago."

Patrik gave his wife a long look as he opened the bag.

"I think it would be best if you read them without taking them out of the plastic. Christian and I have already touched them, but we don't need to add any more fingerprints."

Patrik looked at her again but did as she asked and read the text of the card and letter through the plastic.

"What do you think it means?" asked Erica, scooting forward to sit on the edge of her chair. But when it almost tipped over, she quickly had to redistribute her weight by moving back again.

"Well, they both sound like threats, although they're not very specific."

"Yes, that's what I thought too. And that's definitely Christian's opinion, even though he kept trying to downplay the whole thing. He's refused to show the letters to the police."

"Then how did . . . ?" Patrik held up the plastic bag.

"Oh, er, I guess I just happened to take them by mistake. How silly of me." She tilted her head to one side and turned on the charm, but her husband wasn't so easily fooled.

"So you stole these from Christian?"

"I don't know if I'd use the word 'stole.' I just borrowed them for a while."

"And what exactly do you want me to do about these . . . borrowed materials?" asked Patrik, even though he knew full well what her answer would be.

"Somebody is clearly threatening Christian, and he's scared. I could tell when I saw him today. He's taking these threats very seriously, so I don't know why he won't go to the police. But maybe you could discreetly examine the card and letter to see if you can find anything useful?" Erica was using her most entreating tone of voice, and Patrik already knew that he would give in. Whenever she was in this sort of mood, it was impossible to deal with her, which was something he had learned the hard way.

"Okay, okay," he said, holding his hands in the air. "I surrender. I'll see if we can find out anything. But it's not high on my list of priorities."

Erica smiled. "Thanks, sweetheart."

"Now go on home and get some rest," said Patrik, but he couldn't resist leaning forward to give her a kiss.

After she left, he found himself plucking aimlessly at the plastic bag holding the threatening messages. His brain felt sluggish and obstinate, but something was nonetheless starting to stir inside. Christian and Magnus were friends. Could there be . . . ? Patrik immediately pushed the thought aside, but it kept coming back, and he glanced up at the photograph that was taped to the wall in front of him. Could there be a connection?

Bertil Mellberg pushed the pram as Leo sat inside, happy and contented as usual, and occasionally smiling to show the two lower teeth that had recently come in. Ernst had been left behind at the station today. Otherwise the dog usually walked beside the pram, making sure that nothing threatened what was fast becoming the most important person in his world. For Mellberg, Leo was already the center of his universe.

Mellberg had never known that it was possible to have such strong feelings for anyone. Ever since he had been present at the baby's birth and then been the first to hold the infant, he had felt as if Leo had his heart in an iron grip. It was true that Mellberg also felt great affection for Leo's grandmother, but the tiny tyke was at the very top of the list of people who meant the most to Mellberg.

Reluctantly Mellberg steered the pram back toward the station. His colleague Paula was actually supposed to have taken care of Leo during lunch while her partner, Johanna, tended to some errands. But when Paula had to leave on a domestic violence call, to help a woman whose ex-husband was "beating the shit out of her," Mellberg had quickly stepped in and volunteered to take the baby out for a walk. Now it was time to take him back. Mellberg was deeply jealous of Paula, who would soon be taking maternity leave. He wouldn't have minded cutting back his own hours for a while so he could have more time to spend with Leo. In fact, that might not be such a bad idea. As a good boss, he should give his subordinates a chance to take more training courses. Besides, Leo needed a strong male role model right from the start. With two mothers and no father in sight, they should think about what would be best for the boy and see to it that he was given the opportunity to learn from a solid, real man. Like himself, for example.

Mellberg used his hip to prop open the heavy front door of the station and pulled the pram inside. Annika's face lit up when she saw them, and Mellberg swelled with pride.

"So I see the two of you have been out for a little walk," said Annika, getting up to help Mellberg with the pram.

"Yes, the girls needed some help with him," said Mellberg, as he carefully began removing the baby's outer garments. Annika watched with amusement. Apparently the age of miracles wasn't over.

"Come on, sonny, let's go see if your mother is here," prattled Mellberg as he lifted Leo out of the pram.

"No, Paula's not back yet," said Annika, sitting down at her desk again.

"Oh, what a shame. Looks like you're stuck with your old grandpa a little while longer," said Mellberg, sounding pleased as he headed for the kitchen, carrying Leo in his arms. When he had moved in with Rita a couple of months ago, the girls had suggested that he be called Grandpa Bertil. So now he seized every opportunity to use the name that gave him such joy. Grandpa Bertil.

It was Ludvig's birthday, and Cia was trying to pretend that it was a completely ordinary birthday. He was thirteen. That was how many years it had been since she had given birth in the maternity ward and laughed at how ridiculously similar father and son were in appearance. But now it meant that deep down inside, she had to admit that she was having a hard time even looking at Ludvig. At his brown eyes with the touch of green in them and at his blond hair, which the sun, even in early summer, had bleached almost white. Ludvig's physique and mannerisms were also so similar to Magnus's. They were both tall and lanky, and when her son gave her a hug, his arms felt like her husband's. Even their hands were similar.

With trembling fingers Cia wrote Ludvig's name in icing on the layer cake. That was something else they had in common. Magnus was capable of eating an entire cake all on his own, and it was so unfair that he never gained an ounce. For Cia, all she had to do was look at a cinnamon roll and she'd put on a whole pound. But at the moment she was as thin as she'd always dreamed of being. Ever since Magnus had disappeared, the pounds had seemed to melt away. Every time she tried to eat something, the food practically swelled inside her mouth. And she had a lump in the pit of her stomach from the minute she woke up in the morning until she went to bed at night, falling into an uneasy sleep; that lump seemed to leave little room for food. Yet she cared less and less about her appearance. In fact, she barely glanced at herself in the mirror anymore. What did it matter, now that Magnus was gone?

Sometimes she wished that he had died right before her eyes. Suffered a heart attack or been hit by a car. Anything at all, just so she would have known what happened to him and been able to arrange a funeral, settle his estate, and take care of all the other practical matters that were necessary when somebody died. Then maybe she could have felt the pain of grief, until it gradually faded away, leaving the dull ache of loss, mixed with lovely memories.

Right now she had nothing. She felt as if she were living in a huge void. He was gone, and there was nothing on which to pin her sorrow — no way for her to move on. She felt incapable of going back to work, but she didn't know how long she could stay home on sick leave.

She looked down at the birthday cake. She'd made a real mess with the icing. It was impossible to read anything in the irregular swirls covering the marzipan on top. The sight seemed to sap her of all her remaining strength. She sank to the floor, with her back leaning against the refrigerator and sobs rising up from inside, demanding to be let out.

"Don't cry, Mama." Cia felt a hand on her shoulder. It was Magnus's hand. No, it was Ludvig's. Cia shook her head. She felt reality slipping away from her. She wanted to let it go so she could escape into the darkness that she knew awaited her. A beautiful, warm darkness that would envelop her for ever, if she let it. But through her tears she saw those brown eyes and that blond hair, and she knew that she couldn't give up.

"The cake," she sobbed, trying to get up. Ludvig helped her to her feet and then took the tube of icing out of her hand.

"I'll fix it, Mama. Why don't you go and lie down while I take care of the cake?"

He stroked her cheek. He was thirteen,

but no longer a child. He was his father now. He was Magnus — her rock. She knew that she shouldn't allow him to take on that role; he was still too young. But she didn't have the energy to do anything else but trade roles with him.

She dried her eyes on the sleeve of her shirt while Ludvig got out a knife and carefully scraped off the lumpy icing from his birthday cake. The last thing Cia saw before she left the kitchen was her son concentrating hard to shape the first letter of his own name. L, as in Ludvig.

"You're my handsome little boy, do you know that?" said Mother as she carefully combed his hair.

He merely nodded. Yes, he knew that. He was Mother's handsome little boy. She'd said that over and over ever since he'd been allowed to come home with them, and he never grew tired of hearing it. Sometimes he thought about how things had been before. About the darkness, the loneliness. But all he had to do was take one look at the beautiful apparition who was now his mother, and everything else disappeared, slipped away, and dissolved. As if it had never existed.

He had just climbed out of the bath, and his mother wrapped him in the green robe with the yellow flowers.

"Would my little darling like some ice cream?"

"You're spoiling him." Father's voice came from the doorway.

He huddled inside the terrycloth robe and pulled up the hood in order to hide from the harsh tone of the words that ricocheted off the bathroom tiles. Hiding from the blackness that rose up to the surface again.

"All I'm saying is that you're not doing him any favors by spoiling him like that."

"Are you implying that I don't know how to raise our son?" Mother's eyes turned dark, bottomless. As if she wanted to obliterate Father by simply looking at him. And, as usual, her anger seemed to make Father's own wrath melt away. He seemed to shrink and shrivel up, becoming a little gray father.

"You know best," he muttered and left, his eyes on the floor. Then they heard the sound of his footsteps fading and the front door quietly closing. Father was going out for a walk again.

"We won't pay him any mind," whispered Mother, pressing her lips close to his ear hidden under the green terrycloth. "Because you and I love each other. It's just you and me."

He pressed close to her like a little animal and allowed her to comfort him.

"Just you and me," he whispered.

4

"I won't! I don't wanna!" cried Maja, using up most of her scant vocabulary when Patrik desperately tried to leave her with Ewa, the day-care teacher, on Friday morning. His daughter clung to his trouser legs, howling, until finally he managed to prise her fingers loose, one after the other. His heart ached when she was carried off, still holding her arms out to him. Her tearful "Papa!" echoed in his head as he walked back to the car. For a long moment he just sat there, staring out the windscreen, holding the car keys in his hand. This had been going on for two months now, and it was no doubt Maja's way of reacting to Erika's pregnancy.

Patrik was the one who had to bear the brunt of this struggle every morning. He had actually volunteered for the job. It was just too hard for Erika to get Maja dressed and undressed. And squatting down to help the toddler tie her shoelaces was unthinkable. So there was really no other option. But the daily tussle was beginning to wear on Patrik's nerves, since it started well before they even reached the day-care center. As soon as it was time to get dressed in the morning, Maja would refuse to cooperate. Patrik was ashamed to admit that sometimes he got so frustrated that he would grab her a bit brusquely, making her scream at the top of her lungs. Afterward, he felt like the world's worst parent.

Tiredly he rubbed his eyes, took a deep breath, and turned the key in the ignition. But instead of driving toward Tanumshede, he impulsively turned and headed for the residential area beyond Kullen. He parked in front of the house belonging to the Kjellner family and, feeling a bit unsure of himself, walked up to the front door. He really should have notified them that he was coming, but it was too late now, since he was already here. He raised his hand and gave a sharp rap with his knuckles on the white-painted wooden door. A Christmas wreath was still hanging there; apparently no one had thought to take it down.

Not a sound came from inside the house, so Patrik knocked again. Maybe no one was home. But then he heard footsteps, and Cia opened the door. Her whole body froze when she saw him, and he hurried to shake his head.

"No, that's not why I'm here," he told her, and they both knew what he meant. Her shoulders slumped and she stepped aside to allow him to come in.

Patrik took off his shoes and hung his jacket on one of the few hooks that wasn't already in use, holding coats and jackets belonging to the Kjellner kids.

"I just thought I'd drop by for a chat," he said, suddenly uncertain as to how to present what amounted to little more than vague speculations.

Cia nodded and led the way to the kitchen, which was to the right of the entry. Patrik followed. He'd been here before on a couple of occasions. After Magnus disappeared, they had sat at the kitchen table and gone over everything again and again. He had asked Cia questions about things that should never have been disclosed, but such things had ceased to be private matters the minute Magnus Kjellner walked out the front door and didn't return.

The house looked unchanged. Pleasant and ordinary, a bit untidy, with traces of messy kids everywhere. But the last time Patrik and Cia had sat here together, there had still been a sense of hope. Now resignation had settled over the entire house. Also over Cia.

"There's some cake left. It was Ludvig's birthday yesterday," said Cia listlessly. She got up to take out a quarter of layer cake from the fridge. Patrik tried to protest, but Cia was already setting plates and forks on the table, and he realized that he would have to have cake for lunch today.

"How old is he now?" asked Patrik as he cut himself as thin a piece as seemed polite.

"Thirteen," said Cia, with a hint of a smile on her face as she served herself a small piece of cake too. Patrik wished he could get her to eat more, considering how thin she'd become over the past few months.

"That's a great age. Or maybe not," he said, hearing how strained he sounded. The whipped cream from the cake seemed to swell in his mouth.

"He's so much like his father," said Cia, her fork clanging against her plate. She set it down and looked at Patrik. "What is it you want?"

He cleared his throat. "I may be really off base, but I know that you want us to do everything possible, so you'll have to forgive me if —"

"Just say what you need to say," Cia interrupted him.

"All right. Well, there's something that I've been wondering about. Magnus was friends with Christian Thydell, wasn't he? How did they happen to meet?"

Cia looked at him in surprise, but she didn't counter with any questions of her own. Instead she paused to think about what he'd asked.

"I don't really know. I think they met right after Christian moved here with Sanna. She's a Fjällbacka girl, you know. That must be about seven years ago. Yes, that's right, because Sanna got pregnant with Melker soon afterwards, and he's five now. I remember we thought that happened rather fast."

"Was it through you and Sanna that they met?"

"No, Sanna is ten years younger than me, so we were never really friends before. To be honest, I can't actually recall how they ended up meeting. I just remember that Magnus suggested we should invite Christian and Sanna to dinner, and after that we all saw a lot of each other. Sanna and I don't have much in common, but she's a nice girl, and both Elin and Ludvig think it's fun to play with the little boys. And I have a much better opinion of Christian than of Magnus's other pals."

"And who might they be?"

"His old childhood friends: Erik Lind and Kenneth Bengtsson. I've socialized with them and their wives, but only because Magnus wanted me to. They seem to be a very different sort of people, in my opinion."

"What about Magnus and Christian? Were they close friends?"

Cia smiled. "I don't think Christian has any close friends. He's a rather gloomy person, and it's not easy to get to know him. But he was completely different around Magnus. My husband had that kind of effect on people. Everybody liked him. He made people relax." She swallowed hard, and Patrik realized that she had spoken of her husband in the past tense.

"But why are you asking me about Christian? Don't tell me something has happened to him," Cia added, sounding worried.

"No, no. Nothing serious."

"I heard about what went on at his book launch. I was invited, but I would have felt strange going without Magnus. I hope Christian wasn't offended because I didn't show up."

"I can't imagine that he'd feel that way," said Patrik. "But it seems that someone has been sending him threatening letters for more than a year now. I may be grabbing at straws, but I wanted to find out if Magnus had received anything similar. They knew each other, so there might be some kind of connection."

"Threatening letters?" asked Cia. "Don't you think I would have told you about something like that? Why would I keep back any information that might help you find out what happened to Magnus?" Her voice rose, taking on a shrill note.

"I'm sure that you would have told us about it if you had known," Patrik hastened to interject. "But maybe Magnus didn't say anything because he didn't want to worry you."

"Then why would I be able to tell you anything about it?"

"In my experience, wives can sense things even if their husbands don't specifically talk about what's bothering them. My wife can do that, at any rate."

Cia smiled again. "You have a point there. And it's true. I would have known if something was weighing on Magnus. But he was his usual carefree self. He was the world's most stable and reliable person, almost always cheerful and upbeat. Sometimes I've found that annoying, and I have to admit to occasionally trying to provoke a negative reaction from him if I was feeling angry and upset myself. But I never succeeded. Magnus was the way he was. If something was bothering him, he would have told me about it. If for some reason he decided not to do that, I still would have noticed that something was wrong. He knew everything about me, and I knew everything about him. We had no secrets from each other." She spoke with great confidence, and Patrik could tell that she meant what she said. But he still had his doubts. It was impossible to know everything about another person. Even someone you loved and had chosen to share your life with.

He looked at Cia. "Please forgive me if I'm asking too much, but would you mind if I took a look around the house? Just to get a clearer picture of the kind of person Magnus was." Even though they had already been talking about Magnus as if he were dead, Patrik regretted the way he had formulated his last remark. But Cia didn't comment. Instead, she motioned toward the doorway and said:

"Look around as much as you like. I mean it. Do whatever you want, ask me any questions you can think of, as long as you find him." With an almost aggressive motion she wiped away a tear with the back of her hand.

Patrik sensed that she needed to be alone

for a moment, so he seized the opportunity to get up and leave the room. He started his search in the living room. It looked much like the living room in thousands of other Swedish homes. A big, dark blue sofa from IKEA. Billy bookshelves with built-in lighting. A flat-screen TV on a stand made of the same light-colored wood as the coffee table. Little knick-knacks and travel souvenirs; on the wall, photographs of the children. Patrik went over to a big framed wedding picture hanging over the sofa. It was not a traditional formal portrait. Magnus, wearing a morning coat, was lying on his side in the grass with his head propped on his hand. Cia stood behind him, wearing a frilly wedding dress. She had a big smile on her face, and one foot was planted solidly on top of Magnus.

"Our parents just about died of fright when they saw that wedding picture," said Cia, and Patrik turned around to look at her.

"It's certainly rather . . . different." He glanced again at the photo. He'd met Magnus a few times since he'd moved to Fjällbacka, but had never exchanged more than the usual polite words of greeting with him. Now, as he stood here looking at the man's open and happy expression, Patrik knew at once that he would have liked Magnus.

"Is it okay if I go upstairs?" asked Patrik. Cia nodded from where she stood in the doorway.

The wall of the stairwell was also covered with photographs, and Patrik paused to study them. They bore witness to a rich life that was focused on family and the ordinary joys. And it was obvious that Magnus Kjellner had been tremendously proud of his children. One picture, in particular, made Patrik's stomach knot up. A holiday photo, showing a smiling Magnus standing between Elin and Ludvig, with his arms around both of them. His face was aglow with such happiness that Patrik couldn't bear to look at it any longer. He turned away and continued up the stairs.

The first two rooms belonged to the kids. Ludvig's was surprisingly neat, without any clothes tossed on the floor. The bed was made, and the pen holder and everything else on the desk had been meticulously arranged. The boy was clearly a big sports fan. Pinned up over the bed in the place of honor was a football jersey from the Swedish national team, autographed by Zlatan. Otherwise, photos of the IFK team from Göteborg dominated.

"Ludvig and Magnus used to go to the

games as often as they could."

Patrik gave a start. Once again Cia's voice had caught him by surprise. She seemed able to walk around without making a sound, because he hadn't heard her come up the stairs.

"Quite a tidy young boy."

"Yes, just like his father. Magnus did most of the picking up and cleaning here at home. I'm the messier one. If you have a look in the next room, you'll see which of our children takes after me."

Patrik opened the door to the next bedroom, in spite of the warning posted in big letters: KNOCK BEFORE ENTERING!

"Yikes!" said Patrik, taking a step back.

"Yes, that's the right word for it," sighed Cia, crossing her arms so as to stop herself from trying to clean up the mess. Because Elin's room was indescribably messy. And pink.

"I thought she'd grow out of her pink phase sooner or later, but instead it just seems to have escalated. Now it ranges from pale princess pink to a shocking neon."

Patrik blinked his eyes. Was this how Maja's room was going to look in a few years? And what if the twins turned out to be girls? He was going to drown in pink.

"I've given up. I just ask that she keep the

door closed so I don't have to look at the chaos. I do a 'sniff check' once in a while, to make sure that it doesn't begin to smell like dead bodies in here." She was obviously startled by her own choice of words, but she kept on going. "Magnus couldn't stand knowing what a mess things were in, but I persuaded him to leave her be. I was the same way as a kid, so I knew it would just lead to nothing but nagging and quarrels. In my case, I got neater as soon as I had my own apartment, and I think the same thing will happen with Elin." She closed the door and pointed to the room at the end of the hall.

"That's our bedroom. I haven't touched any of Magnus's things."

The first thing that Patrik noticed was that they had the same bed linens as he and Erica did. Blue-and-white check, bought at IKEA. Somehow that made him very uncomfortable. It made him feel vulnerable.

"Magnus sleeps on the side next to the window."

Patrik went over to his side of the bed. He would have preferred to look things over alone, in peace and quiet. Instead, it felt as if he were snooping around in things that were not his concern, and the feeling grew worse the longer Cia stood in the room star-

80

ing at him. He had no idea what he was looking for. He just felt he needed to get closer to Magnus Kjellner, to see him as a real person, as flesh and blood, not merely a photograph on the wall in the police station. Patrik could still feel Cia's eyes on his back, and finally he turned around to face her.

"I hope you won't be offended, but would you mind leaving while I have a look around?" He sincerely hoped that she would understand.

"I'm sorry. Of course," she said, smiling apologetically. "I realize it must be difficult to have me looking over your shoulder. I'll go downstairs and take care of a few things, so you'll have the place to yourself."

"Thanks," said Patrik. As soon as she left, he sat down on the edge of the bed and started with the bedside table. A pair of glasses, a stack of papers that turned out to be a copy of the manuscript of *The Mermaid,* an empty water glass, and a blister pack of acetaminophen. That was all. Patrik pulled out the drawer and carefully studied what he found inside. Nothing of real interest. A paperback copy of Åsa Larsson's detective novel *Sun Storm,* a little box containing ear plugs, and a package of cough drops.

Patrik got up and went over to the wardrobes that lined one entire wall of the bedroom. He laughed when he slid open the doors and instantly saw a clear example of what Cia had said about how her attitude toward neatness differed from that of her husband. The half of the wardrobe next to the window was a miracle of organization. Everything was carefully folded and arranged in wire baskets: socks, underwear, ties, and belts. Above hung neatly pressed shirts and jackets, along with polo shirts and T-shirts. T-shirts on hangers — the mere thought boggled Patrik's mind. The most he ever did was to stuff his T-shirts into a drawer, only to curse the fact that they ended up looking so wrinkled when he put them on.

In that sense, Cia's half of the wardrobe was more like his own method. Everything was haphazardly jumbled together, as if someone had simply opened the door and tossed everything inside before quickly shutting it again.

He closed the sliding doors and turned to look at the bed. There was something so heartbreaking and sad about a bed that had obviously only been slept in on one side. He wondered if anyone ever got used to sleeping in a double bed that was half empty. The thought of sleeping alone without Erica seemed impossible to him.

When Patrik went back down to the kitchen, Cia was putting away the plates they had used. She gave him an inquisitive look, and he said, in a friendly tone of voice:

"Thanks for letting me take a look around. I don't know whether it will make any difference, but at least now I feel as if I know a little more about Magnus and who he was . . . is."

"That does make a difference. To me, anyway."

Patrik said good-bye and left. He paused on the porch to look at the withered Christmas wreath hanging on the front door. After a moment's hesitation, he lifted it off. Considering what an orderly person Magnus was, he probably wouldn't have wanted to see that old wreath still there.

Both kids were screaming at the top of their lungs. The sound bounced off the walls in the kitchen, and Christian thought his head was going to explode. He hadn't slept well for several nights in a row. Thoughts kept whirling through his mind, around and around, as if he needed to analyze every single thought before he could move on to the next one.

He had even been thinking of retreating

to the boathouse to sit down and write. But the silence of the night and the darkness outside would have given his phantoms free rein, and he didn't have the strength to drown them out with the sentences he constructed. So he'd stayed where he was, staring up at the ceiling while hopelessness descended on him from all directions.

"Stop that right now!" Sanna pulled the boys apart as they fought over a packet of O'Boy which had somehow ended up a little too close to them. Then she turned to Christian, who was sitting at the table and staring into space, his sandwich uneaten on the plate and his coffee untouched in the cup.

"It would be nice if you could help me out a little!"

"I didn't sleep well," he replied, taking a sip of the cold coffee. He got up and dumped the rest in the sink before pouring himself a fresh cup and adding a dash of milk.

"I'm fully aware that you've got a lot on your mind right now, and you know that I've supported you the whole time when you were working on your book. But there's a limit, even for me." Sanna pulled the spoon out of Nils's hand just as he was about to use it to bang his older brother on the forehead. She tossed it with a clatter into the sink. Then she took a deep breath, as if mustering her courage before pouring out everything that she'd been holding inside. Christian wished he could press a PAUSE button to stop her before she spoke. He simply couldn't take any more right now.

"I never said a word whenever you went straight from work to the boathouse and sat there writing all evening. I picked up the kids from day care, cooked dinner, made sure they were fed, tidied up in the house, got them to brush their teeth, read them a story, and then put them to bed. I did all of that without complaint while you devoted yourself to your fucking *creative efforts*!"

Sanna's last words dripped with a sarcasm that Christian had never heard from her before. He closed his eyes and tried to shut out the criticism. But she went on relentlessly:

"I think it's fantastic that everything is going so well. That you got the book published, and that you seem to be a new star on the literary horizon. I think it's great, and I don't begrudge you any of it. But what about me? Where's my place in all of this? Nobody sings my praises, nobody looks at me and says: 'By God, Sanna, you're amazing. Christian is a lucky man to have you.' That's not something that even *you* say to me. You just take it for granted that I'll slave away here at home, taking care of the kids and the house while you do what you 'have to do.' " She sketched two quotation marks in the air. "And it's true. I do handle everything. And I gladly carry the load. You know how much I love taking care of the children, but that doesn't make the burden any easier to bear. I'd at least like to receive a few words of thanks from you! Is that too much to ask?"

"Sanna, I don't think we should let the kids hear. . . ." Christian began, but he realized at once that it was the wrong thing to say.

"Right. You always have some excuse for not talking to me, and not taking me seriously! You're too tired, or you don't have time because you need to work on your book, or you don't want to discuss things in front of the kids, or, or, or. . . ."

The boys didn't make a peep as they stared with frightened eyes at their parents. Christian felt his weariness giving way to anger. This was one thing he detested about Sanna, and they'd discussed it many times before. She never hesitated to draw the children into their arguments. He knew that she was trying to make the boys her allies in the battle that had become more and more vociferous between them. But what could he do? He knew that all their problems were caused by the fact that he didn't love her, and never had. And the fact that she knew this, even though she refused to admit it to herself. He had actually chosen her for that very reason — that she was someone he could never love. Not in the same way as. . . .

He slammed his fist down on the table. Both Sanna and the boys jumped in surprise. His hand stung from the blow, which was exactly what he'd intended. Pain forced out everything else that he couldn't allow himself to think about, and he felt that he was starting to regain control.

"We're not having this conversation right now," he said brusquely. Though he avoided looking Sanna in the eye, he could feel her gaze on his back as he headed for the front hall, put on his jacket and shoes, and went out the door. The last thing he heard before the door slammed shut was Sanna telling the boys that their father was an idiot.

The dreariness of it all was the worst part. Trying to fill the hours while the girls were in school with something that at least seemed to have an iota of meaning. It wasn't that Louise had nothing to do. Ensuring that Erik's life ran smoothly left no room for laziness. His shirts had to be laundered, pressed, and hung up properly; dinners for his business associates had to be planned and successfully hosted; and the whole house had to shine. Of course they had someone who came in to clean once a week — and who was paid under the table — but there were still things that she needed to tend to herself. Millions of minor matters that needed to be handled impeccably so that Erik wouldn't notice that any kind of effort had gone into making everything work as it should. But the problem was that it was all so boring. She had loved being home when the girls were little. Loved taking care of her young daughters. She didn't even mind changing diapers, although Erik had never devoted a single second to that chore. But she hadn't minded, because she had felt needed. She had a purpose. She had been at the center of her children's world, the person who got up in the morning before they did to make the sun shine.

But those days were long gone. The girls were in school. They spent their free time with friends and doing extracurricular activities. Nowadays they regarded her mostly as someone who was at their beck and call. Erik thought of her that way too. And to her sorrow, she was beginning to realize that they were all becoming insufferable. Erik compensated for his lack of involvement in his daughters' lives by buying them everything they wanted, and his contempt for his wife was beginning to rub off on the girls.

Louise ran her hand over the kitchen counter. Italian marble, specially imported. Erik had chosen it himself, during one of his business trips. She didn't really like it. Too cold and too hard. If she'd been allowed to choose, she would have selected something made of wood, perhaps a dark oak. She opened one of the shiny, smooth cupboard doors, which also had a cold appearance. More fashion than feeling. To go with the dark oak countertop that she would have preferred, she would have chosen white cupboard doors in a rustic style, hand-painted so that the brush strokes were visible and gave a certain life to the surface.

She cupped her hand around one of the big wine glasses. A wedding gift from Erik's parents. Hand-blown, of course. At their wedding dinner, she'd been subjected to a lengthy lecture by Erik's mother about the small but exclusive glass-blowing workshop in Denmark where they had specially ordered the expensive glasses.

Something snapped inside her, and her hand opened as if of its own accord. The glass shattered into a thousand pieces on the black pebble-tile floor. The floor was also from Italy, of course. That was one of many things that Erik had in common with his parents: anything Swedish was never good enough. The farther away the origin of something, the better. Just as long as it didn't come from Taiwan. Louise sniggered, reached for another glass, and stepped over the shards on the floor, her feet clad in house slippers. Then she made a beeline for the boxed wine on the counter. Erik always ridiculed her boxed wine. For him, the only acceptable wine came in a bottle and cost hundreds of kronor. He would never dream of sullying his taste buds with wine that cost two hundred kronor per box. Sometimes, out of sheer spite, she would fill his glass with her wine instead of the snooty French or South African variety that was always accompanied by long-winded discourses on their particular characteristics. Strangely enough, it seemed that her cheap wine possessed the exact same qualities, since Erik never noticed the difference.

It was those sorts of minor acts of revenge that made her life bearable — the only way she was able to ignore the fact that he kept trying to turn the girls against her, treated her like shit, and was fucking a bloody hairdresser.

Louise held the glass under the tap of the wine box and filled it to the brim. Then she raised her glass in a toast to her own reflection, visible in the stainless steel door of the fridge.

Erica couldn't stop thinking about the letters. She wandered through the house for a while, until a dull pain started up in the small of her back, forcing her to sit down at the kitchen table. She reached for a notepad and a pen that were lying on the table and began hastily jotting down what she could remember from the letters she'd seen at Christian's house. She had a good memory for text, so she was almost positive that she'd managed to recreate what the letters had said.

She read through what she'd written over and over again, and with each reading the short sentences seemed to sound more and more threatening. Who would have cause to feel such anger toward Christian? Erica shook her head as she sat there at the table. It was impossible to tell whether a woman or a man had written those letters. But there was something about the tone and the way in which the views were expressed that made her think she was reading a woman's hatred. Not a man's.

Hesitantly she reached for the cordless phone, then drew back her hand. Maybe she was just being silly. But after re-reading the words she'd jotted down on the note-pad, she grabbed the phone and punched in the mobile number she knew by heart.

"This is Gaby," said the publishing direc-tor, picking up the phone on the first ring.

"Hi, it's Erica."

"Erica!" Gaby's shrill voice went up another octave, forcing Erica to move the receiver away from her ear in self-defense. "How's it going, dearie? No babies yet? You do know that twins usually arrive early, don't you?" It sounded as if Gaby were run-ning.

"No, the babies aren't here yet," said Erica, trying to restrain her annoyance. She didn't understand why everybody was always telling her that twins were usually born early. If that was the case, she'd find out soon enough. "I'm actually calling you about Christian."

"Oh, how is he?" asked Gaby. "I tried call-ing him several times, but his little wife just told me he wasn't home, which I don't believe for a minute. It was so awful, the way he passed out like that. He has his first book-signings tomorrow, and we really ought to let them know if we need to cancel, which would be terribly unfortunate."

"I went to see him, and I'm sure he'll be fine to attend the book-signings. You don't have to worry about that," said Erica, preparing to bring up the real topic she wanted to discuss. She took in as deep a breath as her highly constricted lung capacity would allow and said "There's something I wanted to talk to you about. . . ."

"Sure, fire away."

"Have you received anything at the publishing house that might concern Christian?"

"What do you mean?"

"Er, well, I was just wondering if you'd received any letters or emails about Christian, or addressed to him. Anything that sounded threatening?"

"Hate mail?"

Erica was starting to feel more and more like a child tattling on a classmate, but it was too late to back out now.

"Yes. The thing is that Christian has been getting threatening letters for the past year and a half, pretty much ever since he started writing his book. And I can tell that he's upset, even though he refuses to admit it. I thought that maybe something might have been sent to the publishing house too."

"I can't believe what you're telling me, but no, we haven't seen anything like that. Is there a name on the letters? Does Christian know who they're from?" Gaby stumbled over her words, and the sound of her high heels clacking on the pavement was gone, so she must have stopped.

"They're all anonymous, and I don't think Christian has any idea who sent them. But you know how he is. I'm not sure he'd tell anyone even if he did know. If it hadn't been for Sanna, I wouldn't have heard a word about it. Or about the fact that he collapsed at the party on Wednesday because the card attached to a bouquet of flowers delivered to him seemed to be from the same person who wrote the letters."

"That sounds totally insane! Does this have anything to do with his book?"

"I asked Christian the same question. But he told me very firmly that no one would be able to recognize themselves in what he's written."

"Well, this is certainly dreadful. You must let me know if you find out anything else, all right?"

"Yes, I'm going to try," said Erica. "And

please don't tell Christian that I said anything about all this."

"Of course not. It's just between you and me. I'll keep an eye on any correspondence we receive that's addressed to Christian. We'll probably be getting a few things now that the book is in the shops."

"Great reviews, by the way," said Erica, to change the subject.

"Yes, it's just wonderful!" exclaimed Gaby with such enthusiasm that again Erica had to move the receiver away from her ear. "I've already heard Christian's name mentioned in connection with the prestigious August Prize. Not to mention that we've printed ten thousand hardbacks that are on their way to the booksellers at this very minute."

"That's incredible," said Erica, her heart leaping with pride. She of all people knew how hard Christian had worked on that manuscript, and she was tremendously pleased that his efforts seemed about to bear fruit.

"It certainly is," chirped Gaby. "Dearie, I can't talk anymore right now. I've got to make a little phone call."

There was something in Gaby's last remark that made Erica uneasy. She should have stopped to consider the situation before phoning the publisher. She shouldn't have allowed herself to get so worked up. As if to confirm her misgivings, one of the twins gave her a hard kick in the ribs.

It was such a strange sensation to be happy. Anna had gradually come to accept the feeling, and she was even starting to get used to it. But it had been a long time since she'd felt this way. If ever.

"Give it back!" Belinda came racing after Lisen, Dan's youngest daughter, who hid behind Anna with a shriek. In her hand she was clutching her older sister's hairbrush.

"I didn't say you could borrow it! Give it back!"

"Anna. . . ." Lisen pleaded, but Anna pulled the child around to face her, keeping a light hold on her shoulder.

"If you took Belinda's brush without asking, you'll have to give it back."

"See, I told you so!" said Belinda.

Anna gave Belinda a warning look.

"As for you, Belinda — you don't really need to go chasing your little sister through the whole house."

Belinda shrugged. "It's her own fault if she takes my things."

"Just wait until little brother is here," said Lisen. "He'll break everything you own!"

"I'm going to be moving out soon, so it's your stuff he's going to be wrecking!" said Belinda, sticking out her tongue.

"Hey, come on, now. Are you eighteen or five?" said Anna, but she couldn't help laughing. "And why are the two of you so sure that it's going to be a boy?"

"Because Mama says that if somebody has as big a rear end as you do, it's bound to be a boy."

"Shhh," said Belinda, glaring at her sister, who couldn't really understand what she'd said wrong. "Sorry," Belinda added.

"That's okay." Anna smiled, but she did feel slightly insulted. So Dan's ex-wife thought she had a big rear end? But not even that sort of remark — and she had to admit there was some truth to it, after all — could put a damper on her good mood. She'd been to hell and back; that was no exaggeration. And her kids had too. Emma and Adrian, in spite of everything they'd been through, were now two very confident and happy children. Sometimes she could hardly believe it was true.

"You'll behave yourself when our guests arrive, won't you?" said his mother, giving him a solemn look.

He nodded. He would never dream of behaving badly and embarrassing his mother. He wanted nothing more than to please her so that she would keep on loving him.

The doorbell rang, and his mother stood up abruptly. "They're here." He heard the anticipation in her voice, a tone that made him uneasy. Sometimes his mother changed into someone else after he heard the sound of that little bell vibrating between the walls in her bedroom. But that might not happen this time.

"Can I take your coat?" He heard his father's voice downstairs in the front hall, along with the murmuring of their guests.

"Go on ahead. I'll be there in a minute." His mother motioned toward him with her hand, and he breathed in the scent of her perfume. She sat down at her dressing table to fix her hair and put the last touches on her makeup as she admired herself in the mirror. He stayed where he was, watching her with fascination. A furrow appeared between her brows as their eyes met in the mirror.

"Didn't I tell you to go downstairs?" she said sharply, and he felt the darkness take hold of him for a moment.

Shamefaced, he bowed his head and headed for the murmur of voices in the front hall. He would behave himself. Mother wouldn't have to be ashamed of him.

5

The cold air tore at his windpipe. He loved that feeling. Everybody thought he was crazy when he went out running in the middle of winter, but he preferred to put in his miles in the frosty weather rather than go out running in the oppressive heat of summer. And on weekends he made a point of running his route twice.

Kenneth cast an eye at his wristwatch. It held everything he needed to know to make the most of his run. It measured his pulse and counted the steps he took; it even kept track of the time from his last session.

His goal right now was to run in the Stockholm Marathon. He'd taken part twice before, and in the Copenhagen Marathon as well. He'd been running for twenty years, and if he had a choice, he'd prefer to die in the middle of a race, twenty or thirty years from now. Because the feeling he had when he ran, when his feet flew over the ground

— rhythmically pounding at a steady pace that in the end seemed to merge with the beat of his heart — was like nothing else in the world. Even the fatigue, the numb sensation in his legs when the lactic acid built up, was something that he'd learned to appreciate more and more with each year that passed. He felt alive whenever he ran. That was the best way he could describe it.

As he drew close to home, he began slowing his pace. When he reached his front door, he jogged in place for a few moments and then held on to the railing to stretch out his thigh muscles. His breath formed a white cloud of ice crystals, and he felt strong and cleansed after running twelve miles at a relatively fast pace.

"Is that you, Kenneth?" He heard Lisbet's voice from the guest room as the front door closed behind him.

"Yes, it's me, dear. I'm just going to take a quick shower, and then I'll come and see you."

He turned the tap until the water was steaming hot and then stood under the needle-like spray of the shower. This was practically the most pleasurable thing of all. It felt so good that it took a real effort for him to turn off the water. He shivered as he stepped out of the shower stall. The bathroom felt like an igloo in comparison.

"Could you bring me the newspaper?"

"Of course, love." Jeans, a T-shirt, and a sweater. He was ready. He stuck his bare feet into a pair of Crocs slippers that he'd bought last summer and went out to the letterbox. When he picked up the newspaper, he noticed a white envelope stuck in the bottom. He must have missed it yesterday. His stomach turned over at the sight of his name written in black ink. Not another one!

As soon as he was back inside, he tore open the envelope and pulled out the card inside. Standing in the front hall, he read what it said. The message was brief and strange.

Kenneth turned the card over to see if there was anything on the back. But there wasn't. The only message was those two cryptic sentences.

"What's keeping you, Kenneth?"

Quickly he stuffed the note back in the envelope.

"I was just checking on something. I'm coming now."

He headed for her door, holding the newspaper in his hand. The white card with the elegant handwriting seemed to burn in his back pocket.

■ ■ ■ ■

It was like a drug. Sanna had become dependent on the high it gave her to check his email, go through his pockets, and surreptitiously examine his phone bill. Every time she didn't find anything, she felt her whole body relax. But that didn't last long. Soon the anxiety would start building again, and with it the tension in her body until all the logical arguments for why she should restrain herself ceased. Then she would sit down at the computer again. She entered Christian's email address and password, which had been easy to crack. He used the same one every time. His birth date, so he would always remember it.

In reality, there was no reason for this feeling that kept tearing at her heart and clawing at her guts until all she wanted to do was scream. Christian had never done anything to give her cause to distrust him. During the years she'd been carrying on this surveillance of his correspondence, she had never once found the slightest trace of anything suspicious. He was an open book. And yet . . . sometimes she had the feeling that he was somewhere else entirely, a place to which she was denied access. And why had he told her so little about his background? He'd said that his parents had died long ago, and she'd never had occasion to meet any of his other relatives, although surely he must have some. He didn't seem to have any childhood friends either, and no old acquaintances had ever gotten in touch. It was almost as if he hadn't existed at all until he met her and moved to Fjällbacka. She hadn't even seen his apartment in Göteborg when they first met. He'd gone there alone with the moving van to pick up his few belongings.

Sanna ran her eyes over the messages in his inbox. A couple of emails from the publisher, several newspapers wanting interviews, some news from the local municipality having to do with his job at the library. That was all.

This time the feeling of relief was just as glorious as ever when she logged out of his account. Before turning off the computer, she did a routine scan of his web browser history, but there was nothing unusual. Christian had checked out the websites for the newspapers *Expressen* and *Aftonbladet,* as well as his publisher's home page. He'd also looked at a new child's car seat online.

But there was still the issue of the letters. He had insisted that he didn't know who had sent those cryptic messages to him. Yet there was something in his tone of voice that contradicted his claim. Sanna couldn't really put her finger on what it might be, and it was driving her nuts. What wasn't he telling her? Who had sent those letters? Was it a woman who had once been his lover? Or someone who was his mistress now?

She clenched and unclenched her hands, forcing herself to breathe calmly. The temporary sense of relief had already vanished, and she tried in vain to convince herself that everything was as it should be. Reassurance. That was the only thing she desired. She just wanted to know that Christian loved her.

But deep inside, she knew that he had never belonged to her. That he had always been searching for something else, someone else, during all the years they had lived together. She knew that he had never loved her. Not really. And one day he would find the person he wanted to be with, the one he actually loved, and then she would be all alone.

Sanna wrapped her arms around herself for a moment as she sat on the desk chair. Then she got up. Christian's mobile phone bill had come in the mail yesterday. It would take her only a minute to peruse it.

■ ■ ■ ■

Erica walked aimlessly through the house. This eternal waiting was going to drive her crazy. She'd finished writing her latest book, but she didn't have the energy to start on a new project right now. And she couldn't do much in the house without her back and joints protesting. She spent her time reading or watching TV. Or she did what she was doing now — wandering around the house out of sheer frustration. At least today was Saturday, and Patrik was home. He'd gone out with Maja for a short walk so she'd get some fresh air. Erica was counting the minutes until they returned.

When the doorbell rang, her heart nearly skipped a beat. Before she managed to respond, the door was thrown open and Anna came into the front hall.

"Are you practically going out of your mind too?" she said, taking off her scarf and jacket.

"How'd you guess?" said Erica, suddenly feeling much more cheerful.

They went into the kitchen, and Anna set a steaming bag on the counter. "Freshly baked buns. Belinda did the baking."

"Really?" said Erica, trying to picture

Anna's eldest stepdaughter wearing an apron and kneading dough with her black-painted fingernails.

"She's in love," said Anna, as if that explained everything. Which, in fact, it actually did.

"Well, I can't recall it ever having that sort of effect on me," said Erica, putting the buns on a plate.

"Apparently he told her yesterday that he likes girls who are the domestic type." Anna raised one eyebrow and gave Erica a knowing look.

"Oh, is that right?"

Anna laughed as she reached for one of the buns. "Hey, calm down, you don't have to go over to his house and give him a thrashing. I've met the boy, and believe me, within a week Belinda is going to get tired of him and go back to her black-clad losers who play in obscure rock bands and don't give a shit whether she's the domestic type or not."

"Let's hope so. But I have to say that these buns aren't bad." Erica closed her eyes as she chewed. In her present condition, a freshly baked bun was as close as she was going to get to an orgasm.

"Well, the one advantage to how we look at the moment is that we can stuff ourselves with as many buns as we like," said Anna, taking a bite of her second one.

"Sure, but we'll have to pay for it later on," replied Erica, although she couldn't help following her sister's example by taking another bun. Belinda really seemed to have a natural talent for baking.

"With twins, you'll soon lose all that weight and more!" laughed Anna.

"You're probably right." Erica found herself thinking about something else, and her sister seemed to guess what it was.

"Don't worry. It'll be fine. Besides, you're not alone this time. You have me to keep you company. We can move two armchairs next to each other in front of the TV and watch *Oprah* as we nurse the babies all day long."

"And take turns ordering takeaway for dinner when our husbands come home."

"Sure. You'll see. Everything's going to be great." Anna licked her fingers and leaned back with a groan. "Ow, I think I ate too much." She propped her swollen feet up on the chair next to her and clasped her hands over her belly. "Have you talked to Christian?"

"Yep. I was over there on Thursday." Erica followed Anna's example and propped her feet on a chair too. Only one bun remained on the plate, and it was practically shouting at her. After a brief battle, she reached for it.

"So, what exactly happened?"

Erica hesitated for a moment, but she wasn't used to keeping secrets from her sister, so in the end she told Anna everything about the letters and their menacing tone.

"Wow, that's horrible," said Anna, shaking her head. "I think it's odd that he started getting them even before his book was published. It would have seemed more logical if they arrived after he attracted attention in the media. I mean, they seem to be from someone who's a little cuckoo."

"I agree. It does sound like that. Christian refuses to take them seriously. At least that's what he told me. But I could tell that Sanna was upset."

"I can believe it," said Anna, licking her index finger and then dabbing up the sugar left on the plate.

"Today he has his first book-signings," said Erica, unable to keep a trace of pride out of her voice. In many ways she felt that she'd contributed to Christian's success, and through him she was reliving her own debut as an author. Those first book-signings. That was a huge deal. Really huge.

"That's great. Where are they going to be held?"

"First at the Böcker och Blad bookshop in Torp, then at Bokia in Uddevalla."

"I hope some people actually turn up. It would be depressing if he had to sit there all alone," said Anna.

Erica grimaced at the thought of her own first signing, at a bookshop in Stockholm. She'd sat there for a whole hour, trying to look unconcerned while all the customers walked past as if she didn't exist.

"There's been so much PR about his book that I'm sure people will come — out of curiosity if nothing else," said Erica, hoping that she was right.

"Well, it's just lucky that the newspapers haven't gotten word of those threatening letters," said Anna.

"Yeah, you're right about that," replied Erica, and then changed the subject. But the uneasy feeling in her chest refused to leave her.

They were going on holiday, and he could hardly wait. He wasn't really sure what it entailed, but the word sounded so promising. Holiday. And they would be taking the travel trailer that was parked outside.

He was never allowed to play in it. A few times he'd tried to peek through the windows, to see what was behind the brown curtains. But he could never actually see anything, and the trailer was always locked. Now the door stood wide open, so as to "give it a proper airing out," as Mother said, and a bunch of cushions had been put in the washing machine to rid them of the smell of winter.

Everything seemed so unreal, like a fairy-tale adventure. He wondered if he'd be permitted to sit inside the trailer as they drove, like traveling inside a little house on wheels, headed for something new and unfamiliar. But he didn't dare ask. Mother had been in a strange mood lately. That sharp, fierce tone in her voice was clearly audible, and Father had been taking more frequent walks, whenever he wasn't hiding behind his newspaper.

Sometimes he'd noticed her staring at him oddly. There was something different about the way she looked at him, and it frightened him, even taking him back to the darkness that he'd left behind.

"Are you just going to stand there gaping, or were you thinking of helping me out?" Mother had her hands on her hips.

He gave a start when he heard that harsh tone once again and ran over to her.

"Take these and put them in the laundry room," she said, tossing some foul-smelling blankets at him with such force that he almost lost his footing.

"Yes, Mother," he said, and hurried into the house.

If only he knew what he'd done wrong. He always obeyed his mother. Never talked back, behaved properly, and never got his clothes dirty. Yet it was as if sometimes she couldn't bear to look at him.

He'd tried to ask his father about this. Mustered his courage on one of the few occasions when they were alone and asked him why Mother didn't like him anymore. For a moment Father had put aside the newspaper to reply curtly that he was being foolish and he didn't want to hear talk of such things again. Mother would be terribly sad if she ever heard him say that. He should be grateful that he had a mother like her.

He didn't ask any more questions. Making his mother sad was the last thing he wanted to do. He just wished that she would be happy and that she would stroke his hair like she used to and call him her handsome little boy. That was all he wanted.

He put the blankets down in front of the washing machine and pushed aside all his gloomy, dark thoughts. They were going on holiday. In the travel trailer.

6

Christian drummed his pen on the top of the small table where he was sitting. Next to him was a big stack of copies of *The Mermaid.* He still couldn't get enough of looking at the book. It seemed so unreal that his name was actually on the cover. The cover of a real book.

There wasn't yet any rush to buy copies, and he didn't think there would be. It was only authors like Liza Marklund and Jan Guillou who attracted large crowds. He was perfectly happy with the five copies that he'd signed so far.

Although he had to admit that he did feel a bit lost as he sat there. People hurried past, giving him curious looks, but they didn't stop. He wasn't sure whether he should say "Hello" when he felt them staring at him, or just pretend that he was busy with something else.

Gunnel, the owner of the bookshop, came

to his rescue. She walked over and nodded at the stack of books.

"Would you mind signing a few of those? It's so nice to have signed copies to sell later."

"Sure. How many should I sign?" asked Christian, happy to have something to do.

"Hmm. Let's say ten," replied Gunnel, straightening the stack, which had gotten a bit crooked.

"That's no problem."

"We did a proper amount of advertising for the book-signing," said Gunnel.

"I have no doubt that you did," Christian told her with a smile. He could see that she was concerned he would think the meager turnout could be blamed on the shop's lack of PR for the event. "I'm not exactly a household name, so I didn't have very high expectations."

"At least we've sold a few copies," she said kindly, heading back to the checkout counter.

He reached for a book, removed the cap on his pen, and began signing. Out of the corner of his eye, he noticed that someone was standing in front of the table. When he looked up, he found a big, yellow microphone thrust in his face.

"We're here in the bookshop where Christian Thydell is signing his first novel, *The Mermaid.* Christian, your name is all over the newspaper placards today. How worried are you about the threats that have been leveled against you? Have the police been brought in?"

The reporter hadn't yet introduced himself, but judging by the label on the microphone, he was from the local radio station. He was peering at Christian with an urgent expression on his face.

Christian felt his mind go blank. "The newspaper placards?" he said.

"Yes, you're on *GT*'s placard. Haven't you seen it?" The reporter didn't wait for Christian to reply but just repeated the question he'd asked initially. "Are you worried about the threats? Have the police provided special protection for you today?"

The reporter glanced around the shop, but then turned back to Christian, who was holding his pen above the book he'd been just about to sign.

"I don't know how —" he stammered.

"But it's true, isn't it? You've received threats while you were writing the book, and you passed out on Wednesday when another letter was delivered to you at the book launch."

"Er, yes, well. . . ." Christian could feel

himself gasping for air.

"Do you know who sent the threats? Do the police know?" The microphone was again only about an inch from Christian's mouth, and he had to restrain himself from shoving it away. He didn't want to answer these questions. He had no idea how the press had found out about any of this. He thought about the letter in his jacket pocket. The letter that had come yesterday and that he'd managed to retrieve from the stack of mail before Sanna discovered it.

Panic-stricken, he looked for some way to escape. He caught Gunnel's eye, and she seemed to realize at once that something was wrong.

She came over to them and asked, "What's going on here?"

"I'm doing an interview," said the reporter.

"Have you asked Christian whether he wants to be interviewed?"

She glanced at Christian, who shook his head.

"He's not interested," she said. She fixed her eyes on the reporter, who had lowered the microphone. "And besides, Christian is busy. He's signing books for our shop. So I'm going to ask you to leave him alone."

"Yes, but . . ." the radio reporter began.

Then he stopped. He pressed one of the buttons on his recording equipment. "We were unable to do a short interview because. . . ."

"Get lost," said Gunnel, and Christian couldn't help grinning.

"Thanks," he said after the reporter had left.

"What was that all about? He seemed really determined."

Christian's feeling of relief that the reporter was gone quickly faded, and he swallowed hard before saying:

"He claimed that my name was on the *GT* placard. I've received a few threatening letters, and apparently the press found out about it."

"Oh, my." Gunnel looked first upset and then worried. "Would you like me to go out and buy you a copy of the newspaper so you can see what they wrote?"

"Would you do that?" he said, his heart pounding.

"Sure. I'll be right back." She gave him a comforting pat on the shoulder and left.

Christian sat motionless for a moment, staring into space. Then he picked up his pen and began writing his signature in the books as Gunnel had requested. After a while, he realized he needed to go to the toilet. Since there were still no customers heading for his table, he didn't think a brief absence would be noticed.

He hurried through the employees' break room at the back of the bookshop. A few minutes later, he was already on his way back to his post. He sat down at the table. Gunnel hadn't yet returned with the newspaper, but he was steeling himself for what was to come.

Christian reached for his pen, but then looked with surprise at the books he was supposed to sign. Had he really left them lying on the table like that? They didn't look the same as when he'd dashed off to the toilet, and he thought that maybe someone had taken the opportunity to swipe a copy while he was gone. Yet the stack didn't look any smaller, so he decided he was just imagining things. He picked up the top copy and opened it to write a greeting to the reader.

The page was no longer blank. And the handwriting was all too familiar. She had been here.

Gunnel was coming toward him with the newspaper, and he saw a big picture of himself on the front page. He knew what the article would say. The past was about to catch up with him. She would never give up.

"Good Lord, do you realize how much money you went through the last time you were in Göteborg?" Erik was holding the credit-card bill in his hand, staring at the figures.

"I think it must have been about ten thousand kronor," said Louise as she calmly continued to paint her nails.

"Ten thousand! How is it possible to spend ten thousand on a single shopping trip?" Erik waved the bill in the air and then tossed it on the kitchen table in front of him.

"If I'd bought the purse I was thinking of getting, it would have been closer to thirty thousand," she said, studying the pink color of her nails with satisfaction.

"You're out of your fucking mind!" He picked up the bill again and stared at it, as if sheer force of will might be able to change the total amount due.

"You mean we can't afford it?" asked his wife, looking at him with a sly smile on her lips.

"It's not a question of whether we can afford it or not. It has to do with the fact that I work around the clock making money, which you then squander on . . . idiotic purchases."

"Oh, right. I do nothing at all at home during the day," said Louise, getting to her feet as she fluttered her hands to make the nail polish dry faster. "I just sit here, eating sweets and watching soap operas all day long. And you've been raising the girls all on your own without any help from me, right? You've changed their diapers, fed them, bathed them, driven them wherever they needed to go, and kept the whole house neat and clean. Is that what you mean?" She swept out of the room without giving him another glance.

This was a conversation that they'd had hundreds of times before. And no doubt they'd have it hundreds of times again, if nothing drastic happened. They were like two well-rehearsed dancers who knew all the steps and were able to carry themselves with consummate elegance.

"This is one of the finds that I made in Göteborg. Nice, isn't it?" She was back, holding a leather jacket that she'd taken from a hanger in the front hall. "It was on sale, reduced to only four thousand." She held it up, then hung it back in the hall and went upstairs.

Presumably neither of them was going to win the argument this time either. They were equal adversaries, and every single row they'd had over the years had ended in a tie. Ironically enough, it might have actually been better if one of them had been weaker than the other. Then their unhappy marriage could have come to an end.

"Next time I'm going to cut up your credit card!" he yelled after her. The girls were at a friend's house, so there was no reason to keep his voice down.

"As long as you continue to spend money on your mistresses, you're not going to do a damn thing with my card. Do you think you're the only one who pays attention to the details on credit-card bills?"

Erik swore. He knew that he should have changed his mailing address so that the bills were sent to his office instead. He couldn't deny that he was a generous man when it came to anyone who happened to have the joy and the honor of sleeping with him. He swore again and stuck his feet in his shoes. He realized that, in spite of everything, Louise had won this round. And she knew it.

"I'm going out to buy the evening paper," he shouted, and then slammed the door after himself.

Gravel flew in all directions as he roared off in his BMW, and his pulse didn't slow until he had almost reached the village. If only he'd been smart enough to demand a prenuptial agreement. Then Louise would be nothing more than a bad memory by this time. But back then, they had been poor students, and when he brought up the subject a few years ago, she had merely laughed in his face. Now he refused to let her get away with half of everything that he'd built up, what he'd fought and slaved for. Never! He pounded his fist on the steering wheel but calmed down as he turned into the car park of the Konsum supermarket.

It was Louise's job to do the grocery shopping, so he moved quickly past the shelves stocked with food items. As he headed toward the stand holding newspapers, which was right next to the checkout counters, he came to an abrupt halt in mid-stride. Big black type on the placards screamed at him: *Rising-star author Christian Thydell fears for his life!* And in smaller type: *Collapsed during book launch party after receiving threatening letter!*

Erik had to force his feet to go closer. It felt as if he were trying to walk through deep water. He picked up a copy of *GT* and with trembling fingers leafed through the paper until he found the right page. When he finished reading the article, he dashed for the exit. He hadn't even paid for the paper, and from somewhere far away he heard the clerk shouting at him. But he kept on running. He had to get home.

"How the hell did the newspapers find out about this?"

Patrik and Maja had been out buying groceries, and now Patrik flung a copy of *GT* on the table before he went on putting food away in the refrigerator. Maja had climbed up on a kitchen chair and was eagerly helping him unload the shopping bags.

"Er . . ." was all Erica could say.

Patrik stopped what he was doing. He knew his wife well enough to be able to decipher what her reticence signified.

"What did you do, Erica?" He was holding a tub of Lätt & Lagom margarine in his hand as he looked her in the eye.

"I think it must have leaked out because of me."

"How did that happen? Who did you talk to?"

Now even Maja was aware of the tension in the kitchen. She sat on the chair, staring at her mother. Erica gulped and then told him. "Gaby."

"Gaby!" Patrik nearly choked. "You told

Gaby? You might as well have called *GT* yourself."

"I didn't think that —"

"No, I'm quite certain you didn't. What does Christian say about all this?" asked Patrik, pointing at the blaring headlines.

"I don't know," said Erica. She felt her insides tie themselves in knots whenever she thought about how Christian would react.

"As a police officer, I have to tell you that this is the worst thing that could have happened. This kind of attention will not only incite the person who sent those letters, but new letter-writers as well."

"Don't yell at me. I know it was a dumb thing to do." Erica could feel the tears rising. She cried easily even under normal circumstances, and all the raging hormones of her pregnancy didn't make things any better. "I just wasn't thinking. I phoned Gaby to find out whether they'd received any threatening letters at the publishing house, and I knew instantly that it was stupid to tell her anything about it. But by then it was too late."

Patrik handed Erica a tissue and then put his arms around her, stroking her hair. He whispered in her ear:

"Don't be upset, sweetheart. I'm sorry I yelled. I know you didn't mean for this to happen. Hush, now. . . ." He rocked her in his arms until her sobs began to fade.

"I never thought she would. . . ."

"I know, I know. But she's a different sort of person than you are. And you need to learn that not everybody thinks the same way." He held her at arm's length and looked at her.

Erica dried her eyes on the tissue he'd given her.

"What should I do now?"

"You need to talk to Christian. Apologize and explain."

"But I can't. . . ."

"Don't argue. It's the only solution."

"You're right," said Erica. "But I have to say, I'm dreading it. And I'm going to have a serious talk with Gaby."

"Above all, you need to stop and think next time before you say anything, and consider who you're talking to. Gaby's top priority is her publishing company, and the rest of you come in second. That's just the way it is."

"Okay, okay, I know that. You don't need to harp on it." Erica glared at her husband.

"We'll leave it at that, then," said Patrik, and he went back to putting away the groceries.

"Have you had a chance to take a closer

look at the letters?"

"No, I haven't had a spare moment," said Patrik.

"But you'll do it, won't you?" Erica persisted.

Patrik nodded as he started cutting up vegetables for dinner. "Sure, of course I will. But it would be easier if Christian were cooperating. Then I could have a look at the other letters too."

"So talk to him about it. Maybe you can persuade him."

"Then he'll realize that you're the one who told me about it."

"And I've hung him out to dry in one of Sweden's biggest newspapers, so you'd better watch out, because he's probably still wishing I'd go to hell."

"It won't be that bad."

"If I were in his shoes, I'd never speak to me again."

"Stop being so dramatic and pessimistic," said Patrik, lifting Maja onto the counter so she could sit there and see what he was doing. She loved to watch him cook and always wanted to "help out." "Go over to see him tomorrow and explain what happened. Tell him it was never your intention for things to get out like this. Then I'll have a talk with him and try to get him to cooperate with us." He handed Maja a slice of cucumber, which she instantly started gnawing on, using the few but very sharp teeth she had.

"Tomorrow? Okay," sighed Erica.

"Yes, tomorrow," said Patrik, bending down to give his wife a kiss on the lips.

Ludvig found himself constantly casting glances at the side of the football pitch. It just wasn't the same without his father.

He had been to every practice session, no matter what the weather. Football was their thing. It was the reason their friendship had lasted, in spite of Ludvig's determination to break free of his parents. Because they had actually been friends, he and his father. Of course they'd quarreled now and then, just like all fathers and sons. But in spite of it, they had still remained friends.

Ludvig closed his eyes, picturing his father in his mind, wearing jeans and a woollen sweater with FJÄLLBACKA across the chest. It was the sweater he'd worn so often, to his wife's regret. His hands stuffed in his pockets and his eyes fixed on the ball. And on Ludvig. But he never yelled at his son — not like the other fathers who turned up at practice and football matches, spending their time screaming from the sidelines.

"You better bloody well pull yourself together, Oscar!" or "Damn it, get moving, Danne!" Nothing like that. Not from his father. All he ever said was: "Good, Ludvig!" "Great pass!" "You show them, Ludde!"

Out of the corner of his eye Ludvig saw that the ball was about to be passed to him, and he automatically kicked it onward. He no longer took any joy in playing football. But he still did his best, running hard and fighting to win in spite of the winter chill. He could have easily thrown in the towel and given up. Stayed away from practice, saying to hell with it and the whole team. No one would have blamed him; everyone would have understood. Except his father. Giving up had never been an option for him.

So here Ludvig was. One of the team. But all his joy was missing, and the sideline was empty. His father was gone. He knew that now. Father was gone.

He wasn't allowed to ride in the trailer. And that was only the first of many disappointments during the so-called holiday. Nothing turned out the way he had hoped. The silence, broken only by harsh words, seemed even more oppressive when it didn't have a whole house to move around in. Being on holiday felt like having more time for quarrels, more time for Mother's outbursts. And Father seemed even smaller and grayer.

This was the first time he had gone along, but as he understood it, every year Mother and Father would take the trailer to the place with the peculiar name. Fjällbacka. The name meant "Mountain Hill" in Swedish, but he saw no mountains and only a few hills. The ground was completely flat in the camping area where they parked the trailer, squeezed in among scores of other campers. He wasn't sure that he liked it. But Father had explained that Mother's family was from the area, and that was why she wanted to go there.

But that was strange too, because he didn't meet any relatives. During one of the arguments inside the cramped space of the trailer, he finally understood that someone called the Old Bitch lived here, and that she was what his mother meant by "family." What a funny name that was. The Old Bitch. But it didn't sound as if his mother cared much for her, because her voice got even harsher when she talked about the woman, and they never did see her. So why did they have to come to this place at all?

Yet what he hated most about Fjällbacka and being on holiday was having to go swimming. He'd never swum in the sea before. At first he wasn't sure what to think. But his mother admonished him. Said she refused to have a wimp for a son, and she told him to stop whining. So he took a deep breath and timidly waded into the frigid water, even though the feeling of cold and salt on his legs made him gasp for air. When the water reached up to his waist, he stopped. It was too cold, he couldn't breathe. And he could feel something moving around his feet, touching the calves of his legs, something creeping and crawling over him. Mother waded out to him from shore, laughing, and then took his hand to lead him further out. All of a sudden he felt happy. She was holding his hand, and her laughter bounced off the surface of the water and off of him too. His feet now seemed to move of their own accord, as if they had left the sandy bottom and were floating. At last he couldn't feel anything solid under his feet, but that didn't matter, because Mother had ahold of him, she was carrying him, she loved him.

Then she let go. He felt the palm of her hand slide over his, then her fingers slipped past his fingertips until not only his feet but his hands were fumbling with nothingness. Again he felt the cold pressing against his chest, and the water seemed to rise up. It reached his shoulders, his neck, and he raised his chin to prevent the water from reaching his mouth, but it rose too fast, and he couldn't stop it. His mouth filled with salt and cold, which raced down his throat, and the water kept rising — over his cheeks, his eyes, and he felt the water close like a lid over his head, until all sound vanished and the only thing he heard was the roar of what was crawling and creeping.

He flailed his arms, lashing out at whatever it was that wanted to pull him downward. But he was no match for the massive wave of water, and when he finally felt someone's skin against his own, a hand on his arm, his first instinct was to defend himself. Then he was yanked upward, and the top of his head surfaced. The first breath was brutal and painful, then he greedily gasped for air. Mother had a tight grip on his arm, but that didn't matter. Because the water was no longer trying to get him.

He looked up at her, grateful that she had rescued him, that she hadn't let him disappear. But what he saw in her eyes was contempt. Somehow he'd done something wrong, he had disappointed her again. If only he knew why.

He had black and blue marks on his arm for days afterward.

7

"Did you really have to drag me over here today?" It was rare for Kenneth to let his annoyance show. He believed in staying calm and focused in every situation. But Lisbet had looked so sad when he told her that Erik had phoned and he'd have to go over to the office for a couple of hours even though it was Sunday. She hadn't complained, and, in a sense, that just made it worse. She knew how few hours they had left together. How important they were, how precious. And yet she offered no objections. Instead, he saw how she summoned the strength to be able to smile and say: "Of course you have to go. I'll be fine."

He almost wished that she had gotten angry and screamed at him. Told him that it was about time for him to get his priorities straight. But she didn't have it in her to do anything like that. He couldn't recall a single occasion in their twenty-year marriage when she had raised her voice to him. Or to anyone else, for that matter. She had accepted all setbacks and sorrows with equanimity, and she'd even comforted him when he was the one to break down. Whenever he lacked the energy to carry on, she had mustered enough strength for both of them.

Now he'd left her at home because he needed to go to work. He was going to waste a few precious hours they could have spent together, and he hated himself because he always came running whenever Erik snapped his fingers. He couldn't understand why. It was a pattern that had been established so early on that by now it was practically part of his personality. And Lisbet was always the one who had to suffer for it.

Erik didn't even bother to answer his question. He just kept staring at the computer screen, as if he were in another world.

"Was it really necessary for me to come in today?" Kenneth repeated. "On a Sunday? Couldn't it wait until tomorrow?"

Erik slowly turned to face Kenneth.

"I have the utmost respect for your personal situation," he said at last. "But if we don't take care of all the arrangements before the bidding this week, we might as well pack up the whole company. We all have to make sacrifices."

Kenneth silently wondered what sort of sacrifices Erik ever made. And nothing was as dire as Erik was predicting. He could have easily put together the documents on Monday. His claim that the company was on the verge of ruin was pure exaggeration. Most likely Erik merely needed a pretext to get out of the house. But why had he felt compelled to drag Kenneth over here too? The answer was obvious: because he could.

Then they each returned to their respective tasks and worked in silence for a while. The office consisted of one large room, so there was no possibility of closing a door for some privacy. Kenneth cast a surreptitious glance at Erik. There was something different about him. It was hard to pinpoint, but Erik looked somehow less distinct, more worn out. His hair was not as perfectly combed as usual, and his shirt was slightly wrinkled. No, he was not himself today. Kenneth considered asking him if everything was okay at home, but he restrained himself. Instead he said, as calmly as he could:

"Did you see the news about Christian yesterday?"

Erik gave a start. "Yes."

136

"How terrible. To be threatened like that by some nutcase," said Kenneth, his tone of voice casual, almost easygoing. But his heart was pounding hard.

"Hmm. . . ." Erik kept his eyes on the computer screen. But he didn't touch the keyboard or the mouse.

"Did Christian mention anything about that to you?" It was like trying to make himself stop picking at a scab. He didn't want to talk about this topic, and Erik clearly didn't want to discuss it either. Yet Kenneth couldn't stop himself. "Did he?"

"No, he never told me about any sort of threats," said Erik, beginning to sort through the documents on his desk. "But he's been really preoccupied with his book, so we haven't seen much of each other lately. And I suppose most people would prefer to keep something like that to themselves."

"Shouldn't he talk to the police about it?"

"How do you know Christian hasn't already done that?" Erik continued aimlessly riffling through the piles of documents.

"True. That's very true. . . ." Kenneth subsided into silence for a moment. "But what could the police do if the letters were anonymous? I mean, they could have come from any lunatic."

"How would I know?" said Erik, swearing as he got a paper cut. "Shit!" He sucked on the injured finger.

"Do you think the threats are serious?"

Erik sighed. "Why do we have to speculate about all this? I told you, I have no idea." His voice rose slightly, quavering on the last words. Kenneth looked at him in surprise. Erik really was not himself. Did it have something to do with the company?

Kenneth had never trusted Erik. Had he done something stupid? He instantly dismissed the idea. He was much too familiar with the firm's accounts; he would have noticed if Erik had decided to make any crazy moves financially. It was probably something to do with Louise. It was a mystery how those two had managed to stay together for so long. Everyone except Erik and Louise could see that the couple would do themselves a big favor if they said goodbye and went their separate ways. But it wasn't Kenneth's place to point this out. He had enough worries of his own.

"I was just wondering," said Kenneth.

He clicked open the Excel file with the latest monthly statements. But his thoughts were somewhere else entirely.

The dress still smelled of her. Christian

pressed it to his nose, inhaling the microscopic traces of her perfume that were embedded in the fabric. Whenever he fell asleep with the scent in his nostrils, he could picture her quite clearly in his mind. The dark hair that reached to her waist and which she usually wore in a plait or gathered in a bun at the back of her neck. It could have looked old-fashioned or even spinsterish, but not on her.

She had moved like a dancer, although she had abandoned her career as a dancer long ago. She claimed that she hadn't been ambitious enough. Not because of lack of talent, but she hadn't had the determination required always to put dance first, to sacrifice love and time and laughter and friends. She had loved life too much.

So she'd stopped dancing. But when they met, and right up until the end, she'd still had the lithe rhythm of a dancer in her body. He could sit and stare at her for hours. Watch her walking around the house, cleaning up and humming while her feet moved so gracefully that she looked like she was floating.

Again he pressed the dress to his face. How refreshing and cool the fabric felt against his feverishly hot skin, catching on the unshaven stubble of his cheek. The last time she had worn the dress was on Midsummer Eve. The blue of the dress had mirrored the color of her eyes, and the dark plait hanging down her back had gleamed as brightly as the lustrous fabric.

It was a fabulous evening. One of the few Midsummers that had offered glorious sunshine, and they'd sat outside in the yard, eating herring and boiled new potatoes. They had cooked the meal together. The baby was lying in the pram, with the mosquito netting firmly in place so that no insects could get in. The child was well protected.

The baby's name fluttered past, and he gave a start, as if he'd jabbed his hand on something sharp. He forced himself to think about the frosty beer glasses and the friends who had raised those glasses in a toast, in honor of summer and love and the two of them. He thought about the strawberries that she brought out in a big bowl. Remembered how she had sat at the kitchen table, cleaning them, and how he had teased her because of the mess she'd made and the fact that every third or fourth strawberry had ended up in her mouth instead of in the bowl. The serving bowl that would later be presented to their guests, along with whipped cream topped with a sprinkling of sugar, just the way she'd been taught by her grandmother. She'd responded to his teasing with a laugh, then pulled him close and kissed him with lips that tasted of ripe berries.

He began to sob as he sat there holding the dress in his hands. He couldn't help it. Little dark spots appeared on the material from his tears, which he quickly wiped away on the sleeve of his shirt, not wanting to soil the dress, refusing to soil what little he had left.

Christian carefully put the dress back in the suitcase. It was all that remained of them. The only thing he could bear to keep. He closed up the suitcase and pushed it back into the corner. He didn't want Sanna to find it. His stomach turned over at the mere thought of her opening it, looking inside, and touching the dress. He knew it was wrong, but he had chosen Sanna for only one reason: the fact that she was completely different in appearance. She didn't have lips that tasted of strawberries, and she didn't move like a dancer.

But it turned out not to be enough. The past had still caught up with him. Just as malevolently as it had caught up with her, wearing that blue dress. And now he could see no way out.

■ ■ ■ ■

"Could you watch Leo for a while?" Paula was looking at her mother, Rita, but then she cast an even more hopeful glance at Mellberg. Soon after their son's birth, both she and Johanna had realized that Rita's new boyfriend was the perfect babysitter. Mellberg was totally incapable of saying no.

"Well, we were actually about to —" Rita began, but Mellberg jumped in and said eagerly:

"No problem. We'll be happy to take care of the little fellow. The two of you should just go off and do whatever you were planning to do."

Rita sighed in resignation, but she couldn't resist casting a look of appreciation at this man — a diamond in the rough, and that was putting it mildly — whom she'd chosen to live with. She knew that many people regarded him as a boor, an unkempt and brash sort of man. But from the very beginning she'd seen other qualities in him, qualities that she as a woman should be able to encourage.

And she was right. Bertil Mellberg treated her like a queen. It was enough for Rita to see him looking at her grandson to know what hidden resources he possessed. His love for the infant was beyond comprehension. The only problem was that she herself had swiftly been demoted to second place, but she could live with that. Besides, she'd begun making progress with Bertil on the dance floor. He'd never be a salsa king, but she no longer had to make sure to wear shoes with steel toes.

"If you wouldn't mind taking care of him on your own for a while, maybe Mama could come with us. We were thinking of driving out to Torp to buy a few things for Leo's room."

"Hand him over," said Bertil enthusiastically, motioning at the baby lying in Paula's arms. "We can manage for a couple of hours. A bottle or two when he gets hungry, and then a little quality time spent with Grandpa Bertil. What more could the boy ask for?"

Paula put her son in Mellberg's arms. Good lord, what an odd couple those two made. But she couldn't deny that there was a special connection between them. Even though, in her eyes, Bertil Mellberg was the worst boss she could imagine, he'd shown himself to be the world's best grandfather.

"So you're sure you'll be all right?" asked Rita, a bit uneasy. Even though Bertil often helped out with Leo, his experience of caring for babies was limited, to say the least. His own son, Simon, had already been a teenager by the time he made an appearance in Mellberg's life.

"Of course I'm sure," said Bertil, sounding offended. "Eat, shit, sleep. How hard could it be? I've been doing exactly the same things for almost sixty years." He more or less shoved the women out of the apartment and then closed the door behind them. Now they'd have some peace and quiet, he and Leo.

Two hours later, he was completely soaked with sweat. Leo was crying at the top of his lungs, and the smell of dirty diapers had settled over the living room like a fog. Grandpa Bertil was desperately trying to lull the baby to sleep, but Leo just cried louder and louder. Mellberg's hair, which was usually combed over into a neat nest on top of his head, had tumbled down over his right ear, and he could feel the sweat spreading under his arms in patches as big as platters.

He was close to panicking, and he cast a sidelong glance at his mobile phone lying on the coffee table. Should he call the girls? They were probably still in Torp, and it would take them a good forty-five minutes to drive home, even if they started out at once. And if he phoned for help, they might not dare leave him alone with their son again. No, he was going to have to find a way to cope on his own. He'd wrestled with quite a few ugly customers in his day. He'd also had to fire his weapon in the line of duty and deal with demented junkies wielding knives. So he should be able to handle this situation. After all, Leo wasn't any bigger than a loaf of bread, even though he had a voice loud enough for a grown man.

"Okay, now, my boy, first we need to analyze the situation," said Mellberg, putting down the furious baby. "Let's see. Looks like you've made a mess in your diaper. And you're probably hungry. In other words, we've got a crisis at both ends. It's just a matter of which one to prioritize." Mellberg was talking loudly, in order to drown out the screaming. "Okay, eating always comes first — at least, for me it does. So let's find you a big bottle of formula."

Bertil lifted Leo up and carried him into the kitchen. He'd been given detailed instructions on how to make the formula and, using the microwave, it took no time at all. He carefully tested the temperature by sucking a little from the bottle himself.

"Hmmm, doesn't really taste like much, my boy. But you'll just have to wait for the good stuff until you're a bit older."

Leo screamed even louder at the sight of the bottle, so Bertil sat down at the kitchen table and nestled the infant in his left arm. When the nipple touched Leo's lips, he began greedily sucking the formula into his stomach. He finished off the whole bottle in a flash, and Mellberg could feel the tiny body relaxing. But soon the boy began squirming again, and the odor was now so strong that Mellberg couldn't stand it any longer. The only problem was that changing diapers wasn't a task that he'd managed very successfully so far.

"All right, now we've satisfied one end. Let's go take care of the other," he said in a sprightly tone of voice that didn't correspond in the slightest to his true feelings about the job.

Mellberg carried the whimpering Leo into the bathroom. He'd helped the girls fasten a changing table to the wall, and there he found everything he needed for Operation Dirty Diaper.

He placed the infant on the table and pulled off his pants, trying to breathe through his mouth, but it didn't help much because the smell was so overwhelming.

Mellberg loosened the tape on the diaper and just about fainted when the whole mess in all its stinky glory appeared before his eyes.

"Dear Jesus," he muttered. He glanced around in desperation and caught sight of a package of wet wipes. When he reached for them, letting go of the baby's legs, Leo took the opportunity to bury his feet in the dirty diaper.

"No, no, don't do that," said Mellberg, grabbing a whole fistful of wipes to dry off the baby's bottom and feet. But all he managed to do was smear the shit around until he realized that he needed to remove the cause of the problem. He lifted Leo by his legs and coaxed out the diaper, which he then dropped into the wastebasket standing on the floor, unable to stop the grimace that appeared on his face.

Having used up half the package of wipes, he finally saw a light at the end of the tunnel. The worst of the mess had been cleaned up, and Leo had calmed down. Mellberg carefully wiped away the last of it and took a new diaper from the shelf above the changing table.

"All right, we're just about done here," he said with satisfaction as Leo kicked his legs, seeming pleased with the chance to air out his bare bottom. "I wonder which way this goes on." Mellberg twisted and turned the diaper, deciding at last that the little animal pictures must go in the back, like the label on a piece of clothing. It didn't seem to fit very well, and the tape didn't close properly. How could it be so hard to make a proper diaper? It was lucky that he was such an efficient person who regarded a problem as a challenge.

Mellberg lifted Leo up, carried him back to the kitchen, and held him against his shoulder as he rummaged in the bottom drawer under the counter. There he found what he was looking for. A roll of tape. He went into the living room, placed Leo on the sofa, and wrapped tape several times around the diaper. Then he sat back to admire his handiwork.

"Okay now. The girls were worried that I wouldn't be able to take care of you. What do you say, Leo? Don't you think we've earned the right to take a little snooze?"

Bertil picked up the now well-taped baby and held him in his arms as he settled himself in a comfortable position on the sofa. Leo rooted around a bit before burrowing his face in the hollow of the police chief's neck.

When the women in their lives came home

half an hour later, they were both sound asleep.

"Is Christian at home?" Erica would have liked nothing better than to turn and run when Sanna opened the door. But Patrik was right. She had no choice.

"Yes, but he's up in the attic. I'll call him." Sanna turned toward the stairs. "Christian! You have a visitor!" she shouted and then looked again at Erica. "Come on in. He'll be down in a minute."

"Thanks." Erica felt awkward standing there in the front hall next to Sanna, but soon they heard footsteps on the stairs. When Christian came into view, she noticed how worn-out he looked, and the guilt she was feeling grew even worse.

"Hi," he said, looking a bit puzzled to see her so soon, but he came to give her a hug.

"There's something I need to talk to you about," said Erica, feeling again an urge to turn on her heel and dash out the door.

"Really? Well, come on in," said Christian, motioning toward the living room. She took off her coat and shoes and followed after him.

"Would you like something to drink?"

"No, thanks." She shook her head. All she

wanted was to get this whole thing over with.

"How did the book-signings go?" she asked, sitting down at one end of the living-room sofa. She sank deep into the cushions.

"Fine," said Christian in a tone of voice that did not invite further questions. "Did you see the newspaper yesterday?" he asked instead. His face was a pallid gray in the winter light filtering through the window.

"Yes, and that's what I wanted to talk to you about." Erica paused to muster her courage to go on. One of the twins gave her a hard kick in the ribs, and she gasped.

"Are the babies kicking?"

"You can say that again." She took a deep breath and went on. "It's my fault that the story got leaked to the press."

"What do you mean?" Christian sat up straighter.

"I wasn't the one who tipped them off," she hurried to explain. "But I was stupid enough to mention it to the wrong person." She didn't dare meet Christian's eyes. Instead, she looked down at her hands.

"You mean Gaby?" said Christian wearily. "But didn't you realize that she would —"

Erica interrupted him. "Patrik said the exact same thing. And you're both right. I should have known not to trust her, that she would view it as an opportunity to get some publicity. I feel like a real fool. I shouldn't have been so naïve."

"Well, there's not much to be done about it now," said Christian.

His resigned attitude made Erica feel even worse. She almost wished that he would yell at her. That would have been preferable to looking at the tired and disappointed expression on his face.

"I'm sorry, Christian. I'm so sorry about all this."

"Let's just hope that she was right, in any case."

"Who?"

"Gaby. Then at least I'll sell more books as a result."

"I don't understand how anyone can be so cynical. To throw you to the wolves like that just because it might be good for business."

"She didn't get to be as successful as she is today by trying to be everybody's friend."

"But still. It can't be worth it." Erica was filled with remorse about what she'd done, even though she'd acted in good faith. For the life of her, she couldn't understand how anyone with a conscience could behave the way Gaby had done. And all for the sake of making a profit.

"I'm sure it will blow over," said Christian, but he didn't sound convinced.

"Were you hounded by reporters today?" Erica shifted her position, trying to get more comfortable. No matter how she sat, it felt like one or another of her internal organs was getting pinched.

"After the first phone call yesterday, I switched off my mobile. I'm not planning to give them any more fuel for the fire."

"So what about . . ." Erica hesitated. "Have you received any more threats? I know that you have no reason to trust me after all this, but believe me when I say that I've learned my lesson."

Christian seemed to shut down. He looked out of the window, as if deciding what to say. When he did answer, his voice sounded weak and exhausted.

"I don't want to dwell on that. It's been blown way out of proportion."

There was a crash upstairs, and a child started crying, loud and shrill. Christian made no move to get up, but Erica heard Sanna dashing upstairs.

"Do the children get along?" Erica asked, motioning toward the room overhead.

"Not really. My older son doesn't like competition. I suppose that's a good way to describe the problem." Christian smiled.

"Most people have a tendency to focus a little too much on the first child right after the birth," replied Erica.

"You're probably right," said Christian, his smile disappearing. He had a strange look on his face, and Erica couldn't really decipher what it might mean. Upstairs, both boys were now crying, joined by Sanna's angry scolding.

"You need to talk to the police," said Erica. "I'm sure you realize that I mentioned the matter to Patrik, and I don't regret doing so. He thinks you should definitely take this whole thing seriously, and the first step is to report it to the police. You could start by just going to see him — unofficially, if you like." She could hear that she sounded like she was pleading with him, but the letters had really upset her, and she had the feeling that Christian felt the same way.

"I don't want to talk about this anymore," he said, getting up. "I know you didn't mean for things to turn out the way they did after you talked to Gaby. But you need to respect the fact that I don't want to make a big deal out of this."

The screams overhead had now gone up several decibels, and Christian headed for the stairs.

"You'll have to excuse me, but I need to

go and help Sanna before the boys kill each other. You can find your way out, can't you?" Then he rushed off without saying good-bye, and Erica had the distinct impression that he was glad to escape.

Weren't they ever going back home? The trailer seemed to get smaller with every day that passed, and he'd already explored every corner of the camping area. Maybe once they were home, they'd start to like him again. Here, it felt as if he didn't exist at all.

Father sat around solving crossword puzzles, and Mother was ill. At least, that was the explanation he'd received when he tried to go in and see her. She spent the days inside the trailer's cramped sleeping area. And she hadn't gone swimming with him again. Even though he couldn't forget the terror or the feeling of something wriggling past his feet, he would have preferred that to being constantly banished from the trailer.

"Mother is ill. Go out and play."

So he would take off, filling the hours of the day on his own. At first the other children at the campground tried to play with him, but he wasn't interested. If he wasn't allowed to be with his mother, then he didn't want to be with anybody.

When she didn't get better, he started to worry more and more. Sometimes he'd hear her throwing up. And she looked so pale. What if it was something serious? What if she too was going to die and leave him behind? Just like his mama had.

The mere thought made him want to crawl into a corner and hide. Shut his eyes tight, so tight that the darkness couldn't grab ahold of him. He refused to think about that. His beautiful mother could not die. Not her too.

He'd found a special place for himself. Up on the slope, with a view of the campground and the water. If he craned his neck, he could even see the roof of their trailer. That's where he now spent his days, in the one place where he was left in peace. Up there, he could make the hours fly by.

Father wanted to go home too. He'd heard him say that. But Mother refused. "I'm not going to give the Old Bitch that satisfaction," Mother said as she lay on the bunk, looking pale and thinner than usual. She wanted the Old Bitch to know that they'd been here all summer, as usual, though they hadn't visited her even once. No, they weren't going home. She'd rather die than leave early.

There was no further discussion. Once

Mother had decided something, that was how it had to be. Each day, he went out to his special place and sat there with his arms wrapped around his knees as all sorts of thoughts and fantasies raced through his mind.

If only they could go back home, then everything would be the way it used to be. He was sure of it.

8

"Don't run off too far, Rocky!" Göte Persson shouted, but the dog wasn't listening, as usual. Göte just managed to catch a glimpse of the golden retriever's tail before Rocky turned left and disappeared behind a boulder. Göte tried to pick up the pace, but his right leg made that impossible. Since his stroke, his leg had had a hard time keeping up with the rest of his body, and yet he still considered himself lucky. The doctors had given him very little hope of ever being able to move much on his own again, because his entire right side had been affected. But they hadn't counted on how stubborn a man he was. Thanks to his God-given tenacity and his physiotherapist, who had pushed him as if he were training for the Olympics, he'd gained greater mobility every week that passed. Occasionally he'd suffered setbacks, and he had to admit that several times he'd been close to giving up. But he had soldiered on, continually making progress that brought him closer to his goal.

By now he was taking daily one-hour walks with Rocky. He walked slowly, and with a noticeable limp, but he kept on going. They went out no matter what the weather was, and each yard forward was a victory.

The dog had come back into view. He was on the beach now, sniffing about near the Sälvik swimming area and glancing up once in a while to make sure his master hadn't gotten lost. Göte took the opportunity to pause and catch his breath. For the hundredth time, he put his hand in his pocket to touch the mobile phone he'd brought along. Yes, it was still there. Just to make sure, he took it out and checked to see that it was switched on and that he hadn't accidentally turned off the ringer. He didn't want to miss a call, but no one had tried to phone him. He impatiently stuffed the mobile back in his pocket.

He knew it was ridiculous to check the phone every five minutes. They'd promised to call when they left for the hospital. His first grandchild. His daughter Ina was almost two weeks past her due date, and Göte couldn't understand how she and her husband could stay so calm. To be honest, he'd heard a trace of annoyance in his daughter's voice when he'd called for the tenth time that day to ask if anything was happening yet. But he seemed to be considerably more concerned than they were. He'd spent the better part of the last few nights wide awake, staring alternately at the alarm clock and his mobile phone. These kinds of things tended to happen in the middle of the night. And what if he was sleeping too soundly to hear when they called?

He yawned. The nighttime vigils had started to take their toll on him. So many emotions had been stirred up inside him when Ina and Jesper announced that they were expecting a child. They'd told him a couple of days after he collapsed and was rushed by ambulance to the hospital in Uddevalla. They had actually planned on waiting to tell him, since it was so early in Ina's pregnancy, and they'd only just found out themselves. But no one had thought that Göte would survive. They weren't even sure that he could hear them as he lay in the hospital bed, hooked up to all sorts of tubes and machines.

But he did hear them; he'd heard every single word. And the news had given his stubborn nature something to hold on to.

Something to live for. He was going to be a grandfather. His only daughter, the light of his life, was going to have a baby. How could he miss such an important occasion? He knew that Britt-Marie was waiting for him, and he actually wouldn't have minded letting go of life so he could see her again. He had missed her every day, every minute since she died and left him and Ina on their own. But he was needed now, as he explained to Britt-Marie, telling her that he couldn't join her yet because their daughter needed him here.

Britt-Marie understood. As he knew she would. He had regained consciousness, waking from the sleep that had been so different and in many ways so enticing. He had climbed out of bed, and every step he'd taken since then was for the sake of the little grandson or granddaughter. He had so much to give, and he was planning to use every extra minute of life he'd been granted to spoil his grandchild. Ina and Jesper could protest as much as they liked. It was a grandfather's prerogative.

The mobile phone in his pocket rang shrilly, making him jump and tearing him away from his thoughts. Eagerly he pulled out the phone, almost dropping it on the ground. He looked at the display. His shoulders sagged with disappointment when he saw the name of a good friend. He didn't dare answer. He didn't want his daughter to get a busy signal if she called.

He couldn't see Rocky anymore, so he put the mobile back in his pocket and limped toward the spot where he'd last seen the dog. Out of the corner of his eye, he caught the flash of something bright, and he turned his head to look at the water.

"Rocky!" he shouted, alarm evident in his voice. The dog had wandered out onto the ice. He was almost twenty yards out, standing there with his head lowered. When he heard Göte yelling, he started barking wildly and pawing at the ice. Göte held his breath. If it had been a bitterly cold winter, he wouldn't have been so concerned. Many times, usually just after New Year's, he and Britt-Marie had packed sandwiches and a thermos of coffee and walked across the ice to one of the nearby islands. But this year the water had alternately frozen and thawed, and he knew the ice wasn't to be trusted.

"Rocky!" he shouted again. "Come here!" He tried to sound as stern as he could, but the dog ignored him.

Göte now had only one thought in his head. He couldn't lose Rocky. The dog would die if he fell through the ice and landed in the frigid water, and Göte simply couldn't bear for that to happen. They'd been companions for ten years, and in his mind he had pictured so many scenes of his future grandchild playing with the dog. He just couldn't imagine being without Rocky.

He walked along the shoreline, then put out one foot to test the ice. Thousands of hairline cracks instantly appeared on the surface, but the ice held. Apparently it was thick enough to bear his weight, so he headed toward Rocky, who was still barking and pawing at the ice.

"Come here, boy," coaxed Göte, but the dog stayed where he was, refusing to budge.

The ice felt more solid here than near the shoreline, but Göte still decided to minimize the risk by lying down on his stomach. With an effort he dropped down and then stretched out, trying to ignore the cold that pierced right through him even though he was bundled up in his winter clothes.

It was difficult to move forward on his stomach. His feet kept slipping when he tried to get some traction, and he wished that he'd been a little less vain and had worn shoes with cleats. That was what every sensible retiree did in Sweden when it was slippery outside.

He glanced about and discovered two

sticks that he might be able to use instead. He managed to drag himself over to them and then began using them as improvised ice cleats. Now it was easier, and inch by inch he made his way toward the dog. Occasionally he tried calling Rocky again, but the dog was so interested in whatever he had found that he refused to take his eyes off it even for a second.

When Göte had almost reached Rocky, he heard the ice start to crack and protest under his weight. He allowed himself to think how ironic it would be if he'd spent months and months regaining his mobility, only to fall through the ice at Sälvik and drown. But the ice continued to hold, and he was now so close that he could stretch out his hand and touch Rocky's fur.

"Okay, boy, you shouldn't be out here," he said soothingly, sliding forward a little more in an attempt to grab the dog's collar. He had no idea how he was going to drag both himself and an intractable dog back to shore. But somehow he would manage.

"Now what's so interesting out here, anyway?" He grabbed Rocky's collar. Then he looked down.

At that moment his mobile rang in his pocket.

■ ■ ■ ■

As usual, it was hard to get anything done on a Monday morning. Patrik was sitting at his desk with his feet propped up on the edge. He was staring at a photo of Magnus Kjellner, as if willing the man to reveal where he was. Or rather, where his remains were.

Patrik was also worried about Christian. He pulled out the right-hand desk drawer and took out the little plastic bag containing the letter and card. He would have liked to send both to the lab for analysis to look for fingerprints. But there was so little to go on, and nothing specific had happened yet. Not even Erica, who unlike Patrik had read all the letters, could say for sure that someone was intending to harm Christian. But her gut told her that he was in danger. And Patrik felt the same way. They both sensed something malevolent in the words. He had to smile at himself. What a word to choose. *Malevolent.* Not a very scientific description. But the letters seemed to convey an intent to do harm. That was the best way he could describe it. And that feeling made him very uneasy.

He'd discussed things with Erica when

she came back from visiting Christian. He had wanted to go over there and have a talk with him too, but Erica had dissuaded him. She didn't think Christian would be receptive to the idea, and she asked Patrik to wait until the newspaper headlines had calmed down a bit. He had agreed. But now that he sat in his office staring at the elegant handwriting, he wondered whether he'd made the right decision.

He gave a start when the phone rang.

"Patrik Hedström," he said. He put the plastic bag back in the desk drawer, which he then closed. Suddenly he froze. "Excuse me? What?" He listened tensely, and as soon as he put down the phone, he went into action. He made several quick calls before dashing out into the hall and knocking on Mellberg's door. He went right in, without waiting for an answer, and woke up both the master and his dog.

"What the devil . . . ?" Mellberg hauled himself upright from his slumped position in his office chair and stared at Patrik. "Didn't you ever learn to knock before entering?" The police chief straightened his comb-over. "Well? Can't you see that I'm busy? What do you want?"

"I think we've found Magnus Kjellner."

Mellberg sat up straighter. "Is that right?

So where is he? On an island in the Caribbean?"

"Not exactly. He's under the ice. Off of Sälvik."

"Under the ice?"

Ernst could sense the tension in the air, and he pricked up his ears.

"An old man who was out there with his dog just called to report finding a body. Of course we can't be sure that it's Magnus Kjellner, since the body hasn't been identified yet. But it seems highly likely."

"So what the hell are we waiting for?" said Mellberg, jumping to his feet. He grabbed his jacket and pushed past Patrik. "I can't understand why you're all such bumblers at this station! How long does it take to spit out the news? Let's go! You're driving!"

Mellberg ran toward the garage while Patrik hurried to his office to get his jacket. He sighed. He would have preferred not to take his boss along, but at the same time he knew that Mellberg wouldn't want to miss the chance to be in the center of all the action. As long as he didn't have to do any of the real work, that is.

"Okay, step on it!" Mellberg was already sitting in the passenger seat. Patrik got in behind the wheel and turned the key in the ignition.

■ ■ ■ ■

"Is this your first time on TV?" chirped the woman doing his makeup.

Christian met her glance in the mirror and nodded. His mouth was dry and his hands sweaty. Two weeks ago, he'd accepted the invitation to appear on the *Morning* show on TV4, a decision that he now bitterly regretted. During the long train ride to Stockholm the night before, he'd had to fight the impulse to turn around and go home.

Gaby had been overjoyed when the producer from TV4 had called. He said they'd heard rumors that a new star in the author firmament was about to be discovered, and they wanted to be the first to book him for a television interview. Gaby had explained to Christian that there was no better marketing opportunity, and he would sell tons of books just from a brief appearance.

And he'd allowed himself to be seduced by the idea. He'd asked for time off from his job at the library, and Gaby had bought his train ticket and made his hotel reservation in Stockholm. At first he'd felt quite excited about being on TV to promote *The Mermaid*. But the newspaper placards over the weekend had ruined everything. How could he have allowed Gaby to talk him into this? He'd lived such a reclusive life for so many years, and he'd convinced himself that by now it would be okay to step forward. Even when the letters started arriving, he had continued to live under the misconception that everything was over, that he was safe.

The newspaper headlines had jolted him out of his delusion. Someone would notice, someone would remember. Everything would be made public again. He shuddered, and the makeup woman looked at him.

"Don't tell me you're freezing when it's so warm in here. Are you coming down with a cold?"

Christian nodded and smiled. That was the easiest way to respond, so he wouldn't have to explain.

The makeup on his face looked thick and unnatural. Some of the flesh-colored cream had even been applied to his ears and hands. Apparently the normal skin tone looked pale and slightly greenish on TV without makeup. In some ways he didn't really mind. It was like putting on a mask that he could hide behind.

"All right. We're done here. The stage manager will come to get you in a minute."

The makeup artist inspected her work as Christian stared at himself in the mirror. The mask stared back.

A few minutes later, he was escorted to the green room just outside the door to the TV studio. An impressive breakfast buffet had been set up, but he made do with a small glass of orange juice. Adrenaline was surging through his body, and his hand shook slightly as he raised the glass.

"It's time," said the stage manager. "Come with me." And she motioned for him to follow. Christian put down his glass, still half-filled with juice. His legs wobbling, he walked behind her to the studio, which was down one flight of stairs.

"You can sit here," she whispered, ushering him to his seat. Christian sat down and then gave a start when he felt a hand on his shoulder.

"Sorry. I just need to attach the microphone," whispered a man wearing a headset. Christian nodded. His mouth was now even drier, if that was possible, and he drank the whole glass of water that was put in front of him.

"Hi, Christian. Great to see you. I read your book, and I have to tell you that I think it's amazing." Kristin Kaspersen held out her hand, and after a moment's hesitation,

170

Christian politely responded. Considering how sweaty his palm was, it must have felt like shaking hands with a wet sponge. Then Anders Kraft, the other talk-show host, came over and sat down as well. He said hello to Christian and introduced himself.

A copy of the book was lying on the table. Behind them, the weather forecaster was delivering his report, so they had to carry on their conversation in a whisper.

"You're not nervous, are you?" asked Kristin with a smile. "You don't need to be. Just stay focused on us, and everything will be fine."

Christian nodded mutely. His water glass had been refilled, and again he drank it down in one go.

"We're on in twenty seconds," said Anders Kraft, giving him a wink. Christian felt himself calmed by the confidence exuded by the man and woman seated across from him. He did everything he could not to think about the cameras surrounding them that were about to broadcast the program live to a large segment of the Swedish population.

Kristin began talking as she looked at a spot behind him, and he realized that the program had started. His heart was pounding, there was a rushing in his ears, and he had to force himself to listen to what Kristin was saying. After a brief introduction, she asked her first question.

"Christian, the critics are raving about your first novel, *The Mermaid.* And there has also been an unusual amount of advance interest from readers. How does it feel?"

His voice quavered a bit as he started talking, but Kristin kept her eyes steadily fixed on his, and he concentrated on looking at her instead of at the camera, which he glimpsed out of the corner of his eye. After stumbling over a few words, he could hear that his voice got stronger.

"It's been incredible. I've always dreamed of being a writer, and to see that dream realized and to get this kind of reception is way beyond my wildest imagination."

"The publisher is putting a lot of PR behind your book. We've been seeing signs in all the bookshop windows, and it's rumored that the first printing was much bigger than usual. The book pages of all the newspapers seem to be competing with each other to compare you with some of the literary greats. Has it been a little overwhelming for you?" Anders Kraft gave him a friendly look.

Christian was feeling more confident, and his heart had returned to its normal rhythm.

"It means a lot that my publisher believes in me and is doing so much promotion for the book. But it does feel a little strange to be compared to other authors. We all have our own unique style of writing." Now he was on solid ground. He began to relax, and after a couple more questions he felt as if he could have sat there and talked all day.

Kristin Kaspersen picked up something from the table and held it up to the camera. When he saw what it was, Christian again broke out in a sweat. Saturday's issue of *GT* with his own name in large letters. The words DEATH THREATS screamed at him. There was no more water in his glass, so he swallowed over and over, trying to wet his dry mouth.

"It's becoming a rather common phenomenon in Sweden for celebrities to be subjected to threats. But this started up even before your name became known to the general public. Who do you think has been sending you these threatening letters?"

At first he uttered only a croaking sound, but then he managed to say:

"This is something that has been taken out of context and blown all out of proportion. There are always people who are jealous or who have psychological problems, and . . . well, I don't really have anything more to say about it." His whole body felt tense, and under the table he wiped his hands on his trousers.

"I'd like to thank you for coming to talk to us about your critically acclaimed novel, *The Mermaid.*" Anders Kraft held up the book to the camera and smiled. Relief flooded over Christian when he realized that the interview was over.

"That went very well," said Kristin Kaspersen, gathering up her papers.

"Yes, it did," said Anders Kraft, standing up. "Excuse me, but I have to go MC the game show now."

The man wearing the headset freed Christian from the microphone cord so he could get up. He thanked Kristin and followed the stage manager out of the studio. His hands were still shaking. They went upstairs, past the catered food area and then out into the chill air. He felt dazed and confused, not sure that he was ready to meet Gaby at the publishing company, which was what they had agreed on.

As the taxi drove toward town, he stared out the window. And he knew that he had now lost all control.

"Okay, how are we going to do this?" Patrik was gazing out across the ice.

As usual, Torbjörn Ruud didn't look the least bit worried. He always maintained a calm demeanor, no matter how difficult the task at hand. As one of the crime-scene technicians in Uddevalla, he was used to solving all sorts of problems.

"We need to make a hole in the ice and pull him out with a rope."

"Will the ice hold up under your weight?"

"With the proper equipment, there shouldn't be any problem for the team. As I see it, the biggest risk is that we make a hole and then the body gets loose and slips away on the current under the ice."

"How are you going to prevent that from happening?" asked Patrik.

"We'll start by making a small hole and getting a firm grip on the body before we break up any more ice."

"Have you ever done this sort of thing before?" Patrik still wasn't totally convinced.

"Hmm. . . ." Torbjörn hesitated, seeming to ponder the question. "No, I don't think we've ever had a body frozen in the ice before. I'd probably remember if we had."

"Right," said Patrik, again fixing his gaze on the spot where the body supposedly lay. "Go ahead and do what you have to do. I need to talk to the witness." Patrik had noticed that Mellberg was having an intense conversation with the man who had found the body. It was never a good idea to allow Bertil to spend too much time with anyone, whether a witness or anyone else.

"Hello. My name is Patrik Hedström," he said as he went over to join Mellberg and the man he was talking to.

"Göte Persson," replied the man, shaking hands. At the same time, he tried to rein in a lively golden retriever.

"Rocky wants to go back out there. I had a lot of trouble getting him to return to dry land," said Göte, giving a sharp jerk on the dog's lead to show him who was in charge.

"Was it your dog who found him?"

Göte nodded. "Yes, he went out on the ice and refused to come in. He just stood there, barking. I was afraid he was going to fall through the ice, so I went after him. And then I saw. . . ." The man turned pale as he recalled the image of the dead face under the icy surface. Then he gave himself a shake, and the color returned to his cheeks. "Do you need me much longer? My daughter is on her way to the maternity clinic. It's my first grandchild."

Patrik smiled. "Then I can understand why you'd like to be off. Just hang on a little bit longer, and then we can let you go so you won't miss anything."

Göte seemed satisfied with that, so Patrik asked him a few more questions. But it was soon evident that the man had nothing more to contribute. He had simply had the bad luck to be in the wrong place at the wrong time, or maybe it was the right place at the right time, depending on the person's point of view. After writing down his contact information, Patrik let Göte, the soon-to-be-grandfather, leave the scene. Limping slightly, but in a big hurry, he headed for the car park.

Patrik went back to the spot on the shoreline that was closest to the place where a tech was now methodically working to lower some sort of hook through a small hole bored in the ice and fasten it to the body. To be on the safe side, the tech was lying on his stomach with a rope around his waist. The rope and the line attached to the hook both ran all the way to shore. Torbjörn wasn't taking any chances with his team.

"As I said, when we've got a good hold on him, we'll cut a bigger hole in the ice and then pull him out." Patrik jumped when he heard Torbjörn's voice on his left. He'd been so focused on what was happening out on the ice that he hadn't heard him approach.

"Will you bring him ashore then?"

"No, because we might end up losing any evidence that's on his clothing. Instead, we'll try to put him in a body bag out there on the ice before we bring him in."

"Would there really be any evidence left after he's been in the water this long?" asked Patrik skeptically.

"Most of it has probably been destroyed. But you never know. There might be something in his pockets or in the folds of his clothes. It's best not to take any chances."

"I'm sure you're right about that." Patrik didn't think it very likely that they'd find anything. He'd seen corpses get pulled out of the water before, and if they'd been there a while, there was never much left.

He shaded his eyes with his hand. The sun had climbed a little higher in the sky, and the blinding reflection off the ice brought tears to his eyes. He squinted and saw that the hook must now be securely fastened to the body, because a bigger hole was being cut in the ice. Slowly, very slowly, the body was pulled from the water. It was too far away for Patrik to see any details, and for that he was grateful.

Another tech cautiously crawled out on to the ice, and when the body was all the way out of the water, two pairs of hands carefully placed it inside a black body bag, which was then scrupulously closed. A nod to the men on shore, and the line went taut. Inch by inch, the bag was hauled toward land. Patrik instinctively backed up when it came close, but then cursed himself for being such a wimp. He asked the techs to open the bag and forced himself to look down at the man who had been under the ice. His suspicions were confirmed. He was almost positive that they had found Magnus Kjellner.

Patrik felt completely empty inside as he watched the techs seal the body bag closed, then lift it up and carry it over to the lawn above the beach which served as a parking area. Ten minutes later, the body was on its way to the forensics lab in Göteborg for the postmortem. On the one hand, it meant that they would be able to provide some answers and follow some leads. There would be a resolution. On the other hand, as soon as the identity of the body was confirmed, he would have to tell the family. And that was not something he looked forward to doing.

Finally the holiday was over. Father had packed up all their things, stowing them away inside the car and the trailer. Mother was lying in bed, as usual. She was even thinner, even paler. Now she said that all she wanted was to go home.

At last Father had told him why she looked so ill. It turned out that she wasn't really sick. She had a baby inside her stomach. A little brother or little sister. He didn't understand why that should make her feel so bad. But Father said that it did.

At first he was happy. A brother or sister to play with. But then he heard them talking, Mother and Father, and he understood. He now knew why he was not his mother's handsome little boy any more, why she no longer stroked his hair, and why she looked at him the way she did. He knew who had taken her away from him.

Yesterday he had returned to the trailer moving like an Indian brave. He sneaked up without making a sound, tiptoeing in his moccasins with a feather stuck in his hair. He was Angry Cloud, and Mother and Father were the palefaces. He could see them moving around inside the trailer behind the curtains. Mother was not in bed. She was up, talking, and Angry Cloud was glad, because maybe now she was feeling better, maybe the baby wasn't making her sick any more. And she sounded happy, tired but happy. Angry Cloud crept closer, wanting to hear more of the paleface's joyful voice. One step at a time, he moved closer until he was right under the open window. With his back pressed against the trailer, he shut his eyes and listened.

But he opened his eyes when they started talking about him. Then all the blackness came pouring over him full force. He was back with her again, he had the horrid smell in his nostrils, he heard the silence echoing in his head.

Mother's voice pierced through the silence, pierced through the darkness. As young as he was, he understood exactly what she was saying. She regretted becoming his mother, now they were going to have a child of their own. If only she'd known ahead of time, she would never have brought him home. And Father, with his gray and tired-sounding voice, said: "But the boy is here now, so we'll just have to make the best of things."

Angry Cloud didn't move as he sat there, and at that moment his hatred was born. He couldn't have put the feeling into words, but he knew that it felt both wonderful and terribly painful.

So while Father packed the car with the camp stove and their clothes and the cans of food and all sorts of other stuff, he packed his hatred. It filled up the entire seat where he was sitting in back. But he didn't hate Mother. How could he? He loved her.

He hated the one who had taken her away from him.

9

Erica had driven over to the Fjällbacka library. She knew that Christian wasn't at work. He'd done a good job on the *Morning* show, at least up until the end. When they started asking him about the threats, his nervousness became all too obvious. In fact, it was so painful to watch him turning bright red and starting to sweat that Erica had turned off the TV even before the interview was over.

And now here she was, pretending to scan the titles of the books on the shelves while she worked out how she was going to broach the real purpose of her visit: talking to Christian's colleague, May. Because the more Erica thought about the letters, the more convinced she was that it couldn't be a stranger who was threatening Christian. No, it felt too personal; the culprit had to be found among people who were part of Christian's life, now or in the past.

The problem was that he'd always been extremely reluctant to talk about himself. This morning, she'd decided to write down everything she'd ever heard about Christian and his background. She ended up sitting in front of a blank piece of paper, holding her pen in her hand. She realized that she really knew nothing about him. Even though she and Christian had spent a lot of time together editing his manuscript, and even though, in her opinion, they had become good friends, he had never told her anything about his private life. He never mentioned where he was from or the names of his parents or what sort of work they did. He hadn't said where he'd gone to school, or whether he'd played any sports in his younger days. He never talked about friends he'd had or mentioned whether he was still in contact with any of them. She knew nothing about him.

That in itself set off the alarm bells. Because people always reveal little tidbits about themselves in conversation, scraps of information that show what they were once like and what had made them who they'd become. The fact that Christian was so guarded about what he said made Erica even more certain that he was hiding something. The question was whether he'd been equally successful in keeping up his guard with everybody else. Maybe a colleague who worked with him every day might have learned something.

Erica cast a sidelong glance at May, who was typing at her computer. Fortunately they were the only two people in the library at the moment, so they could talk undisturbed. Finally she decided on a possible tactic. She couldn't very well just come right out and ask May about Christian; she needed to take a more circuitous approach.

She pressed her hand to the small of her back, sighed heavily, and sank onto one of the chairs in front of the counter where May was sitting.

"It must be hard for you. I heard you're having twins," said May, giving Erica a look of maternal sympathy.

"That's right. I've got two of them inside here." Erica patted her belly, trying to look as though she really needed to rest for a while. It didn't take much acting on her part. Whenever she sat down, her whole back would relax in gratitude.

"Just sit there and rest for a while."

"Thanks, I will," said Erica with a smile. After a moment she added, "Did you see Christian on TV this morning?"

"No, I missed it, unfortunately. I was here

at work. But I set up my DVD player to record the program. At least I think it will. I'll never be comfortable with all these modern machines. Did he do a good job?"

"He certainly did. It's great that his book is getting so much attention."

"Yes, I'm really proud of him," said May, her face lighting up. "I had no idea that he was a writer until I heard about his book being published. And what a book! The reviews have been fantastic."

"It's really amazing, isn't it?" Erica fell silent for a moment. "Everybody who knows Christian must be so happy for him. I hope his former colleagues are too. Where was it he worked before he came to Fjällbacka?" She tried to look as if she knew but just couldn't remember.

"Hmm. . . ." Unlike Erica, May seemed to be actually searching her memory. "You know what? Now that I think of it, I've actually never heard where he used to work. How strange. But Christian was already working here at the library by the time I was hired, and we've never talked about what he did before."

"So you don't know where he's from, or where he lived before moving to Fjällbacka?" Erica could tell that she sounded a bit too interested, so she fought to maintain a more neutral tone. "I just happened to think about it today as I was watching the interview. I've always thought that he speaks with a Småland accent, but I suddenly seemed to hear traces of a different dialect, and I couldn't really place it." Not a very good lie, but it would have to do.

May seemed to accept her explanation. "Well, he's not from Småland, that much I can say with certainty. But otherwise I have no idea. Of course we talk to each other here at work, and Christian is so pleasant and amiable." She looked as if she were considering how to put her next thought into words. "Yet he always seems to put up a barrier with other people. As if he's saying: 'It's okay to come this close, but no closer.' Maybe I'm being silly, but I've never asked him about personal matters because he has somehow signaled that those types of questions wouldn't be welcome."

"I know what you mean," replied Erica. "So he's never mentioned anything in passing?"

May paused to think. "No, I can't recall. . . . Wait a minute. . . ."

"Yes?" said Erica, silently cursing her own impatience.

"It was just a little thing. But I got the feeling that. . . . One time, we were talking about Trollhättan because I'd gone to visit my sister, who lives there. And he seemed to know the town. Then he looked as if he'd been caught off guard, and he started talking about something else. I specifically remember noticing that. The fact that he changed the subject so abruptly."

"Did you have the feeling that he might have lived there?"

"I think so. Although, as I said, I can't be sure."

It wasn't much to go on. But at least it gave her somewhere to start. In Trollhättan.

"Come in, Christian!" Gaby met him at the door, and he cautiously entered the white landscape that was the publishing company's domicile. Even though Gaby, who was head of the company, preferred strong colors and an extravagant personal style, the office was spartanly furnished and tended toward pale pastel hues. But maybe that was intentional, because it provided the perfect backdrop for her to shine.

"Would you like some coffee?" She pointed to a coat rack with hangers and a shelf for hats. He hung up his jacket.

"Yes, thanks. That would be nice." He followed Gaby as she led the way, her high heels clacking down the long corridor. The kitchen was decorated in colors as pale as the rest of the place, but the cups she took from the cupboard were a shocking pink, and there didn't seem to be any others to choose from.

"Latte? Cappuccino? Espresso?" Gaby pointed at a gigantic coffee machine that dominated the counter. Christian paused to consider.

"I'll have a latte, please."

"Coming right up." She reached for his cup and began pressing buttons. When the coffee machine had stopped huffing and puffing, she motioned for Christian to follow her.

"We'll go to my office. There are too many people running around here." She nodded pointedly at a young woman in her thirties who had come into the kitchen. Judging by the woman's alarmed expression, Christian thought Gaby must keep a tight rein on her employees.

"Have a seat." Gaby's office was right next door to the kitchen. It was neat and pleasant but impersonal. No photographs of family members, no odd little knick-knacks. Nothing that would give any hint as to who Gaby really was, and Christian suspected that was exactly the way she wanted it.

"You were great this morning!" She sat

down behind the desk, beaming at him.

He nodded, fully aware that she'd noticed his nervousness. He wondered if she had any pangs of conscience about the way she'd thrown him to the media, leaving him defenseless for what was to come.

"You have such a presence." Her teeth flashed a dazzling white as she smiled at him. Too white, an unnatural white.

He clutched the pink coffee cup in his sweaty hands.

"We're going to try to get you a few more TV spots," Gaby prattled on. "*Carin,* at nine thirty in the evening, *Malou* on Channel 4, maybe some kind of game show. I think you —"

"I'm not doing any more TV shows."

Gaby stared at him. "Sorry? I must have heard wrong. Did you just say that you're not doing any more TV?"

"That's right. You saw what happened this morning. I'm not going to subject myself to that again."

"But TV sells books." Gaby's nostrils flared. "Just that one short interview this morning is going to really spark sales of your book." She was impatiently tapping her long fingernails on the desktop.

"I'm sure that's true, but it doesn't matter. I'm not doing anything like that again."

And he really meant what he said. He didn't want to appear in the spotlight anymore. He couldn't. Even that one interview was too much; it had been enough to provoke a reaction. Maybe he could still keep fate at bay if he put a stop to it. But he had to do it now.

"I must say, you're not being very co-operative. I can't sell your book or get readers to notice it if you won't help me. And that means taking part in the promotional efforts." Gaby's voice was ice-cold.

Christian felt a buzzing start up inside his head. He stared at Gaby's pink nails against the light-colored desktop, and he tried to stop the roar that kept getting louder and louder. He began scratching the palm of his left hand. He felt a prickling under his skin. Like an invisible eczema that got worse the more he touched it.

"I'm not doing anything like that again," he repeated. He didn't dare meet her eye. The slight nervousness he'd felt before coming to this meeting had now turned to panic. She couldn't force him. Or could she? What exactly did it say in the contract that he'd signed? He hadn't really read it, he'd been so thrilled about getting his book accepted for publication.

Gaby's voice cut through the roaring

sound. "We expect you to show up, Christian. I expect you to show up." Her annoyance provided more impetus for the prickling and itching sensation inside of him. He scratched even harder at the palm of his hand, until he felt it sting. When he glanced down, he saw bloody streaks left by his fingernails. He looked up.

"I need to go home now."

Gaby studied him with a frown on her face. "How are you doing, actually?" The furrow on her brow deepened when she saw the blood on the palm of his hand. "Christian. . . ." She seemed at a loss for what to say, and he couldn't take it any longer. The thoughts were buzzing louder and louder, saying things that he didn't want to hear. All the question marks, all the connections, everything merged together until the itching under his skin was the only thing he noticed.

He jumped up and ran out of the room.

Patrik stared at the phone. It would take quite a while to get a complete report on the body that they'd found under the ice, but he was counting on receiving confirmation very soon that it really was Magnus Kjellner. Rumors were no doubt already flying through Fjällbacka, and he didn't want Cia to hear about it from anyone other than the police.

But so far his phone had remained silent.

"Nothing yet?" Annika stuck her head in the door, giving him an enquiring look.

Patrik shook his head. "Nope. But I'm expecting to hear from Pedersen any minute."

"Let's hope you do," said Annika. The second she turned to go back to the reception area, the phone rang. Patrik grabbed the receiver.

"Hedström." He listened, motioning for Annika to wait. It was Tord Pedersen from the forensics lab on the line. "Yes . . . okay . . . I understand . . . thanks." He put down the phone and exhaled loudly. "Pedersen confirmed that it's Magnus Kjellner. He won't be able to give us a time of death until after the postmortem, but he can say with certainty that Kjellner was the victim of a violent assault. His body has a number of stab wounds on it."

"Poor Cia."

Patrik nodded. His heart felt heavy as he thought about the task ahead of him. Even so, he wanted to tell her himself. He owed it to her after all the times she'd come to the police station, each time looking a little sadder, a little more haggard, but still holding out hope. Now there was no longer any hope, and the only thing he could offer her was the certain knowledge that her husband was dead.

"I'd better go over there and have a talk with Cia right away," he said, standing up. "Before somebody else tells her."

"Are you going alone?"

"No, I'll take Paula with me."

He went to his colleague's office and knocked on the open door.

"Is it him?" As usual, Paula got right to the point.

"Yes. I'm going to have a talk with his wife. Could you come along?"

"Sure. Of course," she said, pulling on her jacket and following Patrik, who was already moving toward the front door.

In the reception area they were stopped by Mellberg.

"Have you heard anything?" he wanted to know.

"Yes. Pedersen has confirmed that the victim is Magnus Kjellner." Patrik turned away to head for the police car parked outside the station, but Mellberg wasn't ready to let him go.

"So he drowned, right? I knew he killed himself. Probably some sort of woman trouble, or maybe he lost a bundle playing poker on the Internet. I just knew it."

"It doesn't appear to be a suicide." Patrik weighed his words carefully. From bitter experience, he knew that Mellberg did whatever he liked with information he obtained, and it could easily lead to disastrous results.

"Bloody hell! You mean it was murder?"

"We don't really know very much at this point." Patrik's voice had taken on an admonitory tone. "The only thing Pedersen could tell me was that Magnus Kjellner had suffered extensive wounds."

"Bloody hell," Mellberg said again. "That means this investigation is going to get a lot of attention. We need to pick up the pace. We need to put everything that has already been done, or not done, under the microscope. I haven't really been involved very much so far, but now we need to focus all of the station's resources on the case."

Patrik and Paula exchanged glances. As usual, Mellberg was oblivious to their lack of confidence in his leadership abilities. He went on enthusiastically:

"We need to call a meeting and go through all the material we have on hand. I'll expect everyone to be present and accounted for at three P.M., eager to get to work. We've wasted too much time already. Good Lord, should it really take three months to find a man? It makes me downright ashamed." He cast a stern look at Patrik, who fought to control a childish impulse to give his boss a good kick in the shin.

"Three o'clock," said Patrik. "Understood. But if you don't mind, we need to get going now. Paula and I are on our way over to see Kjellner's wife."

"Go, go," said Mellberg impatiently, waving them out. He seemed to already be lost in thought, deciding how to delegate the work in what had now turned out to be a murder investigation.

All his life, Erik had been in control. He was the one who decided. He was the hunter. Now somebody was hunting him, some unknown person that he couldn't see. And that frightened him more than anything else. Everything would have been easier if he'd known who was after him. But he honestly didn't know.

He had devoted a lot of time to pondering the situation, even taking an inventory of his life. In his mind he'd listed all the women he'd known, his business contacts, his friends, and his enemies. He couldn't deny that he'd left a trail of bitterness and anger in his wake. But hatred? He wasn't so sure about that. The letters he'd received practically smoldered with hatred and a resolve to do harm. There was no question about that.

For the first time, Erik felt alone in the world. For the first time, he realized how thin a protective veneer he possessed, and just how little all the success and pats on the back meant in the long run. He had even considered confiding in Louise. Or Kenneth. But he never seemed to find a moment when his wife wasn't looking at him with scorn. And Kenneth was always so submissive. Neither seemed fertile ground for confiding his concerns. Or for sharing the uneasiness that he'd felt ever since the first letters had arrived.

There was no one he could turn to. He realized that he alone was to blame for his isolation, but he had enough self-awareness to know that he wouldn't have acted differently even if he could. The taste of success was too sweet. The feeling of being superior and idolized was too intoxicating. He had no regrets, but he still wished he could talk to someone.

For lack of anything else, he decided to seek out the second-best thing. Sex. Nothing else made him feel so invincible yet at the same time allowed him to relinquish control in a way that was otherwise foreign to him. It had nothing to do with whoever his partner happened to be. They had changed so often over the years that he could no longer put names and faces together. He could remember that one woman had perfect breasts, but no matter how hard he searched his memory, he couldn't recall the face that went with the breasts. Another woman had tasted incredibly delicious, making him want to use his tongue, breathe in her scent. But her name? He had no idea.

At the moment, Cecilia was his lover, but he didn't think he'd remember anything special about her either. She was merely expedient. In every way. Completely acceptable in bed, but nothing that would make the angels sing. A body that was sufficiently well-shaped to give him a hard-on, but it wasn't her body that he pictured in his mind when he was home in bed with his eyes closed, jerking off. She was here, she was available and willing. That was the extent of her attraction, and he knew that he would soon grow tired of her.

But at the moment that was certainly good enough. Impatiently he rang her doorbell, hoping he wouldn't have to put up with much small talk before he could get inside her and feel all his tension released.

The minute she opened the door, he saw

that his hopes would be dashed. He'd sent her a text message, asking if he could drop by, and received a "yes" in reply. Now he realized that he should have phoned instead to see what sort of mood she was in. Because she had a determined air about her. Not angry or annoyed. That wasn't it. Just determined and calm — which was far more worrisome than if she had been furious.

"Come in, Erik," she said, stepping aside to let him in.

Erik. It was never a good sign when someone said his name in that way. It meant that she wanted to put special emphasis on what she was going to say. That she wanted his full attention. He considered turning on his heel, saying that he suddenly had to take off, anything to avoid entering into this resolute scheming of hers.

But the door stood wide open, and Cecilia was on her way to the kitchen. He had no choice. Reluctantly he closed the front door behind him, hung up his coat, and went to join her.

"It's good you came. I was just thinking of phoning you," she said.

He stood leaning against the counter, his arms crossed. Waiting. Now it would come. Just like always. The waltz. When the woman wanted to start leading, taking charge and moving forward; when she stated terms and demanded promises that he could never keep. Sometimes these kinds of moments gave him a sense of satisfaction. He enjoyed slowly and meticulously crushing the woman's pathetic hopes. But not today. Today he wanted to feel naked skin and inhale sweet scents; he needed to climb to the top and experience an exhausted release. He needed this to keep at bay whoever it was who was hunting him. Why did this stupid woman have to choose this particular day to have his dreams dashed?

Erik stood still, glaring coldly at Cecilia, who stared back with great composure. That was something new. He was used to seeing nervous eyes and flushed cheeks in anticipation of the leap about to be made, combined with elation because the woman had found her "inner courage" to demand what she thought was her right. But Cecilia just stood there, facing him, her eyes steady.

She opened her mouth to speak just as the mobile phone in his trouser pocket began vibrating. He clicked on the message and read what it said. A single sentence. A sentence that almost made his knees buckle. At the same time, from far away, he heard Cecilia's voice. She was talking to him, saying something. It was impossible to take in her words. But he forced himself to listen, forced his brain to give meaning to the syllables she was saying.

"I'm pregnant, Erik."

Not a word was spoken as they drove to Fjällbacka. Before they left, Paula had asked Patrik if he wanted her to deliver the news, but he merely shook his head. They had picked up Lena Appelgren, the pastor, who was now sitting in the back seat. She too had remained silent after she heard what she needed to know about the circumstances.

As they turned into the driveway in front of the Kjellner home, Patrik regretted having taken a police vehicle instead of his own Volvo. There was only one way that Cia would interpret seeing a police car driving up to her house.

Patrik rang the doorbell, and in less than five seconds Cia opened the door. He could tell from her expression that she'd seen the car and had already come to a conclusion.

"You found him, didn't you?" she said, drawing her cardigan tighter around her as the cold winter wind blew in the open doorway.

"Yes," Patrik told her. "We found him."

For a moment Cia retained her composure, but then her legs seemed to give way beneath her, and she collapsed onto the floor. Patrik and Paula lifted her up. Leaning on them, she headed for the kitchen, where they set her down on a chair.

"Would you like us to call anyone?" Patrik sat down next to Cia and took her hand in his.

She seemed to consider the question. Her eyes were glassy, and Patrik surmised that she was having a hard time collecting her thoughts.

"Would you like us to bring Magnus's parents over here?" he said kindly, and she nodded.

"Do they know yet?" she asked, her voice quavering.

"No," said Patrik. "But two police officers have also gone over to their place, so I can phone and ask them if they'd like to come here."

It turned out that wasn't necessary. Just then another police car pulled up next to Patrik's, and he realized that Gösta and Martin had already informed Magnus's parents, who climbed out of the vehicle. They came into the house without stopping to ring the bell. Paula went out to the hall to have a whispered conversation with her colleagues. Through the kitchen window,

Patrik saw Gösta and Martin go back out into the cold and drive off.

Paula came back to the kitchen, accompanied by Margareta and Torsten Kjellner.

"I thought having four officers here would be too much, so I sent them back to the station," Paula told Patrik. "I hope that's okay." He nodded.

Margareta went straight over to Cia and put her arms around her. As soon as her mother-in-law did that, Cia began to cry, and then the dam burst and the tears flowed freely in awful, wrenching sobs. Torsten looked pale and upset. The pastor went over to him and introduced herself.

"Why don't you sit down, and I'll make all of us some coffee," said Lena. They knew each other only by name, and the pastor was aware that her job at the moment was to stay in the background, stepping forward only if necessary. Everyone reacted differently to the news of a death, and sometimes all she had to do was to provide something hot and soothing to drink. She began rummaging around in the cupboards, soon finding everything she needed to make the coffee.

"Hush now, Cia," said Margareta, stroking her daughter-in-law's back. Over Cia's head she met Patrik's gaze, and it took a great effort for him not to look away from the deep sorrow he saw in the eyes of a mother who had just learned that she'd lost a son. Yet Margareta was strong enough to offer comfort to her son's wife. Some women possessed such fortitude that nothing could break them. Bend them perhaps, yes. But they didn't break.

"I'm so sorry." Patrik turned to Magnus's father, who was staring blankly straight ahead as he sat at the kitchen table. Torsten didn't respond.

"Here's some coffee for you." Lena set the cup in front of Torsten and then placed her hand on his shoulder for a moment. At first he didn't react, but then he said, faintly, "Sugar?"

"I'll get it." Lena again looked through the cupboards until she found a box of sugar.

"I don't understand . . . ," said Torsten, closing his eyes. Then he opened them. "I don't understand. Who would want to hurt Magnus? Who would want to harm our boy?" He looked at his wife, but she didn't hear him. She still had her arms around Cia, while a wet patch was growing bigger on her gray jumper.

"We don't know, Torsten," said Patrik. He nodded gratefully to the pastor, who handed him a cup of coffee before she sat down at the table with them.

"So what *do* we know?" The words seemed to stick in Torsten's throat from anger and grief.

Margareta gave him a warning look. As if to say: Not now. This isn't the proper time or place.

He bowed to his wife's stern gaze and instead reached for the sugar, pouring some into his coffee and stirring it with a spoon.

Silence descended over the room. Cia's sobs had diminished, but Margareta still held her close, putting her own sorrow aside for the moment.

Cia raised her head. Her cheeks were streaked with tears, and her words were barely audible as she said:

"The children. They don't know yet. They're in school. They have to come home."

Patrik nodded. He stood up, and then he and Paula headed back outside to the car.

He held his hands over his ears. He couldn't understand how something so tiny could produce such a racket, and how something so ugly could attract so much attention.

Everything had changed after those holiday weeks spent at the campground. Mother got fatter and fatter until she disappeared for a week and then came home with little sister. He'd wondered a bit about that, but no one had bothered to answer his questions.

Nobody paid the slightest attention to him anymore. Father was the same as always. And Mother only had eyes for the wrinkled little bundle. She was always walking about, carrying little sister, who never stopped crying. She was always holding her and feeding her and changing her and cuddling her and cooing to her. He was just in the way. The only time he caught his mother's attention was when she scolded him. He didn't like it when she did that, but anything was better than when she looked right through him, as if he were nothing but air.

What angered her the most was when he ate too much. She was very finicky about food. "You need to pay attention to your weight," she always said when Father asked for another helping of gravy.

Nowadays he always helped himself to more food. Not just once, but two or three times. At first, Mother had tried to stop him. But he simply stared at her as he slowly and deliberately poured himself more gravy or shoveled more mashed potatoes onto his plate. Finally she'd given up and merely glared at him angrily. And the servings got bigger and bigger. Part of him enjoyed the disgust he saw in her eyes whenever he opened his mouth wide and stuffed in the food. At least she was looking at him. But nobody called him "my handsome little boy" anymore. He was no longer handsome. He was ugly. Both inside and out. But at least she didn't ignore him.

After putting the baby in her cot, Mother often lay down to take a nap. Then he would go over to look at little sister. Otherwise he wasn't allowed to touch her, not when Mother was looking. "Take your hands away, they might be dirty." But when Mother was asleep, he could look at the baby. And touch her.

He tilted his head to one side and studied

her. Her face looked like an old woman's. Slightly chapped and red. As she slept, she clenched her hands into little fists and moved about a bit. She had kicked off the blanket. He didn't pull it back over her. Why should he do that? She'd taken everything away from him.

Alice. Even her name filled him with disgust. He hated Alice.

10

"I want you to give my jewelry to Laila's girls."

"Lisbet, sweetheart, can't this wait?" He took her hand, which was lying on top of the covers. He squeezed it gently, feeling how fragile her bones were. Like bird bones.

"No, Kenneth, it can't wait. I can't rest until I know that everything is in order. I'll never find peace if I know that I've left you with a big mess." She smiled.

"But. . . ." He cleared his throat and tried again. "It's so. . . ." Again his voice broke, and he could feel tears filling his eyes. He quickly wiped them away. He needed to remain in control, he had to be strong. But the tears fell onto the flowered duvet cover, which they'd had from the very beginning. By now, it was faded from being laundered so many times. He always put it on her bed, because he knew how much she loved it.

"You don't need to pretend in front of

me," she said, stroking his head.

"Are you rubbing my bald spot again?" he said, attempting to smile. She gave him a wink.

"I've always thought that hair on the head is overrated. You know that. A nice, shiny head is much more attractive."

He laughed. She'd always been able to make him laugh. Who was going to do that now? Who would stroke his head and say it was lucky that God had made a landing strip for her caresses in the middle of his head? Kenneth knew he wasn't the most attractive man in the world. But in Lisbet's eyes he was. And he still marveled at the fact that he had such a beautiful wife. Even now, after the cancer had stripped her of everything it could take, eaten away at every part of her body. She had been so unhappy to lose her hair, and he'd tried to make the same joke about her. Telling her that God had now made a landing strip for *his* caresses. But her smile had not reached her eyes.

Her hair had always been her pride and joy. Blond and curly. He saw her eyes fill with tears when she stood in front of the mirror and slowly ran her hand over the sparse wisps that remained after the treatment. He still found her beautiful, but he knew that it made her sad. So the first thing he did when he had occasion to drive to Göteborg was to go into a shop and buy her a Hermès scarf. She had been longing for a scarf like that but had always objected when he wanted to buy her one. "It's not right to pay so much money for a small piece of fabric," she had told him when he tried to insist.

Nonetheless, when he went to Göteborg he bought her a scarf. The most expensive one in the shop. With an effort, she had climbed out of bed and opened the package, taking out the scarf and carrying it over to the mirror. With her eyes fixed on her own face, she had wrapped the glossy silk square with the yellow-and-gold pattern around her head. It had hidden the hair loss and dulled the cold. And it had brought back the gleam in her eye, which the harsh treatment had taken away, along with her hair.

She hadn't said a word, just walked over to him as he sat on her bed, leaned down, and kissed him on the top of his head. Then she had crawled back into bed. Ever since, she had always worn that scarf wrapped around her head.

"I want Annette to have that heavy gold necklace, and give Josefine the pearls. They can divide up the rest as they see fit. Let's just hope that they don't end up fighting as a result." Lisbet laughed, certain that her sister's daughters would be able to agree on how to share the jewelry she was leaving behind.

Kenneth gave a start. He'd been lost in his own memories, and her words came as a cruel awakening. He understood his wife and her need to make arrangements for everything before she died. At the same time, he couldn't bear being reminded of the inevitable, which was no longer very far away, according to those who knew about such things. He would have given anything not to be sitting here, holding her frail hand in his own and listening to his beloved wife dividing up her earthly goods.

"And I don't want you to live alone for the rest of your life. Get out once in a while so you have a chance to see what's available. But stay away from those Internet dating services, because I think that —"

"Okay, that's enough of that," he said, stroking her cheek. "Do you really think any other woman could ever measure up to you? It's better not even to go looking."

"I don't want you to be alone," she said solemnly, gripping his hand as hard as she could. "Do you hear me? You have to go on with your life." Beads of sweat appeared on her forehead, and he gently wiped them away with the handkerchief lying on the bedside table.

"You're here with me right now. And that's the only thing that matters."

They sat in silence for a while, gazing into each other's eyes and seeing their whole life together. The great passion in the beginning, which had never really disappeared, even though daily life sometimes nibbled away at the edges. All the laughter, all the friendship, all the companionship. All the nights they had lain close, so close to each other as she rested her cheek on his chest. All the years of yearning for children that never came, their hopes flushed away in torrents of red, until finally they had reached a stage of calm acceptance. Their lives filled with friends, shared interests, and love for each other.

His mobile was ringing out in the front hall. He didn't get up, though he let go of her hand. But the phone kept ringing, and finally she nodded at him.

"You might as well take the call. It sounds like someone is really trying to get ahold of you."

Kenneth reluctantly stood up, went out to the hall, and picked up his mobile from the bureau. "Erik," it said on the display. Again he felt annoyance wash over him. Even now he insisted on intruding.

"Yes?" he said, making no effort to hide his feelings. But his mood changed as he listened to what Erik had to say. He asked a few brief questions and then ended the conversation before going back into Lisbet's room. He took a deep breath as he fixed his gaze on her face, so ravaged by illness but in his eyes so beautiful, framed by a halo of yellow and gold.

"It seems that they've found Magnus. And he's dead."

Erica had tried to call Patrik several times, but there was no answer. He must be really busy down at the station.

She was at home, sitting in front of her computer and doing a search on the Internet. Though she stubbornly tried to focus on the task, there was no denying that it was distracting to have two sets of feet kicking inside her belly. It was hard to keep her thoughts in check. And her worries. She recalled the early days with Maja, which hadn't been anything like the rosy visions of baby bliss that she'd imagined. That period was like a black hole, when she thought back on it, and now it was going to be doubled. Two to feed, two babies waking up in the middle of the night, two demanding all her attention, all her time. Maybe she was selfish, maybe that was why she had such a hard time placing her very existence, her whole life in someone else's hands. The hands of her children. She cringed at the idea, and then instantly felt guilty. Why on earth did she feel so anxious about something as incredible as having two more children, two gifts at one time? But she did. She was so worried that it was practically tearing her apart. Yet this time she knew the result. Maja was such a joy that Erica didn't regret for one second the difficult period she'd been through. But she still had the memories of what it had been like, and they continued to bother her.

Suddenly she felt a kick that was so hard, she had to gasp for breath. One of the babies, or maybe both of them, seemed to have a talent for football. The pain brought her back to the present. She was well aware that she was preoccupied with her speculations about Christian and the letters because it kept other thoughts and worries away. But she didn't see anything wrong with that.

She opened Google and typed in his name: Christian Thydell. She got several pages of hits. All of them had to do with his book; none of them mentioned anything about his past. She tried adding "Trollhättan." No hits. But if he had lived there, he must have left some traces behind. And she should be able to find out more about him. She chewed on her thumbnail as she thought. Could it be that she was on the wrong track? There was really nothing in the letters to indicate that they'd come from someone Christian had known before he moved to Fjällbacka.

She kept coming back to the question: Why was he so secretive about his past? It felt as though Christian had erased the life he'd lived before he arrived in Fjällbacka. Or was she the only one he refused to talk to? The thought stung, but she couldn't get it out of her mind. Of course, he hadn't been particularly open with his colleague at work either, but that was a whole different matter. Erica felt that she and Christian had become friends when they worked on his manuscript, tossing around thoughts and ideas, discussing tone and nuances in his writing. But maybe that wasn't the case after all.

Erica realized that she ought to talk to more of Christian's friends before she let her imagination run wild. But who? She had only a vague notion of who belonged to

Christian's circle of friends. Magnus Kjellner was the first person who came to mind, but unless some sort of miracle occurred, that wasn't an option. Christian and Sanna also seemed to socialize with Erik Lind, the man who owned that construction company, and his partner, Kenneth Bengtsson. Erica had no idea how close they were to Christian, or which of them she should talk to in order to obtain the most information. And besides, how would Christian react if he found out that she was going around questioning everyone he knew?

She decided to ignore any such scruples, which were far outweighed by her curiosity. And it was in Christian's own best interest, after all. If he refused to get to the bottom of who was sending those threatening letters, then she would just have to do it for him.

Suddenly she knew who she would talk to first.

Ludvig glanced at the clock again. It would soon be time for break. Math was his absolute worst subject, and the hour was dragging along, as usual. Five more minutes. Today his class had break time together with 7A, which meant the same time as Sussie. Her locker was in the next row over, and if he was lucky, they'd arrive there at the same time to put their books away after class. He'd had a crush on her for more than six months now. Nobody knew about it, except for his best friend Tom. And Tom knew that he would die a slow and painful death if he ever told anyone.

The bell rang, and Ludvig gratefully picked up his math book and dashed out of the classroom. He kept looking around as he walked toward his locker, but Sussie was nowhere in sight. Maybe her class wasn't over yet.

Soon he was going to get up the courage to talk to her. That's what he'd decided. He just wasn't sure how to begin or what he would say. He'd tried to get Tom to run into one of her friends, so that he could approach her that way. But Tom had refused, so Ludvig was forced to come up with some other plan.

The area around his locker was deserted. He opened the padlock, put his books inside, and carefully locked it again. Maybe she wasn't in school today. He hadn't seen her earlier either, so maybe she was sick or had the day off. The thought made him feel so depressed that he considered cutting his last class. He jumped when someone tapped him on the shoulder.

"Sorry, Ludvig. I didn't mean to scare you."

The principal was standing behind him. She looked pale and tense, and in a fraction of a second, Ludvig knew why she wanted to talk to him. His thoughts of Sussie and everything else, which only a moment ago had seemed so important, instantly vanished, to be replaced by a pain so strong that he felt it would never let him go.

"I'd like you to come with me to my office. Elin is waiting for us there."

He nodded. There was no reason to ask what this was all about, since he already knew. The pain seemed to radiate from his fingertips, and he couldn't feel his feet as he followed the principal. He was moving his feet forward, as he knew he had to, but they were completely numb.

In the corridor, halfway to the principal's office, he saw Sussie. She looked at him, staring him right in the eye. But it felt like an eternity ago that such an encounter had meant anything to him, and he looked right through her. Nothing existed but the pain. Everything else was a reverberating void.

Elin burst into tears when she saw him. She had probably been sitting there, fighting back the sobs, and when he entered the room she rushed into his arms. He hugged her tight, stroking her back as she cried.

The police officers, whom he'd met a few times before, were standing nearby, giving the two siblings a moment to comfort each other. He still hadn't uttered a word.

"Where did you find him?" Ludvig asked at last, even though he wasn't aware of having formulated the question. He wasn't even sure that he wanted to hear the answer.

"Down by Sälvik," said the officer whose name was apparently Patrik. His colleague took a couple of steps back. She seemed at a loss for words. Ludvig understood how she felt. He didn't know what to say either. Or what to do.

"We thought we'd drive you home now." Patrik nodded at Paula to lead the way. Elin and Ludvig followed. In the doorway Elin stopped and turned toward Patrik.

"Did Papa drown?"

Ludvig stopped too, but he could see that the officer had no intention of saying anything more at the moment.

"Let's go home, Elin. We'll find out all the details later," Ludvig said quietly, taking his sister's hand. At first, she resisted. She didn't want to leave. She wanted to know what had happened. But then she turned again to follow Paula.

■ ■ ■ ■

"All right. Let's have a look. . . ." Mellberg paused for effect. He pointed at the cork-board where Patrik had carefully pinned up all the material they'd collected pertaining to Magnus Kjellner's disappearance. "I've gathered here what we know so far, and there's not much to write home about. Three months on the case, and this is all you've managed to dig up? It's just as well you're all out here in the sticks — back in Göteborg we knew what it was to work in a pressure-cooker environment. We would have solved a case like this in a week!"

Patrik and Annika exchanged glances. As the police chief in Tanumshede, Mellberg was constantly reminding his colleagues of the time he'd spent working in Göteborg. Although by now it seemed he'd given up any hopes of being transferred back to the city. He was the only one who had ever believed that might happen.

"We've done everything we could," said Patrik wearily. He was aware how pointless it was to try to counter Mellberg's accusations. "Besides, it wasn't until today that it became a murder investigation. We've been treating it as a missing-persons case."

"Okay, okay. Would you mind reviewing what exactly happened? Where was his body found, who found it, and what has Pedersen told you so far? I'll give him a ring later, of course. I just haven't had time yet. So we'll have to make do with the information you have at the moment."

Patrik reported on the events of the day.

"Was he really stuck in the ice?" Martin Molin shuddered as he looked at Patrik.

"We'll have photographs of the crime scene later, but yes, he was frozen solid. If the dog hadn't gone out on the ice, it would have taken a long time before we found Magnus Kjellner. If ever. As soon as the ice thawed, his body would have come loose and then drifted away. He could have ended up anywhere." Patrik shook his head.

"So I suppose that means we won't be able to work out where or when he was tossed into the water, right?" Gösta had a gloomy look on his face as he absentmindedly patted Ernst, who was pressed against his leg.

"The ice didn't set in until December. We'll have to wait for Pedersen's report to hear how long he thinks Magnus has been dead, but my guess is that he died right after he went missing." Patrik raised an admonitory finger. "But as I said, we have no facts to support that theory, so we can't really use it as a basis for our investigation."

"But it does sound like a reasonable assumption," said Gösta.

"You mentioned stab wounds. What do we know about that?" Paula's brown eyes narrowed as she impatiently tapped her pen on the notepad lying on the table in front of her.

"I didn't find out a lot about that either. You know how Pedersen is. He doesn't really like to say anything until he's done a thorough examination. The only thing he told me was that Kjellner had been assaulted and multiple stab wounds had been inflicted."

"Which seems to indicate that he'd been stabbed with a knife," Gösta added.

"Most likely, yes."

"When are we going to get more information from Pedersen?" Mellberg now sat at the head of the table and snapped his fingers to summon Ernst to his side. The dog instantly left Gösta and trotted over to place his head on his master's knee.

"He said he'd get to the postmortem at the end of the week. So we might know more by the weekend, if we're lucky. Otherwise, early next week." Patrik sighed. Sometimes the constraints of the job taxed his patience. He wanted answers now, not in a week.

"All right. What do you know about his disappearance?" Mellberg made a show of holding up his empty coffee cup toward Annika, who pretended not to notice. Next he tried Martin, with better results. Martin hadn't yet achieved the status required to ignore his boss. Mellberg leaned back with satisfaction as his youngest colleague got up and headed for the kitchen.

"We know that Kjellner left home just after eight in the morning. Cia had already left at seven thirty to drive to her job in Grebbestad. She works part-time in a real estate agency there. The children had to leave by seven to catch the bus to school." Patrik paused to take a sip of his coffee after Martin had refilled everyone's cups. Paula took the opportunity to jump in with a question.

"How do you know that Magnus Kjellner left just after eight?"

"That's when a neighbor saw him leaving the house."

"Did he drive off?"

"No, Cia had taken the family's only car, and according to her, Magnus usually walked."

"But he didn't walk all the way to Tanum,

did he?" asked Martin.

"No, he rode to work with a colleague of his, Ulf Rosander, who lives over by the mini-golf course. That was where he walked. But on that particular morning, he phoned Rosander to say he'd be late. And he never showed up."

"Do we know that?" asked Mellberg. "Have we taken a proper look at this Rosander? After all, we have only his word that Magnus never turned up."

"Gösta went out to interview Rosander, and there's nothing to indicate that he's lying, either from what he said or the way he acted," said Patrik.

"Maybe you haven't pressured him enough," said Mellberg, writing something on his notepad. He glanced up and fixed his gaze on Patrik. "Let's bring him in and grill him a little more."

"Isn't that a bit drastic? People might hesitate to talk to the police in the future if they hear that we've started hauling witnesses down to the station," Paula objected. "How about if you and Patrik drive out to his place in Fjällbacka? Of course, I know that you're extremely busy at the moment, so I could go with Patrik instead, if you like." She gave Patrik a discreet wink.

"Hmmm, that's true. I do have quite a lot

on my plate right now. That's a good idea, Paula. You and Patrik can drive over there and have another chat with . . . Rosell."

"Rosander," Patrik corrected him.

"Right. That's what I said." Mellberg glared at Patrik. "At any rate, I want you and Paula to talk to him. I think that could be productive." He waved his hand impatiently. "So, what else? What more do we know?"

"We've knocked on doors all along the route that Magnus used to take when he walked over to Rosander's house. Nobody saw anything, but that doesn't necessarily mean anything. People are always busy with their own morning routines," said Patrik.

"It seems Magnus just disappeared in a puff of smoke the minute he stepped out the front door. Until we found him in the ice, that is." Martin had a resigned expression on his face as he looked at Patrik, who made an effort to sound more positive than he actually felt.

"No one just disappears. Somewhere there are traces of what happened. We just have to find them."

Patrik could hear the platitudes rolling a bit too glibly from his lips, but he had nothing else to offer.

"What about his personal life? Have we

dug deep enough? Pulled all the skeletons out of the wardrobe?" Mellberg laughed at his own joke, but no one joined in.

"Magnus and Cia's closest friends are Erik Lind, Kenneth Bengtsson, and Christian Thydell. And their wives. We've talked to all of them, along with Magnus's family members. But the only thing we've learned is that Magnus was a devoted father and a good friend. No gossip, no secrets, no rumors."

"Rubbish!" Mellberg snorted. "Everybody has something to hide. It's just a matter of digging it out. You clearly haven't tried hard enough."

"Of course . . ." Patrik began. But then he fell silent as he realized that Mellberg might actually be right, for a change. Maybe they *hadn't* dug deep enough, maybe they hadn't asked the right questions. "Of course we'll do another round of interviews with his family and friends," he went on. He suddenly pictured Christian Thydell, and the letter that lay in the top drawer of his desk. But Patrik didn't want to say anything about that yet, not until he had something more concrete to go on. So far it was just a gut feeling.

"Okay then. Let's do it over, and do it right!" Mellberg stood up so fast that Ernst, who had been resting his head on his master's knee, almost toppled over. The police chief was halfway out of the door when he turned and gave his subordinates a stern look as they sat around the table. "And let's pick up the pace a bit, too."

Dark had fallen outside the train windows. He'd gotten up so early that morning that it now felt more like evening, even though his watch told him it was only late afternoon. In his pocket, his phone stubbornly buzzed again and again, but he ignored it. No matter who was trying to call, it was bound to be someone who wanted something from him. Someone trying to chase him down and make demands.

Christian stared out of the window. They had just passed Herrljunga. He'd left his car in Uddevalla. From there it was about a 45-minute drive home to Fjällbacka. He leaned his forehead on the pane and closed his eyes. The glass felt cold against his skin. The darkness outside seemed to be forcing its way inward, toward him. He gasped for breath, opened his eyes, and moved his head back. His forehead and the tip of his nose had left a visible print on the windowpane. He raised his hand and rubbed it off. He didn't want to look at that, didn't want to see any trace of himself.

When the train arrived in Uddevalla, he was so tired that he could barely see straight. He'd tried to doze during the last hour of the trip, but images kept flickering through his mind, keeping him awake. He stopped at the McDonald's on the road to Torp and bought a large coffee, which he quickly downed for the sake of the caffeine.

His mobile was buzzing again, but he didn't feel like taking the phone out of his pocket, much less talking to whoever was so persistently trying to reach him. It was probably Sanna. She would be annoyed with him when he finally got home, but he didn't care.

He could feel a prickling sensation in his body, and he shifted position in the driver's seat. The headlights from the car behind him were shining in his rear-view mirror, and he was temporarily blinded when he shifted his gaze to the road ahead. There was something about those headlights — the steadily maintained distance, and the glare — that made him glance in the rear-view mirror again. It was the same car that had been behind him ever since he stopped in Torp. Or was it? He rubbed his eyes. He was no longer sure about anything.

The lights stayed with him as he turned

off the highway at the sign for Fjällbacka. Christian squinted, trying to make out what model car was following him. But it was too dark, and the headlights were too bright. His hands were sweaty as he tightened his grip on the steering wheel. He was holding on so hard that his hands started to ache, and he briefly let go to flex his fingers.

He pictured her in his mind. She was wearing the blue dress, holding the child in her arms. The scent of strawberries, the taste of her lips. The feeling of the dress fabric against his skin. Her hair, long and brown.

Something jumped out in front of his car. Christian braked hard, and for several seconds the tires lost contact with the road. The car slid toward the ditch, and he could feel that he'd lost control of the vehicle; he just let it happen. But an inch or two from the edge, the car came to a halt. The white rump of a deer was clearly visible in the light of the headlights, and he watched the animal leaping with fright across the field.

The engine was still running, but the sound was drowned out by the roar inside his head. In his rear-view mirror he noticed that the car behind him had also stopped, and he knew that he ought to get going.

Away from those headlights shining in the mirror.

A car door opened and someone got out of the other car. Who was that coming toward him? It was so dark outside, and he couldn't tell if it was a man or a woman approaching. A few more steps and the dark figure would reach his door.

Christian's hands began shaking as he continued to grip the wheel. He looked away from the mirror to stare out across the open field at the edge of the forest, which was vaguely discernible a short distance away. He stared and waited. The door on the passenger side of his car opened.

"Are you all right? Everything okay? It looks like you almost hit that deer."

Christian turned his head toward the voice. A white-haired man in his sixties was standing there, looking at him.

"I'm fine," Christian muttered. "I was just a bit shocked. That's all."

"I can understand that. It's awful when something jumps out in front of your car like that. Are you sure you're all right, though?"

"Absolutely. I'm going to head for home now. I'm on my way to Fjällbacka."

"Ah, I see. I'm going to Hamburgsund. Drive carefully."

The man shut the door, and Christian could feel his pulse begin to slow down. It was only ghosts, memories from the past. Nothing that could harm him.

A little voice in his head tried to talk about the letters. They were not figments of his imagination. But he turned a deaf ear, refusing to listen to the voice. If he started thinking about that, she would be in control again. And that was something he could not allow. He had worked so hard to forget. She wasn't going to get ahold of him again.

He started driving, headed for Fjällbacka. In his jacket pocket, his mobile was buzzing.

Alice kept on crying, both day and night. He heard Mother and Father talking about it. They said she had something called colic. No matter what that meant, it was unbearable, listening to the racket she made. The sound was encroaching on his whole life, taking everything away from him.

Why didn't Mother hate her when she cried so much? Why did she hold her, sing to her, rock her to sleep, and look at her with such a gentle expression, as if she felt sorry for the baby?

There was no reason to feel sorry for Alice. She behaved that way on purpose. He was convinced of that. Sometimes when he leaned over her cot and peered down at her as she lay there like an ugly little beetle, she would stare back at him. She gave him a look that said she didn't want Mother to love him. That was why she cried and demanded everything from her. So that there would be nothing left for him.

Now and then he could see that Father felt the same way. That he too knew that Alice was acting like that on purpose, so that Father would have no share of Mother either. Yet Father did nothing. Why didn't he do anything? He was big and grown up. He should be able to make Alice stop.

Father was hardly allowed to touch the baby either. Occasionally he would try, picking her up and patting her bottom and stroking her back to get her to calm down. But Mother always said that he was doing it wrong, that he should leave Alice to her. And then Father would retreat again.

But one day Father decided to take charge of her. Alice had been crying worse than ever, for three whole nights in a row.

He had lain awake in his room, pressing the pillow over his head to block out the sound. And under the pillow, his hatred had grown. It began spreading, settling so heavily on top of him that he could hardly breathe, and he had to lift the pillow away to gasp for air. By now Mother was worn out after being awake for three nights. So she had made an exception, leaving the baby to Father while she went to bed. And Father had decided to give Alice a bath, asking him if he'd like to watch.

Father carefully tested the temperature of the water before filling the bathtub. He looked at Alice — who for once was quiet — with the same expression on his face as Mother usually had. Never before had Father seemed so important. He was usually an invisible figure who disappeared in Mother's radiance, someone who had also been shut out from the relationship that Mother and Alice shared. But now he was suddenly important. He smiled at Alice, and she smiled back.

Father cautiously lowered the tiny naked body into the water. He placed her in a baby bath seat lined with terrycloth, almost like a little hammock, so she was partially sitting up. Tenderly he washed her arms, her legs, her plump little belly. She waved her hands and kicked her feet. She wasn't crying. Finally she had stopped crying. But that didn't matter. She had won. Even Father had left his place of refuge behind the newspaper to come out and smile at her.

He stood quietly in the doorway. Couldn't take his eyes off Father's hands touching that little body. Father, who had been the closest thing to an ally after Mother had stopped looking at him. The doorbell rang, and he gave a start. Father looked from the bathroom door to Alice, unsure what to do. Finally he said:

"Could you look after your little sister for a

minute? I just need to go see who that is. I'll be right back."

He hesitated a second. Then he felt his head nodding. Father got up from where he was kneeling beside the tub and told him to come closer. His feet moved automatically to carry him the short distance over to the tub. Alice looked up at him. Out of the corner of his eye, he saw Father leave the bathroom.

They were alone now, he and Alice.

11

Erica stared at Patrik in disbelief.

"In the ice?"

"Yes. The poor man who found him must have had a real shock." Patrik had given Erica a brief summary of the day's events.

"I guess he did!" She dropped heavily on to the sofa, and Maja immediately tried to climb onto her lap. And that was not an easy task.

"Hello! Hello!" shouted Maja, pressing her mouth against her mother's belly. Ever since they'd explained to her that the babies could hear her, she'd seized every opportunity to communicate with them. Since her vocabulary was limited, and that was putting it mildly, there wasn't much variety to her conversations.

"They're probably sleeping, so let's not wake them," said Erica, holding her finger to her lips.

Maja imitated the gesture, and then

pressed her ear against her mother's belly to hear if the babies really were asleep.

"Sounds like it was a terrible day," said Erica in a low voice.

"Yes, it was," said Patrik, trying to push aside his memory of the expressions he'd seen on the faces of Cia and her children. Especially the look in Ludvig's eyes. He was so much like Magnus, and that look was going to stay with Patrik for a very long time. "At least now they know. Sometimes I think uncertainty is worse," he said, sitting down next to Erica so that Maja ended up between them. She slid happily onto his lap, which offered a little more room, and burrowed her head into his chest. He stroked her blond hair.

"You're probably right. At the same time, it's hard when hope disappears." Erica hesitated, then asked: "Do the police have any idea what happened?"

Patrik shook his head. "No, at this point we know nothing. Absolutely nothing."

"What about the letters that were sent to Christian?" she asked, wrestling a bit with herself. Should she say anything about her excursion to the library today and what she'd been thinking about Christian's past? She decided not to mention either of those things until she'd found out a bit more.

"I still haven't had time to think about the letters. But we're going to have another talk with Magnus's family and friends, so I can take up the subject when I interview Christian."

"They asked him about the letters this morning on the TV talk show," said Erica, shuddering when she thought about her own role in provoking the questions that Christian had been subjected to on live television.

"What did he say?"

"He dismissed the whole thing, even when they pressured him to discuss it."

"I'm not surprised." Patrik kissed his daughter on the top of her head. "So, what do you think, Maja? Shall we go and cook dinner for Mama and the babies?" He got up, holding Maja in his arms. She nodded eagerly. "What shall we make? Poop sausages with onions?"

Maja laughed so hard that she hiccupped. She was bright for her age and had recently discovered the pleasures of poop and pee humor.

"Hmm. . . ." said Patrik. "No, I think we'll cook fish sticks and mashed potatoes instead. Okay? We'll save the poop sausages for another day."

His daughter thought about this for a moment and then graciously nodded her agreement. Fish sticks it was.

Sanna paced back and forth. The boys were sitting in front of the TV in the living room, watching *Bolibompa*. But she just couldn't settle in one place. She kept wandering through the house, gripping her mobile phone in one hand. Every once in a while, she would punch in his number.

No answer. Christian hadn't answered his phone all day, and one disaster scene after another had played out in her mind. Especially after the news about Magnus, which had shocked all of Fjällbacka. She'd checked Christian's email at least ten times during the day. It felt as if something was building up inside of her, growing stronger and stronger until it demanded to be either denied or confirmed. Deep inside, she almost wished she could find something to blame him for. Then at least she would know and have some outlet for the anxiety and fear that kept gnawing at her.

In reality, she knew that she was going about things all wrong. With her need to be in control and her constant questions about who he had met and what he'd been thinking, she was driving him further away. She knew this on a rational level, but the emotions she had were so overwhelming. She felt that she couldn't trust him, that he was hiding something from her, that she wasn't good enough. That he didn't love her.

The thought hurt so much that she sat down on the kitchen floor and wrapped her arms around her knees. The refrigerator was humming behind her back, but she hardly noticed. The only thing she was aware of was the hollowness inside her.

Where was he? Why hadn't he called? Why couldn't she get ahold of him? Resolutely she tapped in his number again. Christian's mobile rang and rang, but there was still no answer. She stood up and went over to look at the letter lying on the kitchen table. It had arrived today, and she had opened it at once. The message was as cryptic as ever. *You know you can't escape. I'm inside your heart, and that's why you can never hide, no matter where in the world you may go.* The handwriting in black ink was very familiar. With trembling fingers, Sanna picked up the letter and held it to her nose. It smelled of paper and ink. No perfume or anything else that might hint at the identity of the sender.

Though Christian persisted in maintaining that he didn't know who had written the letters, she didn't believe him. It was that simple. Fury rose up inside her, and she flung the letter on to the table, turned on her heel, and dashed upstairs. One of the boys called to her from the living room, but she ignored him. She had to know, she had to find out the answer. It was as if someone else had taken over her body, as if she no longer had control of herself.

She started with the bedroom, pulling out the drawers in Christian's bureau and tearing through the contents. She took everything out, carefully examining each item, and then ran her hand over the inside of the empty drawers. Nothing. Absolutely nothing other than T-shirts, socks, and underwear.

She stood in the middle of the room and looked around. What about the wardrobes? Sanna went over to the large pieces of furniture that covered one entire wall and methodically went through them. Everything that belonged to Christian ended up tossed on the floor. Shirts, trousers, belts, and shoes. She found nothing personal, nothing that would tell her anything more about her husband or help her penetrate the wall that he'd constructed around himself.

Faster and faster she pulled out his clothes. Finally only her own dresses and other clothing were left. She sank down onto the bed and ran her hand over the coverlet that her grandmother had stitched. She possessed so many things that revealed who she was and where she had come from. The coverlet, the dressing table that had once belonged to her other grandmother, the necklace that her mother had given her. Not to mention all the letters from friends and family members, which she kept in boxes in the wardrobe. There were also school yearbooks neatly stacked on a shelf, and her graduation cap safely stored away in a hatbox next to her dried bridal bouquet. So many little things that were part of her personal history, part of her life.

She suddenly realized that her husband didn't have any such things. Apparently he wasn't as sentimental as she was. Nor was he inclined to collect things. But there had to be something. No one went through life without holding on to at least a few mementos.

She jabbed at the coverlet with her fists. The suspense was making her heart beat faster. Who was Christian? Who was he really? An idea occurred to her, and she suddenly sat very still. There was one place she hadn't yet searched. The attic.

■ ■ ■ ■

Erik swirled the glass in his hand, studying the deep red color of the wine, which was lighter toward the rim. The sign of a young wine, he'd learned at one of the countless wine classes that he'd attended.

His whole life was on the verge of collapsing, and he couldn't really understand how this had happened. He felt he was being carried by a current so strong that there was nothing he could do to resist.

Magnus was dead. One shock had merged with another, so it was only now that he could really take in what Louise had texted to his phone. First the news that she'd heard Magnus's body had been found, and almost at the same time Cecilia had announced that she was pregnant. Two events that had shaken him to the core and that he'd learned within thirty seconds of each other.

"You could at least answer me." Louise's voice was harsh now.

"What?" he replied, realizing that his wife had said something to him, but he'd obviously missed what it was. "What did you say?"

"I asked you where you were today when I sent you the message about Magnus. I called your office first, but you weren't there. Then I tried you several times on your mobile, but I just got your voicemail." She was slurring her words, as she'd done all evening. She had probably started drinking sometime in the afternoon.

Disgust welled up in his mouth, mixing with the wine and giving it a bitter bouquet of steel. He found it nauseating that she had lost control of her life so badly. Why couldn't she just pull herself together, instead of looking at him with that martyr expression and her body full of wine from a box?

"I was out running an errand."

"An errand?" Louise took another sip of her wine. "Oh, right. I can just imagine what sort of errand that might be."

"Stop," he said wearily. "Not today. Not today of all days."

"Why not today?" She sounded like she was eager for a fight. The girls had gone to bed a while ago, and now it was just the two of them. Erik and Louise.

"One of our closest friends was found dead today. Can't we have a little peace and quiet tonight?"

Louise didn't reply. He saw that she was embarrassed. For a moment he pictured her as the young girl he'd met at the university: sweet, intelligent, quick-witted. But the image quickly vanished, and what he saw was the slack skin and the teeth stained purple by the wine. Again he had that bitter taste in his mouth.

And then there was Cecilia. What was he going to do about her? As far as he knew, this was the first time that any of his mistresses had gotten pregnant. Maybe he'd just been lucky. But now his luck had run out. She said she wanted to keep the child. She had stood there in her kitchen and coldly told him that. No argument, no discussion. She told him because she felt that she had to, and to offer him the opportunity to participate. Or not.

All of a sudden Cecilia seemed so grown-up. The giggling, naïve demeanor was gone. He stood there, facing her, and he could tell from her expression that for the first time she was seeing him for who he really was. And it had made him squirm. He didn't want to see himself through her eyes. He didn't want to see himself at all.

People had admired him his whole life, and he'd always taken their praise for granted. Some people feared him, and that had been equally rewarding. But Cecilia, holding a protective hand over her belly, had looked at him with contempt. Their affair was over. She had presented the options open to him. She could keep quiet about who was the father of her child, in return for a significant sum of money deposited in her bank account on a monthly basis, starting with the birth and continuing until the child turned eighteen. Or else Cecilia would tell Louise and then do everything she could to rob him of all honor and respect.

As Erik looked at his wife, he wondered if he'd made the right choice. He didn't love Louise. He constantly betrayed her and hurt her, and he knew that she would be happier without him. But it would be difficult to give up what he was used to. There was nothing appealing about a bachelor's life, with stacks of dirty dishes and mountains of laundry waiting to be washed. Or eating Findus frozen meals in front of the TV, and seeing the girls only on the weekends. Louise had won because it was more convenient, and because she was entitled to half of his assets. It was the simpler solution. But he was going to be paying big-time for this convenience for the next eighteen years.

For almost an hour, Christian sat in the car a short distance from the house. He could see Sanna moving around inside. He could tell from her body language that she was upset.

He didn't have the energy to deal with her anger, her weeping and accusations. If it hadn't been for the boys. . . . Christian started up the car and headed up the driveway to prevent himself from completing that thought. Every time he felt the love for his sons swelling inside his chest, he was overcome with fear. He had tried not to let them come too close. Tried to keep the danger and the evil at bay. But the letters had made him realize that the evil was already here. And his love for his sons was deep and irrevocable.

He had to protect them, no matter what the cost. He couldn't fail again. Then his whole life and everything he believed in would be changed forever. He leaned his head against the steering wheel, felt the plastic touching his forehead, and waited to hear the front door open at any moment. But apparently Sanna hadn't heard the car, and he had a few more seconds to compose himself.

He had thought that he could create a sense of security by shutting off the part of his heart that belonged to his sons. But he was wrong. There was no escape. And he couldn't help loving them. So he was forced to fight, facing the evil, eye to eye. Confront what for so long he had held inside of him;

but now the book had opened it up. For the first time, he thought he shouldn't have written that novel. Everything would have been different if it didn't exist. At the same time, he knew that he hadn't acted of his own free will. He had been forced to write it; he had been forced to write about her.

Now the front door opened. He raised his face from the steering wheel. Sanna stood in the doorway, shivering, with her cardigan wrapped tightly around herself. The light from the hall made her look like a madonna, albeit clad in a nubbly jumper and with slippers on her feet. She was safe. He knew that as he looked at her. Because she didn't touch anything inside of him. She had never been able to do that and she never would. She wasn't someone that he needed to protect.

But he did have to answer to her for his actions. His legs felt heavy and numb as he climbed out of the car. He pressed the remote to lock the doors and walked toward the light. Sanna took a step back into the hall, staring at him. Her face was very pale.

"I've been trying to reach you. Over and over again. I've tried since lunchtime, and you haven't bothered to answer. Tell me that your mobile was stolen, or that it was broken. Tell me anything that could reasonably explain why I haven't been able to get ahold of you."

Christian shrugged. He had no explanation.

"I don't know," he said, taking off his jacket. His arms felt numb too.

"You don't know?" She spoke the words haltingly, and even though he had closed the front door, she was still hugging her arms around her body as if she were freezing.

"I was tired," he said, well aware of how lame that sounded. "It was a rough interview this morning, and then I had to meet with Gaby, and . . . I was tired." He didn't have the energy to tell her what had happened at the meeting with his publisher. All he really wanted to do right now was go upstairs and crawl under the covers so he could fall asleep and forget about everything else.

"Have the boys gone to bed?" he asked, walking past Sanna. He accidentally brushed against her, and she wavered but stayed on her feet. When she didn't answer his question, he repeated it. "Have the boys gone to bed?"

"Yes."

Christian went upstairs to his sons' room. They looked like little angels as they lay in their beds, their cheeks flushed and their eyelashes like tiny black fans. He sat down on the edge of Nils's bed and stroked his blond hair as he listened to Melker snuffling in his sleep. Then he stood up and tucked the covers more snugly around both boys before he went back downstairs. Sanna was still standing in the same spot in the front hall. He began to sense that her attitude wasn't due to the usual complaints and accusations. He knew that she checked up on him in every way she could, that she read his emails and phoned the library with contrived excuses just to see if he was really at work. He knew all about this and had accepted it. But something else was going on now.

If he'd had a choice, he would have turned on his heel and gone back upstairs to make good on his thoughts of climbing into bed. But he knew it was no use. Sanna had something she wanted to say, and she was going to tell him what it was, whether he stood here in the hall or lay in bed.

"Has something happened?" he asked, and suddenly his whole body went cold. Could she really have done it? He knew what she was capable of.

"A letter came today," said Sanna, finally deciding to move. She went into the kitchen, and he assumed that he was supposed to follow.

"A letter?" Christian sighed with relief. Was that all it was?

"The same as usual," said Sanna, tossing the envelope down on the table in front of him. "Who keeps sending you these letters? And don't tell me that you don't know. I don't believe it for a second." Her voice rose to a falsetto. "Who is she, Christian? Is she the one you went to see today? Is that why I haven't been able to get ahold of you? Why is she sending you these letters?" The questions and accusations poured out of her. Christian wearily sank on to the chair closest to the window. He held the letter in his hand without looking at it or reading it.

"I have no idea, Sanna." Deep in his heart he almost had an urge to tell her. But he couldn't.

"You're lying." Sanna began to sob. Her head drooped, and she wiped her nose on the sleeve of her jumper. Then she looked up. "I know that you're lying. There's some woman, or at least there has been. Today I ran around the house like crazy, looking for something that would give me the slightest hint about the man I'm married to. And you know what? There was nothing. Nothing! I have no idea who you are!"

Sanna was screaming at him now, and Christian let her anger wash over him. She was right. He'd left everything behind — who he was and who he had been. He'd left them all behind. But he should have realized that she would refuse to be forgotten, to remain in the past. He should have known.

"So say something!"

Christian gave a start. Sanna was leaning forward, spraying saliva as she shouted at him. Slowly he raised his arm to wipe off his face. Then she moved her face even closer and lowered her voice so she was almost whispering.

"But I kept on looking. Everybody has something they don't want to reveal. So what I want to know is. . . ." She paused, and he felt his skin prickling with alarm. She had a look of satisfaction on her face that was new and frightening. He didn't want to hear any more, didn't want to play this game any longer, but he knew that Sanna would proceed relentlessly toward her goal.

She reached for something lying on one of the chairs on the other side of the kitchen table. Her eyes were shining with all the emotions that had been stored up during their years together.

"What I want to know is, who does *this*

belong to?" Sanna said, holding up something blue.

Christian saw at once what it was. He had to fight his instinct to tear it out of her hands. She had no right to touch that dress! He wanted to tell her that, shout the words at her, and make her understand that she had crossed a line. But his mouth was dry, and he couldn't utter a single word. He stretched out his hand for the blue fabric, which he knew would feel so soft against his cheek and which would rest so lightly in his hand. She took a step back, holding it out of reach.

"Who does this belong to?" Her voice was even lower now, barely audible. Sanna unfolded the dress and held it up in front of her, as if she were in a shop and wanted to see if the color suited her.

Christian didn't look at her; his eyes were fixed on the dress. He couldn't bear to see it sullied by anyone else's hands. At the same time, his brain was working in a surprisingly cold and methodical way. The two worlds, which he had so carefully kept separate, were about to collide, and he couldn't reveal the truth. It could never be spoken aloud. Yet the best lie was always the one that held fragments of truth.

Suddenly he felt completely calm. He

would give Sanna what she wanted. He would give her a small piece of his past. So he started talking, and after a while she sat down to listen to his story, although he told her only part of it.

Lisbet's breathing was irregular. It had been months since she had slept in the double bed upstairs. Eventually her illness had made it impossible for her to manage the climb to the bedroom, so he'd fixed up the guest room on the ground floor for her. He'd made the small room as comfortable as possible, but no matter what he did, it was still the guest room. And this time the cancer was the guest. It occupied the room with its smell, its tenacity, and its portent of death.

Soon the cancer would leave them, but as Kenneth lay there listening to Lisbet's halting breath, he wished that the guest would stay. Because it wouldn't be leaving alone; it would take along the dearest person in his life.

The yellow scarf lay on the bedside table. He turned on his side, propped his head on his hand, and studied his wife in the faint light coming from the streetlights outside the window. He reached out his hand and gently caressed the downy fuzz on her head.

She stirred uneasily, and he hastily withdrew his hand, afraid of waking her from the sleep that she needed so badly, though she seldom slept for more than a few hours at a time.

He couldn't sleep close to her anymore — not like they'd done in the past. It was something that they both had loved; and at first they had tried, moving close under the covers. He had put his arm around her the way he always had done, ever since their first night together. But the illness had robbed them of that joy too. It hurt her to be touched, and she had jerked away every time he nestled close. So he had set up a bed next to hers. The thought of not sleeping in the same room with her was unbearable. The thought of sleeping alone upstairs, in their bed, never even occurred to him.

He slept badly on the cot. His back ached every morning, and his joints were always stiff. He'd considered buying a real bed to put next to hers, but he knew it would be pointless. Even though he didn't like to think about it, he knew that soon there would be no more need for an extra bed. Soon he would be sleeping alone upstairs.

Kenneth blinked away his tears as he watched Lisbet's breathing, shallow and strained. Her eyes moved under her lids, as if she were dreaming. He wondered what she saw in her dreams. Was she healthy? Was she running with the yellow scarf tied around her long hair?

He turned away. He had to try to get some sleep; he had a job to tend to, after all. For too many nights he had lain here, tossing and turning on the cot and watching her, afraid to miss out on a single minute. Fatigue had settled over him, and it never seemed to let up.

He realized that he had to pee, so he might as well get up. He wouldn't be able to sleep until he'd relieved himself. With an effort, he turned over so he could sit up. His back creaked, and the cot did too. He sat on the edge for a moment to stretch out his muscles, which were clenched up tight. The floor felt cold under his feet as he stood up and padded out to the hall. The bathroom was right next door, on the left, and he blinked in the glare when he switched on the light. He raised the toilet lid, pulled down his pajama trousers, and shut his eyes as he felt the pressure ease.

Suddenly he noticed a draft on his legs. He opened his eyes and looked up. The bathroom door stood open, and it felt like an icy wind had blown in. He cast a quick glance over his shoulder, but he wasn't done pissing, and he didn't want to miss the toilet. When he was finished, he shook off the last drops, pulled up his pajama trousers, and turned toward the doorway. It was probably just his imagination, because he didn't feel the cold anymore. Yet something told him to be wary.

The hall was dimly lit. The glow from the bathroom light reached only a short distance ahead of him, and the rest of the house was in darkness. Lisbet always used to hang Advent stars in the windows in November, and they stayed there until March because she loved the way they shone. But this year she hadn't had the energy, and he had never gotten around to it either.

Kenneth tiptoed out into the entry. It wasn't his imagination. The temperature was definitely lower here, as if the front door had stood open. He went over and tried the handle. Not locked. That wasn't unusual, since he sometimes forgot to lock the door, even at night.

For safety's sake, he now made sure the door was properly closed and then turned the lock. He was about to go back to bed, but he suddenly had goose bumps. Something still didn't feel right. He looked at the doorway leading to the kitchen, which was lit only by the faint light from the streetlamp outside. Kenneth squinted and took a step closer. There was something shiny white lying on the kitchen table, something that hadn't been there when he cleared away the dishes before going to bed. He took a few more steps. Fear surged in waves through his body.

In the middle of the table he saw a letter. Another letter. And next to the envelope someone had carefully placed a kitchen knife. The blade gleamed in the glow of the streetlamp. Kenneth looked around, but he realized that whoever the intruder had been, he or she had now gone. Leaving behind a letter and a knife.

Kenneth wished he understood what the message was intended to be.

She smiled at him. A big smile, no teeth, just gums. But he wasn't fooled. He knew what she wanted. She wanted to take and take until he no longer had anything left.

Suddenly he noticed the smell in his nostrils. That sweet, repulsive smell. It had been there back then, and it was here now. It must be coming from her. He looked down at the soft, shiny little body. Everything about her disgusted him. The plump belly, the notch between her legs, the hair that was dark and unevenly sprinkled over her head.

He put his hand on her head. He felt a pulsing under the skin. Close and fragile. His hand pressed harder, and she slid farther down. Still she laughed at him. The water closed around her legs, splashing as her heels struck the bottom of the tub.

He could hear Father's voice, far far away, at the front door. It rose and fell and didn't sound as if it would return for a few minutes yet. He could still feel the pulsing under his palm, and she had started to whimper. Her smile came and went, as if she wasn't sure whether she was happy or sad. Maybe she could feel through his hand how much he hated her, how much he detested every second he had to spend in her presence.

It would be so much better without her, and without all that crying. He wouldn't have to see the joy on Mother's face when she looked at the baby, or the absence of joy when Mother turned to look at him. It was so obvious. Whenever Mother shifted her gaze from Alice to him, it was as if a light went out. The light died.

Again he listened for Father. Alice seemed to have decided not to burst into tears yet, and he smiled back at her. Then he carefully placed his arm under her head, for support, just as he'd seen Mother do. With his other hand he pulled away the seat that was holding her in a reclining position. It wasn't easy. She was slippery and kept squirming about.

At last he got the bath seat out and cautiously pushed it aside. Now all of her weight was resting on his left arm. The sweet, suffocating smell was getting stronger. Feeling sick, he turned his head away. He felt her eyes burning his cheek, and her skin was wet and slippery against his arm. He loathed her because she brought that smell back to him, because she forced him to remember.

Slowly he pulled his arm away and looked at her. Her head fell back toward the tub, and just before it struck the water, she took a breath to scream. But by then it was too late, and her little face disappeared under the surface. Her eyes stared up at him through the rippling water. She flailed her arms and legs, but she couldn't pull herself up. She was too little, too weak. He didn't even have to hold her head down. It came to rest on the bottom, and the only thing she could do was move it from side to side.

He squatted down, leaned his chin on the edge of the bathtub, and watched her struggle. She shouldn't have tried to take his beautiful mother away from him. She deserved to die. It wasn't his fault.

After a while her arms and legs stopped moving and slowly sank. He felt a great calm spread through him. The smell was gone and he could breathe again. Everything would be the way it used to be. With his head tilted, resting against the cold enamel, he looked at Alice, who now lay very still.

12

"Come in, come in," said Ulf Rosander, looking groggy with sleep, although he was fully dressed. He motioned for Patrik and Paula to enter.

"Thanks for agreeing to see us on such short notice," said Paula.

"No problem. I just had to phone my workplace to say that I'd be a little late. Considering the circumstances, they understood completely. We've all lost a colleague." He headed for the living room, and they followed.

It looked as if a bomb had gone off in the room. Toys and all sorts of other items were scattered everywhere. Ulf shoved aside a pile of children's clothing so they could sit down on the sofa.

"It's always chaotic in the morning before the kids have to go off to the day-care center," he apologized.

"How old are they?" asked Paula as Patrik

leaned back, letting her take the lead. As a police officer, he never underestimated the value of small talk.

"Three and five," said Rosander, his face lighting up. "Two girls. They're my second brood. I also have two sons from a previous marriage who are fourteen and sixteen. But they're living with their mother at the moment, or the house would look even worse."

"How do the kids get along, since there's such a big age difference?" wondered Patrik.

"Much better than expected, actually. The boys are real teenagers, so things don't always go smoothly. But the girls worship them, and the boys like their little sisters too. In fact, the girls call them the Elk Brothers."

Patrik laughed, but Paula looked mystified. "It's from a children's book," he told her. "Just wait a few years, and you'll understand."

Then he turned serious as he said to Rosander, "Well, as you probably heard, we've found Magnus."

The smile on Rosander's face instantly disappeared. He ran his hand through his hair, which was disheveled enough already.

"Do you know how he died? Did he go down in the sea?"

That was an old-fashioned way of referring to a shipwreck, but a common expression for people who lived in a community so close to the water.

Patrik shook his head. "We don't know yet. But right now it's more important to find out what happened on the morning he disappeared."

"I understand. But I don't really know how I can help." Rosander threw out his hands. "The only thing I know is that he phoned to tell me he was running late."

"Was that unusual?" asked Paula.

"For Magnus to be late?" Rosander frowned. "Now that you mention it, I don't think it had ever happened before."

"How long had you been driving to work together?" Patrik discreetly removed a little plastic ladybird that he'd been sitting on.

"Ever since I started working at Tanum Windows five years ago. Before that, Magnus always took the bus, but we got to talking at work, and I said that he could ride with me. In return he could pay his share of the gas."

"And during these five years, had he ever phoned before to say that he'd be late?" Paula repeated her question.

"No, not once. I should have thought of that earlier."

"How did he sound when he called?"

asked Patrik. "Calm? Upset? Did he say why he was delayed?"

"No, he didn't. I can't be sure about this, because it's been a while now, but I don't think he sounded quite himself."

"What do you mean by that?" Patrik leaned forward.

" 'Upset' is probably too strong a word, but I got the impression that something was wrong. I thought maybe he'd had a row with Cia or the kids."

"Was there something he said to give you that idea?" asked Paula, exchanging a glance with Patrik.

"No, not really. The conversation lasted about five seconds. Magnus phoned and said that he was running late and that I should just go on ahead if he took too long. He'd make it to work on his own. Then he hung up. I waited for a while, and then I left. That was all. I assume it was his tone of voice that made me think there'd been some sort of trouble at home."

"Do you know whether they had any problems in their marriage?"

"I never heard Magnus say a single bad thing about Cia. On the contrary. They seemed to get on really well. Of course it's impossible to tell what goes on in other families, but I've always thought of Magnus as a happily married man. Mind you, we didn't talk much about those sorts of things. It was more about the weather and football."

"Would you say that the two of you were friends?" asked Patrik.

Rosander hesitated before answering. "No, I wouldn't really say that. We drove to work together and we chatted now and then at lunch, but we never socialized or anything like that. I don't really know why not, because we enjoyed each other's company. But everyone has their own circle of friends, and it's hard to change things like that."

"So if something was bothering him, or if someone had upset him, he wouldn't have confided in you?" Paula asked.

"No, I don't think he would have. But I did see him five days a week, so I should have been able to tell if he was worried about something. But he was just the same as always. Cheerful, calm, and confident. A really great guy, to put it simply." Rosander looked down at his hands. "I'm sorry I can't be of more help."

"You've been extremely cooperative." Patrik got up, and Paula followed suit. They shook hands with Rosander and thanked him for his time.

Back in the car, they went over what they'd heard as they drove.

"So, what do you think?" said Paula, glancing at Patrik's profile as he sat next to her in the passenger seat.

"Hey, keep your eyes on the road!" Patrik grabbed the door handle as Paula barely managed to avoid colliding with a truck in the narrow curve just before Mörhult.

"Whoops," said Paula, all of her attention now fixed on the windshield and the road ahead.

"Women drivers," muttered Patrik.

Paula knew he was just teasing her and chose to ignore his remark. Besides, she'd been a passenger in the car when Patrik was driving, and she thought it was a miracle he even had a license.

"I don't think Ulf Rosander has anything at all to do with the murder," said Patrik, in answer to her question.

Paula nodded. "I agree. In this instance, Mellberg is really barking up the wrong tree."

"So we'll just have to convince him of that."

"But it was still good that we went out there. Gösta must have missed that bit of information. There has to be a reason why Magnus was late for the first time in five years. It was Rosander's impression that he sounded upset, or at least not like himself when he phoned. I don't think it's a co-incidence that he disappeared that very morning."

"You're right. I just don't know how we should go about finding out what had upset him. I asked Cia the same question earlier, whether anything in particular happened that morning, and she said no. She did leave for work before Magnus did, but what could have happened in the short period of time when he was home alone?"

"Has anyone checked the phone records?" asked Paula, careful to keep her eyes focused on the road.

"Several times. No one phoned their house that morning. No one called his mobile. The only phone call was when Magnus called Rosander. After that, nothing."

"Do you think someone came over to see him in person?"

"I don't think so." Patrik shook his head. "The neighbors had a good view of the house. They were eating breakfast when Magnus left. Of course, it's possible that they might have missed seeing someone who rang the doorbell, but they were quite confident they hadn't."

"What about his email?"

Again Patrik shook his head. "Cia gave us

permission to look through his computer, but there were no emails that aroused any interest."

They drove in silence for a while, both of them lost in thought. What could have happened to make Magnus Kjellner disappear one day without a trace, only to turn up three months later, his body frozen in the ice? What had actually happened on that morning?

Foolishly, Erica had decided to walk. In her mind, the distance between her house in Sälvik and her destination had seemed no more than a stone's throw away. But it seemed it would have to have been a world-record-breaking stone's throw.

Erica pressed a hand to the small of her back as she paused to catch her breath. She looked in the direction of the Ocean View Development office, which was still a long way off. But she'd have just as far to go if she turned around and went back home, so she could either sit down here in the snow-drift or just push on.

Ten minutes later, feeling exhausted, she stepped inside the office. She hadn't phoned in advance, thinking that she might win an advantage by making a surprise visit. She had made sure that Erik's car wasn't parked outside. Kenneth was the one she wanted to talk to. Preferably without being interrupted.

"Hello?" No one seemed to have heard the door close behind her, so she made her way farther inside. It appeared to be an ordinary house that had been converted into office space. A large section of the ground floor now had an open-floor plan, and the walls were lined with shelves holding three-ring binders. There were also large posters of the structures the company had built, and a desk stood at either end of the room. Kenneth was sitting at one of them. He seemed unaware of Erica's presence, because he carried on staring straight ahead without moving.

"Hello?" she tried again.

Kenneth gave a start. "Oh, hello! I'm sorry, but I didn't hear you come in." He got up and came toward her. "Erica Falck, if I'm not mistaken."

"That's right." She shook hands with him and smiled. Kenneth noticed that she was eagerly eyeing one of the visitor's chairs, and he motioned for her to have a seat.

"Please sit down. It must be difficult carrying around the extra weight. Looks like your due date must be pretty soon."

Erica gratefully leaned back in the chair,

feeling the pressure ease in her back.

"I've still got a little while to go. But I'm having twins," she said, looking a bit surprised by her own words.

"In that case, you're certainly going to be busy," said Kenneth kindly, sitting down next to her. "Are you in the market for a new house?"

Erica was startled by the way his face looked when she saw him up close, in the light from the nearby lamp. He looked tired and haggard. "Hunted" was actually the word she was looking for. Suddenly she remembered hearing that his wife was seriously ill. She resisted the impulse to put her hand over his, suspecting that he might not appreciate such a gesture of sympathy. But she couldn't help saying something. His sorrow and fatigue were so obvious, so deeply etched into the lines of his face.

"How is your wife doing?" Erica asked, hoping he wouldn't be offended by the question.

"Things are bad. She's not doing well at all."

Neither of them spoke for a moment. Then Kenneth sat up straight and attempted a smile, although it didn't hide the pain he was feeling.

"So, are you and Patrik thinking about a

new house? The one you have is really very nice. But no matter what, Erik is really the one you and your husband need to talk to. I handle the finances and the account books, and I'm not much of a talker. But Erik will be here after lunch, I think, so if you'd like to come back then. . . ."

"No, I'm not here about buying a house."

"Oh? Then why exactly are you here?"

Erica hesitated. Why the hell did she have to be so curious that she couldn't help sticking her nose in everybody else's business? How was she going to explain this?

"I suppose you've heard about Magnus Kjellner? That his body was found?" she began.

Kenneth's face turned a shade grayer as he nodded.

"And as I understand it, the two of you saw quite a lot of each other. Is that right?"

"Why are you asking me about this?" said Kenneth, his expression suddenly wary.

"I just. . . ." Erica searched for a good explanation but didn't find one. She'd have to settle for telling a lie. "Did you read what it said in the newspapers about the threatening letters that Christian Thydell has received?"

Kenneth nodded, still looking circumspect. Something flashed in his eyes, but it was gone so fast that Erica wasn't even sure she'd seen anything.

"Christian is my friend, and I want to help him," she went on. "I think there's a connection between the threats he's been receiving and what happened to Magnus."

"What sort of connection?" asked Kenneth, leaning forward.

"I can't go into that right now," she said evasively. "But it would really help if you could tell me a little about Magnus. Did he have any enemies? Is there anyone who might have wanted to harm him?"

"No, that doesn't seem at all likely." Kenneth leaned back in his chair again. His whole posture signaled his unwillingness to continue with this topic.

"How long have you known each other?" Erica was trying to steer the conversation toward less-charged territory. Sometimes it was best to take a roundabout approach.

And it worked. Kenneth seemed to relax. "In principle, our whole lives. We're the same age, so we were in the same class in grade school and also in secondary school. The three of us have always been friends."

"The three of you? You mean you, Magnus, and Erik Lind?"

"Yes, that's right. If we'd first met as adults, I don't think we would have become friends, but Fjällbacka is so small, and we more or less grew up together, so we've always stayed in touch. When Erik lived in Göteborg, we didn't see much of him, but since he moved back here we've seen rather a good deal of each other, getting together with our families. Out of habit, I suppose."

"Would you say that the three of you are close?"

Kenneth paused to think, glancing out of the window and staring across the ice before he answered. "No, I wouldn't say that. Erik and I work together, of course, so we have a lot of contact with each other. But we're not close friends. I don't think anyone is close to Erik. And Magnus and I were so different. I don't have a bad word to say about Magnus; I don't think anyone does. We always got on well together, but we've never been what you'd call confidants. In that sense, it was Magnus and the newcomer in the group, Christian, who spent the most time together."

"How did Christian come into the picture?"

"I don't really know. Magnus was the one who decided to include him and Sanna, right after Christian moved here. After that, he became a regular."

"Do you know anything about his background?"

"No," he said and then fell silent for a moment. "Now that you mention it . . . I really know nothing about what he did before he moved to Fjällbacka. We never talked about it." Kenneth seemed surprised by what he'd just said.

"How do you and Erik get along with Christian?"

"He's a bit difficult to get to know, and he can be really gloomy. But he's a nice guy, and if he just has a couple of glasses of wine, he loosens up and we usually have a great time."

"Do you think he's seemed stressed lately? Worried about anything?"

"Christian, you mean?" Again a flash of something in Kenneth's eyes, but it disappeared so quickly.

"Yes. He's been getting these threatening letters for almost a year and a half."

"That long? I didn't know that."

"So you and Erik haven't noticed anything?"

He shook his head. "As I said, Christian is rather . . . complicated, you might say. It's hard to know what's going on inside his head. For instance, I had no idea that he was writing a book until it was just about to be published."

"Have you read it? It's really creepy," said Erica.

Kenneth shook his head. "I'm not much of a reader. But I heard that the reviews have been great."

"Yes, really incredible," Erica replied. "But Christian didn't tell you or Erik about the letters?"

"No, he never mentioned them. But as I said, we've mostly seen each other at social events. Dinner parties, celebrations, and at New Year's and Midsummer. Things like that. Magnus was probably the one person that Christian might have talked to."

"And Magnus didn't say anything to you either?"

"No, he didn't." Kenneth got up. "I'm sorry, but I really need to get back to work now. Are you sure that you and Patrik wouldn't like to consider a new house?" He smiled and gestured toward the advertising posters on the wall.

"We're very comfortable where we are, but thanks. And your houses certainly are attractive." Erica made an effort to stand up, but with the usual awkward result. Kenneth held out his hand and helped her get to her feet.

"Thank you." Erica wrapped her scarf around her neck. "I'm really sorry," she said then. "About your wife, I mean. I hope that. . . ." She didn't know what else to say, and Kenneth merely nodded.

Erica shivered as she stepped back out into the cold.

Christian was having a hard time concentrating. Normally he enjoyed his job at the library, but today he was finding it impossible to focus, impossible to keep his mind on anything.

Everybody who came in wanted to say something about *The Mermaid*. Some had already read the book, some were planning to read it, some had seen him on the TV talk show. And he always responded politely, thanking people for their favorable comments, and offering a brief summary of his novel for those who asked. But in reality, he just wanted to scream.

He couldn't stop thinking about the terrible thing that had happened to Magnus. The prickling sensation had started up in his hands again, and it was spreading. To his arms, over his torso, down into his legs. At times it felt as if his whole body was itching and burning. He was having a hard time sitting still. That's why he kept getting up to go over to the shelves, reshelving books that had ended up in the wrong place and straightening the spines so the books formed nice, even rows.

All of a sudden he stopped. He was standing there with one hand raised, resting on top of some books, and he was incapable of taking it down. That's when the thoughts came, the ones that had been appearing more and more often. What was he doing here? Why was he here, in this particular place, at this particular moment? He shook his head to push the thoughts away, but they just burrowed deeper into his mind.

Someone walked by outside, going past the library entrance. He caught only a glimpse of the person, sensing a movement rather than actually seeing anything. But the feeling that instantly came over him was the same as when he had driven home the night before. The feeling of something hostile, yet at the same time familiar.

He dashed over to the entrance and peered out in the direction the person had gone. Nobody there. No footsteps or any other sound. No one in sight. Was he imagining things? Christian pressed his fingertips to his temples. He closed his eyes and in his mind he pictured Sanna, seeing again the expression on her face when he'd told her what was half true and half lies. Her mouth agape, sympathy mixed with horror.

She wouldn't be asking him any more questions. At least not for a while. And the blue dress was back upstairs in the attic, where it belonged. By revealing a little bit of the truth, he had bought himself a temporary respite. But sooner or later she would start questioning what he'd told her, looking for answers and the part of the story that he hadn't wanted to tell. That part had to stay buried. There was no other option.

He still had his eyes closed when he heard someone clearing their throat. Christian opened his eyes.

"Excuse me, but my name is Lars Olsson. I'm a reporter. I was just wondering if we could have a little chat. I've tried to reach you by phone, but nobody answers."

"I've switched off my mobile." Christian took his hands away from his temples. "What do you want?"

"Yesterday a man was found frozen in the ice. Magnus Kjellner. He's been missing since November. As I understand it, the two of you were good friends."

"Why are you talking to me about this?" Christian backed away, retreating behind the library counter.

"It seems a strange coincidence, don't you think? The fact that you've been receiving threats for a long period of time, and then one of your closest friends is found dead? We've also learned that he was most likely murdered."

"Murdered?" said Christian, hiding his hands under the counter. They were shaking badly.

"Yes, there were wounds on the body that indicate he was the victim of an attack. Do you know whether Magnus Kjellner had also been threatened? Or who might have sent those letters to you?" The journalist was using an aggressive tone of voice, leaving no doubt that he expected Christian to answer.

"I know nothing about that. Nothing at all."

"But it seems that somebody is fixated on you, and then it's not a big leap to assume that people close to you might be targeted too. Has anyone in your family been threatened in any way?"

All Christian could do was mutely shake his head. Images began crowding into his mind, and he swiftly pushed them away. He couldn't allow them to take over.

"From what I understand, the threats began arriving before all the media attention started when your book came out. So that seems to indicate this is a personal matter. Do you have any comment about that?"

Again Christian shook his head, this time even more vigorously. He was clenching his jaw so tight that his face felt like a frozen mask. He wanted to run away from all these questions, stop thinking about her and the fact that, after so many years, she had finally caught up with him. He refused to let her in again. At the same time, he knew it was too late. She was already here; he couldn't escape. Maybe he had never actually been able to flee.

"So you have no idea who might be behind the threatening letters? Or whether there's any connection to the murder of Magnus Kjellner?"

"I thought you said you had information indicating he was murdered. Not that it was an established fact."

"Right. But that's a reasonable assumption," replied the reporter. "And you have to agree that in a small town like Fjällbacka, it's a strange coincidence that a man would receive threats and then one of his friends is found murdered. That stirs up a whole lot of questions."

Christian felt his anger growing. What right did they have to come barging into his life, demanding answers and asking him to produce something that he didn't have?

"I have nothing more to say about any of this."

"You do realize that we're going to write about it whether you cooperate or not? It would be in your own best interest to give us your view of the matter."

"I've said everything that I'm going to say," Christian replied, but the journalist didn't look as if he was going to back off.

Then Christian stood up. He walked through the library and went into the toilet, locking the door behind him. He gave a start when he saw his face in the mirror. It looked like a complete stranger staring back at him. He didn't recognize himself at all.

He closed his eyes, leaning with his hands on the sink. His breathing was fast and shallow. By sheer force of will, he tried to slow his pulse and regain control. But his life was about to be taken away from him. He knew that. Once upon a time she had taken everything, and now she was here to do it again.

Images danced on the inside of his eyelids. He heard the voices too. Hers and theirs. Without being able to stop himself, he tilted his head back. And then with great force he threw himself forward. He heard the sound of the mirror shattering, felt the blood on his forehead. But it didn't hurt. Because in the seconds when the glass pierced his skin, the voices fell silent. A blessed silence.

It was just past noon, and Louise was marvelously drunk. To precisely the right extent. Relaxed, numbed, but without losing her grip on reality.

Louise filled her glass again. The house was empty. The girls were in school, and Erik was at the office. Or somewhere else, maybe with his whore.

He'd been acting strangely the past few days. Quieter and more subdued. And her sense of dread was mixed with hope. That was how she always felt when she thought Erik might actually leave her. It was as if she were two people. One of them felt relief at being able to escape the prison that their marriage had become, with nothing but betrayal and lies; the other person was panic-stricken at being abandoned. Of course she would get a large portion of Erik's money, but what would she do with it when she was all on her own?

There wasn't much companionship in her present life, but it was still better than nothing. She had a warm body next to her in bed at night and someone sitting at the kitchen table, reading the newspaper at breakfast. She had somebody. If he left her, she would be utterly forsaken. The girls were growing up; they were like temporary guests in the house, always on their way to see friends or go to school. They had already begun to adopt the taciturn behavior of teenagers, barely answering at all when she spoke to them. When they were home, she mostly saw the closed doors to their rooms, and the only sign of life was the constant thudding of the music they had playing.

One more glass of wine had disappeared, and she poured herself another. Where was Erik right now? Was he at the office, or was he with her? Was he rolling over Cecilia's naked body, entering her, caressing her breasts? Here at home he never did any of those things. He hadn't touched her in two years. At first she had tried slipping her hand under the covers to touch him. But after being rejected a few times, when he demonstratively rolled over on his side so his back was turned, or simply pushed away her hand, she had given up.

She could see her own reflection in the shiny stainless steel of the refrigerator. As usual, she studied herself, raising her hand to touch her face. She didn't look that bad, did she? Once, she had been quite attractive. And she'd kept off the pounds, been careful about what she ate, disdaining her contemporaries who allowed buns and sweet rolls to add extra padding to their figures, which they then tried to conceal under a floral tent dress bought at Lindex. She, on the other hand, could still put on a pair of tight jeans and look respectable. She raised her chin. It had actually started to sag a bit. She raised it again. All right, that's how it should look.

She lowered her chin, noticing how the skin relaxed into a small fold. She had to resist an impulse to take one of the knives out of the holder in front of her and cut off the repulsive flap of skin. She was suddenly disgusted by her own reflection. No wonder Erik didn't want to touch her anymore. No wonder he'd rather have firm skin under his fingers, wanting to touch something that was not slowly decaying and rotting from the inside.

She lifted her wine glass and tossed the contents at the fridge, erasing her reflection and replacing it with the gleaming red liquid that ran down the smooth surface. The phone was on the counter in front of her, and she punched in the number to the office. She had to find out where he was.

"Hi, Kenneth. Is Erik there?"

Her heart was pounding hard as she put down the phone, even though by now she should be used to the situation. Poor Kenneth. How many times over the years had he been forced to cover for Erik? To quickly come up with some lie about where Erik was and what sort of task he was taking care of, assuring her that he was bound to be back in the office soon.

She filled her glass without bothering to wipe up what she'd thrown at the fridge and resolutely headed for Erik's workroom. She wasn't really supposed to go in there. He claimed that it disturbed the order of things if anyone else used the room, so she was strictly forbidden from even setting foot inside. And that was exactly why she was going there now.

Fumbling, she set down her wine glass on the desk and began pulling out the drawers. In all the doubt-filled years she'd spent with Erik, she had never gone through his things. She had preferred not to know. Suspicions were better than knowledge, even though in her case there was very little difference. Somehow she had always known who he happened to be seeing at the moment. Two of his secretaries, when they had lived in Göteborg; one of the teachers at the day-care center; the mother of one of the girls' classmates. She could tell because of the evasive and slightly guilty expressions the women wore when they saw her. She had smelled their perfume, noticed a hasty touch that wasn't appropriate.

Now, for the first time, she pulled out Erik's desk drawers and rummaged through his papers, not caring whether he noticed what she'd done. Because she was becoming convinced that the oppressive silence of the past few days could mean only one thing. He was thinking of leaving her. Throwing her away like rubbish, used goods — and yet she had given birth to his children, kept his home clean, cooked all those fucking dinners for his fucking business contacts who were usually so boring that she felt as if her head would explode when she was forced to converse with them. If he thought that she would just step aside like some wounded animal and not put up a fight, he was sorely mistaken. And besides, she knew about business agreements that he'd made over the years that wouldn't stand closer examination. It would cost him dearly if he made the mistake of underestimating her.

The last drawer was locked. She tugged on it, harder and harder, but it refused to yield. She knew that she had to get it open. There was some reason why Erik had locked it, there was something that he didn't want her to see. She looked at the surface of the desk, which was a modern piece of furniture — in other words, not such a challenge to break into as an older, more solid desk would have been. Her eyes were drawn to a letter opener. That would do. She pulled at the drawer until the lock stopped it from moving. Then she inserted the letter opener into the crack and began prising at the lock. At first it looked like the drawer would refuse to give, but then she tried a little harder, and her hopes rose when the wood began to crack. When the lock finally let go, it happened so suddenly that she almost fell over backwards. At the last instant she grabbed the edge of the desk and managed to stay upright.

Curiosity mounting, she peered inside the drawer. Something white was lying on the bottom. She stretched out her hand, trying to focus because her vision had gone a bit hazy. White envelopes. The drawer contained nothing but letters in white envelopes. She actually recalled seeing them arrive in the mail, but she had paid little attention at the time. They were all addressed to Erik, so she had simply added them to his stack of mail, which he always opened when he came home from work. Why had he put them inside a locked drawer?

Louise took out the letters and sat down

on the floor, spreading them out in front of her. Five of them, all with Erik's name and address on the envelope, written with black ink in an elegant script.

For a moment she considered stuffing them back in the drawer and continuing on, ignoring everything. But she had broken the desk lock, and as soon as Erik came home, he would know that she had been in here. So she might as well have a look.

She reached for her wine glass, needing to feel the alcohol running down her throat and into her stomach, soothing the place where it hurt. Three sips. Then she set the glass on the floor beside her and opened the first letter.

After she had read them all, she stacked them on top of each other. She didn't understand a thing. Except it was clear that somebody wanted to harm Erik. Something evil was threatening their life, their family, and he had said nothing about it. That filled her with a rage greater than any anger she might have felt. He hadn't considered her an equal, not enough to tell her about something important like this. But now he was going to have to answer to her. He could no longer treat her with such meager respect.

She decided to drive into town, to Erik's

office. She placed the letters next to her on the passenger seat in the car. It took a moment for her to insert the key in the ignition, but after taking a couple of deep breaths, she managed it. She knew that she shouldn't be driving right now, but, like so many times before, she pushed aside any scruples and pulled out into the street.

He thought she looked rather sweet as she lay there so still, no longer crying or demanding or taking. He reached out his hand to touch her forehead. His movement stirred up the water again, and her features were blurred by the ripples on the surface.

It sounded like Father was saying good-bye to whoever it was at the front door. He could hear footsteps approaching. Father would understand. He too had been shut out. She had taken from him too.

He drew his fingers through the water, making patterns and waves. Her hands and feet were resting on the bottom. Only her knees and a small part of her forehead stuck out of the water.

Now he heard Father just outside the bathroom door. He didn't look up. Suddenly it felt like he couldn't take his eyes off her. He liked her this way. For the first time, he liked her. He pressed his cheek even harder against the edge of the tub. Listening and waiting for Father to realize that they were free of her now. They had Mother back, both he and Father. Father would be happy; he was sure of that.

Then he felt someone yanking him away from the bathtub. Surprised, he looked up. Father's face was contorted with so many feelings that he didn't know how to interpret them. But he didn't look happy.

"What have you done?" Father's voice roared and he grabbed Alice out of the tub. Helplessly he held her slack body in his arms, and then he gently set her down on the rug. "What have you done?" Father said again, without looking at him.

"She took Mother away." He felt the words stick in his throat, unable to come out. He didn't understand a thing. He had thought Father would be pleased.

Father didn't say a word. Just gave him a quick glance, a look of disbelief on his face. Then he leaned down and pressed his fingers lightly on the baby's chest. He held her nose, blew gently into her mouth, and then pressed on her chest again.

"Why are you doing that, Father?" He could hear how whiny his voice sounded. Mother didn't like it when he whined. He pulled his knees to his chest, wrapping his arms around them as he leaned his back against the tub. This wasn't how it was supposed to go. Why was Father giving him such strange looks? He wasn't just angry at him; Father also looked scared of him.

Father kept on blowing into Alice's mouth. Her hands and feet lay motionless on the rug, just as still as when they were resting on the bottom of the tub. Every once in a while they jerked a bit when Father pressed his fingers on her chest, but that was Father moving them. She wasn't moving them on her own.

But the fourth time that Father stopped blowing, one of her hands quivered. Then came the coughing, and after that the scream. That oh-so-familiar, shrill, demanding scream. He didn't like her anymore.

Mother's footsteps could be heard coming down the stairs. Father picked up Alice, holding her so close that the front of his shirt was soaked. She was shrieking so loudly that the bathroom seemed to vibrate, and he wished she would stop, that she would be as quiet and sweet as she had been before Father did what he had done to her.

As Mother approached, Father squatted down in front of him. His eyes were big and frightened as he leaned forward and whispered: "We will never talk about what happened here. And if you ever do it again, I'm going to send you away so fast that you won't even hear the door close after you. Do you understand? You are never to touch her again!"

"What's going on here?" Mother's voice in the doorway. "The minute I go upstairs to take a nap for a moment's respite, pure hysteria breaks out down here. What's wrong with her? Did he do something?" She turned to look at him sitting on the floor.

For several seconds the only answer was Alice screaming. Then Father stood up, still holding her in his arms, and said, "No, I just didn't get the towel wrapped around her fast enough when I took her out of the bath. She's just angry."

"Are you sure he didn't do anything?" She stared at him, but he just bowed his head and pretended to be busy tugging at the fringe of the rug.

"No, he was just helping me out. He's been very nice with her." Out of the corner of his eye, Father gave him a warning look.

Mother seemed satisfied with that response. Impatiently she reached out for Alice, and after a moment's hesitation Father handed the baby to her. When she had left the room to calm the child, they looked at each other. Neither of them said a word. But he saw in Father's eyes that he meant what he had said.

They would never speak of what had just happened.

13

"Kenneth?" Her voice broke as she tried to call her husband's name.

No answer. Was she imagining things? No, she was sure that she'd heard the door open and then close again.

"Hello?"

Still no answer. Lisbet attempted to sit up, but her strength had been seeping away so fast over the past few days that she couldn't manage it. What energy she had left, she saved for the hours when Kenneth was at home. All for the purpose of convincing him that she was doing better than she actually was, so that he'd let her stay home a little while longer. So she could escape the smell of the hospital and the feel of the starched sheets against her skin. She knew Kenneth so well. He would drive her to the hospital in an instant if he knew how bad she was really feeling. He would do it because he was still clinging desperately to hope.

But Lisbet's body told her that her time was near. She'd used up all her reserves, and the disease had taken over. Victorious. All she wanted was to die at home, with her own blanket over her body and her own pillow under her head. And with Kenneth sleeping next to her in the night. She often lay awake, listening, trying to memorize the sound of each breath he took. She knew how uncomfortable it was for him to sleep on that rickety cot. But she couldn't get herself to tell him to go upstairs to sleep. Maybe she was being selfish, but she loved him too much to be away from him in these last hours that she had left.

"Kenneth?" she called out again. She had just persuaded herself that it was all in her imagination when she heard the familiar creak of the loose floorboard out in the hall. It always protested whenever anyone stepped on it.

"Hello?" Now she was starting to get scared. She looked around for the telephone, which Kenneth usually remembered to leave within reach. But lately he'd been so tired in the morning that he sometimes forgot. Like today.

"Is someone there?" She gripped the edge

of the bed and again tried to sit up. She felt like the main character in one of her favorite stories, *The Metamorphosis* by Franz Kafka, in which Gregor Samsa is changed into a beetle and can't turn over if he lands on his back. He just lies there, helpless.

Now she heard footsteps in the hall. Whoever it was moved cautiously, but was still getting closer and closer. Lisbet felt panic taking over. Who would refuse to answer her cries? Surely Kenneth wouldn't try to tease her in that way. He had never subjected her to any sort of practical jokes or surprises, so she didn't think he would start now.

The footsteps were very close. She stared at the old wooden door, which she had personally sanded and painted what now seemed like an entire lifetime ago. When the door didn't move, she again thought that her brain must be playing tricks on her, that the cancer had spread there too, so that she could no longer think clearly or tell what was real and what wasn't.

But then, very slowly, the door began to open. Someone was standing on the other side, pushing it open. She screamed for help, screamed as loud as she could, trying to drown out the terrifying silence. When the door swung all the way open, she stopped. And the person began to speak. The voice was familiar and yet not, and she squinted to see better. The long dark hair she saw made Lisbet instinctively touch her own head to make sure the yellow scarf was in place.

"Who are you?" she asked, but the person held up a finger. And Lisbet fell silent.

The voice spoke again. Now it was coming from the edge of the bed, speaking close to her face, saying things that made her want to cover her ears with her hands. Lisbet shook her head, didn't want to listen, but the voice continued. It was spellbinding and relentless. It told a story, and something about its tone and the narrative's movement, both backward and forward, made her understand that the story was true. And the truth was more than she could bear.

Paralyzed, she listened to the inexorable outpouring of words. The more she heard, the weaker was her hold on the fragile lifeline that had been keeping her going. She'd been living on borrowed time and sheer force of will, relying on love and her faith in it. Now that it had been taken from her, she let go of her grip. The last thing Lisbet heard was the voice. And then her heart burst.

14

"When do you think we can talk to Cia again?" Patrik looked at his colleague.

"I'm afraid we can't wait," said Paula. "I'm sure she understands that we need to keep working on the investigation."

"You're probably right," said Patrik, but he didn't sound convinced. It was always a difficult balance. Doing his job, which might involve intruding on someone's grief, or showing compassion and thereby putting his work in second place. At the same time, Cia's steadfast Wednesday visits to the police station had shown him what she considered the top priority.

"What should we do?" Paula asked. "What haven't we done yet? Or is there anything we need to do over? Have we missed something?"

"Well, to begin with, Magnus spent his whole life here in Fjällbacka, so if he had any secrets, either now or in the past, we should be able to find them here. And that makes things easier. The local gossip mill is usually highly efficient, and yet we haven't found out a single thing about him. Nothing that might give us a motive for why someone would want to harm him, much less take the drastic step of killing him."

"He seems to have been a real family man. A stable marriage, well-behaved children, a normal social circle. But in spite of all that, somebody went at him with a knife. Could it have been an act of insanity? Some mentally deranged person who snapped and then chose a victim at random?" Paula presented this theory without a great deal of confidence.

"We can't rule that out, but I don't think so," Patrik said. "The most significant thing contradicting that premise is the fact that Magnus phoned Rosander to say that he'd be late. And besides, Rosander said that Kjellner didn't sound like himself. No, something happened that morning."

"In other words, we need to focus on the people he knew."

"Easier said than done," replied Patrik. "Fjällbacka has approximately a thousand inhabitants. And everybody knows everybody else, more or less."

"Oh, great. I'm beginning to see the

problem," laughed Paula. She was a relative newcomer in Tanumshede, which itself had fewer than two thousand, and she was still trying to get used to the shock of losing the anonymity of a big city.

"But in principle, you're right. So I suggest that we start at the center and then make our way outwards. We'll talk to Cia as soon as we can. And to the children, if Cia will allow it. Then we'll move on to Magnus's closest friends: Erik Lind, Kenneth Bengtsson, and especially Christian Thydell. There's something about those threatening letters. . . ."

Patrik opened his top desk drawer and took out the plastic bag containing the letter and the card. He told his colleague the whole story about how Erica had acquired them. Paula listened in disbelief. In silence she read the hostile words.

"This is serious," she said then. "We should send these to the lab for analysis."

"I know," said Patrik. "But let's not jump to any hasty conclusions. I just have a feeling that everything might be connected somehow."

"I agree," said Paula, getting up. "I don't think it's a coincidence either." She paused before leaving Patrik's office. "Should we talk to Christian today?"

"No, I'd like us to spend the rest of the day gathering all the information we can find about all three of them: Christian, Erik, and Kenneth. Then we'll go through all the material together tomorrow morning, to see whether there's anything we can use. I also think both of us should read through all the notes from the interviews that were conducted right after Magnus disappeared. Then we'll be able to catch anything that doesn't jibe with what people said the first time around."

"I'll talk to Annika. I'm sure she can help with the background material."

"Good. I'll phone Cia and find out if she can bear to meet with us."

With a meditative expression on his face, Patrik sat and stared at the phone for a long time after Paula had left.

"Stop calling here!" Sanna slammed down the phone. It had been ringing nonstop all day. Journalists wanting to talk to Christian. They never said exactly what they wanted, but it wasn't hard to guess. The fact that Magnus had been found dead so soon after the existence of the threatening letters was revealed had prompted the reporters to link the two events. But that was absurd. They had nothing to do with each other. It was also rumored that Magnus had been murdered; but until she heard it from more reliable sources than the gossipmongers in town, Sanna refused to believe it. Even if such an unthinkable thing was actually true, why should there be a link to the letters that Christian had received? In an attempt to reassure her, Christian had said that the letters were probably sent by a mentally disturbed person who had decided to target him for some reason. A person who was most likely quite harmless.

She had wanted to ask him why, if that was the case, he had reacted so strongly at the book launch. Didn't he believe his own theory? But all her questions had vanished as soon as he told her where the blue dress had come from. In light of that revelation, all else had paled. It was horrifying, and her heart had ached when she heard his explanation. At the same time, it was comforting to know the real story, because it clarified so much. And excused a good deal.

Her worries also seemed insignificant when she thought about Cia and what she'd been going through. Christian was going to miss Magnus. She would too, even though their relationship had at times been a little strained, but that was only natural. Erik, Kenneth, and Magnus had grown up together and shared a past. Sanna had been aware of them; but because she was so much younger, she had never spent time with them until Christian came into the picture and got to know the other men. Of course she knew that their wives thought she was young and perhaps a bit naïve. But they had always welcomed her with open arms, and over the years that particular group of friends had become a regular part of their lives. They celebrated holidays together, and occasionally they ate dinner together on the weekends.

Of the other wives, Sanna liked Lisbet best. She was a quiet person with a droll sense of humor, and she always treated Sanna as an equal. Besides, Nils and Melker worshipped her. It seemed so unfair that she and Kenneth had no children of their own. But Sanna had a guilty conscience because she couldn't bear to visit Lisbet. She had tried at Christmastime, going over there with a poinsettia and a box of chocolates. But as soon as she saw Lisbet lying in bed, looking more dead than alive, she wanted to back out and run as far away as possible. Lisbet noticed her reaction. Sanna could tell by her expression, which was a combination of understanding and disappointment. She couldn't stand to see that disappointed look again, couldn't stand to meet death disguised as a person and then pretend that it was still her friend lying in that bed.

"Hey, how come you're home already?" Sanna looked up in surprise as Christian came in the front door and mutely hung up his coat. "Are you sick? Aren't you supposed to work until five today?"

"I'm just not feeling well," he muttered.

"You don't look so good, either," she said worriedly as she studied his face. "What did you do to your forehead?"

He dismissed her question with a wave of his hand. "It's nothing."

"Did you scratch yourself?"

"Let's just drop it, okay? I'm not in the mood for an interrogation." He took a deep breath and then said, in a calmer tone of voice, "A reporter came to the library today, asking about Magnus and the letters. I'm sick and tired of the whole thing."

"They've been phoning here too, like crazy. What did you say to him?"

"As little as possible." Then he cringed. "There's probably going to be something in tomorrow's paper anyway. They just write whatever they want."

"At least Gaby will be happy," said Sanna acidly. "How did your meeting go with her, by the way?"

"Fine," said Christian curtly. But something about his tone told her that he wasn't being completely truthful.

"Really? I can understand if you were mad because of the way she threw you to the wolves like that. . . ."

"I said it went fine!" snapped Christian. "Do you always have to dissect everything I say?"

Anger surged up inside him again, and Sanna could only stand there and stare. His expression was thunderous as he came closer and kept on shouting.

"For God's sake, can't you just leave me alone? Don't you understand? Stop poking your nose into something that's none of your bloody business!"

She looked into the eyes of her husband, whom she ought to know so well after all the years they'd spent together. But the person staring back at her was now a stranger. And for the first time, Sanna was afraid of him.

Anna squinted her eyes as she rounded the curve just past the Sailing Club and headed toward Sälvik. The person she saw in the distance bore a striking likeness to her sister, judging by the hair color and clothing. And the body was rather reminiscent of Barbamama on TV. Anna slowed to a stop as she rolled down the car window.

"Hi! I was just on my way over to your house. Looks like you could use a lift the rest of the way."

"That would be great," said Erica, opening the door on the passenger side and sinking onto the seat. "I severely overestimated my ability to walk. I'm completely done in and soaked with sweat."

"So where have you been?" Anna shifted into first and drove toward the house that had once been her childhood home but now belonged to Erica and Patrik. The house had almost been sold out from under them, but Anna quickly pushed aside all thoughts of her former husband Lucas and the past. Those days were over. Forever.

"I went over to have a little chat with Kenneth. At Ocean View Development, you know."

"Why? You're not going to sell the house, are you?"

"No, no," Erica hastened to reassure her. "I just wanted to talk to him about Christian. And Magnus."

Anna parked the car in front of the beautiful old house. "But why?" she asked, almost instantly regretting that she'd asked. Her big sister's inquisitive nature had occasionally landed her in situations that Anna preferred not to know about.

"I realized that I know nothing about Christian's background. He has never said a single thing about his past," replied Erica, climbing out of the car with a groan. "And besides, I think the whole thing is a bit odd. Magnus has presumably been murdered, and Christian has been threatened. Considering that the two of them were close friends, I don't really buy the idea that it's just a coincidence."

"Yes, but did Magnus get any threatening letters?" Anna followed Erica into the front hall and hung up her coat.

"Not that I've heard. I'm sure Patrik would know about it if he had."

"And do you think Patrik would have told you if something like that came to light during the investigation?"

Erica smiled. "You mean because my dear husband is so good at keeping things to himself?"

"You have a point there," laughed Anna, sitting down at the kitchen table. Patrik never held out for long, especially once Erica had decided to finagle some piece of information out of him.

"Besides, I could tell that Christian's letters came as a surprise when I showed them to Patrik. If he'd found out that Magnus had received something similar, he would have reacted differently."

"Hmm, you're probably right. So did you find out anything from Kenneth?"

"No, not much. But I got the feeling that he found all my questions very uncomfortable. There seems to be some sort of sensitive issue here, but I can't put my finger on what it could be."

"How well do they know each other?"

"I'm not really sure. I can't see what Christian would have in common with either Kenneth or Erik. Magnus seems a more likely friend for him."

"I've always thought that Christian and Sanna are an odd couple too."

Erica paused for a moment, searching for the right response. She didn't want to sound as if she were bad-mouthing anyone. "Sanna just seems a bit young," she said at last. "I also think she's terribly jealous. And to a certain extent, I can understand why. Christian is a handsome guy, and their relationship doesn't seem very equal." She'd made a pot of tea and now set it on the table along with some honey and milk.

"What do you mean by equal?" asked Anna.

"I haven't spent a lot of time with them, but I have a feeling that Sanna adores Christian, while he seems to treat her with a certain indifference."

"That doesn't sound pleasant," said Anna, taking a sip of the tea, but it was still too hot. She set down her cup to let it cool off a bit.

"No, it doesn't. And maybe I'm making a hasty judgment, based on the little that I've seen. But there's something about their interaction that makes it seem more like a parent and child than two adults."

"Well, at least his book is selling well."

"Yes, and his success is well deserved," said Erica. "Christian is one of the most talented writers I've ever come across, and I'm so glad that readers like his work."

"All the PR has helped a lot too. You should never underestimate the level of people's curiosity when it comes to a scandal."

"That's true, but as long as they find out about his book, I don't care how it happens," said Erica, helping herself to another spoonful of honey. She had tried to get used to drinking tea without making it so sweet that the honey stuck to her teeth, but she just couldn't do it.

"How's it going with those two?" Anna

pointed at Erica's belly, unable to hide the concern in her voice. She hadn't been around much to help Erica out in the difficult period after Maja was born, since she'd had her own problems to deal with. But this time she was actually rather worried about her sister. She didn't want to see Erica sink into a fog of depression again.

"I'd be lying if I said that I'm not anxious," replied Erica hesitantly. "But I feel more mentally prepared this time around. I know what to expect, and how tough the first few months can be. At the same time, it's really impossible to imagine what it'll be like with two babies at once. It might be ten times worse, no matter how prepared I think I am."

She too remembered how she had felt right after Maja's birth. She had no memory of any details or any specific moments from her daily life during that time. In that sense, all she saw was blackness when she tried to think back. But the feeling was still very strong, and she panicked at the mere thought of falling once again into the bottomless despair and total obliteration of self that she'd experienced before.

Anna sensed what Erica was thinking. She reached out and put her hand on her sister's.

"It won't be the same this time. Of course

it will involve more work than with Maja; I can't imagine otherwise. But I'll be here for you, Patrik will be here for you, and we'll both help you if it looks like you might fall into that deep pit again. I promise. Look at me, Erica." Anna forced her sister to raise her head and meet her eyes. When she had her full attention, Anna calmly reiterated: "We won't let you end up like that again."

Erica blinked away a few tears and squeezed her sister's hand. So much had changed between them over the past few years. She was no longer like a surrogate mother to Anna. She was hardly even a big sister anymore. They were just sisters, plain and simple. And friends.

"I've got a container of Ben & Jerry's Chocolate Fudge Brownie in the freezer. Shall I get it out?"

"And you waited until now to tell me this?" said Anna, pretending to look insulted. "Bring out the ice cream before I disown you!"

Erik sighed when he saw Louise's car skid into the parking area in front of the office. She almost never came here, so the fact that she was here now did not bode well. She'd also tried to reach him by phone a little while ago. Kenneth had mentioned it when

Erik came back after a quick trip to the shops. For once, he'd been able to tell his colleague the truth about where he'd been.

He wondered why Louise was so determined to get ahold of him. Could she have found out about his affair with Cecilia? No, the fact that he was sleeping with some other woman wasn't enough of a motivation to make her get in the car and go driving through the slushy snow. He suddenly froze. Could she have found out that Cecilia was pregnant? Had Cecilia broken their agreement, even though it had been her idea in the first place? Had her desire to hurt him and to seek revenge turned out to be greater than her wish to receive a monthly payment to support herself and the child?

He saw Louise get out of her car. He was paralyzed by the thought that Cecilia might have given him away. He should never underestimate a woman. The more he thought about it, the more likely it seemed that she had sacrificed the money for the satisfaction of destroying his life.

Louise came in the front door. She looked upset. When she got closer, he could smell how the stench of wine enveloped her like a thick miasma.

"Are you out of your mind? Did you drive here drunk?" he snarled. Out of the corner of his eye, he saw that Kenneth was pretending to be very interested in whatever was on his computer screen. But it didn't make any difference, because he couldn't help hearing what was being said.

"To hell with that," replied Louise, slurring her words. "I drive better when I'm drunk than you do sober." She swayed a bit, and Erik glanced at his watch. Three in the afternoon, and she was already sloshed.

"What do you want?" He just wanted to get this over with. If she was going to rip apart his world, she might as well get on with it. He had always been a man of action, never flinching from unpleasantness.

But she didn't heap accusations upon him about Cecilia and say that she knew about the child; she didn't tell him to go to hell and say that she was going to take everything he owned. Instead, she put her hand in her coat pocket and pulled out something white. Five white envelopes. Erik knew at once what they were.

"You were in my workroom? You went through my desk?"

"Isn't it obvious? You never tell me anything. Not even who has been sending you threatening letters. Do you think I'm crazy? Do you think I don't know that these are the same letters they've been writing about in all the newspapers? Just like the ones that Christian got. And now Magnus is dead." Her anger boiled over. "Why didn't you ever show them to me? Some sick person is sending threats to our house, and you don't think I have the right to know about it? When I'm home alone all day, unprotected?"

Erik cast a glance at Kenneth, annoyed that his colleague could hear Louise yelling at him. But when he saw Kenneth's expression, he froze. He wasn't looking at the computer screen anymore. He was staring at the five white envelopes that Louise had tossed on the desk. His face was pale. For a moment he looked at Erik, then he turned away. But it was too late. Erik understood.

"Have you received letters like this too?"

Louise was startled by Erik's question. She turned to look at Kenneth. At first he didn't seem to have heard, because he continued to study a complicated Excel chart showing a breakdown of income and expenses. But Erik wasn't about to let him off the hook.

"Kenneth, I asked you a question!" It was Erik's voice of command. The same as it had always been for all the years they'd known each other. And Kenneth reacted in the same way as he had when they were

317

boys. Still the compliant one who always followed, submitting to Erik's authority and need to control. Slowly he spun his chair around until he was facing Erik and Louise. He clasped his hands in his lap and said in a low voice:

"I've received four. Three in the mail and one that was left on my kitchen table."

Louise turned pale. Her anger toward Erik had just been given more fuel, and she turned to face him. "What is this all about? First Christian, then you and Kenneth? What have the three of you done? And what about Magnus? Did he get letters like this too?" She glared at her husband, then at Kenneth, and then back at Erik.

None of them spoke for a moment. Then Kenneth looked at his colleague and shrugged.

Erik shook his head. "Not that I know of. Magnus never mentioned it, but that doesn't really mean anything. Do you know?" He directed his question at Kenneth, who also shook his head.

"No. If Magnus ever told anyone about something like this, it would have been Christian."

"When did you get the first one?" Erik's mind had started working through the new information. Twisting and turning it, trying to come up with a solution and then take control.

"I don't really recall. But before Christmas, at any rate. Sometime in December."

Erik reached for the letters lying on his desk. Louise had retreated into herself, all her anger sapped. She was still standing in front of her husband, watching him sort through the letters according to the date they were sent. He put the earliest one on the bottom and then picked it up to peer at the postmark again.

"December fifteenth."

"So that's about the same time as the one I got," said Kenneth, his eyes on the floor.

"Do you still have the letters? Can you check the dates on the ones that were delivered in the mail?" asked Erik, speaking in his most efficient and businesslike voice.

Kenneth nodded and took a deep breath. "When the fourth letter was delivered, it was lying next to one of our kitchen knives."

"Are you sure you didn't put the knife there yourself?" Louise was no longer slurring her words. Fear had sobered her up, lifting the fog from her brain.

"No, I'm positive that I cleared everything away, and there was nothing on the table when I went to bed."

"Was the front door locked?" Erik still

sounded cold and matter-of-fact.

"No, it wasn't. I don't always remember to lock up at night."

"Well, all of the letters I got came in the mail," said Erik, riffling through the envelopes. Then he happened to recall something he'd read in the articles about Christian.

"Christian was the first one to get threatening letters. They started arriving a year and a half ago. You and I didn't get any until three months ago. So what if this whole thing has to do with him? What if he's the real target of whoever is sending these letters, and we're just mixed up in this mess because we know him?" Erik's voice took on an indignant tone. "Damn him if he knows something about this and isn't talking. Subjecting me and my family to some lunatic without warning us."

"But he doesn't know that we've received letters too," Kenneth objected, and Erik had to admit that he was right.

"No, but he's going to find out now, in any case." Erik gathered up the envelopes in a neat stack and slapped them against the desktop.

"So you're thinking of going to talk to him?" Kenneth sounded anxious, and Erik sighed. Sometimes he really couldn't stand his colleague's fear of any sort of conflict.

He'd always been that way. Kenneth always went with the flow, never said no, always said yes. Which had actually worked to Erik's advantage, since there could only be one person in charge. So far he had been that person, and that's the way it was going to stay.

"Of course I'm going to talk to him. And to the police too. I should have done that long ago, but it wasn't until I read about Christian's letters that I started taking the whole thing seriously."

"And it's about time," muttered Louise. Erik glared at her.

"I don't want to upset Lisbet." Kenneth raised his chin, and there was a defiant glint in his eye.

"Someone went into your house, put a letter on the kitchen table, and set a knife next to it. If I were you, I'd be more worried about that than about whether Lisbet might get upset. She's home alone for a large part of the day. What if someone gets in while you're not there?"

Erik saw that Kenneth had already had the same thought. At the same time that he was annoyed by his colleague's lack of enterprise, he was trying to ignore the fact that he too had failed to report the letters. On the other hand, none of them had been placed directly inside his house.

"All right, let's do this. You go home and pick up the letters that you've received, and we can take all of them over to the police station together. Then they can get started on this whole matter at once."

Kenneth stood up. "I'll leave now and be right back."

"Good. You do that," said Erik.

After Kenneth left and the door closed behind him, Erik turned to Louise and studied her for several seconds.

"There's a lot we need to talk about."

Louise looked at him for a moment. Then she raised her hand and slapped his face.

"I said there's nothing wrong with her!" Mother's voice was angry and she was on the verge of tears. He slipped away and sat down behind the sofa some distance away. But not so far that he couldn't hear what they said. Everything having to do with Alice was important.

He liked her better now. She never gave him that look anymore that meant she wanted to take something from him. Mostly she lay still and made very little noise, and he thought that was wonderful.

"She's eight months old, and she hasn't made a single attempt to crawl or move about. We need to have a doctor take a look at her." Father was speaking in a low voice. The voice he used when he wanted to persuade Mother to do something that she didn't want to do. He placed his hands on her shoulders so she would be forced to listen to what he was saying.

"Something isn't quite right with Alice. The sooner we get help, the better. You're not doing her any good by closing your eyes to what's wrong."

His mother shook her head. Her shiny dark hair hung down her back, and he wished that he could reach out and touch it. But he knew that she wouldn't like it; she would pull away from his touch.

Mother kept on shaking her head. The tears rolled down her cheeks, and he knew that in spite of everything, she had begun to relent. Father turned to look over his shoulder, casting a swift glance at him as he sat behind the sofa. He smiled at Father, not knowing what he meant. But apparently it was wrong to smile, because Father frowned and looked angry, as if wishing his expression were different.

Nor did he understand why Mother and Father were so worried and sad. Alice was so calm and nice now. Mother didn't have to carry her around all the time, and she lay peacefully wherever they put her. But Mother and Father weren't happy. And even though there was now space for him too, they treated him like he was air. He didn't really care so much that Father did that; Father wasn't the one who mattered. But Mother didn't see him either, and if she did, it was only with a look of disgust and loathing on her face.

Because he couldn't seem to stop himself. He couldn't resist lifting his fork again and again, stuffing the food in his mouth, chewing, swallowing, taking more, feeling his body filling out. The fear was too great, the fear that she would never see him. He was no longer Mother's handsome little boy. But he was here, and he took up space.

15

It was quiet when he came home. Lisbet was probably sleeping. He considered going in to see her right away, but he didn't want to wake her if she'd just fallen asleep. It would be better to do it just before he left. She needed all the rest she could get.

Kenneth paused in the front hall for a moment. This was the silence that he would soon have to live with. Of course he'd been home alone in the past. Lisbet had been very involved with her job as a teacher, and she'd often worked overtime in the evenings. But it was a different sort of silence when he'd arrived home before she did. It was a silence full of promise, full of anticipation, waiting for that moment when the front door opened and she would come in, saying "Hi, sweetheart, I'm home."

He would never again hear those words. Lisbet would leave this house, but she would never come home again.

Suddenly he was overcome with grief. He had put so much energy into keeping his sorrow at bay, not wanting to let it in ahead of time. But now he couldn't stop it. He leaned his forehead against the wall and felt the tears rising. And he let them come, weeping silently, the tears falling to his feet. For the first time, he allowed himself to feel what it would be like when she was gone. In many ways, she was already gone. Their love was as great as ever, but it was different. Because the Lisbet who lay in the guest-room bed was only a shadow of the woman he had loved. She no longer existed, and he missed her terribly.

He stood there for a long time with his forehead pressed against the wall. After a while his sobs subsided, the tears fell more slowly. When they stopped altogether, he took a deep breath, raised his head, and wiped his wet cheeks with his hand. That was enough. That was all he could allow himself right now.

He went into the workroom. The letters were in the top desk drawer. His first instinct had been to throw them out, to ignore them. But something had stopped him. And when the fourth one arrived the other night, delivered inside his home, he was glad that he'd kept the others. Because now he realized that he needed to take them seriously. Someone wanted to harm him.

He knew that he should have turned over the letters to the police right away, and not worried so much about upsetting Lisbet as she waited to die. He should have protected her by taking the matter seriously. It was lucky that he'd realized this in time, that Erik had made him realize it in time. If anything had happened to her because, as usual, he had failed to act, he would never have forgiven himself.

With trembling fingers he picked up the letters, walked quietly down the hall to the kitchen, and placed all of them inside an ordinary one-gallon plastic bag. He considered leaving immediately so as not to wake Lisbet. But he couldn't go without looking in on her. He needed to make sure that everything was all right, to see her face, he hoped peacefully asleep.

Cautiously he opened the door to the guest room. It opened without a sound, and gradually more and more of his wife came into view. She was sleeping. Her eyes were closed, and he took in every feature, every detail of her face. She was gaunt and her skin was parched, but she was still beautiful.

He quietly took a few steps inside the

room, unable to resist the urge to touch her. But suddenly he sensed that something was wrong. Lisbet looked the way she always did when she slept, but now he realized what was different. It was so silent. He didn't hear a sound. Not even a breath.

Kenneth rushed forward. He placed two fingers on her throat, moved his fingers to the wrist of her left hand, fumbling, moved his hand back to her throat, wishing with all his heart that he would find the life-giving pulse. But in vain. There was nothing. It was silent in the room and silent in her body. She had left him.

He heard a sobbing sound, as if from an animal. Guttural and filled with despair. And he realized that the sound was coming from himself. He sat down on the edge of the bed and lifted her up, cautiously, as if she could still feel pain.

Her head rested heavily on his lap. He stroked her cheek and felt his tears return. Grief overcame him with a force that erased everything he had ever felt before; he was consumed by sorrow. It was a physical sorrow that spread through his whole body, wringing every nerve. The pain made him scream out loud. The sound of his cries echoed through the small room, bouncing off the floral coverlet and the pale wallpaper to be thrown back at him.

Her hands were clasped over her breast, and gently he pulled them apart. He wanted to hold her hand one last time. He felt her rough skin against his own. Her skin had lost its softness after the treatments, but it still felt so familiar.

He lifted her hand to his lips, kissing the back of it, as his tears fell on both of their hands, joining them together. He closed his eyes and tasted the salt of his tears mixing with her scent. He would have liked to sit there forever, never letting go. But he knew that was impossible. Lisbet was no longer his, she was no longer here, and he had to let her go. At least she was no longer in pain; that was over now. The cancer had won, but it had also lost because it was forced to die with her.

He put her hand down, placing it gently at her side. Her right hand still lay on her breast, and he picked it up to move it to her other side.

But he gave a start when he noticed something in her hand, something white. His heart began pounding wildly. He wanted to clasp her hands again and hide what he saw, but he couldn't. With trembling fingers he opened her right hand. The white object tumbled out and fell onto the coverlet. A small piece of paper, folded in half so the message was hidden. But he knew what it was. He could feel the presence of evil in the room.

Kenneth reached for the slip of paper. He hesitated for a moment, and then he read what it said.

Anna had just left when the doorbell rang. At first Erica thought that her sister must have forgotten something, but Anna never bothered about such trivial matters as waiting for permission to enter the house; she usually just opened the door and walked in.

Erica put down the cups she had started to clear away and went to open the door.

"Gaby? What are you doing here?" She stepped aside to allow the publishing director to enter. Today she lit up the drab of winter with a bright turquoise coat and enormous glittery gold earrings.

"I was in Göteborg for a meeting, so I thought I'd just drop by and have a little chat."

Drop by? It was an hour-and-a-half drive from Göteborg, and she hadn't even phoned ahead to make sure that Erica would be home. What could possibly be so urgent?

"I wanted to talk to you about Christian," Gaby said, answering Erica's unspoken question as she came inside. "Do you have any coffee?"

"Oh, of course."

As usual, dealing with Gaby felt like being hit by a train. She didn't bother to take off her boots, just gave them a superficial wipe on the rug before stepping on to the hardwood floor with her clacking heels. Erica cast a nervous glance at the polished planks of her floor, hoping her publisher wasn't going to leave any ugly marks behind. But it would be fruitless to say anything to Gaby. Erica couldn't recall ever seeing her in her stocking feet, and she wondered if Gaby even took off her boots when she went to bed.

"How . . . cosy you've made things here," said Gaby, smiling broadly. But Erica could tell that she was actually horrified by the sight of all the toys, Maja's clothes, Patrik's papers, and everything else scattered all over. Gaby had visited them before, but on those occasions Erica had expected her arrival and had cleaned up ahead of time.

The publishing director brushed a few crumbs from a chair before sitting down at the kitchen table. Erica quickly grabbed a dishcloth and ran it over the tabletop, which she hadn't had time to do since breakfast and then Anna's visit.

"My sister was just here," she explained, removing the empty ice-cream container.

"I hope you know it's a myth that you can eat for two when you're pregnant," said Gaby, staring at Erica's enormous belly.

"Hmm," said Erica, restraining herself from giving a caustic reply. Gaby wasn't known for being particularly tactful. Her own slender figure was the result of a disciplined diet and regular workouts with a personal trainer at the downtown Stockholm health club Sturebadet three times a week. Nor did her body show any signs of past pregnancies. Her career had always been her highest priority.

Out of pure spite, Erica set a platter of pastries on the table and pushed it over toward Gaby.

"Wouldn't you like a pastry?" She watched as Gaby was torn between her desire to be polite and a desperate urge to say "No, thanks." Finally she reached a compromise.

"I'll take half of one, if you don't mind." Gaby carefully broke off a piece, with a look on her face as if she were about to stuff a cockroach in her mouth.

"So you said you wanted to talk to me about Christian, right?" said Erica. She couldn't restrain her curiosity.

"Yes. I can't understand what's going on

with him." Gaby seemed relieved that the pastry dilemma was over, and she took a big gulp of coffee to wash down the piece she had eaten. "He says he refuses to do any more promotion for his book, but that's just not right. It's unprofessional!"

"He does seem to be taking all the media attention rather hard," Erica ventured, again feeling guilty about her own part in the whole affair.

Gaby gestured with her well-manicured fingers. "I know. And I do understand that. But it'll soon blow over, and all the fuss has given book sales a real boost. People are curious about him and about his novel. I mean, in the end, Christian is going to reap the benefits. And he must realize that we've put a tremendous amount of time and money into launching him and his work. So we expect some cooperation from him in return."

"Sure, of course," murmured Erica, although she was unsure of her own stand on this issue. On the one hand, she understood Christian's attitude. It must be awful to have his personal life exposed in the media like that. He was just starting his writing career, and the attention he received at this point was supposed to serve him well for many years to come.

"Why don't you talk to him about this yourself?" she asked cautiously. "Shouldn't you be having this discussion with Christian?"

"We had a meeting yesterday," replied Gaby curtly. "And you might say that it didn't go very well." She pressed her lips together as if to underscore what she'd just said. Erica realized that it must have been a real disaster.

"Oh, that's unfortunate. But I think Christian is under a lot of stress right now, and maybe we should overlook —"

"I understand; but at the same time, I'm running a business and we have a contract with Christian. Even though it doesn't spell out in detail what his obligations are regarding dealing with the press, helping with marketing efforts, and so on, it's understood that we expect certain things from him. Some authors may get away with acting like hermits and not participating in events that they consider beneath them. But those writers are already established and have a big audience for their books. Christian isn't there yet, not by a long shot. He may reach that position some day, but an author's career isn't built overnight, and with the flying start that he's had with *The Mermaid,* he owes it to himself and to his publishing house to make certain sacrifices." Gaby paused, giving Erica a stern look. "I was hoping that you might explain this to him."

"Me?" Erica didn't know what to say. She wasn't at all convinced that she was the right person to persuade Christian to throw himself to the wolves again. Especially since she was the one who had lured them to his door in the first place.

"I don't know if that would be such a good —" She searched for a diplomatic way of declining the task, but Gaby cut her off.

"Excellent. Then that's decided. You'll go see him and explain what we expect from him."

"But what. . . ." Erica looked at Gaby, wondering what on earth she had said that might be interpreted as an affirmative response. But Gaby was already getting to her feet. She smoothed down her skirt, picked up her purse, and slung the strap over her shoulder.

"Thanks for the coffee and the chat. I'm glad we have such a great working relationship, you and I." She leaned down and air-kissed Erica on both cheeks and then clacked across the floor, heading for the front door.

"Don't bother getting up. I can find my

way out," she called over her shoulder. "Bye-bye."

"Bye-bye," replied Erica with a wave. This time it wasn't like being hit by a train — it was like being smashed completely flat.

Patrik and Gösta jumped in the car and headed out within five minutes of receiving the call. At first, Kenneth Bengtsson could hardly manage more than a few words, but after a moment Patrik understood what he was trying to say. His wife had been murdered.

"What the hell is going on here, anyway?" Gösta shook his head, keeping a tight grip on the handle fastened above the window on the passenger side of the car. He always did that when Patrik was driving. "Do you really need to take the curves so fast? I'm practically plastered to the windshield."

"Sorry." Patrik slowed down a bit, but it wasn't long before his foot was again pressing down on the accelerator. "What's going on, you ask? That's what I'd like to know too," he said with a grimace as he cast a glance in the rear-view mirror to make sure that Paula and Martin were close behind.

"What did he say? Did she have stab wounds too?" asked Gösta.

"I couldn't get much out of him. He

sounded like he was in shock. He just said that he came home to find his wife murdered."

"From what I've heard, she didn't have long to live," said Gösta. He loathed anything having to do with illness and death. For most of his life he'd been waiting to come down with some sort of incurable disease. All he wanted was to get in as many games of golf as possible before that happened. But right now Patrik looked more like a victim of ill health than he did.

"You don't look so good, by the way."

"You don't know what the hell you're talking about," said Patrik, annoyed. "You have no idea what it's like to have both a full-time job and a toddler at home. Impossible to keep up, impossible to get enough sleep." Patrik regretted his words as soon as they left his lips. He knew that the greatest sorrow in Gösta's life was that his son had died shortly after birth.

"Forgive me. That was stupid," he said.

Gösta nodded. "That's okay."

Neither of them spoke for a while. They listened to the sound of the tires on the road as they drove along the highway, heading for Fjällbacka.

"It's nice about Annika and the little girl she's going to adopt," said Gösta at last, his

338

expression softening.

"Yes, but it certainly is a long wait," said Patrik, glad to talk about something else.

"I'm surprised it takes so long. I had no idea. I mean, the child is there, so what's the problem?" Gösta was almost as frustrated about it as Annika and her husband Lennart were.

"Bureaucracy," said Patrik. "And I suppose we should be grateful that they check up on everyone properly and don't hand over the children to just anybody."

"You're right about that."

"Okay, we're here." Patrik turned into the drive in front of the Bengtssons' house and parked the car. A second later the other police car pulled up, with Paula at the wheel. When she turned off the engine, the only sound was the soughing of the wind in the nearby woods.

Kenneth Bengtsson opened the front door. His face was pale, and he looked confused.

"Patrik Hedström," said Patrik, shaking hands with Kenneth. "Where is she?" He motioned for his colleagues to wait outside. It would create problems for the crime-scene techs if they all tromped about inside the house. Kenneth opened the door wider and pointed down the hallway.

"In there. I . . . would it be all right if I stay here?" He was looking at Patrik, but his eyes had a blank look.

"Stay here with my colleagues, and I'll go inside," said Patrik, glancing at Gösta to get him to take charge of the victim's spouse. Gösta's skills as a police officer left a lot to be desired, but he had a talent for dealing with people, and Patrik knew that Kenneth would be in good hands. The medics would be arriving any minute. He had phoned them before leaving the station, so the ambulance should be here soon.

Patrik cautiously stepped inside and took off his shoes. He headed in the direction that Kenneth had indicated, assuming he meant the door at the end of the hall. It was closed, and Patrik stopped himself as he was about to touch the door handle. There might be fingerprints. Using his elbow, he pushed down on the handle and opened the door by leaning against it.

She was lying in bed with her eyes closed and her arms at her sides. She looked like she was sleeping. He took a couple of steps closer, looking for any injuries on the body. There was no blood, no wounds. But her body did show clear signs of her illness. Her bones were visible under the taut, dry skin, and her head looked bald under the scarf she was wearing. His heart ached at the thought of what she must have suffered, and what Kenneth must have suffered as he was forced to see his wife in this state. But there was nothing to indicate anything except that she had died in her sleep. Patrik carefully backed out of the room.

When he stepped outside into the cold again, Gösta was speaking in a soothing voice to Kenneth while Paula and Martin were helping the ambulance driver back his vehicle into the drive.

"I went in to see her," Patrik told Kenneth in a low voice, putting his hand on the man's shoulder. "And I don't see any sign that she was murdered, as you said on the phone. From what I understand, your wife was seriously ill. Is that right?"

Kenneth nodded mutely.

"Isn't it more likely that she simply died in her sleep?"

"No, she was murdered," Kenneth replied vehemently.

Patrik exchanged glances with Gösta. It wasn't unusual for someone in shock to react strangely and say strange things.

"Why do you think so? As I said, I just went in to see your wife, and there are no obvious injuries to her body, nothing to indicate anything . . . out of the ordinary."

"She was murdered!" Kenneth insisted, and Patrik began to realize that there was nothing more they could do here. He would ask the medics to tend to the poor man.

"Take a look at this!" Kenneth pulled something out of his pocket and held it out to Patrik, who took it without thinking. It was a small white piece of paper, folded in half. Patrik gave Kenneth an inquisitive look and then opened the paper. In black cursive script it said: *The truth about you killed her.*

Patrik instantly recognized the handwriting.

"Where did you find this?"

"In Lisbet's hand. I took it out of her hand," Kenneth stammered.

"And she didn't write this herself?" Patrik already knew the answer, but he still felt that he had to ask the question to remove any doubt. The handwriting was the same, and the few words conveyed the same sense of evil, as the letter that Erica had taken from Christian.

As expected, Kenneth shook his head. "No," he said, holding up something else that Patrik hadn't noticed he was clutching in his hand. "The same person sent these."

Inside the plastic bag were several white envelopes. The address had been written with black ink in an elegant script. The same as on the piece of paper that Patrik was holding.

"When did you get these?" he asked, feeling his heart pounding hard.

"We were just going to turn them over to the police," said Kenneth quietly, handing the plastic bag to Patrik.

"Who do you mean by 'we'?"

"Erik and I. He received similar letters."

"Erik Lind? He has letters too?" Patrik repeated, wanting to make sure that he'd heard correctly.

Kenneth nodded.

"Why didn't you tell the police about this before?" Patrik tried to keep his frustration out of his voice. The man standing in front of him had just lost his wife, so this was not the proper time for reproaches.

"I . . . we . . . it wasn't until today that Erik and I realized that we'd both received these sorts of letters. And we only heard about Christian getting threats when we read about it in the paper this weekend. I can't speak for Erik, but for my part, I didn't want to upset. . . ." His voice trailed off.

Patrik took another look at the letters inside the plastic bag. "Only three of them have an address and postmark on them. One of them just has your name on the envelope. How did that letter arrive?"

"Someone came into the house last night and left it on the kitchen table." He hesitated, but Patrik didn't speak, sensing that Kenneth had more to say. "And there was a knife lying next to the letter. One of our kitchen knives. I suppose that's a message that could be interpreted several different ways." He began to cry as he went on. "I thought it was me that someone wanted to harm. Why Lisbet? Why kill Lisbet?" He wiped away a tear with the back of his hand, apparently embarrassed to be crying in front of Patrik and the other officers.

"We don't know whether she was actually murdered," said Patrik gently. "But someone has definitely been inside your house. Do you have any idea who that might be? Or who would have sent you these letters?" He kept his eyes fixed on Kenneth, wanting to see if there was any change in his expression. As far as he could tell, Kenneth was speaking the truth when he said:

"I've thought a lot about it ever since the first letter appeared. That was right before Christmas. But I can't think of anyone who would want to harm me. No one at all. I've never made any enemies in that way. I'm too . . . unimportant."

"What about Erik? How long has he been

getting these letters?"

"About the same as me. He has them over at the office. I was just coming home to pick mine up and then we were going to contact the police. . . ." His voice faded again, and Patrik could see his thoughts were back in that room where he'd found his wife dead.

"What do you think the message on this note means?" asked Patrik cautiously. "It refers to a 'truth about yourself' — what do you think that could be?"

"I don't know," said Kenneth quietly. "I really have no idea." Then he took a deep breath. "What will you do with her now?"

"She'll be taken to Göteborg for closer examination."

"Closer examination? Do you mean a postmortem?" Kenneth grimaced.

"Yes. A postmortem. I'm afraid it's necessary so we can work out what actually happened here."

Kenneth nodded, but his eyes were glazed, and his lips were looking slightly blue. Realizing that they'd been standing outdoors in the cold too long, considering the thin clothing that Kenneth was wearing, Patrick added:

"It's cold out here, and you need to go inside." He paused for a moment. "Would you like to drive over to the office with me?

To your office, I mean? Then we can have a talk with Erik. Feel free to say no if you're not up to it, and I'll go over there myself. Is there anyone you'd like to phone, by the way?"

"No. I'd like to go with you," said Kenneth, almost defiantly. "I want to know who did this."

"All right, then." Patrik took him lightly by the arm to steer him toward the car. He opened the door on the passenger side so Kenneth could get in. Then he went over to Martin and Paula to give them some brief instructions. He went inside to get a jacket for Kenneth before he motioned for Gösta to come with him. The tech team was on its way, and Patrik hoped to get back before they were finished. Otherwise he'd have to talk to them later. Right now going to see Erik was so urgent that it couldn't wait.

As they backed out of the driveway, Kenneth cast a long look at the house. His lips moved, as if forming the words of a silent farewell.

Nothing had really changed; it felt just as empty as before. The only difference was that now there was a body to bury and the last glimmer of hope had vanished. Cia's premonitions had turned out to be right, after all. Dear God, how she wished she'd been wrong.

How was she going to live without Magnus? How would her life look without him? It seemed so unreal that her husband, the father of her children, would be lying in a grave in the cemetery. Magnus, who had always been so full of life, who had always wanted to have fun and make sure that everyone else enjoyed themselves too. Of course she had been annoyed with him on occasion, irritated by his carefree attitude and constant teasing. It drove her crazy whenever she wanted to talk about something serious and he just played around and teased her until she couldn't help laughing even though she didn't want to. At the same time, she had never wanted to change anything about him.

What she wouldn't give for just one more hour with him! Half an hour, even one minute! They weren't finished with their life together; in fact, they had just begun. They'd only had the chance to make half the journey they'd envisioned for themselves. The exhilarating first meeting when they were nineteen. The first years when they were so in love. Magnus proposing to her, and then their wedding in Fjällbacka church. The children. The nights filled with crying infants, when they'd taken turns getting some sleep. All the hours of playing and laughing with Elin and Ludvig. The nights when they had made love or just fallen asleep, holding hands. And the last few years when the children were getting older and she and Magnus had been able to get to know each other again.

But there was so much more they had wanted to do; the road ahead had seemed long and filled with anticipated experiences. Magnus was looking forward to teasing his children's first boyfriend and girlfriend, respectively, who would turn up at their house to be introduced, awkward and shy and stammering. They were planning to help Elin and Ludvig when they moved into their first apartments, carrying in furniture, painting the walls, and sewing curtains. As the father, Magnus would give a speech when each of his children married. He would talk too long, get too sentimental, and tell too many details about their childhood. Cia and Magnus had even imagined their first grandchild, even though it would be years until that happened. But it was there in the future, like a promise, sparkling like a jewel. And they would be the world's best grandparents. Always ready to lend a hand and spoil the grandchildren. Give them cake for dinner and buy them far too many toys. Offering their time, all the time that they had.

All of that was now gone. Their dreams for the future would never be realized. Suddenly Cia felt a hand on her shoulder. She heard his voice, but it sounded so unbearably like Magnus that she shut it out, refused to listen. After a while the voice fell silent and the hand was taken away. In front of her she saw that the road had vanished, as if it had never existed.

On the last stretch of the drive to Christian's house, Erica felt as if she were heading toward Golgotha. She had phoned the library to speak to him, but was told that he'd gone home. So she had squeezed herself in behind the wheel to drive over there. She still wasn't sure that it was a good idea to do as Gaby had asked. At the same time, she didn't really see how she could get out of the situation. Gaby never took no for an answer.

"What do you want?" asked Sanna when she opened the door. She looked even sadder than usual.

"I need to talk to Christian," Erica told her, hoping that she wouldn't be asked to explain why.

"He's not home."

"When do you expect him?" asked Erica patiently, feeling almost grateful for the chance to postpone the meeting.

"He's writing. Over in the boathouse. You can go down there if you want to, but you'll be disturbing him at your own risk."

"That's okay. I'll take the risk." Erica hesitated. "It's important," she added.

Sanna shrugged. "Do whatever you like. Do you know where it is?"

Erica nodded. She had visited Christian in his little writer's den a couple of times before.

Five minutes later, she parked the car next to the row of boathouses. The one Christian was working in had been inherited from Sanna's family. Her maternal grandfather had bought it for a song, and now it was one of the few still owned by someone who lived in Fjällbacka year-round.

Christian must have heard her car, because he opened the door even before she could knock. Erica noticed that he had a cut on his forehead, but she decided that it wasn't the right time to ask him about it.

"What are you doing here?" he asked with the same lack of enthusiasm that Sanna had displayed.

Erica was starting to feel as if she were

carrying the plague. "It's just me and a couple of others," she tried to joke, but Christian didn't look amused.

"I'm working," he said, making no sign of inviting her inside.

"I'll only bother you for a few minutes."

"You of all people should know what it's like to be in the middle of writing something," he said.

This was going a lot worse than Erica had expected. "I had a visit from Gaby a while ago. She told me about your meeting."

Christian's shoulders sagged and he sighed. "She came all the way here just to tell you about that?"

"She was in Göteborg for a meeting. She's really upset. And she thought that I could . . . er, couldn't we go inside to talk instead of just standing here in the doorway?"

Without saying a word, Christian finally stepped aside and let her come in. The ceiling was so low that he had to bow his head a bit, but Erica, who was half a head shorter, was able to stand up straight. He turned his back to her and led the way into the room facing the sea. The computer was on and manuscript pages lay strewn over the drop-leaf table in front of the window, indicating that he really had been working.

"All right, what did she say?" He sat down, crossed his long legs, and folded his arms. His whole body radiated antipathy.

"As I mentioned, she's very upset. Or maybe concerned is a better word. She says that you refuse to do any more interviews or other promotion for your book."

"That's right," replied Christian, looking even more defiant.

"May I ask why?"

"I'm sure you know why," he snapped, and Erica gave a start. He noticed her reaction and seemed to regret his tone of voice. "You know why," he repeated dully. "I can't . . . I just can't. Not after everything that has been said in the media."

"Are you worried about attracting more attention? Is that it? Have you received more threats? Do you know who's sending them?" The questions poured out of her.

Christian shook his head vigorously. "I have no idea." His voice rose again. "I have absolutely no idea! I just want a little peace and quiet so I can work undisturbed and not have to. . . ." He turned away.

Erica studied Christian in silence. He didn't really fit in with this setting. That was something she'd thought about before, when she met him here at the boathouse, and the feeling was even stronger this time.

He looked so out of place among all the fishing gear and nets adorning the walls. The little shed seemed like a doll's house into which he had squeezed his long limbs and then got stuck so he couldn't get out. In a sense, that might have been exactly what happened. She glanced at the manuscript on the table. It was impossible to see what the text was about, but she estimated that there were about a hundred pages.

"Is that a new book?" She had no intention of dropping the topic that seemed to upset him so much, but she was willing to give him a short breathing space so he could calm down.

"Yes," he said, and he seemed to relax a bit.

"Is it a sequel? To *The Mermaid*?"

Christian smiled. "There is no sequel to *The Mermaid*," he told her, turning to look out at the sea. Then he added, hesitantly, "I don't understand how anyone would dare."

"Sorry?" Erica didn't think she'd said anything that would cause him to smile. "What do you mean by 'dare'?"

"Dive."

Erica turned to see what he was looking at, and suddenly she understood what he meant.

"You mean from the diving tower? At Badholmen?"

"Yes." Christian was staring at it without blinking.

"I've never dared. But on the other hand, I have to admit that I'm afraid of the water, which is rather embarrassing considering that I grew up here."

"I've never dared either." Christian spoke in a voice that sounded far away, almost dreamy. Erica waited anxiously for him to say more. There was something in the air, a tension that seemed close to the bursting point. She didn't dare move; she hardly dared breathe. After a few moments Christian went on. But he no longer seemed aware of her presence.

"She dared."

"Who?" Erica whispered the question. At first she didn't think she'd get an answer. Silence settled between them. Then Christian said, in such a low voice that his words were barely audible:

"The Mermaid."

"In the book?" Erica didn't understand. What was he trying to say? And where was he? Not here, at any rate. Not in the present moment, not with her. He was someplace else, and she sincerely wished she knew where that was.

The next instant, the mood had passed.

Christian took a deep breath and turned to face her. He was back.

"I want to focus on my new manuscript. Not sit around giving interviews and writing birthday greetings in the books that I'm asked to sign."

"That's all part of the job, Christian," Erica calmly pointed out. She couldn't help feeling a bit annoyed at his arrogance.

"You mean I have no choice in the matter?" He spoke calmly, but there was still an underlying tension.

"If you weren't prepared to take on that part of the job, you should have said so from the beginning. The publisher, the marketplace, and the readers — and, for God's sake, they're the most important of all — expect us to devote some of our time to them. If an author doesn't want to do that, he needs to make it clear right from the start. You can't change the rules in the middle of the game."

Christian looked down at the floor, and she saw that he was listening carefully, taking in what she was saying. When he raised his head, he had tears in his eyes.

"I can't, Erica. It's impossible for me to explain, but. . . ." He shook his head and tried again. "I can't. They can ostracize me, blacklist me, I don't care. I'll keep on writing, because that's what I have to do. But I can't play their game." He began vigorously scratching his arms as if there were ants swarming under his skin.

Erica looked at him with concern. Christian was like a taut string that might snap at any moment. But she realized that there was nothing she could do about it. He didn't want to talk to her. If she was going to solve the mystery of the letters, she would have to look for answers on her own, without his help.

He stared at her for a moment and then abruptly pulled his chair closer to the table with the computer.

"I have to get back to work now." His face was expressionless. Closed.

Erica stood up. She wished she could see inside his head and pluck out his secrets, which she knew had to be in there. She was sure they were the key to everything. But he had turned his attention to the computer screen, focusing intently on the words that he'd written, as if they were the last things he would ever read.

She left without saying another word. Not even good-bye.

Patrik sat in his office, trying to fight off an overwhelming feeling of fatigue. He needed to concentrate and be alert, now that the investigation had reached a critical stage. Paula stuck her head in the door.

"What's happening?" she asked, taking in Patrik's unhealthy pallor and the beads of sweat on his forehead. She was worried about him. It was impossible not to notice that he'd been looking worn-out lately.

Patrik took a deep breath and forced his thoughts back to the latest development.

"Lisbet Bengtsson's body has been taken to Göteborg for a postmortem. I haven't talked to Pedersen, but considering that it'll be a few days yet before we have the results on Magnus Kjellner, I'm not counting on anything regarding Lisbet until the beginning of next week at the earliest."

"So what do you think? Was she murdered?"

Patrik hesitated. "When it comes to Magnus, I'm sure it was homicide. The injuries he sustained couldn't possibly have been self-inflicted; they could only be the result of an assault. As for Lisbet . . . I don't really know what to say. She had no visible injuries that I could see, and she was seriously ill, so she could have simply died from her disease. If it weren't for that note, that is. Someone had been in her room and put that piece of paper in her hand. But whether that was

357

done before she died, as she was dying, or after her death, it's impossible to say. We'll have to wait for Pedersen to give us more information."

"What about the letters? What did Erik and Kenneth say? Did they have any theory about who might have sent them? Or why?"

"No. They both say they haven't a clue. And right now I see no reason not to believe them. But it seems incredible that three people would be selected at random to receive letters like that. They know each other and spend time together. There must be some sort of common denominator. Something that we've overlooked."

"In that case, why didn't Magnus receive any letters?" Paula asked.

"I don't know. He may have gotten some but didn't tell anyone about them."

"Have you asked Cia?"

"Yes, I asked her as soon as I heard about the threatening letters that had been sent to Christian. She claimed that her husband hadn't received any such thing: if he had, she would have known about it and reported it to us in the very beginning. But it's hard to know for sure. Magnus may have kept quiet in order to protect her."

"It feels like the whole thing has started to escalate. Entering someone's house in the middle of the night is a lot more serious than sending a letter in the mail."

"You're right," said Patrik. "I'd like to give Kenneth police protection, but we just don't have the staff to do that."

"No, we really don't," Paula agreed. "But if it turns out that his wife was actually murdered, then. . . ."

"We'll have to rethink the whole case if that's true," replied Patrik wearily.

"Have you sent the letters to the lab for analysis, by the way?"

"Yes, I sent them off at once. And I included the letter that Erica took from Christian."

"That Erica stole, you mean," said Paula, trying to hide her smile. She'd teased Patrik mercilessly when he'd tried to defend his wife's actions.

"Okay, yes, she stole the letter." Patrik blushed. "But I don't think we should get our hopes up. So many people have already handled those letters, and it's hard to trace ordinary white paper and black ink. You can buy them just about anywhere in Sweden."

"True," said Paula. "There's also a risk that we're dealing with someone who is very careful to erase their tracks."

"That's possible, but we might also get a lucky break."

"So far, that hasn't happened," muttered Paula.

"No, it hasn't. . . ." Patrik sank back on his chair, and they both pondered the case in silence.

"Tomorrow we'll make a fresh start. We'll meet at seven o'clock to go over all the material and then proceed from there."

"A fresh start tomorrow," Paula repeated and then went back to her own office. They really needed some sort of breakthrough right now. And Patrik looked as though he needed a good night's rest. She resolved to keep an eye on him. He didn't look at all well.

The writing was going slowly. Words collected in his head but without forming into sentences. The cursor on the screen was annoying as it kept blinking at him. This book was proving much harder to write; it contained very little of himself. On the other hand, *The Mermaid* had contained too much. It surprised Christian that no one had noticed that. They had read the book as a story, a dark fantasy. His greatest fear had proved baseless. The whole time he had carried out the difficult but necessary work on the novel, he had struggled with the fear of what might happen when he lifted up the rock. What would crawl out when the light of day touched what was hiding underneath?

But nothing had happened. People were so naïve, so used to being fed fictionalized accounts, that they couldn't recognize reality even under the skimpiest of disguises. He looked at the computer screen again. Tried to summon forth the words, get back to what was truly a made-up story. It was like he'd told Erica: there was no sequel to *The Mermaid.* That story was over.

He had played with fire, and the flames had burned his feet. She was very close now; he knew that. She had found him, and he had only himself to blame.

With a sigh, he turned off the computer. He needed to clear his mind. He threw on his jacket and zipped it up to his chin. Then he left the boathouse, and with his hands in his pockets he set off at a brisk pace for Ingrid Bergman Square. The streets were crowded and lively during the summer, but right now they were deserted. That actually suited him better.

He had no idea where he was going until he turned off at the wharf where the Coast Guard boats were docked. His feet had carried him to Badholmen and the diving tower, which loomed against the gray winter sky. The wind was blowing hard. As he walked along the stone jetty that took him over to the little island, a strong gust seized hold of his jacket, making it billow like a sail. He found shelter between the wooden walls separating the changing booths; but as soon as he stepped out onto the rocks facing the tower, the wind again struck him full force. He stood still, allowing himself to be buffeted back and forth as he tilted his head back to stare up at the tower. It wasn't exactly beautiful, but it definitely had a certain presence. From the uppermost platform, there was an impressive view of all of Fjällbacka and the bay opening onto the sea. And it still had a worn dignity about it. Like an old woman who had lived a long life, and lived it well, and wasn't ashamed to show it.

He hesitated for a moment before moving forward to climb the first step. He held on to the railing with cold hands. The tower creaked and protested. In the summertime it withstood hordes of eager teenagers running up and down, but right now the wind was tearing at it with such force that he wasn't sure it would even hold his weight. But that didn't matter. He had to go up to the top.

Christian climbed higher. Now there was no doubt that the tower was actually swaying in the wind. It was moving like a pendulum, swinging his body from side to side. But he kept on going until he reached the top. He closed his eyes for a moment as he sat down on the platform and exhaled. Then he opened his eyes.

She was there, wearing the blue dress. She was dancing on the ice, holding the child in her arms, without leaving any tracks in the snow. Even though she was barefoot, just like on that Midsummer day, she didn't seem to be cold. And the child was wearing light clothes, white trousers and a little shirt, but smiling in the wintry wind as if nothing could touch him.

Christian stood up, his legs unsteady. His eyes were fixed on her. He wanted to scream a warning. The ice was thin, she shouldn't be out there, she shouldn't be dancing on the ice. He saw the cracks, some of them spreading, some of them opening wide. But she kept on dancing with the child in her arms, her dress fluttering around her legs. She laughed and waved, and the dark hair framed her face.

The tower swayed. But he stood upright, countering the movement by holding out his arms to either side. He tried shouting to her, but only a raspy sound came out of his throat. Then he saw her. A soft white hand.

It rose out of the water, trying to catch hold of the feet of the woman who was dancing, trying to grab her dress, wanting to drag her down into the deep. He saw the Mermaid. Her pale face that covetously reached for the woman and the child, reached for what he loved.

But the woman didn't see her. She just kept on dancing, took the child's hand and waved to him, moving her feet across the ice, sometimes only inches from the white hand trying to catch her.

Something flashed inside his head. There was nothing he could do. He was helpless. Christian pressed his hands over his ears and shut his eyes. And then came the scream. Loud and shrill, it rose out of his throat, bouncing off the ice and the rocks below, ripping open the wound in his chest. When he stopped screaming, he cautiously took his hands away from his ears. Then he opened his eyes. The woman and the child were gone. But now he knew. She would never give up until she had taken everything that was his.

Alice still demanded so much. Mother devoted hours to training her, bending her joints, doing exercises with pictures and music. She had moved heaven and earth before she finally accepted the situation. Things were not as they should be with Alice.

But he no longer got so angry. He didn't hate his sister, in spite of all the time she required from Mother. Because the look of triumph in her eyes was gone. She was calm and quiet. She mostly sat by herself, plucking at something, repeating the same movement for hours, staring out of the window or straight at the wall, looking at something only she could see.

And she did learn things. First how to sit up, then how to wriggle forward, finally how to walk. The same as other children. It just took longer for Alice.

Now and then Father would happen to look at him over her head. For a moment, just an instant, their eyes would meet, and there was something in Father's expression that he couldn't decipher. But he understood that Father was keeping watch over him, keeping watch over Alice. He wanted to tell Father that it wasn't necessary. Why would he do anything to her, now that she was so nice?

He didn't love her. He loved only Mother. But he tolerated her. Alice was now part of his world, a small part of his reality, in the same way as the TV set with its noise, the bed he crawled into at night, or the rustling of the newspapers that Father read. She was just as much a natural part of daily life, and she meant just as little.

Alice, on the other hand, adored him. He couldn't understand it. Why had she chosen him instead of their beautiful mother? Alice's face lit up whenever she saw him, and she would stretch out her arms to him, wanting to be picked up. Otherwise, she didn't like to be touched. She often recoiled and pulled away when Mother came near, wanting to caress her and hold her. He didn't understand it. If Mother had wanted to touch him and caress him in that way, he would have crept into her embrace and closed his eyes, never wanting to leave.

Alice's unconditional love for him was surprising. And yet it gave him a certain feeling of satisfaction that at least somebody wanted him. Sometimes he would test her love. On those few occasions when Father forgot to keep an eye on them and went to the toilet or out to the kitchen to get something, he would test how far her love extended. He would see how far he could go before the light in her eyes was extinguished. Sometimes he would pinch her, sometimes he would pull her hair. Once he had cautiously removed her shoe and scratched the sole of her foot with the little pocket knife he had found and always carried in his pocket.

He didn't really like hurting her, but he knew how shallow love could be, and how easily it could be blown away. To his great amazement, Alice never cried; she didn't even give him a reproachful look. She simply put up with whatever he did. Silently, with those bright eyes staring at him.

And no one ever took any notice of the little black and blue marks or the tiny cuts on her body. She was constantly getting bumps and bruises, toppling over, running into things, and cutting herself. It was as if she moved about with a couple of seconds' time lag in her awareness, and she often didn't react until she was already knocking into something. But she never cried, even then.

There were no signs on the outside, nothing

that was visible. Even he had to admit that she looked like an angel. If Mother took Alice out in her stroller — and she was really too big for it by now, but she was still allowed to ride in it because she took so long to walk anywhere on her own — strangers would always comment on the way Alice looked.

"What a lovely child," they would chirp. Leaning over her, they would look at Alice with hungry eyes, as if they wanted to inhale all her sweetness. And he used to glance up at Mother, noticing how for a second she would beam with pride as she nodded.

Then everything would be destroyed in an instant. Alice would reach out toward her admirers with drool hanging from her lips. Then they would abruptly step back, casting first a shocked and then a sympathetic glance at Mother, while her proud expression vanished.

They never looked at him at all. He was just somebody walking behind Mother and Alice, if he was even allowed to go along. A fat, shapeless mass, and no one gave him a thought. But he didn't care. It was as if the anger that had burned inside his chest had died the moment the water had covered Alice's face. He never noticed the smell in his nostrils anymore. That sweet smell had disappeared, as if it had never existed. That too the water had washed away. Although the memory was still there. Not like a memory of something real, but more like a feeling of something displaced. He was someone else now. Someone who knew that Mother no longer loved him.

16

They got started early. Patrik had refused to listen to any protests about holding the meeting at seven o'clock sharp.

"I have a very ambiguous picture of who's behind all of this," he said after having summarized the case. "We seem to be dealing with an individual who is seriously mentally unbalanced but at the same time extremely cautious and well organized. And that's a dangerous combination."

"We don't know for sure that the same person who killed Magnus is also responsible for the letters and the break-in at Kenneth's house," said Martin.

"No, but there's nothing to contradict that theory either. I suggest that for the present we assume there's a connection." Patrik rubbed his face with his hand. He'd lain in bed tossing and turning most of the night, and he felt more tired than ever. "I'll phone Pedersen after we're done here and find out if we can get a definitive answer about the cause of death for Magnus."

"It's probably going to take a few more days to get Pedersen's report," said Paula.

"I know, but it doesn't hurt to lean on him a bit." Patrik pointed at the corkboard on the wall. "We've wasted far too much time already. It's been three months since Magnus disappeared, but only in the past few days did we find out about the threats to other individuals."

Everyone's eyes were fixed on the photographs that were pinned up next to each other.

"We have four friends: Magnus Kjellner, Christian Thydell, Kenneth Bengtsson, and Erik Lind. One is dead. The other three have received threatening letters from someone who we believe to be a woman. Unfortunately, we don't know whether Magnus received similar letters. At any rate, his wife, Cia, isn't aware of any. So it's unlikely we'll ever know for sure."

"But why these four?" Paula squinted her eyes at the photos.

"If we knew that, we'd probably know who's behind everything," said Patrik. "Annika, have you found out anything interesting about their backgrounds?"

"Not really. At least not yet. No surprises

when it comes to Kenneth Bengtsson. There's a lot about Erik Lind, but nothing that seems relevant for us. Mostly suspicions regarding shady financial dealings and that sort of thing."

"I'll bet Erik is involved in some way," said Mellberg. "He's a slippery devil. I've heard plenty of rumors about his business enterprises. He's also a real ladies' man. So obviously we ought to take a closer look at him." He tapped his finger against the side of his nose.

"But why was Magnus murdered?" asked Patrik, receiving an annoyed look in reply.

"I haven't found much on Christian so far," Annika went on calmly. "But I'll keep at it, and of course I'll let you know if I find out anything that might be useful."

"Don't forget that he was the first to receive a letter." Paula was still staring at the corkboard. "They started arriving a year and a half ago. Christian has also received more letters than his friends. At the same time, it seems odd that the others would be dragged into the situation if only one person was the target. I have a strong feeling that there's something linking all four of them together."

"I agree. And it also seems significant that it was Christian who first drew the attention of whoever this person is." Patrik wiped his forehead. It was hot and stuffy in the room, and he'd begun to sweat. He turned to Annika. "Focus on Christian for now."

"I still think we need to concentrate on Erik," said Mellberg. He glared at Gösta. "What do you say, Flygare? You and I are the ones with the most experience. Don't you think Erik Lind should be given some extra attention?"

Gösta squirmed. He'd made it through his whole career as a police officer by adopting the policy of always taking the path of least resistance. But after wrestling with himself for a few seconds, he finally shook his head.

"Well, even though I see your point, I'm afraid I'll have to agree with Hedström that Christian Thydell seems the most interesting at the moment."

"All right, if you want to waste more time, then go ahead," said Mellberg, getting up with a hurt expression on his face. "I have better things to do than to sit here casting pearls before swine." And he left the room.

What Mellberg apparently regarded as "better things to do" involved taking a lengthy nap. But Patrik had no intention of stopping him. The more Mellberg kept out of the investigation, the better.

"Okay, so you'll focus on Christian," Patrik reiterated, nodding at Annika. "When do you think you'll have something for me?"

"By tomorrow I should have a much clearer picture of his background."

"That's great. Martin and Gösta, I'd like you to go and see Kenneth at his home. Try to find out more details about what happened yesterday, and about the letters. Eventually we should also have another talk with Erik Lind. For my part, I'm going to phone Pedersen as soon as it's eight o'clock." Patrik cast a glance at his watch. Only another half-hour. "Then I think Paula and I should drive over to see Cia."

Paula nodded. "Just let me know when you're ready, and we'll head over there."

"Good. So now everyone knows what they should be doing."

Martin raised his hand.

"Yes?"

"Shouldn't we provide some sort of police protection for Christian and the others?"

"I've thought of that, of course. But we just don't have the resources, and we don't have much to go on yet. So we'll wait on that. Anything else?"

No one spoke.

"Okay, then let's get busy." Patrik wiped the sweat from his brow again. Next time, in spite of the winter weather, they would really need to open one of the windows to let in some air.

After the others had left, Patrik remained seated at the table for a while, studying what was posted on the corkboard. Four men. Four friends. One of them dead.

What was it that linked all of them together?

Sanna felt like she was always tiptoeing around him. Their marriage had never been good, not even in the beginning. It took courage to admit that, but she could no longer ignore the truth. Christian had never let her into his life.

He'd always said what was expected of him, done the things he was supposed to do, courted her and given her compliments. But she had never really believed him, although in the past she refused to admit as much to herself. Because he was more than she had ever allowed herself to dream of. His profession might give the impression of a boring and dusty person, but he was the polar opposite. Unattainable and handsome, with eyes that seemed to have seen everything. And when he looked at her with those eyes, she had done her best to fill in the void herself. He had never loved her, and she realized that she'd known this all along. Yet she had fooled herself, seeing only those things she wanted to see and ignoring whatever had rung false.

Now Sanna had no idea what to do. She didn't want to leave Christian. Even though her love was not returned, she still loved him; and she told herself that would be enough, if only he would stay. At the same time, she felt empty and cold inside at the thought of living with him that way, being the only one who gave any love.

She sat up in bed and looked at her husband. He was sound asleep. Slowly she reached out her hand to touch his hair. His thick, dark hair with the traces of gray. A stray lock had tumbled down over one eye, and she gently pushed it back.

Things had not gone well last night, and that was becoming a more and more frequent occurrence. She never knew when he might explode over something, whether large or small. Yesterday the children had been making too much noise. Then he didn't like the dinner she'd made, and she'd said something to him in the wrong tone of voice. Things couldn't continue like this. Everything that had been difficult during their years together had suddenly taken over, and soon there would be nothing good left. It was as if they were rushing at the speed of light toward something unknown, toward the darkness, and she wanted to yell "Stop!" and put an end to it. She wanted their life to be the way it used to be.

Yet, in spite of everything, she understood more now. Christian had given her a small piece of his past. And no matter how terrible the story was, she felt as if she'd received a beautifully wrapped gift. He had told her something about himself, shared something with her that he'd never shared with anyone else. And she treasured that.

But she didn't really know what to do with the information he had confided in her. She wanted to help him, to talk more about it and find out other things that nobody else knew. But he gave her nothing. She had tried again yesterday, with the result that Christian had left the house, slamming the door behind him so hard that the windows rattled. She had no idea when he had finally come home. By eleven o'clock she had cried herself to sleep, and when she had woken up a little while ago, there he was in bed next to her. Now it was almost seven. If Christian was going to work today, he should be getting up. She glanced at the alarm clock, but it hadn't been set for a specific time. Should she wake him?

Sanna hesitated as she sat on the edge of the bed. His eyes were moving rapidly under his eyelids. She would have given anything to know what he was dreaming, what images he saw. His body twitched, and his face looked pained. Slowly she lifted her hand, placing it lightly on his shoulder. He would be angry if he was late for work because she hadn't woken him. But if he had the day off, he'd be angry that she hadn't let him sleep. She wished she knew how to please Christian, how to make him happy.

She jumped at the sound of Nils's voice coming from the children's room. He was shouting for her, sounding scared. Sanna stood up and listened. For a second she thought she had imagined it, that Nils's voice was an echo from her own dreams, in which the kids were always calling her, needing her. But there it was again.

"Mama!"

Why did he sound scared? Sanna's heart began pounding hard, and her feet moved swiftly. She threw on her bathrobe and rushed into the next room, which the boys shared. Nils was sitting up in bed. His eyes were wide as he looked toward the doorway, staring at her. He was holding out his arms, like a little Christ figure on the cross. Sanna felt the shock descend on her like a punch in the stomach. She saw her son's trembling, splayed fingers, his chest, his teddy-bear pajamas, which he loved. By now she had washed them so many times that they were beginning to fray at the wrists. She saw the red. Her brain was hardly able to take in the scene. Then she raised her eyes to the opposite wall, and a scream rose up inside of her, reaching her throat and then bursting out of her.

"Christian! CHRISTIAN!"

Kenneth's lungs were burning. It was a strange feeling in the midst of the haze that enveloped him. Ever since yesterday afternoon, when he'd found Lisbet dead in her bed, his life had seem shrouded in fog. The house was so quiet when he returned home after going to the office with the police. They had taken her away. She was gone.

He had considered going somewhere else. It had suddenly felt impossible for him to step inside their home. But where could he have gone? There was no one he could stay with. Besides, it was here in the house that he would find her. In the pictures on the walls and the curtains in the windows, in the handwriting on the little labels on the packages of food in the freezer. In the radio station that he would hear when he switched it on in the kitchen, and in all the strange foodstuffs that filled the pantry: truffle oil, whole-grain biscuits, and peculiar canned goods. Items that she had brought home with the greatest satisfaction but then never used. He had teased her so many times about her big culinary plans and ambitious recipes that always gave way to much simpler meals. He wished he could tease her one more time.

Kenneth took longer strides. Erik had said that he didn't have to come in to work today, but he needed routines. What was he supposed to do with himself at home? He had gotten up as usual when the alarm clock rang, climbing out of the cot next to his wife's bed, now empty. He had even welcomed the ache in his back. It was the same sore muscles that he'd had when she was still alive. In an hour, he had to be at the office. It took him forty minutes every morning to make his usual run through the woods. He had passed the football field a few minutes ago, which meant that he was about halfway. He picked up the pace. His lungs were telling him that he was approaching the limits of his endurance, but his feet continued to pound against the ground. That was good. The pain in his lungs forced out some of the pain in his heart. Enough so that he didn't simply lie down, curl up in a ball, and let his grief take over.

He didn't know how he was going to live without her. It was like having to live without oxygen. Just as impossible, just as suffocating. His feet moved even faster. Tiny dots of light flickered in front of his eyes, and his field of vision contracted. He fixed his eyes on a spot far away, an opening in the branches where the first glimmer of morning light was filtering through. The harsh light from the lamps that lit up the route still dominated.

The track narrowed to a path, and the ground became more uneven, peppered with hollows and holes. It was also a bit icy, but he was so familiar with the route that he didn't bother to look down. He was staring at the light, focused on the approaching dawn.

At first, Kenneth didn't understand what was happening. It was as if someone had suddenly put up an invisible wall right in front of him. He was caught in mid-stride, with his feet in the air. Then he toppled forward. Instinctively he put out his hands to break his fall, and the jolt when his palms struck the ground sent pain up through his arms and into his shoulders. After that, he felt a different kind of pain. A searing, burning sensation that made him gasp for breath. He looked down at his hands. Both palms were covered with glass. Big and small pieces of clear glass that were slowly turning red from the blood seeping out of the cuts where the shards had torn into his skin. He didn't move, and there was not a sound to be heard.

When he finally tried to sit up, he realized that his feet were tangled in something. He looked down at his legs. There too the glass had punctured his skin, going right through his trousers. Then he let his gaze wander farther over the ground. And that's when he saw the cord.

"Come on, you have to help out a little!" Erica was drenched in sweat. Maja had fought against every garment, from panties to sweatsuit, as her mother tried to get her dressed. By now she was bright red in the face and crying as Erica tried to put mittens on her hands.

"It's cold outside. You have to wear mittens," she said, even though no amount of verbal persuasion had done any good this morning.

Erica felt on the verge of tears herself. She was feeling guilty about all the scolding and arguing, and she would have liked nothing better than to take off Maja's outdoor clothes and let her stay home from the day-care center. Then the two of them could spend a cozy day together. But she knew that wasn't a good idea. She didn't have the energy to take care of Maja for a whole day on her own, and besides, things would be even worse tomorrow if she gave in right now. If this was what Patrik went through every morning, she could understand why he was looking so worn-out.

With an effort she hauled herself up from a seated position, and without further discussion she took her daughter by the hand and led her to the door. She stuffed the mittens into her pocket. Maybe things would be better by the time they got to the day-care center; at least she hoped that the teachers would have greater success than she'd had.

On their way out to the car, Maja dug in her heels and refused to budge.

"Come on now, Maja. I can't carry you." Erica took a tighter grip, with the result that Maja toppled over and started to sob. And now Erica was crying too. If anyone had seen her at that moment, they would have phoned the social welfare authorities at once.

Slowly she squatted down, trying to ignore the pinching and squeezing of her intestines. She helped Maja get up and said in a gentler voice:

"I'm sorry that Mama was being so stupid. Would you like a hug?"

Maja never turned down an opportunity to cuddle, but now she just glared at Erica and cried even louder. She sounded like a foghorn.

"Now, now, sweetie," said Erica, patting Maja's cheek. After a few minutes she began to calm down, and the wailing gave way to sniffling. Erica made another attempt:

"Won't you give Mama a hug?"

Maja hesitated for a moment but then allowed Erica to hug her. She burrowed her face against her mother's throat, and Erica felt herself getting soaked with snot and tears.

"I'm sorry. I didn't mean to make you fall. Did you hurt yourself?"

"Um-hmm," snuffled Maja, looking pitiful.

"Shall I blow on it?" asked Erica. That usually did the trick.

Maja nodded.

"Where should I blow? Where does it hurt?"

Maja thought for a moment and then

started pointing at every part of her body that she could reach. Erica blew on them all and then brushed the snow off Maja's red sweatsuit.

"Don't you think your friends are waiting for you at the day-care center?" said Erica. And then she played her trump card: "I'll bet Ture is there, hoping to see you soon."

Maja stopped sniffling. Ture was her great love. He was three months older, with more energy than most kids and a fondness for Maja that matched her feelings for him.

Erica held her breath. Then Maja suddenly smiled. "Go see Ture."

"Yes, that's right," said Erica. "We're going to go see Ture. And we'd better hurry up or else Ture might get a job in some foreign country or something like that."

Maja gave her mother a puzzled look, and Erica couldn't help laughing.

"Don't pay any attention to your silly mama. Now let's go see Ture."

He was ten years old when everything changed. He had actually adapted quite well by that time. He wasn't happy, not the way he thought he would be when he saw his beautiful mother for the first time, or the way he had been before Alice started growing inside her stomach. But he wasn't unhappy either. He had a place in life, able to dream himself far away through the world of books, and he was content with that. And the fat on his body protected him; it was an armor against what was chafing inside.

Alice loved him as much as always. She followed him like a shadow but didn't say much, which suited him just fine. If he needed anything, she was right there. If he was thirsty, she would bring him some water; if he wanted something to eat, she would slip into the pantry and fetch the pastries that Mother had hidden away.

Occasionally Father would still have that

strange look in his eyes, but he no longer kept watch over him. Alice was big now. She was five years old, and she had finally learned to walk and talk. But she looked like other children only if she stood still and didn't speak. Then she looked so sweet that people would stop and stare at her, just as they had done when she was little and sat in the stroller. If she moved or said something, a look of pity would appear on their faces as they shook their heads.

The doctor had said that she would never be right. Of course he wasn't allowed to go to the doctor appointments. He was never allowed to go with them anywhere, but he hadn't forgotten how to creep about like an Indian brave. He moved through the house without making a sound, and he was always listening. He heard their discussions and knew everything that was said about Alice. It was mostly Mother who talked. She was the one who took Alice to all the doctor appointments, trying to find some new treatment, a new method or new type of exercise that might help Alice and make her movements, her speech, and her abilities better match the way she looked.

No one ever talked about him. That was also something he learned by eavesdropping. It was as if he didn't exist; he merely took up space. But he had learned to live with that.

The few times that he felt hurt, he would think about the smell and what was now starting to seem more and more like an evil fairy tale. A distant memory. That was enough to enable him to live with being invisible to everyone except Alice. Now that he had made her be nice.

A phone call changed everything. The Old Bitch had died, and her house now belonged to Mother. The house in Fjällbacka. They hadn't been there since Alice was born, not since that summer in the trailer when he had lost everything. Now they were going to move there. Mother was the one who made the decision. Father tried to object, but as usual nobody listened to him.

Alice didn't like change. She wanted everything to always remain the same, the same things every day, the same routines. So when all her possessions were packed up and they were sitting in the car with Father behind the wheel, Alice turned around and pressed her nose against the back window, peering at the house until it was lost from sight. Then she turned around to face forward again, moving close to him. She laid her cheek on his shoulder, and for a moment he considered consoling her, giving her a little pat on the head or taking her hand. But he didn't do it.

She leaned against him all the way to Fjäll-backa.

17

"You certainly embarrassed me yesterday," said Erik. He was standing in front of the mirror in the bedroom, trying to knot his tie.

Louise didn't respond. She merely turned her back to him, rolling over onto her side.

"Did you hear what I just said?" He raised his voice a bit, but not enough so the girls could hear him from their rooms across the hall.

"I heard you," she said in a low voice.

"Don't do that again. Ever! It's one thing for you to behave like a drunk here at home in the daytime. As long as you can stay on your feet when the girls are around, I don't care what else you do. But I bloody well won't have you coming over to the office."

No answer. It annoyed him that she offered no defense. He preferred her caustic remarks to this silence.

"You disgust me. Do you know that?" The

knot of his tie ended up too far down, and he swore as he tore it apart to try again. He cast a glance at Louise. She was still lying on the bed with her back turned, but now he saw that her shoulders were shaking. Damn it. This morning was just getting better and better. He despised her hangovers, which were always accompanied by tears and self-pity.

"Stop that. You need to pull yourself together." He could feel how the same old admonitions, repeated over and over, were starting to wear out his patience.

"Are you still seeing Cecilia?" Her voice was muffled by the pillow. Then she turned over to face him to hear his answer.

Erik looked at her with distaste. Without makeup and without the disguise of expensive clothes, she looked ghastly.

She repeated her question. "Are you still seeing her? Are you fucking her?"

So she knew. That was more than he'd expected from her.

"No." He thought about the last conversation that he'd had with Cecilia. He didn't want to talk about it.

"Why not? Are you already tired of her?" Louise had taken hold of the topic like a pit bull.

"Let's just drop it!"

There was no sound from the girls' rooms, and he hoped that they hadn't heard. He realized that he must have been shouting. But he didn't want to think about Cecilia or the child that he was going to be forced to support in secret.

"I don't want to talk about her," he said in a calmer tone of voice as he finally got his tie knotted.

Louise was staring at him, her mouth agape. She looked old. Tears had collected at the corners of her eyes. Her lower lip was quivering as she kept looking at him without saying a word.

"I'm going to the office now. Get your ass out of bed and make sure the girls get to school on time. If you can manage that." He gave her a cold stare and then turned away. Maybe it would be worth the money to be rid of her after all. There were plenty of women who would be overjoyed to accept what he had to offer. She would be easy to replace.

"Do you think he's in any shape to talk to us?" Martin asked Gösta. They were driving out to Kenneth's house, even though neither of them really wanted to disturb him so soon after his wife's death.

"I don't know," replied Gösta, his voice

392

clearly indicating that he didn't want to talk about it. Both of them fell silent.

After a while Gösta asked, "So, how's it going with the little girl?"

"Great!" Martin's face lit up. After a long series of unsuccessful relationships, he had almost given up hope of ever having a family of his own. But Pia had changed all that, and in the fall she'd given birth to a baby girl. His bachelor life now seemed like a distant and not particularly pleasant dream.

Silence again. Gösta drummed his fingers on the steering wheel but stopped after Martin gave him an annoyed look.

Both of them jumped when Martin's mobile rang. When Martin answered, his expression grew more and more somber.

"We've got to go," said Martin as he ended the call.

"What do you mean? What's going on?"

"That was Patrik. Something has happened over at Christian Thydell's house. He phoned the station and was practically incoherent. But it's something to do with his kids."

"Bloody hell." Gösta stomped on the gas pedal. "Hold on," he told Martin and drove even faster. He could feel his stomach starting to clench up. He'd always had a hard time dealing with cases involving children.

And it hadn't gotten any easier over the years. "Couldn't Patrik tell you anything more?"

"No," said Martin. "Christian was in such a state that Patrik couldn't get a sensible word out of him. He and Paula are also on their way, but we'll get there first. Patrik said not to wait for them." Martin was looking pale too. It was bad enough to arrive at a crime scene if they were prepared for what they were going to see. But right now they had no idea what was in store for them.

When they drove up in front of the Thydell house, they didn't bother to park the car properly. Gösta brought it to a skidding halt, and they both jumped out. No one answered when they rang the bell, so they opened the door.

"Hello! Anyone home?"

They heard sounds coming from overhead, so they dashed upstairs.

"Hello? It's the police." They shouted again, but there was still no answer. From one of the rooms they heard sobs and the high-pitched screams of a child interspersed with the sound of splashing water.

Gösta took a deep breath and looked inside. Sanna was sitting on the bathroom floor, crying so hard that her whole body shook. In the bathtub sat the two little boys.

The water was a faint pink color, and Sanna was vigorously scrubbing their small bodies.

"What happened? Are they hurt?" Gösta stared at the children in the tub.

Sanna turned around, gave them a hasty look, and then turned back to her sons.

"Are they hurt, Sanna? Should we call an ambulance?" Gösta went over to her, squatted down, and put his hand on her shoulder. But Sanna didn't reply. She just kept on scrubbing, without much result. The red wasn't coming off. In fact, it just seemed to be spreading.

Gösta took a closer look at the boys and felt his pulse start to slow down. The red color wasn't blood.

"Who did this?"

Sanna sobbed as she used the back of her hand to wipe away the drops of pink water that had sprayed her face.

"They . . . they. . . ." Her teeth were chattering, and Gösta squeezed her shoulder to reassure her. Out of the corner of his eye, he saw that Martin was standing in the doorway.

"It's paint," he told Martin. Then he looked again at Sanna. She took a deep breath and made another attempt to speak.

"Nils was calling for me. He was sitting up in bed. This . . . this is how they looked.

Somebody had written on the wall, and some of the paint must have spattered on to their beds. I thought it was blood."

"But you and Christian didn't hear anything during the night? Or this morning?"

"No, nothing."

"Where is the children's room?" asked Gösta.

Sanna pointed out into the hall.

"I'll go take a look," said Martin, turning around to leave.

"I'll come too." Gösta forced Sanna to meet his gaze before he stood up. "We'll be right back. Okay?"

She nodded. Gösta stood up and went out into the hall. From the children's room he could hear loud voices.

"Christian, put that down."

"I have to get this off. . . ." Christian sounded just as confused as Sanna, and when Gösta entered the room he saw him holding a big bucket of water, ready to toss the contents at the wall.

"We need to have a look at it first." Martin held up his hand toward Christian, who was wearing only his underwear. On his chest were red flecks of paint that he'd no doubt acquired when he helped Sanna carry the boys to the bathroom.

Now he made an attempt to throw the

water at the wall, but Martin leaped forward and grabbed the bucket. Christian offered no resistance. He let go of the handle and just stood there, swaying slightly.

With Christian under control, Gösta could concentrate on what he'd been trying to wash away. On the wall above the boys' beds someone had written: *You don't deserve them.*

The red paint had dripped down from the letters, which looked as if they'd been written in blood. The same impression was made by the paint on the children's bed. Gösta now understood the extent of the shock that Sanna must have had when she came into the room. And he also understood Christian's reaction. His face was now expressionless as he stared at the words on the wall, but he was muttering to himself. Gösta moved a little closer to hear what he was saying.

"I don't deserve them. I don't deserve them."

Gösta cautiously took him by the arm. "Go and put on some clothes, Christian, and then we'll talk." Gently but firmly Gösta ushered him out the door and over to the room that he had noticed belonged to Christian and Sanna.

Christian followed obediently, but then he

just sat down on the bed, without making any attempt to get dressed. Gösta looked around until he found a bathrobe hanging from a hook behind the door. He handed the robe to Christian, who put it on, his movements listless and slow.

"I need to have another look at Sanna and the children. Then we'll go down to the kitchen and talk."

Christian nodded. His eyes were vacant, as if covered by a glassy membrane. Gösta left him sitting on the bed and went back to find Martin, who was still in the children's room.

"What the hell is going on here?" Gösta asked.

Martin shook his head. "This is sick. Whoever did this must be insane. And what does it mean? 'You don't deserve them.' Deserve what? The children?"

"That's what we need to find out. Patrik and Paula should be here any minute. Could you go downstairs and let them in? And phone for a doctor, too. I don't think the kids are hurt, but the whole family has received a bad shock. It's probably best to have a doctor look at them. I'm going to help Sanna get the paint washed off of the boys. She's scrubbing so hard that she's going to flay the skin off them."

"We need to get the crime techs out here too."

"Exactly. As soon as Patrik gets here, ask him to contact Torbjörn ASAP so they'll send over a team. And we should try not to walk around in here any more than we have to."

"At least we managed to save the wall," said Martin.

"Yes. That was damn lucky."

They went downstairs together, and Gösta quickly managed to locate the door that led down to the basement. Only a bare bulb lit the stairs, so he descended cautiously. Like most people's basements, the one belonging to the Thydell family was filled with all sorts of junk: cardboard boxes, discarded toys, containers labeled "Christmas decorations," tools that didn't look as if they were used very often, and a shelf holding painting equipment: cans, bottles, brushes, and rags. Gösta reached for a bottle half-filled with paint thinner, but the moment his fingers closed around the bottle, he caught sight of something out of the corner of his eye. A rag was lying on the floor. Spattered with red paint.

He quickly scanned the cans of paint on the shelf. None of them held red paint. But Gösta was positive that the red color on the rag was the same as he'd seen in the boys' room. Whoever had painted those words on the wall must have brought the paint along and then come down here to wash up. He looked at the bottle he was holding. Shit. It might have fingerprints on it. But he needed the thinner. The boys had to have the paint removed from their skin so they could get out of the bath. An empty cola bottle solved the problem. Without changing his grip on the bottle of thinner, he poured the contents into the plastic cola bottle and then set it back on the shelf. If he was lucky, he hadn't ruined all the prints. And the rag might also give them something to go on.

Carrying the cola bottle, Gösta went back upstairs. Patrik and Paula hadn't yet arrived, but they couldn't be far away.

Sanna was still stubbornly scrubbing her sons when he came into the bathroom. The boys were crying desperately. Gösta squatted down next to the tub and said gently:

"You're not going to get the paint off just by scrubbing with soap. We need to use paint thinner." He held up the bottle that he'd brought from the basement. Sanna stopped what she was doing and stared at him. Gösta took a hand towel from a hook next to the sink and poured some of the fluid onto the cloth as Sanna watched. He held up the towel to show it to her and then took hold of the older boy's arm. There was no use trying to calm them down right now. He just had to work fast.

"See? The paint comes right off." Even though the boy was wriggling like a worm, Gösta managed to wipe off a good deal of the paint. "This is what we need to do."

He realized that he was speaking to Sanna as if she were a child, but it seemed to work because she was starting to look less and less distraught.

"Okay. So he's done now." Gösta put down the towel and picked up the handheld shower hose to rinse the solvent off the boy's body. The child began wildly kicking when Gösta lifted him out of the tub, but Sanna reacted by swiftly wrapping her son in a bathrobe. She pulled him onto her lap and rocked him as she held him close.

"Okay, little guy. Now it's your turn." The younger boy seemed to understand that if he let the policeman wash him off, he'd be allowed out of the bathtub and could sit on his mother's lap. He abruptly stopped crying and sat perfectly still as Gösta poured more thinner on the towel and then began wiping off the paint. Soon he too was only a faint shade of pink, and he was allowed to sit on Sanna's lap, wrapped from head to toe in a big bath towel.

From downstairs, Gösta could now hear voices and then footsteps approaching. Patrik appeared in the doorway.

"What happened?" he asked, out of breath. "Is everybody okay? Martin said the children didn't seem to be hurt." Patrik's eyes were fixed on the bathtub filled with crimson water.

"The kids are fine. Just a little shocked. Like their parents." Gösta stood up and went out into the hall with Patrik. Briefly he told his colleague what had happened.

"This is crazy. Who would do such a thing?"

"Martin and I said the same thing. Something isn't right, and that's putting it mildly. I think Christian knows more than he's telling us." He repeated what he'd heard Christian mumbling.

"I agree," said Patrik. "I've had that feeling for a while now. Where is he?"

"In the bedroom. We need to see if he's in good enough shape that we can have a talk with him."

"I reckon it's high time we did just that."

Patrik's mobile rang. He took it out of his pocket and answered. Then he gave a start.

"What did you say? Can you repeat that?"

He glanced at Gösta, a look of dismay on his face. Gösta tried in vain to hear what the other person was saying. "Okay. Understood. We're over at the Thydell home. Something has happened here too, but we'll deal with it."

He ended the call.

"Kenneth Bengtsson has been taken to the Uddevalla hospital. He was out running this morning, and someone had set a trap for him, a cord that tripped him so he fell headlong onto a bed of broken glass."

"Good God," whispered Gösta. And for the second time that morning, he said "What the hell is going on here?"

Erik stared at his mobile phone. Kenneth was on his way to the hospital. Dutiful as ever, he had persuaded the ambulance medics to call the office to say that he couldn't make it to work.

Somebody had set a trap for him that he was bound to encounter on his run. Erik didn't even consider the possibility that it could be a mistake, a practical joke that had gone too far. Kenneth always took the same route every morning. Everyone in the area knew that, and anyone else could have found out. So there was no doubt that somebody wanted to harm Kenneth. Which meant that he too was in danger.

This was getting out of hand. Over the years, Erik had taken many risks and stepped on plenty of people along the way. But he never would have foreseen something like this, or the terror that he now felt.

He turned to his computer and logged on to his bank's website. He needed to get an idea of the possibilities open to him. Thoughts were whirling through his mind, but he tried to focus on the amounts in his bank accounts so as to channel his fear into a plan, a means of escape. For a moment, he allowed himself to ponder who could have sent those letters and, most likely, murdered Magnus. Evidently that person had now shifted his or her attention to Kenneth. At least for the moment. Then Erik pushed those thoughts aside. It would serve no useful purpose to keep speculating. It could be anybody. Right now he had to save his own skin, take what funds he could and leave the country for some warmer place where no one could touch him. And stay there until this whole thing had blown over.

Of course, he would miss the girls while he was away. But they were older now, and maybe it would make Louise pull herself together if she had the primary responsibility for their daughters instead of being able to lean on him. And he wouldn't be leaving them with nothing. He would see to it that they had enough money in the bank to live on for quite a while. Then Louise would have to get a job. It would do her good. After all, she couldn't very well expect him to support her for the rest of her life. He had every right to do this, and the money that he'd saved up over the years would be sufficient to create a whole new life for himself. And keep him safe.

He had the situation under control; all he needed to do was take care of a few practical matters. For one thing, he needed to talk to Kenneth. Erik decided to go to the hospital in the morning and hope that his colleague would be feeling well enough to review some figures. Of course it was going to be hard on Kenneth, having to leave the company so soon after Lisbet's death, and no doubt there would be some tiresome repercussions. But Kenneth was a big boy now, and maybe Erik was actually doing him a favor by forcing him to stand on his own two feet. The more he thought about it, this was bound to be good for both Louise and Kenneth, since he would no longer be available to hold their hands.

Then there was Cecilia. But she had

already told him in no uncertain terms that she didn't need his help, other than financially. And he should be able to set aside a small sum for her.

So that's what he would do. Cecilia could take care of herself; they could all take care of themselves. And the girls would probably understand. Over time they would understand.

It had taken a long time to remove all the pieces of glass. Two still remained. They were so deeply embedded that it would take a more serious procedure to get them out. But everyone said that he'd been extremely lucky. The glass had missed the major arteries. Otherwise things could have gone very badly. That was exactly what the doctor had so cheerfully told him.

Kenneth turned his face to the wall. Didn't they understand that this was as bad as it could get? If he'd had his way, the glass would have sliced through one of his arteries, cutting off the pain and taking away the evil in his heart. Purging the evil memory. Because in the ambulance, while the sirens wailed in his ears and he grimaced at every jolt as the vehicle roared along at high speed, he had suddenly understood. And he knew who it was that was hunting them.

Who hated all of them and wanted to harm both him and the others. And who had taken Lisbet from him. The idea that his wife had died with the truth ringing in her ears was more than he could bear.

He looked down at his arms resting on top of the blanket. They were covered with bandages. His legs were too. He had run his last marathon. The doctor said it would be a miracle if his wounds healed properly. But that didn't matter now. He had no desire to do any more running.

He had no intention of running away from her, either. She had already taken what mattered most to him. The rest was unimportant. There was some sort of biblical justice that was impossible to combat. An eye for an eye, a tooth for a tooth.

Kenneth closed his eyes and saw the images that he had banished to a far corner of his memory. After so many years, it was as if it had never even happened. Only once had the memories resurfaced. That was on that midsummer day when the whole thing had nearly fallen apart. But the walls had held, and he had suppressed those images once again, storing them away in the darkest recesses of his brain.

Now they were back. She had brought them out into the light, forcing him to look at them. And he couldn't stand what he saw. Above all, he couldn't bear knowing that this had been the last thing Lisbet had heard. Had it changed everything? Had she died with a black hole in her heart where her love had once been? Had he become a stranger to her at that moment?

He opened his eyes again. Staring up at the ceiling, he felt tears running down his cheeks. She could come and take him now. He wasn't going to run away.

An eye for an eye, a tooth for a tooth.

"Out of the way, Fatty!"

The boys deliberately bumped into him as they passed in the corridor. He tried to ignore them, to be as invisible at school as he was at home. But it didn't work. It was as if they had been waiting for someone like him, someone who stuck out, a scapegoat they could pick on. He understood. After spending so many hours reading books, he knew more and understood more than most kids his age. He excelled in all his classes, and the teachers loved him. But what good was that when he couldn't kick a ball, run fast, or spit far? Those were the sorts of skills that counted, the talents that mattered.

Slowly he made his way home. He kept looking around to see if anyone was waiting to ambush him. Luckily he didn't have a long walk to school. The route was filled with dangers, but at least it was short. All he had to do was go down the slope of Håckebacken, head left toward the wharf that faced Badholmen, and there was his house. The house they had inherited from the Old Bitch.

Mother still called her by that name. She had said that name every time she discarded, with great satisfaction, any of the old woman's possessions, tossing them into the big trash bin they had placed in the yard when they moved in.

"If only the Old Bitch could see this. Here go all her fancy chairs," said Mother, cleaning and clearing things out as if she'd gone mad. "Now I'm throwing away your grandmother's china. See that?"

He had never heard why she'd been given that name: the Old Bitch. Or why Mother was so angry with her. Once he had timidly asked Father, but he had merely muttered something in reply.

"You're already home?" Mother was combing Alice's hair when he came in.

"School was out the same time as always," he said, ignoring Alice's smile. "What's for dinner?"

"You look like you've already eaten enough for the rest of the year. No dinner for you today. You can just live on your fat."

It was only four o'clock, and already he could feel how hungry he was going to be. But when he looked at Mother, he could tell that it would do no good to protest.

He went up to his room, closed the door, and lay down on his bed with a book. Filled with hope, he stuck his hand under the mattress. If he was lucky, he might have missed something. But there was nothing there. She was very clever. She always found the food and sweets that he stashed away, no matter where he tried to hide them.

A couple of hours later, his stomach was growling noisily. He was so hungry that he was on the verge of tears. From downstairs came the smell of freshly baked buns, and he knew that Mother was making cinnamon rolls just so the fragrance would drive him crazy with hunger. He sniffed at the air, then turned onto his side and buried his face in the pillow. Sometimes he thought about running away. No one would care. Alice might miss him, but he didn't give a damn about her. She had Mother.

Mother devoted all her free time to Alice. So why couldn't Alice look at her instead of him with those adoring eyes of hers? And why did she take for granted what he would have given anything to have?

He must have dozed off, because he was awakened by a light tap on the door. His book had fallen over his face, and he had been drooling in his sleep, because the pillow was wet with saliva. He wiped his cheek with his hand and groggily got up to open the door. Alice was standing there. In one hand she had a bun, which she held out to him. His mouth watered, but he hesitated. Mother would be angry if she found out that Alice had slipped upstairs to bring him something to eat.

Alice stared at him with her eyes wide. She wanted him to see her, to love her. An image appeared in his mind. An image and the feeling of a baby's slippery, wet body. Alice staring up at him from the water. The way she flailed about and then lay still.

He grabbed the bun and closed the door in her face. But it didn't help. The images were still there.

18

Patrik had sent Gösta and Martin to Udde-valla to see if Kenneth was feeling well enough to talk to them. Torbjörn Ruud's team of crime techs was on the way. The team would have to split up in order to deal with both the place where Kenneth had fallen and the house belonging to Christian and Sanna. Gösta hadn't wanted to leave; he would have preferred to stay and have a talk with Christian. But Patrik wanted Paula to stay instead. He thought it would be good to have a woman speak with Sanna and the children. Nevertheless he had been im-pressed with Gösta's handling of the situa-tion, and especially his finding the rag and bottle in the basement. With luck, these items would give them the perpetrator's fingerprints and DNA. Up until now, he or she had been too careful to leave a trace.

He stared at the man sitting at the kitchen table facing him. Christian looked worn out and old. He seemed to have aged ten years since Patrik last saw him. He hadn't bothered to tie the belt of his bathrobe properly, and his bare chest made him look even more vulnerable. Patrik wondered if he ought to tell Christian, for his own sake, to close up his bathrobe, but he decided not to say anything. His clothing was undoubtedly the last thing on Christian's mind at the moment.

"The boys have calmed down. My colleague Paula is going to talk to them and your wife. She'll be careful what she says and do her best to make sure they won't be further frightened or upset. Okay?" Patrik tried to catch Christian's eye to see if he was listening. At first there was no response, and he considered repeating what he'd just said. But finally Christian nodded.

"In the meantime, I thought you and I should have a little chat," Patrik went on. "I know that you haven't been keen to talk to us before, but this time you really have no choice. Someone came into your house and went into the room where your sons were sleeping. The boys weren't harmed physically, but it must have been a terribly scary experience for them. If you have any idea about who might be behind this, you need to tell me. Don't you understand that?"

Again a long pause before Christian finally nodded. He cleared his throat as if to speak, but no words came.

Patrik continued: "It was only yesterday that we found out that Kenneth and Erik had also received threatening letters from the same person who sent letters to you. And this morning Kenneth was seriously injured while he was out taking a run. Someone set a trap for him."

Christian glanced up, looking startled, but then lowered his eyes again.

"We have no information that Magnus received similar threats, but we're working from the assumption that the same person was involved with his death. And I have a feeling that you know more than you're telling us. Maybe because it's something you don't want to drag out into the light, or it's something you think is trivial, but you need to let us decide what's important. Even the slightest lead could be significant."

Christian was tracing circles on the table with his finger. Then he raised his head and met Patrik's glance. For a moment it looked as though there was something Christian wanted to say. Then he shut down again.

"I have no idea," he said. "I don't know any more than you do who could be doing this."

"Are you aware that both you and your family are in grave danger as long as this person is at large?"

An uncanny calm had settled over Christian's face. All trace of worry or concern had vanished. Instead, his expression was what Patrik could only describe as determined.

"I understand. And I'm sure that you'll do your best to find out who the guilty party is. But I'm afraid I can't help you. I just don't know anything."

"I don't believe you," said Patrik bluntly.

Christian shrugged. "Well, there's nothing I can do about that. I'm just telling you how it is. I don't know anything." As if suddenly aware that he was practically naked, he closed up his bathrobe and pulled the belt tight.

Patrik felt like shaking the man, out of sheer frustration. He was convinced that Christian was holding something back. He didn't know what it was, or even if it was relevant to the case. But there was definitely something he didn't want to discuss.

"What time did all of you go to bed last night?" asked Patrik, deciding to move on to another topic, but only for the moment. He wasn't going to let Christian off the hook so easily. He'd seen how terrified the children were as they sat in the bathtub. Next time it might not be a question of red paint. He had to make Christian understand how serious the situation was.

"I went to bed late, just after one o'clock. I have no idea when Sanna went to bed."

"Were you home all evening?"

"No, I went out for a walk. Sanna and I are having a few . . . problems. I needed to get some air."

"Where did you go?"

"I'm not really sure. No place in particular. I just wandered around a bit, and then I walked through town."

"Alone? In the middle of the night?"

"I didn't want to be in the house. Where was I supposed to go?"

"So you came back home around one? And you're sure about the time?"

"I'm positive. I looked at the clock over on Ingrid Bergman Square, and it said quarter to one. It takes about ten or fifteen minutes to walk home from there. So it should have been just about one o'clock when I got back."

"Was Sanna asleep?"

Christian nodded. "Yes, she was asleep. And the boys were too. The house was quiet."

"Did you look in on the kids when you

417

came home?"

"I always do that. Nils had kicked off the covers, as usual, so I tucked him in."

"And you didn't notice anything odd or out of the ordinary?"

"You mean like big red letters on the wall?" he said sarcastically.

Patrik could feel himself getting annoyed.

"I'll repeat my question: You didn't see anything unusual, anything you reacted to, when you came home?"

"No," said Christian. "I didn't see anything that I reacted to. If I had, do you think I would have just gone to bed?"

"No, probably not." Patrik was sweating again. Why did everyone have to keep their homes so hot? He tugged at his shirt collar. It felt like he wasn't getting enough air.

"Did you lock the door after you got home?"

Christian paused to think. "I don't know," he said. "I think so. I usually lock the door. But . . . but I don't really recall doing it." Now all sarcasm was gone from his voice. He was almost whispering when he said "I don't remember locking the door."

"And you didn't hear anything during the night?"

"No, nothing. At least *I* didn't. I don't think Sanna did either. We're both very sound sleepers. I didn't wake up until Sanna started screaming this morning. I didn't even hear Nils. . . ."

Patrik decided to try again. "And you have no idea why anyone would do this? Or why someone would send you threatening letters for a year and a half? No suspicions at all?"

"Why the hell aren't you listening to what I'm saying?"

The outburst came out of the blue, and Patrik actually jumped. Christian had shouted so loudly that Paula called from upstairs:

"Is everything okay?"

"We're fine," Patrik called in reply, hoping he was right. Christian looked on the verge of collapse. His face was bright red, and he was vigorously scratching the palm of his hand.

"I don't know anything," Christian repeated, as if he were trying desperately not to shout. He was scratching so hard that he was leaving marks on his skin.

Patrik waited for Christian to relax a bit, and for the color of his face to return more or less to normal. When he stopped scratching, he looked in surprise at the marks on the palm of his hand, as if he couldn't understand where they'd come from.

"Is there anywhere you and your family

could stay until we find out more?" asked Patrik.

"Sanna and the boys could go to her sister's house in Hamburgsund and stay there for a while."

"What about you?"

"I'm staying here." Christian sounded as if he'd made up his mind.

"That doesn't seem like a good idea," said Patrik, his voice equally firm. "We can't offer you police protection twenty-four/seven. I'd rather you stayed at a different location where you would feel safer."

"I'm staying here."

Christian's tone of voice indicated that there was no room for discussion.

"All right," said Patrik reluctantly. "Make sure your family leaves as soon as possible. We'll try to keep an eye on the house as best we can, but we don't have the resources to —"

"I don't need police protection," Christian interrupted him. "I'll be fine."

Patrik fixed his eyes on him. "A seriously disturbed person is on the loose. This individual has already committed one murder, possibly two, and seems determined to make sure that you and Kenneth, and maybe Erik, end up dead too. This is not a game. You don't seem to understand that."

He spoke slowly, clearly enunciating every word to make sure his message got through.

"I assure you that I fully understand how serious this is. But I'm staying here."

"If you change your mind, you know where to find me. And as I said, I don't believe you for a minute when you say that you know nothing about this. I hope you realize what you're putting at risk by not speaking up. No matter what it is you're keeping back, we'll find out what it is sooner or later. It's just a matter of whether we find out before or after somebody else gets hurt."

"How's Kenneth?" muttered Christian, avoiding looking Patrik in the eye.

"All I know is that he was injured. Nothing more."

"What happened?"

"Someone stretched a cord across the path and spread a thick layer of broken glass on the ground. So maybe now you'll understand why I'm asking for your cooperation."

Christian didn't reply. He turned away and looked out of the window. His face was as pale as the snow outside, and his jaws were clenched. But his voice was cold and devoid of any emotion as he repeated, his eyes fixed on some distant spot:

"I know nothing. I. Know. Nothing."

■ ■ ■

"Does it hurt?" Martin looked at the man's bandaged arms resting on top of the blanket. Kenneth nodded.

"Are you up to answering a few questions?" Gösta pulled over a chair and motioned for Martin to do the same.

"Seeing as how you've already sat down, it seems that you assume I'm up to it," said Kenneth with a faint smile.

Martin couldn't take his eyes off the bandages. It must have hurt like hell, falling onto all that glass and then having the pieces removed.

He cast an uncertain glance at Gösta. Sometimes it felt as if he'd never have enough experience to know how to proceed in the situations that he landed in as a police officer. Should he just plunge in and start asking questions? Or should he show respect for his older colleague and let him steer the conversation? It was such a balancing act. He was always the youngest, always the one sent off to do one thing or another. He too would have preferred to stay at Christian's house, which was what Gösta had been muttering about all the way out to Uddevalla. He would have liked to interview

Christian and his wife, to talk with Torbjörn and his team when they arrived; to have been in the thick of things.

He was disappointed that Patrik usually chose to work with Paula, even though Martin had joined the station a couple of years before she arrived. Of course, she had experience from working in Stockholm, while he had spent his entire brief career on the Tanumshede police force. But was that necessarily such a negative thing? He knew the area, he was familiar with all the resident troublemakers, he knew how people thought and how a small town operated. In fact, he had even gone to school with a couple of the worst offenders, while they were complete unknowns to Paula. And after the rumors about her personal life had spread through the district like wildfire, many people had started eyeing her with suspicion. Martin himself had nothing against those who chose to live with a partner of the same sex, but many of the people they dealt with on a daily basis were not as understanding. So it seemed a little odd that Patrik kept on choosing Paula to work with him. All Martin wanted was to get a certain amount of respect from his colleagues. He wished they would stop treating him like some young whippersnapper. He really wasn't all that young anymore. And now he was a father too.

"I'm sorry?" Martin was so immersed in his own gloomy thoughts that he'd missed what Gösta had said to him.

"I was just saying that maybe you'd like to start."

Martin stared at Gösta in surprise. Was he a mind-reader? But he seized the opportunity and asked:

"Could you tell us in your own words what happened?"

Kenneth reached for a glass of water standing on the table next to his bed before he realized that he couldn't use his hands.

"Wait, let me do it." Martin picked up the glass and helped him take a drink through a straw. Then Kenneth leaned back against the pillows. In a calm and matter-of-fact voice, he recounted what had happened to him, starting with tying his shoes before going out for his usual morning run.

"What time did you leave the house?" Martin had taken out a notebook and pen.

"Six forty-five," replied Kenneth, and Martin wrote down the time without hesitation. It was his impression that if Kenneth said it was six forty-five, then that was the time. Without a doubt.

"Do you always go running at the same

time each morning?" Gösta leaned back with his arms crossed.

"Yes, give or take ten minutes or so."

"And you didn't consider not . . . I mean, given that. . . ." Martin stammered.

"You didn't consider skipping your run, given that your wife died yesterday?" Gösta interjected, without sounding unkind. And without turning the question into an accusation.

Kenneth didn't respond immediately. He swallowed hard and then said in a low voice:

"If there was ever a morning when I needed to go running, it was today."

"I understand," said Gösta. "Do you always take the same route?"

"Yes, except sometimes on the weekend, when I do it twice. I suppose I'm a bit of a stick-in-the-mud. I don't like surprises, adventures, or things that change." He fell silent. Gösta and Martin both knew what he was thinking about and didn't say a word.

Kenneth cleared his throat and turned away so they wouldn't see the tears welling up in his eyes. He cleared his throat again so he'd be able to speak without faltering.

"As I said, I like routines. I've been running the same route now for over ten years."

"And I assume that plenty of people are aware of that, right?" Martin looked up from his notebook after jotting down *10 years* and drawing a circle around it.

"There's never been any reason to keep it a secret." A smile suddenly appeared on Kenneth's face, but vanished just as swiftly.

"Did you meet anyone while you were out running this morning?" asked Gösta.

"No, not a soul. I seldom do. Sometimes I'll see someone who's up early walking their dog, or someone out pushing a baby carriage. But that rarely happens. Usually I'm alone on the path. Like this morning."

"And you didn't see a car parked somewhere near your route?" Martin received an appreciative glance from Gösta when he asked that question.

Kenneth paused to consider. "No, I don't think so. I can't say for sure. It's possible that someone was there and I just didn't see them. But no, I'm sure I would have noticed."

"So there was nothing out of the ordinary?" Gösta persisted.

"No, it was just like every other morning. Except that. . . ." His words hung in the air and tears began spilling down his cheeks.

Martin was ashamed that he found it embarrassing to see Kenneth cry. He felt at a loss for words and didn't know whether he should do something or not. But Gösta calmly reached across Kenneth and took a tissue from the table. Then he gently wiped the tears from Kenneth's face. After that, he again reached across and put the tissue back on the table.

"Have you heard anything yet?" whispered Kenneth. "About Lisbet?"

"No, it's much too early for that. It'll be a while before we know what the medical examiner can tell us."

"She killed her." The man in the bed flinched and then seemed to shrivel up, staring into space.

"Sorry, what did you just say?" asked Gösta, leaning forward. "Who is 'she'? Do you know who did this to you and your wife?"

Martin could tell that Gösta was holding his breath. He was too.

Something flashed in Kenneth's eyes.

"I have no idea," he said firmly.

"You said 'she,' " Gösta pointed out.

Kenneth avoided looking at him. "The handwriting on the letters looks like it was done by a woman. So I'm just assuming that it's a 'she.' "

"Ah, so that's it," said Gösta, making it clear to Kenneth that he didn't believe him, although he wasn't going to say that to the man's face. "There must be something that has made the four of you the targets. Magnus, Christian, Erik, and you. Someone has unfinished business with you. And all of you — well, except for Magnus — insist that you have no idea who is doing this, or why. But there must be an intense hatred behind such actions. The question is: What prompted that hatred? I have a hard time believing that none of you knows anything. You must at least have a theory." He leaned close to Kenneth.

"It must be someone who's mentally disturbed. I can't think of any other explanation." Kenneth turned away again, pressing his lips tight.

Martin exchanged glances with Gösta. They both knew they weren't going to get anything more out of Kenneth. At least not for the time being.

Erica stared at the phone in shock. Patrik had called from the station to tell her that he was going to be late. Briefly he had also explained why, and she could hardly believe what she'd heard. To think that someone had gone after Christian's children. And after Kenneth too. A cord strung across the path — simple but brilliant.

Her brain immediately began working overtime. There must be some way to make the investigation go faster. She could hear how frustrated Patrik had sounded, and she sympathized. The chain of events had begun to escalate, and the police were no closer to a solution.

She weighed the mobile in her hand as she thought things over. Patrik would be furious if she interfered in any way. But she was used to doing research for her books. Of course, what she wrote dealt with crimes that had already been solved, but it shouldn't be much different to take a closer look at an ongoing investigation. And besides, it was so dreary just to hang around the house. She was itching to do something useful.

She could also rely on her gut instinct. It had helped her so many times in the past. Right now it was telling her that the answer would be found with Christian. After all, he had been the first to receive letters, he was very secretive about his past, and he was clearly nervous. Small but crucial factors. And after their conversation in the boathouse, she'd had the feeling that Christian knew something; there was something he was hiding.

Quickly, so as not to have time to regret her decision, she threw on her winter coat. As she drove, she would call Anna and ask her if she could pick up Maja from the day-care center. Erica would be home before evening, but not in time to collect her daughter. It took an hour and a half to drive to Göteborg; that was quite a distance to go, just on a whim. But if she didn't find out anything, she could always drop by to see Göran, her newly discovered half-brother.

The idea that she and Anna had a big brother was still almost incomprehensible. It had been upsetting to find out that during the Second World War their mother had given birth to a son and then given him up for adoption. But the dramatic events that had led to all this coming to light last summer had ended up producing something positive, and she and Anna had developed a close relationship with Göran. Erica knew that she was always welcome to stop by to see him and the woman he had grown up calling his mother.

Anna agreed at once to pick up Maja, who was much beloved by all the children, both Anna's and Dan's. Erica had no doubt that her daughter would come home worn out from playing, and stuffed with sweets.

Then Erica turned her attention to the task at hand. The work she had done writing books about real murders — books that had proved a big hit with the public — had provided good training in doing research. She just wished she knew Christian's civil registration number; that would have saved her a number of conversations. But she'd have to make do with his name. It suddenly came to her that Sanna had once mentioned that Christian had been living in Göteborg when they met. At the library, May had mentioned Trollhättan, and that was still nagging at Erica, but she decided that Göteborg had to be the logical place to start. That was where he had lived before coming to Fjällbacka, so she would begin there. She hoped she could then backtrack if necessary. She had absolutely no doubt that the truth lay in Christian's past.

After speaking to four different people, she finally had something: the address where Christian used to live before he moved to Fjällbacka with Sanna. Erica stopped at a Statoil gas station just outside of Göteborg and bought a map of the city. She also took time to use the restroom and stretch her legs. It was terribly uncomfortable to drive with two babies in between herself and the steering wheel. Her back and legs felt stiff and achy.

Just as she had wedged herself back into the driver's seat, her mobile rang. Balancing her paper coffee cup in one hand, she grabbed the phone with the other and looked at the display. Patrik. She'd better let her voicemail take the call. She'd explain things later. Especially if she came home with something that might help the investigation. Then she could at least avoid some of the reproaches that she sensed were in the offing.

After one last glance at the map, she started up the car and pulled back onto the highway. It was a little more than seven years since Christian had lived at the address where she was now headed. She suddenly had some doubts. What were the odds that she'd find anything that Christian might have left there? People moved all the time without leaving any trace behind.

Erica sighed. Well, she was already here, and Göran was sure to offer her a cup of coffee before she drove back home. So the drive wouldn't have been totally in vain.

She heard a beep. Patrik had left a message on her mobile.

"Where is everybody?" Mellberg was still feeling groggy as he looked around. He'd dozed off for just a few minutes, and when he awoke the station was deserted. Had the others gone off to the café without asking his permission?

He rushed out to the reception area, where he found Annika.

"What's going on here? Does everybody think it's already the weekend? Why isn't anyone working? If they're over at the bakery, they're in for a reprimand when they get back. The municipality expects us to be on the job at all times, and we have an obligation" — he started waving his finger in the air — "to be here when our fellow citizens need us." Mellberg loved to hear the sound of his own voice, particularly when he adopted an authoritative tone.

Annika stared at him without saying a word. Mellberg began to fidget. He'd expected her to shower him with excuses and apologies on behalf of her colleagues. Instead, he suddenly had a most unpleasant feeling come over him.

After a moment, Annika said calmly:

"They were called out to Fjällbacka. A lot of things have happened while you were working in your office." She said the word "working" without a hint of sarcasm, but something told him that she was fully aware that he'd been taking a little siesta. So it was up to him to salvage the situation.

"Why didn't anyone tell me?"

"Patrik tried. He knocked on your door

for a long time. But you had locked the door, and there was no answer. Finally he was forced to leave."

"Er . . . yes, well, sometimes I get so immersed in my work that I don't hear a thing," said Mellberg, swearing to himself. Why did he have to be such a bloody sound sleeper? It was both a gift and a curse.

"Hmmm . . . ," replied Annika, turning back to her computer screen.

"So what's happened?" Mellberg demanded, still feeling that he'd been played for a fool.

Annika quickly gave him a summary of what had happened at Christian's house and to Kenneth on the jogging trail. Mellberg listened, openmouthed. Things were getting stranger and stranger.

"They'll be back soon; at least, Patrik and Paula will. They'll be able to tell you more of the details. Martin and Gösta drove down to Uddevalla to have a talk with Kenneth, so it might be a while before they get back."

"Tell Patrik to come and see me as soon as he gets in," said Mellberg. "And tell him to knock louder this time."

"Okay, I'll tell him. And I'll make sure that he does knock louder. In case you're engrossed in your work again."

Annika looked at him with a serious

expression, but Mellberg still couldn't shake the feeling that she was mocking him.

"Can't you come with us? Why do you have to stay here?" Sanna tossed a couple of shirts into her suitcase.

Christian didn't reply, which just made her more upset.

"Answer me! Why do you have to stay here all alone in the house? It's so crazy, so. . . ." Angrily she threw a pair of jeans at the suitcase, but she missed and they landed on the floor at Christian's feet. She went over to pick them up, but instead cupped his face in her hands. She tried to catch his eye, but he refused to look at her.

"Christian, sweetheart. I don't understand. Why won't you come with us? It's not safe for you to stay here."

"There's nothing to understand," he said, removing her hands. "I'm staying here, and that's all there is to it. I have no intention of running away."

"Running away from whom? From what? I hope to God you don't know who is doing this and you're just not telling us." Tears were streaming down her cheeks, and she could still feel the warmth of Christian's face on the palms of her hands. He never let her come close, and that stung. In situations like this, they ought to be able to support each other. But he was turning his back on her, refusing to let her in. Humiliation made Sanna's cheeks turn red, and she looked away. Then she went back to her packing.

"How long do you think we need to stay there?" she asked, stuffing into the suitcase a fistful of panties and stockings that she'd taken from the top drawer.

"How should I know?" Christian had taken off his bathrobe, washed the red paint from his chest, and put on jeans and a T-shirt. She still thought he was the handsomest man she'd ever seen. She loved him so much, it hurt.

Sanna closed the drawer and glanced out into the hall where the boys were playing. They were quieter than usual. More serious. Nils was pushing his cars back and forth, while Melker was making his action figures fight with each other. Both were playing without making the normal sound effects, and without quarreling, which almost never happened.

"Do you think they . . . ?" She started to cry again and had to start over. "Do you think they were harmed?"

"They don't have a scratch on them."

"I don't mean physically." Sanna couldn't

understand how Christian could be so cold, so calm. This morning he had seemed just as shocked, confused, and scared as she was. Now he was acting as if nothing had happened, or as if it were a mere trifle.

Someone had come into their home while they were asleep and gone into the boys' room. And now they might feel scared and unsafe forever after, no longer secure in the knowledge that nothing could happen to them when they were at home in their own beds. That nothing could happen when their parents were only a few yards away. That feeling of security might now be gone for good. Yet their father sat there, so calm and distant, as if he didn't care. And because of that, right now, at this particular moment, she hated him.

"Children forget so quickly," said Christian, looking down at his hands.

She saw that he had deep scratches on the palm of one hand, and she wondered how he'd gotten them. But she didn't ask. For once she didn't ask. Could it be that their marriage was over? If Christian couldn't let her in and love her even when something evil and horrible was threatening them, maybe it was time for her to give up.

She kept on tossing things into the suitcase, not caring what sort of clothes she was packing. Her tears made everything look blurry, and she simply grabbed whatever she could pull off the hangers. Finally the suitcase was filled to overflowing, and she had to sit on it to close it properly.

"Wait, let me help you." Christian got up and added his weight to the suitcase so that Sanna could close the zipper. "I'll take it downstairs." He grabbed the handle and carried it out of the room, past the boys.

"Why do we have to go to Aunt Agneta's? Why are we taking so many things with us? Are we going to be gone for a long time?" Melker sounded so anxious that Christian stopped halfway down the stairs. Then he continued on, without saying a word.

Sanna went over to her sons and squatted down next to them. She tried to sound calm as she said:

"Let's pretend that we're going on holiday. But we're not going far away, just over to visit your aunt and cousins. You usually think that's lots of fun. And I'll make you a special treat for dinner tonight. Since we're on holiday, you can have some sweets after dinner, even though it's not Saturday."

The boys looked at her a bit suspiciously at first, but the promise of sweets seemed to work magic. "Are we all going?" asked Melker, and then his brother repeated, with a slight lisp: "Are we all going?"

Sanna took a deep breath. "No, just the three of us. Papa has to stay here."

"That's right. Papa has to stay here and fight with those stupid people," said Melker.

"What stupid people?" said Sanna, patting his cheek.

"The people who messed up our room." He crossed his arms and looked angry. "If they come back, Papa can beat them up!"

"Papa isn't going to fight with any stupid people, because they're not coming back." She stroked Melker's hair, silently cursing Christian. Why wouldn't he go with them? Why didn't he say anything? She stood up.

"This is going to be so much fun. A real adventure. I just need to go and help Papa load everything in the car, then I'll come back and get you. Okay?"

"Okay," both boys said, but they didn't sound very enthusiastic. She could feel them watching her as she went downstairs.

She found Christian at the car, loading the suitcases in the trunk. Sanna went over to him and took him by the arm.

"This is your last chance, Christian. If you know something, if you have the slightest clue about who is doing these things to us, I beg you to tell me now. For our sake. If you don't tell me, and later I find out that

439

you did know something, then it's over. Do you understand? It's over!"

Christian stopped, the suitcase he was holding hovering halfway inside the trunk. For a moment she thought that he was really going to tell her something. Then he shook off her hand and dropped the suitcase inside.

"I don't know anything. Stop nagging me!"

He slammed the trunk shut.

When Patrik and Paula arrived back at the station, Annika stopped Patrik before he headed to his office.

"Mellberg woke up while all of you were gone. He was a bit upset that he hadn't been informed."

"I stood outside his office and pounded on the door, but he never opened it."

"That's what I told him, but he claimed that he must have been so engrossed in his work that he didn't hear you."

"Oh, right," said Patrik, noticing once again how sick and tired he was of his incompetent boss. But to be honest, it had been a relief not to have Mellberg in tow. He cast a quick glance at his watch. "Okay, I'll go and inform our honorable leader now. Let's meet in the kitchen for a quick briefing in fifteen minutes. Please tell Gösta and Martin too. They're on their way back right now."

He headed straight for Mellberg's office and loudly knocked on the door.

"Come in." Mellberg looked as if he were deeply immersed in studying a stack of documents. "I heard that things are heating up, and I must say that it doesn't look good for the police to respond to important emergency calls without the chief in attendance."

Patrik opened his mouth to reply, but Mellberg held up one hand. Apparently he wasn't done yet.

"It sends the wrong signal to the citizens if we don't take such situations seriously."

"But —"

"No, not another word. I accept your apology. Just don't do it again."

Patrik could feel his pulse hammering in his ears. The bastard! He clenched his fists, but then opened them again and took a deep breath. He had to try to ignore Mellberg and focus on what was important — i.e., the investigation.

"Tell me what happened. What have you found out?" Mellberg leaned forward eagerly.

"I was thinking we should all get together

for a meeting in the kitchen. If that works for you?" said Patrik, his jaw tight.

Mellberg thought for a moment. "That might actually be a good idea. Then we won't have to go over everything twice. All right, shall we get going, Hedström? Time is of the essence, you know, when it comes to this type of investigation."

Patrik turned his back on his boss and left the room. Mellberg was undeniably right about one thing. Time was of the essence.

All that mattered was to survive. But it required more effort with each year that passed. The move had been good for everyone but him. Father had found a job he enjoyed, and Mother liked living in the Old Bitch's house, remodeling it until the place was no longer recognizable since she had erased all trace of the woman. Alice seemed to be doing well in the calm and peaceful atmosphere in Fjäll-backa, at least for nine months of the year.

Mother was teaching her at home. At first Father had been against the idea, saying that Alice needed to get out and meet children her own age. She needed to be around other people. But Mother had merely looked at him and said in a cold voice:

"I'm the only one Alice needs."

That was the end of the discussion.

In the meantime, he kept getting fatter, and he was constantly eating. It was as if his craving for food had taken on a life of its own. He stuffed into his mouth everything he could get his hands on. But it no longer drew any attention from Mother. Occasionally she would cast a disgusted glance in his direction, but she mostly ignored him. It had been a long time since he'd thought of her as his beautiful mother and yearned for her love. He had given up, accepting the fact that he was someone that nobody could love; he didn't deserve to be loved.

The only person who loved him was Alice. And she was a monstrosity, just like him. She lurched about, slurring her words, and she couldn't manage even the most basic tasks. She was eight years old and couldn't even tie her shoes. She was always following him like a shadow. In the morning when he left to catch the school bus, she would sit in the window to watch him, the palms of her hands pressed against the glass and a wistful expression on her face. He didn't understand it, but he didn't try to make her stop.

School was a torment. Every morning when he got off the school bus, it felt like he was on his way to prison. He looked forward to the classes, but the rest filled him with terror. They were always after him, teasing and punching him, vandalizing his locker and yelling taunts at him in the school yard. He wasn't stupid; he knew that he was the perfect scapegoat.

His fat body made him guilty of the worst sin of all: he stood out. He understood it, but that didn't make things any easier.

"Can you find your dick when you have to piss, or does your stomach get in the way?"

Erik. Perched on one of the tables out in the schoolyard, where he was surrounded by a bunch of eager hangers-on, as usual. He was the worst of the lot. The most popular boy, handsome and self-confident. He talked back to the teachers and had ready access to cigarettes, which he smoked and also handed out to his followers. He didn't know who he detested most. Erik, who seemed driven by sheer wickedness and was always looking for new ways to hurt him. Or the sneering idiots who sat next to Erik, filled with admiration for their popular classmate and basking in his glory.

At the same time, he knew that he'd give anything to be one of them. To be allowed to sit on the table with Erik, accept the cigarette he offered, and comment on the girls going past, who would respond with delighted giggles and flushed cheeks.

"Hey! I'm talking to you. Answer me when I ask you a question!" Erik got down from the table, and the two others watched him with excitement. The athletic one, Magnus, actually met his eyes. Sometimes he thought he saw a glimpse of sympathy in the boy's expression, but if so, it wasn't enough to make Magnus risk falling out of favor with Erik. Kenneth was simply a coward and always avoided looking him in the eye. Right now he was staring at Erik, as if waiting to follow orders. But today Erik didn't seem to have the energy to cause any trouble, because he sat down again and said with a laugh:

"Get out of here, you disgusting fatso! If you hurry up and take off now, you won't get a beating today."

He wanted nothing more than to stand his ground and tell Erik to go to hell. With precise and powerful movements, he would give Erik such a thrashing that everyone standing around would realize that their hero was heading for a fall. Then with great effort Erik would lift his head up from the ground, with blood running from his nose, and look at him with new respect. After that, he would have a place in the group. He would belong.

Instead, he turned tail and ran. As fast as he could, he lumbered across the schoolyard. His chest hurt, and the rolls of fat on his body jiggled up and down. Behind him he could hear them laughing.

19

Erica drove past the roundabout at Korsvägen, with her heart in her throat. The traffic in Göteborg always made her nervous, and this particular junction was the worst. But she got through it without a problem and then drove slowly up Eklandagatan, looking for the street where she needed to turn.

Rosenhillsgatan. The block of apartments stood at the end of the street, facing Korsvägen and Liseberg. She checked the address and then parked her car right in front. She glanced at her watch. The plan was to ring the doorbell and hope that someone was at home. If not, she and Göran had agreed that she'd spend a couple of hours visiting with him and his mother before trying again. If that proved necessary, she wasn't going to get home until late in the evening, so she crossed her fingers that she'd be lucky enough to find the current tenant at home. She had memorized the name from the phone calls she'd made on her way to Göteborg, and she found it at once on the building intercom. Janos Kovács.

She pushed the button. No answer. She tried again, and then she heard a crackling sound, and a voice with a strong accent said: "Who is there?"

"My name is Erica Falck. I'd like to ask you a few questions about someone who used to live in your apartment. Christian Thydell." She waited tensely. Her explanation sounded a bit fishy, even to her own ears, but she hoped the man would be curious enough to let her in. A buzzing sound from the door showed that she was in luck.

The elevator stopped at the second floor, and she got out. One of the three doors was ajar, and peering at her through the gap was a short and slightly overweight man in his sixties. When he caught sight of her enormous belly, he lifted off the safety chain and opened the door wide.

"Come in, come in," he said earnestly.

"Thank you," said Erica and stepped inside. A heavy aroma from many years of cooking spicy food reached her nostrils, and she felt her stomach turn over. The smell wasn't really unpleasant, but her pregnancy had made her nose sensitive to particularly pungent odors.

"I have coffee. Good strong coffee." He pointed toward a small kitchen right across the hall. She followed him, casting a glance inside what appeared to be the only other room in the apartment, functioning as both living room and bedroom.

So it was here that Christian had lived before he moved to Fjällbacka. Erica felt her heart beating faster with anticipation.

"Sit." Janos Kovács more or less pushed her down onto a straight-backed chair and then served her coffee. With a triumphant whoop he set a big plate of small cakes in front of her.

"Poppyseed cakes. Hungarian specialty! My mother often sends me packages of poppyseed cakes because she knows that I love them. Have one." He motioned for her to help herself, so she took a cake from the plate and tentatively bit into it. Definitely a new taste, but good. She suddenly realized that she hadn't eaten anything since breakfast, and her stomach rumbled gratefully as she swallowed the first bite of cake.

"You're eating for two. Take another, take two, take as many as you want!" Janos Kovács pushed the plate closer to her, his eyes sparkling. "Big baby," he said with a smile as he pointed at her belly.

Erica smiled back. His good humor was infectious. "Well, I'm actually carrying two, you see."

"Ah, twins." He clapped his hands with delight. "What a blessing."

"Do you have children?" asked Erica, her mouth full of cake.

Janos Kovács lifted his chin and said proudly, "I have two fine sons. Grown up now. Both have good jobs. At Volvo. And I have five grandchildren."

"And your wife?" said Erica cautiously, glancing around. It didn't look as if any woman lived in the apartment. Kovács was still smiling, but his smile was not as bright.

"About seven years ago she came home one day and said 'I'm moving out.' And then she was gone." He threw out his hands. "That's when I moved here. We lived in this building, in a three-room apartment downstairs." He pointed to the floor. "But when I had to take early retirement, and my wife left me, I couldn't stay there anymore. And since Christian met a girl at the same time and was going to move, well, I moved in here. Everything turned out for the best," he exclaimed, looking as if he truly meant it.

"So you knew Christian before he moved?" asked Erica, sipping her coffee, which was delicious.

"Well, I wouldn't say that I really knew him. But we often ran into each other here in the building. I'm very handy." Kovács held up his hands. "So I help out when I can. And Christian couldn't even change a light bulb."

"I can imagine," said Erica, smiling.

"Do you know Christian? Why are you asking me questions about him? It was many years ago that he lived here. I hope nothing has happened to him."

"I'm a journalist," said Erica, assuming the role that she'd decided on during the drive to the city. "Christian is an author now, and I'm writing a big article about him, so I'm trying to find out a little about his background."

"Christian is an author? How about that! He always did have a book in his hand. And one whole wall in the apartment was covered with books."

"Do you know what he did when he lived here? Where he worked?"

Janos Kovács shook his head. "No, I don't know. And I never asked. It's important to respect a neighbor's privacy. Not get too nosy. If someone wants to talk about himself, he will."

That sounded like a healthy philosophy,

and Erica wished that more people in Fjäll-backa shared his attitude.

"Did he have a lot of visitors?"

"Never. I actually felt a little sorry for him. He was always alone. That's not good for people. We all need company."

He's certainly right about that, thought Erica, hoping that Janos Kovács himself had someone who came to visit now and then.

"Did he leave anything behind when he moved? Maybe in the storage room?"

"No, the apartment was empty when I moved in. There was nothing."

Erica decided to give up. Janos Kovács didn't seem to have any more information about Christian's life. She thanked him and then politely but firmly refused his offer to take a sack of poppyseed cakes home with her.

She was just stepping out the door when Kovács stopped her.

"Wait! I don't know how I could have forgotten. Maybe I'm starting to get a little senile." He tapped his finger on his temple, then turned around and went into the main room of the apartment. After a moment he came back, holding something in his hand.

"When you see Christian, could you give these to him? Tell him that I did as he said and threw out all the mail that came for him. But these . . . well, I thought it seemed a bit odd to toss them in the wastebasket. Considering that one or two have arrived every year since he moved out, it seems clear that someone is really trying to get ahold of him. I never did get Christian's new address, so I just put them aside. So if you wouldn't mind giving them to him with my greetings." He smiled cheerfully and handed her a bundle of white envelopes.

Erica felt her hands start to shake as she took them from Janos.

20

There was suddenly an echoing silence in the house. Christian sat down at the kitchen table and rested his head in his hands. His temples were throbbing, and the itching had started up again. His whole body was burning, and he felt a stinging sensation when he began rubbing the cuts on the palm of his hand. He closed his eyes and leaned forward, laying his cheek against the table-top. He tried to sink into the silence and push away the feeling that something was trying to crawl out of his skin.

A blue dress. It fluttered past under his eyelids. Disappeared and then came back. The child in her arms. Why didn't he ever see the child's face? It was blank and featureless. Had he ever been able to picture it properly? Or had the child always been overshadowed by his enormous love for her? He couldn't remember. It was so long ago.

He began to weep quietly, his tears slowly

making a little puddle on the table. Then the sobs came, rising up from his chest and pouring out until his whole body was shaking. Christian raised his head. He had to make the images go away, make her go away. Otherwise he would burst and fall apart. He let his head sink heavily back onto the table, letting his cheek strike the surface full force. He felt the wood against his skin, and he raised his head again and again, pounding it against the hard tabletop. Compared with the itching and the burning inside his body, the pain almost felt good. But it did nothing to get rid of the images. She stood there just as clearly, large as life, right in front of him. She smiled and held out her hand toward him, so close that she could have touched him if only she reached a bit farther.

Was that a sound from upstairs? Abruptly he stopped moving, with his head only an inch or two from the table, as if someone had suddenly pressed the pause button on the film of his life. He listened, not moving a muscle. Yes, he did hear something overhead. It sounded like faint footsteps.

Christian slowly sat up. His entire body was tensed, on high alert. Then he got up from his chair and as quietly as possible made his way to the stairs. Holding on to the banister, he started up, keeping close to the wall where the creaking would be less. Out of the corner of his eye he saw something fluttering, quickly slipping past upstairs in the hall. Or was he imagining things? It was gone now, and the house was again silent.

A step creaked underfoot, and he held his breath. If she was up there, she would know that he was coming. Was she waiting for him? He felt a strange calm settle over him. His family was gone now. She couldn't harm them anymore. He was the only one here; it was between the two of them, just as it had been from the beginning.

A child whimpered. Was it really a child? He heard it again, but now it was more like one of the many sounds that an old house makes. Christian slowly climbed a few more steps to reach the next floor. The hallway was empty. The only sound was his own breathing.

The door to the boys' room stood open. It was a mess inside. The techs from the police had made things even worse, with black spots from the fingerprint powder now covering the whole room. He sat down in the middle of the floor, facing the words written on the wall. At first glance, the paint still looked like blood. *You don't deserve them.*

He knew she was right. He didn't deserve them. Christian kept on staring at the words, letting the message sink into his consciousness. He needed to put everything right. Only he could make everything right. In silence he read the words again. He was the one she was after. And he knew where she wanted him to go. He would give her what she wanted.

"This is going to be a short meeting." Patrik reached for a paper towel from the kitchen roll on the counter to wipe his forehead. He was sweating like crazy. He must be in much worse shape than he thought. "Here's the situation: Kenneth Bengtsson is in the hospital. Gösta and Martin will tell us more about that in a minute." He gave them a nod. "And someone broke into Christian Thydell's house last night. Whoever it was didn't physically harm anyone, but they wrote a message in red paint on the wall in the children's room. Obviously, the whole family is in shock. We have to assume that we're dealing with someone who has a screw loose, and that means they're dangerous."

"Of course I would have liked to come along this morning when you were called out." Mellberg cleared his throat. "Unfortunately, I was not informed about what was happening."

Patrik chose to ignore him and went on, turning to look at Annika.

"Have you found out anything more about Christian's background?"

Annika hesitated. "Possibly, but I'd like to double-check a few things first."

"Do that," said Patrik, and then turned to Gösta and Martin. "What did you find out when you talked to Kenneth? And how is he, by the way?"

Martin glanced at Gösta, who motioned for him to start.

"His injuries aren't life-threatening, but according to his doctors, it's pure luck that he's still alive. The pieces of glass really cut up his arms and legs badly. If any of the glass had punctured a major artery, he would have died out there on the jogging trail."

"The question is: what did the perpetrator intend? Did he, or she, merely want to injure Kenneth? Or was it attempted murder?"

No one even tried to answer Patrik's question, so Martin continued:

"Kenneth said that it was generally known that he took the same route every morning, and at exactly the same time. So in that sense, we can treat everyone in Fjällbacka as suspects."

"But we shouldn't assume that whoever did this is from here. It could be someone who happens to be visiting," Gösta interjected.

"How would a visitor to the area know about Kenneth's morning routines? Doesn't it seem more likely that the perpetrator lives here?" asked Martin.

Patrik thought for a moment. "Well, I don't think we can rule out someone who doesn't live here. They may have been here just long enough to watch Kenneth for a few days and confirm that he's a creature of habit." Then he added: "What did Kenneth have to say about it? Does he have any idea what might be behind the attack?"

Gösta and Martin exchanged glances again, but this time Gösta did the talking.

"He says he doesn't have a clue, but both Martin and I got the impression that he's lying. He knows something, but for some reason he's keeping it to himself. He did use the word 'she' about the perpetrator."

"He did?" A deep furrow appeared between Patrik's eyebrows. "I got the same feeling when I talked to Christian — that he's hiding something. In Christian's case, his entire family seems to be in danger. And Kenneth is convinced that his wife was murdered, even though we haven't yet determined whether that's true or not. So why aren't they cooperating with us?"

"Christian didn't say anything either?" Gösta carefully pulled apart the two sections of a Ballerina cookie and licked off the filling. He slipped the vanilla half to Ernst, who lay at his feet under the table.

"No, I couldn't get anything out of him," said Patrik. "He was clearly in a state of shock. But he steadfastly maintains that he doesn't know who is doing these things, or why, and so far there's nothing to contradict him. Only a gut feeling I have, just like you had with Kenneth. And he stubbornly insists on staying in the house. Thankfully, he sent Sanna and the kids to stay with her sister Agneta in Hamburgsund. Hopefully they'll be safe there."

"Did the techs find anything of interest? You told them about the rag, didn't you? And the bottle?" asked Gösta.

"They were there quite a long time, at any rate. And yes, they took the items you found in the basement. Torbjörn said to tell you 'good job,' by the way. But as usual it's going to take a while before we have any concrete results. I plan to call Pedersen again and ask him to hurry things up a bit. I couldn't get ahold of him this morning. Hopefully they can get a move on with this investigation so that we'll have the postmortem reports very soon. Considering how things are starting to escalate, we can't afford to waste any more time."

"Let me know if you want me to phone him instead. Just to give the request a little more weight," said Mellberg.

"Thanks, but I'll try and do it myself. It'll be difficult, but I'll do my best."

"All right. Just so you know that I'm here to help. In any way I can," said Mellberg.

"Paula, what did Christian's wife say?" Patrik asked, turning to his colleague. They had driven back together from Fjällbacka, but he hadn't had time to ask about Sanna. His mobile phone had been ringing nonstop.

"I don't think she knows anything," said Paula. "She's very confused and upset. And scared. She doesn't think Christian knows who it was, but she hesitated a bit when she said that — which makes me suspect that she's not quite sure. It might be good to talk to her again under calmer circumstances, after the worst of the shock has worn off. By the way, I recorded our conversation, so you can listen to it yourself if you like. The tape is on my desk. Maybe you might pick up something I missed."

"Thanks," said Patrik again, but this time he meant it. Paula was always reliable, and it was great to have her on the investigative team.

He looked at the small group gathered in the kitchen. "All right, then, we're finished here. Annika, keep working on the background material and we'll check with you again in a couple of hours. I think I'll take Paula along and go to see Cia. We haven't made it out to her house yet today, and now it seems even more urgent, after what happened this morning. Magnus's death is somehow linked to all of this. That's one thing I know for certain."

Erica went to a café and ordered a coffee so she could sit in peace and quiet as she read the letters. She had no scruples about opening somebody else's mail. If Christian had been anxious to have those letters, he would have given Janos Kovács his new address, or had the post office forward them.

Her hands shook a bit as she set about slitting open the first envelope. She had put on a pair of thin leather gloves, which she always kept in her car. She had trouble getting the envelope open all the way, and when she tried using a table knife, she almost spilled her big latte over the rest of the letters. She quickly moved the glass a safe distance away.

She didn't recognize the handwriting on the envelope. It wasn't the same as the threatening letters she'd seen, and she thought it looked more like a man's script than a woman's. She pulled out the sheet of paper and unfolded it. She was surprised. She'd been expecting a letter, but instead she found herself looking at a child's drawing. She was holding it upside down, so now she turned it around to look at it properly. Two people, two stick figures. One big and one little. The big one was holding the smaller one's hand, and both of them looked happy. There were flowers around them, and the sun was shining from the upper right-hand corner. They were standing on a green line, that was apparently supposed to be grass. Above the big figure someone had printed "Christian" in scraggly letters. Over the smaller figure it said "Me."

Erica reached for her latte glass and took a sip. She could tell that the thick froth had left a milk mustache above her lip, and she absentmindedly wiped it off on the sleeve of her sweater. Who was "Me"? Who was the shorter person next to Christian?

She set down her glass and reached for the other envelopes, which she quickly slit open. She ended up with a small stack of drawings on the table in front of her. As far as she could tell, they had all been done by the same person. Each picture showed two figures: the tall Christian and the short "Me." Otherwise, the scene was different in each drawing. In one of them, the larger figure was standing on what looked like a beach, with the smaller figure's head and arms sticking out of the water. Another had buildings in the background, including a church. Only in the last picture were there more figures. But it was hard to tell exactly how many there were, because the scene was a hodgepodge of legs and arms. That drawing was also darker than the others, with no flowers or sun. The bigger figure had been banished to the left-hand corner. He no longer had a smiling mouth, and the little figure didn't look happy either. Another corner was covered with black lines. Erica squinted, trying to work out what they could be, but they were clumsily drawn, and it was impossible to know what they represented.

She glanced at her watch, suddenly realizing that she wanted to go home. There was something about the last drawing that made her feel sick to her stomach. She couldn't put her finger on why, but that particular picture had a deep effect on her.

With an effort, Erica got to her feet. She decided to skip paying a visit to Göran today. He would undoubtedly be disappointed, but they would just have to get together another time.

On the drive back to Fjällbacka, she couldn't help thinking about everything. The drawings kept flitting through her mind. The big figure of Christian and the smaller "Me." She knew instinctively that this "Me" was the key to everything. And there was only one person who could tell her who it was. First thing tomorrow, she would go and have a talk with Christian. This time he would have to answer her questions.

"What a coincidence. I was just about to give you a call." Pedersen's voice was as dry and correct as always. But Patrik knew that under the laconic façade there was a sense of humor. He'd actually heard Pedersen make a joke on a few occasions, although it didn't happen often.

"Is that so? Well, I was just wondering whether I could hurry you up a bit. We need information. Anything you can give us might help us to move forward with the investigation."

"I'm not sure how helpful I can be. But I did take it upon myself to put a rush on the postmortems pertaining to your case. We completed our report on Magnus Kjellner late last night, and I just finished with Lisbet Bengtsson."

Patrik suddenly pictured Pedersen talking to him on the phone while clad in blood-stained scrubs and wearing surgical gloves.

"So what's the verdict?"

"Let's start with the obvious: Kjellner was definitely murdered. I could have reached that conclusion just from a cursory visual examination, but you never know. Over the years I've encountered a number of cases where the individual died from perfectly natural causes, and then ended up getting injured after death."

"But that's not the case in this instance?"

"No, absolutely not. The victim had a number of stab wounds on the chest and stomach which were made by a sharp instrument, probably a knife. That was without a doubt what killed him. The attack came from the front, and he also had classic defense wounds on his hands and forearms."

"Are you able to tell what sort of knife

was used?"

"I'd prefer not to speculate, but, judging by the injuries, I can say that it had to be a knife with a smooth blade. And. . . ." He paused for effect. "I'd guess that it was some kind of fish knife," Pedersen said with satisfaction.

"How can you tell?" asked Patrik. "There must be a million different kinds of knives."

"You're right. And I can't prove that it was an actual fish knife. But I do know that it was a knife that had been used to clean fish."

"Okay, but how do you know that?" Patrik was feeling impatient, and he wished that Pedersen wasn't so fond of injecting drama into his reports. The medical examiner already had his full attention.

"I found fish scales," said Pedersen.

"You did? But how could they still be inside the body after it was in the water so long?" Patrik could feel his pulse quicken. He wanted so badly to hear something, anything at all, that would give them a lead so they'd know what direction to take.

"Probably a lot did disappear in the water. But I found several scales embedded deep in the wounds. I've sent them to the lab to see if the type of fish can be determined. I hope that might be useful to you."

"It's possible," said Patrik, although he thought the information was basically unimportant. This was Fjällbacka, after all. A community in which fish scales were a regular part of daily life.

"Anything more about Kjellner?"

"Not really." Pedersen sounded a bit disappointed that Patrik wasn't more enthusiastic about his find. "He was stabbed to death and presumably died instantly. He seems to have bled a great deal. The crime scene must have looked like a slaughterhouse."

"Was his body tossed into the water right afterwards?"

"Impossible to know," replied Pedersen. "The only thing I can tell you is that he'd been in the water a long time, and it seems most likely that his body was dumped there soon after he died. But that's based more on how the killer would most likely react, and not on any scientific evidence. So it'll be hard to prove. I'll fax over my report, as usual."

"What about Lisbet? What did you decide about her?"

"She died of natural causes."

"Are you sure?"

"I performed a very meticulous postmortem on her body." Now Pedersen sounded insulted.

"So you're saying that she wasn't murdered?"

"That's correct," replied Pedersen, still a bit miffed. "To be quite honest, it was a small miracle that she lived as long as she did. The cancer had spread to all the vital organs in her body. Lisbet Bengtsson was a very sick woman. She simply passed away in her sleep."

"So Kenneth was wrong," Patrik murmured to himself.

"What did you say?"

"It's nothing. I was just thinking out loud. Thanks for giving our case priority. We need all the help we can get at the moment."

"It's that bad?" asked Pedersen.

"Yes, it really is that bad."

He and Alice had something in common. They both loved summertime. In his case, it was because he was out of school and free from his tormenters. For Alice, it was because she could go swimming in the sea. She spent every possible minute in the water. Swimming back and forth and tumbling about. All the awkwardness that her body displayed on land instantly disappeared as soon as she slipped into the water. There she could move about unhindered and with ease.

Mother would sit and watch her for hours, clapping her hands at her daughter's tricks in the water and encouraging her to practice her swimming. She called Alice her mermaid.

But Alice didn't care much about her mother's enthusiasm. Instead, she would look toward him and call:

"Watch this!" Then she would dive off the rocks, and when she resurfaced, she would smile.

"Did you see that? Did you see what I did?" she'd ask eagerly, giving him that hungry look of hers. But he never answered. Just glanced up for a moment from the book he was reading as he sat on a towel that he'd spread out on the flat rocks. He didn't know what she wanted from him.

Mother used to reply in his stead, after first casting an annoyed and astonished look in his direction. She didn't understand it. She was the one who gave all her time and love to Alice.

"I saw it, sweetie! That was wonderful!" she would shout. But it was as if Alice didn't hear her mother's voice. Then she would call to him again:

"Watch me now! Watch what I can do!" And she would start swimming the crawl, heading toward the horizon. The movement of her arms was perfectly coordinated and rhythmic.

Mother would stand up, looking nervous. "Alice, sweetie, don't go any farther than that." She held up one hand to shade her eyes.

"She's swimming too far out. Go get her!"

He tried to be like Alice and pretend that he hadn't heard. Slowly he turned the page, focusing on the words, the black type on the white paper. Then he felt a burning pain on his scalp. Mother had taken a firm grip on his hair and was pulling as hard as she could. He

471

sprang to his feet, and she let go.

"Go get your sister. Move that fat ass of yours and make sure she swims back to shore."

For a moment he remembered her hand holding his that time when they went swimming together — the way she had let go, and he had been dragged under. Ever since that day, he hadn't liked to swim. There was something terrifying about the water. There were things below the surface that he couldn't see and didn't trust.

Mama grabbed ahold of the roll of fat around his waist and squeezed hard.

"Go get her. Now. Otherwise I'll leave you here when we go home." The tone of her voice gave him no choice. He knew that she meant it. If he didn't do as she said, she really would leave him here on this island.

With his heart pounding, he headed for the water. It took all his willpower to make his feet move forward and then jump in. He didn't dare dive in head first, like Alice; he simply dropped feet first into the blue and green. He got water in his eyes and had to blink so he could see again. He felt panic coming over him. His breathing was fast and shallow. He squinted. Far away, moving toward the sun, was Alice. Clumsily he started swimming in her direction. He could feel his mother watching, standing on the rocks behind him with her hands on her hips.

He couldn't swim the crawl. His strokes were uneven and choppy. But he kept moving forward, the whole time aware of the depths beneath him. The sun dazzled his eyes, and he could no longer see Alice. He saw only the white, blinding light that brought tears to his eyes. All he wanted to do was turn around, but he couldn't. He had to reach Alice and make her go back to Mother. Because Mother loved Alice, and he loved Mother. In spite of everything, he loved her.

Suddenly he felt something around his neck. Something holding on hard, pulling his head underwater. Now panic really set in, and he flailed his arms, trying to escape and get back up to the surface. Then the pressure around his neck was gone as swiftly as it had appeared, and he gasped for breath as he felt the air on his face.

"It's just me, stupid."

Alice was treading water without any effort at all, looking at him with those bright eyes of hers. The dark hair that she'd inherited from Mother gleamed in the sun, and salt water glittered on her lashes.

He saw those eyes again. The eyes staring up at him from under the water. The body was limp and lifeless, not moving, just resting on the bottom of the bathtub. He shook his head, not wanting to see those images.

"Mother wants you to come back," he said, out of breath. He couldn't tread water as easily as Alice could, and his heavy body was being tugged downward, as if weights were attached to his limbs.

"Then you'll have to tow me in," said Alice in that special way of hers, as if her tongue couldn't find the right place in her mouth when she spoke.

"I can't do that. Come on, now."

She laughed and tossed back her wet hair.

"I'll only come if you tow me."

"But you swim much better than I do. Why should I have to tow you?" But he knew that he'd lost the argument. He motioned for her to put her arms around his neck again. Now that he knew it was her, he didn't panic.

He started swimming. It was slow going, but he managed. Alice's arms felt strong around his neck. She had swum so much all summer that she had visibly developed muscles in her upper arms. She hung on to him, letting him tow her to shore like a little skiff. She rested her cheek against his back.

"I'm your mermaid," she said. "Not Mama's."

21

"I don't really know. . . ." Cia was staring at a spot behind Patrik's shoulder, and he noticed that the pupils of her eyes were big. He assumed that she'd been given some sort of sedative that was contributing to her distracted air.

"I know we keep asking you the same questions over and over. But we need to find the connection between Magnus's death and what happened today. It's even more important now that we've determined that Magnus really was murdered. It might be something that you haven't thought about before, some tiny detail that could help us move forward," Paula pleaded with her.

Ludvig came sauntering into the kitchen and sat down next to Cia. Presumably he'd been listening from outside the room.

"We want to help," he said, his voice somber. The look in his eyes made him seem much older than his thirteen years.

"How are Sanna and the children?" asked Cia.

"They had a bad shock, of course," said Patrik.

On their drive to Fjällbacka, Patrik and Paula had discussed whether they should tell Cia about what had happened. She didn't need any more bad news at the moment. At the same time, they really did have to tell her, because she'd hear about it soon enough from friends and acquaintances. And maybe these new events would make her recall something she'd forgotten.

"Who would do such a thing? And to children . . . ," she said, her voice sounding both compassionate and hollow. The sedative was blunting her emotions, making things less overwhelming. Less painful.

"We don't know," Patrik told her. His words seemed to echo in the kitchen.

"And Kenneth . . ." she shook her head.

"That's why we have to ask you these questions. Someone has targeted Kenneth and Christian and Erik. And most likely Magnus too," said Paula.

"But Magnus never received any letters. Not like the ones the others got."

"We know that. But we still think that his death is linked to the threats against the others," said Paula.

"What do Erik and Kenneth say? Don't they know what it's about? Or Christian? One of them ought to have some idea," said Ludvig. He had put his arm protectively around his mother's shoulders.

"You'd think so, yes," said Patrik. "But they all say that they haven't a clue."

"Then how could I. . . ." Cia's voice faded away.

"Did anything strange ever happen in all the years you were together? Anything that you reacted to? Anything at all?" asked Patrik.

"No, there was never anything unusual. I've already told you that." She took a deep breath. "Magnus, Kenneth, and Erik have known each other since they were schoolboys. From the very beginning, it was always the three of them who stuck together. I never thought Magnus had much in common with the other two, but they probably stayed friends out of force of habit. There aren't many new people to make friends with here in Fjällbacka."

"What was their relationship like?" Paula leaned forward.

"What do you mean?"

"Well, all relationships have a certain dynamic, with each person taking on a different role. So what was their friendship like, before Christian came into the picture?"

Cia paused to think, her expression serious. Then she said:

"Erik was always the leader. The one who decided. Kenneth was . . . the lapdog. That sounds mean, but he obeys the slightest command from Erik, and I've always pictured him as a little dog, wagging his tail and begging for attention from Erik."

"What about Magnus?" asked Patrik.

Cia paused again before answering. "I know that he thought Erik could be a real bully, and occasionally he'd tell him that he'd gone too far. Unlike Kenneth, Magnus was able to speak up and make Erik listen."

"Did they ever quarrel?" Patrik went on. He had a strong feeling that the answer lay in the past of these four men, and in their relationship to each other. But it seemed to be buried very deep, and it was proving difficult to bring whatever it was out into the light. The whole thing was driving him crazy.

"Well, I suppose they argued once in a while, the way people do when they've known each other a long time. Erik can get a bit hot-tempered. But Magnus was always so calm. I've never seen him flare up or even raise his voice. Not once, in all the years we were together. And Ludvig is just like his

478

father." She turned to her son and stroked his cheek. He smiled at her, but he seemed to be thinking about something.

"I once saw Papa get upset. With Kenneth."

"You did? When?" Cia asked in surprise.

"Don't you remember the summer when Papa bought the video camera, and I was running around filming things all the time?"

"Oh, yes. Dear God, you were a real pest. You even went into the bathroom and started filming Elin sitting on the toilet. Your life was hanging by a thread when you pulled that stunt." Her eyes brightened, and a smile brought some color to her cheeks.

Ludvig stood up so abruptly that his chair almost toppled over backwards.

"I've got an idea. I want to show you something!" He was already on his way out of the kitchen. "Go in the living room. I'll be right back."

They heard him running up the stairs. Patrik and Paula got up to do as he'd asked. After a moment, Cia followed suit.

"Here it is." Ludvig had come back downstairs, holding a small cassette in one hand and a video camera in the other.

He got out a cord and attached the camera to the TV. Patrik and Paula watched him in silence. Patrik could feel his pulse starting to quicken.

"What are you going to show us?" asked Cia, sitting down on the sofa.

"You'll see," said Ludvig. He put in the videocassette and pressed the PLAY button. Suddenly Magnus's face filled the screen. They heard Cia gasp, and Ludvig turned around, looking worried.

"Are you okay, Mama? Otherwise you could go wait in the kitchen."

"It's okay," she said, but her eyes filled with tears as she stared at the TV.

Magnus was clowning around, making faces and talking to the person holding the camera.

"I filmed the whole Midsummer Eve party," said Ludvig quietly, and Patrik saw that his eyes were tearful too. "Watch, here come Erik and Louise," he said, pointing.

Erik came through the patio door and waved to Magnus. Louise and Cia hugged, and Louise handed a package to her hostess.

"I need to fast-forward. It's further along," said Ludvig, pressing a button on the video camera so the film began speeding ahead. They watched dusk fall, and then it got darker.

"You thought we'd gone to bed," said Ludvig to his mother. "But we sneaked out

480

and eavesdropped on what you were saying. You were all drunk and acting silly, and we thought it was hilarious."

"Ludvig!" said Cia, embarrassed.

"But you were drunk," her son repeated. And judging by all the commotion, Ludvig had certainly captured their condition on the video. Loud voices and laughter were heard through the summertime dusk; it sounded as if the party was a good one.

Cia tried to say something, but Ludvig held his finger to his lips.

"Shh, we're almost there."

They all stared at the screen without speaking. The only sound was the noise of the party from the video they were watching. Then two people got up, picked up their plates, and came toward the house.

"Where were you hiding?" asked Patrik.

"In the playroom. It was perfect. I could shoot through the window." He put his finger to his lips again. "Listen."

Two voices, separated a bit from the others. Both sounded upset. Patrik gave Ludvig an enquiring glance.

"Papa and Kenneth," Ludvig explained without taking his eyes off the TV. "They slipped away to have a smoke."

"I think Papa had stopped smoking by

then," said Cia, leaning forward to see better.

"Sometimes he'd have a cigarette or two, at parties and things like that. Didn't you ever notice?" Ludvig paused the tape so their talk wouldn't interrupt.

"He did?" said Cia in dismay. "I didn't know that."

"Well, on this occasion at any rate, he and Kenneth went around the corner to have a smoke." He pointed the remote control at the screen and started the tape rolling again.

Two voices. It was very hard to distinguish one from the other.

"Do you ever think about it?" That was Magnus.

"What are you talking about?" said Kenneth, slurring his words.

"You know what I mean." Magnus also sounded very drunk.

"I don't want to talk about that."

"But we have to talk about it sometime," said Magnus. There was something pleading, almost vulnerable in his voice that made the hairs on Patrik's arms stand on end.

"Who says we have to? What's done is done."

"But I don't know how we can live with it. For God's sake, we have to. . . ." The rest of the sentence disappeared in an inaudible mumble.

Then Kenneth spoke again. Now he sounded annoyed. But there was something else in his voice. Fear.

"Pull yourself together, Magnus! It won't do any good to talk about it. Think of Cia and the children. And Lisbet."

"I know, but what the hell should I do? Sometimes I can't help thinking about it, and then in here it feels like. . . ." It was too dark to see what he was pointing at.

After that, it was impossible to make out any more of the conversation. They lowered their voices, mumbling their words, and then went back to join the others. Ludvig pressed the pause button and froze the image of two shadowy figures, seen from the back.

"Did your father ever see this?" asked Patrik.

"No, I kept it to myself. Usually he was the one in charge of the videocassettes, but I shot this one on the sly, so I hid it in my room. I have a few more in the wardrobe."

"And you've never seen this before?" Paula sat down next to Cia, who was staring at the TV, her mouth agape.

"No," she said. "No."

"Do you know what they were talking

about?" asked Paula, placing her hand on Cia's.

"I . . . no." Her eyes were fixed on the dark figures of Magnus and Kenneth. "I have no idea."

Patrik believed her. Whatever it was that Magnus was talking about, he had kept it well hidden from his wife.

"Kenneth must know," said Ludvig. He pressed the stop button, took out the cassette, and placed it back in its holder.

"I'd like to borrow that," said Patrik.

Ludvig hesitated for a moment before he put the cassette in Patrik's outstretched hand.

"You won't wreck it, will you?"

"I promise that we'll take good care of it. And you'll get it back in the same shape it's in right now."

"Are you going to talk to Kenneth about it?" asked Ludvig, and Patrik nodded.

"Yes, we are."

"Why hasn't he mentioned anything about this before?" Cia sounded confused.

"That's what we'd like to know too." Paula patted her hand again. "And we're going to find out."

"Thank you, Ludvig," said Patrik, holding up the cassette. "This might turn out to be important."

"You're welcome. I just happened to think of it because you asked if they'd ever quarreled." He blushed to the roots of his hair.

"Shall we go?" Patrik said to Paula, who stood up. To Ludvig he added in a low voice, "Take care of your mother. Call me if you need anything." And he pressed his business card into the boy's hand.

Ludvig stood in the doorway, watching the police officers drive away. Then he closed the door and went inside.

Time passed slowly in the hospital. The TV was on, showing an American soap opera. The nurse had come in and asked Kenneth if he'd like her to change the channel. But when he didn't answer, she had left.

The loneliness was worse than he'd ever imagined. His grief was so great that the only thing he could manage was to focus on his breathing.

And he knew that she would come. She had waited a long time, and now there was nowhere to run to. But he wasn't afraid; he welcomed her appearance. It would rescue him from the loneliness and the sorrow that were tearing him apart. He wanted to go to Lisbet so he could explain what had happened. He hoped she would understand that he had been a different person back then, and it was because of her that he had changed. He couldn't bear the thought that she had died with his sins before her eyes. That weighed on him more than anything else, making each breath an effort.

He heard a knock on the door, and Patrik Hedström, the police officer, came into his field of vision. Behind him was a short, dark-haired female colleague.

"Hi, Kenneth. How are you feeling?" Hedström had a serious expression on his face. He went to get two chairs and brought them over to the bed.

Kenneth didn't reply. He just kept looking at the TV. The actors were performing in front of a background of poorly constructed stage sets. Patrik repeated his question, and finally Kenneth turned his head toward his visitors.

"I've felt better." What was he supposed to say? How could he describe what it really felt like? How it burned and stung inside of him, how it felt like his heart was about to burst? Any answer would sound like a cliché.

"Our colleagues have already been here to see you today. You met with Gösta and Martin earlier." Kenneth saw Patrik glancing at his bandages, as if trying to imagine what it must have felt like to have hundreds of glass shards piercing his skin.

"Right," said Kenneth listlessly. He hadn't said anything then, and he wasn't going to say anything now. He was just going to wait. For her.

"You told them that you didn't know who could be behind what happened this morning." Patrik looked at him, and Kenneth stubbornly met his gaze.

"That's right."

The police officer cleared his throat. "We don't think you're telling the truth."

What had they found out? Suddenly Kenneth panicked. He didn't want them to know, didn't want them to find her. She had to finish what she'd begun. That was his only salvation. If he paid the price for what he'd done, he would be able to explain it to Lisbet.

"I don't know what you're talking about." He looked away, but he knew they'd seen the fear in his eyes. Both of the officers had noticed. They took it as a sign of weakness, as an opportunity to get at him. They were mistaken. He had everything to win and nothing to lose by keeping silent. For a moment he thought about Erik and Christian. Above all, Christian. He'd been dragged into this even though he was not to blame. Not like Erik. But he couldn't take the others into consideration. Lisbet was the only one who mattered.

"We've just paid a visit to Cia. We saw a video that was taken at a Midsummer party at their house." Patrik seemed to be expecting a reaction, but Kenneth had no idea what he was talking about. His old life, with parties and friends, now seemed so far away.

"Magnus was drunk, and the two of you slipped away to have a smoke. It seemed that you wanted to make sure no one could hear you."

He still didn't understand what Patrik was getting at. Everything was a hazy blur. Nothing was distinct or clear any more.

"Magnus's son, Ludvig, filmed the two of you without your knowledge. Magnus was upset. He wanted to talk to you about something that had happened. You got annoyed with him and said that what was done was done. You told him to think about his family. Do you remember any of this?"

Oh yes, Kenneth did remember. It was still a bit vague, but he recalled how he had felt when he saw the panic in Magnus's eyes. He could never work out why the topic had come up on that particular evening. Magnus had been aching to talk about it, to make amends. And that had scared him. He had thought about Lisbet, about what she would say, how she would look at him.

Finally he'd been able to calm Magnus down — that much he remembered. But from that moment on, he had expected something to happen that would make everything crack wide open. And that's exactly what had happened, only not in the way he'd imagined. Because even in the worst possible scenarios he had pictured in his mind, Lisbet had still been alive to reproach him. Leaving always a slim chance that he'd be able to explain. Now things were different, and justice would have to be done for him to be able to explain. He couldn't let the police ruin his chances.

So he shook his head, pretending that he was trying to recall.

"No, I don't remember that."

"We can arrange for you to watch the tape, if that might jog your memory," said Paula.

"Sure, I can look at it. But I can't imagine that it was anything important, or I would have remembered. It was probably just drunken rambling. Magnus got like that once in a while when he was drinking. Melodramatic and sentimental. Trivial matters got blown all out of proportion."

He could see that they didn't believe him, but it didn't matter, because they couldn't read his mind. The secret would come out sooner or later — he knew that too. The police wouldn't give up until they found out everything. But that didn't have to happen until she came to give him what he deserved.

The officers stayed a little while longer, but it was easy to fend off their questions. He wasn't about to do their job for them; he had to think of himself and Lisbet. Erik and Christian would have to manage on their own as best they could.

Before leaving, Patrik looked at him kindly and said: "We also wanted to tell you that we received the report from Lisbet's postmortem. She wasn't murdered. She died of natural causes."

Kenneth turned his face away. He knew they were wrong.

Patrik was on the verge of falling asleep as they headed back to Uddevalla. For a moment, his eyes actually fell shut and he drove into the oncoming lane.

"What are you doing!" cried Paula, grabbing the wheel to steer the car back where it belonged.

Patrik gave a start and gasped.

"Bloody hell! I don't know what's going on. I'm just so tired."

Paula looked at him with concern. "Okay,

let's head over to your house, and I'll drop you off there. And tomorrow you need to stay home. You don't look well."

"I can't do that. I've got lots of things to do." He blinked his eyes, trying to focus on the road.

"All right, here's what we're going to do right now," said Paula firmly. "Turn in at the next gas station and we'll change places. I'll drive you home, and then I'll go to the office and pick up all the materials you need and bring them back to Fjällbacka. I'll also make sure the videocassette is sent to the lab for analysis. But you have to promise to take it easy. You've been working too much, and I'm sure it's been tough at home too. I know how hard it was for Johanna when she was expecting Leo, and I'm sure you're having to carry an extra-heavy load right now."

Patrik nodded reluctantly and did as she said. He turned in at the gas station at the Hogstorp exit and got out of the car. He was simply too worn out to argue. It was actually impossible for him to take a day off, or even a couple of hours, but his body refused to cooperate. If he could just get some rest and have time to go through all the documentation, maybe he'd regain some of the energy he needed to proceed with the investigation.

Patrik leaned his head against the window on the passenger side and had almost dozed off even before Paula pulled out onto the highway. When he opened his eyes, they were parked in front of his house. Feeling groggy, he climbed out.

"Go on in and lie down. I'll be back in an hour. Don't lock the door, so I can leave the papers for you inside," said Paula.

"Okay. Thanks." That was all he could manage to say.

Patrik opened the door and went in.

"Erica!"

No answer. He had phoned her in the afternoon, but hadn't been able to get ahold of her. Maybe she'd gone over to Anna's house and had ended up staying a while. For safety's sake, he decided to leave her a note on the bureau in the front hall, just so she wouldn't get scared if she came home and heard somebody in the house. Then he walked numbly up the stairs and fell into bed. He was asleep as soon as his head hit the pillow. But it was not a deep or restful sleep.

Something was about to change. Louise couldn't say that she liked her life as it had been over the past few years, but at least it was familiar. With the coldness, the indifference, the exchange of caustic and well-rehearsed remarks.

Now she could feel the ground under her feet starting to shake, and the cracks were getting wider. During their last argument, she'd seen a sense of finality in Erik's eyes. His disdain wasn't new, and it no longer really affected her, but this time something was different. And it scared her more than she'd ever imagined was possible. Because deep in her heart, she had always believed that they would continue to dance this dance of death with ever-greater elegance.

He had reacted strangely when she mentioned Cecilia. Usually he didn't care if she talked about his mistresses. He just pretended not to hear her. Why had he become so angry this morning? Was it a sign that Cecilia actually meant something to him?

Louise drained her glass. She was already having a hard time gathering her thoughts. Everything was wrapped in a pleasant woolliness, in the warmth spreading through her limbs. She poured herself more wine, looking out of the window across the ice that embraced the islands, while her hand as if of its own accord raised the glass to her lips.

She had to find out what was going on. Whether the cracks beneath her feet were real or imagined. But one thing she knew for sure: if the dance was about to end, it wouldn't happen with a quiet pirouette. She was planning to dance with stomping feet and flailing arms until there were only crumbs left of their marriage. She didn't want him, but that didn't mean she was planning to let him go.

Maja had not come away without protest when Erica went to pick her up at Anna's house. She was having too much fun playing with her cousins to want to go home willingly. But after a little negotiating, Erica managed to get her daughter into her outdoor garments and settled in the car. She thought it was a bit odd that she hadn't heard from Patrik, but she hadn't taken the time to phone him either. She hadn't yet worked out how she was going to explain her expedition to Göteborg. But she was going to have to say something, because she needed to hand over the drawings to Patrik at once. Something told her that they were important and that the police should see them. Above all, they needed to talk to Christian about the pictures. She had to admit that she was actually eager to do that herself, but she knew that she'd already gone too far by making the trip to Göteborg. She couldn't go behind Patrik's back again.

As she pulled into the drive in front of their house, she saw in the rear-view mirror that a police car was not far behind. That must be Patrik, she thought. But why wasn't he driving his own car? She lifted Maja out of the car seat as she cast a glance at the vehicle, which drove up and parked nearby. She was surprised to see Paula in the car instead of Patrik.

"Hi, where's Patrik?" asked Erica.

"He's in the house," said Paula, getting out of the car. "He was so tired that I ordered him to go home and get some rest. I know I was overstepping my authority, but he didn't offer any objections." She laughed, but the laugh didn't chase away the concern in her eyes.

"Is something wrong?" asked Erica, suddenly seized by misgiving. As far as she knew, Patrik had never come home early from work like this.

"No, no. I think he's just been working too hard lately. He looks a bit run-down. So I managed to convince him that he's no good to anyone if he doesn't get some rest."

"And he agreed? Just like that?"

"Well, we compromised. He agreed as long as I drove back to the station and picked up the materials he wants to look at. I was just going to leave them inside the door, but now I can give them to you." And she handed a paper sack to Erica.

"Okay, that sounds more like Patrik," said Erica, feeling immediately calmer. If he couldn't stop working, that meant that his health couldn't be all that bad.

She thanked Paula and lugged the sack into the front hall. Maja scampered after her. Erica smiled when she saw the note that Patrik had left for her on the bureau. He knew that she would have been scared to death if she hadn't known he was home and suddenly heard someone moving about upstairs.

Maja began to cry with frustration because she couldn't get her shoes off. Erica hurried to hush her.

"Shhh, sweetie. Papa is asleep upstairs. We don't want to wake him."

Maja stared at her, wide-eyed, and put her finger to her lips. "Shhh," she said loudly as she peeked up the stairs. Erica helped her take off her shoes and outdoor clothes. Then Maja ran inside to play with her toys, which were scattered all over the living-room floor.

Erica took off her jacket and tugged at her shirt a bit. She was always sweating these days. She had a deep-seated aversion to the smell of sweat, so she changed her shirt two or three times a day. She also applied such a generous amount of deodorant under her arms that Nivea must have experienced a noticeable upswing in sales during her pregnancy.

She cast a glance upstairs. Then she looked at the paper sack that Paula had left. Again she looked upstairs, then at the sack. She was waging an inner battle, even though she honestly knew beforehand that it was a battle doomed to failure. A temptation like this was too much to resist.

An hour later, she had gone through all the documents in the sack, but she felt none the wiser. In fact, even more questions had piled up. Among the documents, she'd also found notes that Patrik had made: What is the link between the four men? Why did Magnus die first? Why was he upset the morning that he disappeared? Why did he phone to say he'd be late? Why did Christian start getting letters so much earlier than the others? Did Magnus ever receive any letters? If not, why not? Page after page of questions, and it bothered Erica that she didn't know the answer to a single one of them. And she had questions of her own to add: Why did Christian move without leaving his new address? Who sent the drawings to him? Who was the little figure in the pictures? And above all: Why was Christian so secretive about his past?

Erica made sure that Maja was still busy playing with her toys before she went back to the investigative materials. The only thing left was an unmarked cassette tape. She got up from the sofa to get out her tape recorder. Luckily it was the right kind of tape for the player. She cast a nervous glance up at the ceiling before she pressed the PLAY button, turning down the volume as much as possible and then holding the tape recorder up to her ear.

The tape lasted twenty minutes, and she listened tensely to the whole thing. What she heard didn't really tell her any new information. But there was one thing that made her suddenly freeze, and she pressed REWIND to listen to it again.

After she was done with the tape, she carefully removed the cassette from the player and put it back in its case, which she then placed in the paper sack along with everything else. Having spent several years interviewing people for her books, she was good at catching details and nuances in a conversation. What she had just heard was important. She was sure of that.

She would have to deal with it tomorrow

morning. Right now she could hear Patrik moving around upstairs, and with greater speed than she'd been able to muster for several months, she returned the sack to the front hall, went back to the sofa, and tried to look as if she were deeply engrossed in playing with Maja.

Darkness had settled over the house. He hadn't switched on any lights; it seemed pointless to do so. At the end of the road, lights weren't necessary.

Christian was sitting semi-nude on the floor, staring at the wall. He had painted over her words. In the basement he'd found a brush and a can of black paint. Three times he had painted the black over the red. Three times he had blotted out her judgment of him. Yet he still thought he could see the words as clearly as before.

He had paint smeared on his hand and his body. Black as tar. He looked at his right hand. It was sticky, and he wiped it off on his chest, but the black just seemed to spread.

She was waiting for him now. He had known that all along. All he had done was postpone things, fooling himself and almost dragging his sons into the trap. The message was clear. *You don't deserve them.*

He saw the child carried in the arms of the woman he had loved. Suddenly he wished that he could have loved Sanna. He had never meant her any harm, yet he had betrayed her. Not with other women, the way Erik frequently did, but in the worst imaginable way. Because he knew that Sanna loved him, and he'd always given her just enough to allow her to live with the hope that someday he might love her — even though that was an impossibility. It was something he was no longer capable of. It had disappeared with the blue dress.

The boys were a different story. They were his flesh and blood and the reason why he had to let her take him. It was the only way to save his sons, and he should have understood that before things went so far. He shouldn't have told himself that it was all just a bad dream, and that he was safe. That they were safe.

It had been a mistake to come back, to try again. But it had seemed like such an irresistible temptation to return here and be so close. He didn't really understand it himself, but he'd felt an urge to return from the moment the opportunity presented itself. And he had thought that there might be a second chance for him. A second chance to have a family, as long as he kept them at a distance and chose a wife who meant very little to him. But he was wrong.

The words on the wall told the truth. He loved the boys, but he didn't deserve them. He hadn't deserved the other child either, or the woman whose lips tasted of strawberries. And they had paid the price. This time he would see to it that he was the one who paid.

Christian slowly stood up and looked around the room. A ragged-looking teddy bear sat in one corner. It had been a present to Nils when he was born, and he had loved it so hard that by now it had lost almost all its fur. Melker's action figures were carefully lined up in a box. He took such good care of them, and his fist would immediately appear if his little brother touched them. Christian could feel himself waver as doubts began to build, and he realized that he needed to leave. He had to meet her before he lost his nerve.

He went into the bedroom to put on some clothes. It didn't matter what he chose; that was no longer important. Then he went downstairs, grabbed his jacket from the hanger, and took one last look around the house. Dark and silent. He didn't bother to lock the door behind him.

During the short walk he kept his eyes

fixed on the ground, not wanting to look at anyone, not wanting to talk. He needed to concentrate on what he was about to do and the person he was about to meet. The palms of his hands had started itching again, but this time he had no trouble ignoring the sensation. His brain felt as if it had switched off all communication with his body, which was now superfluous. The only thing of importance was what was inside his head, the images and memories. He was no longer living in the present. He saw only what had once been, like a film slowly playing as the snow squeaked under his feet.

The wind had started to gust as he walked across the dock toward Badholmen. He knew that he was cold because his body was shivering, but he didn't feel the chill. The place was deserted. It was dark and quiet, with not a person in sight. But he could feel her presence, just as he always had. His guilt had to be settled here. It was the only possible place. From the top of the diving tower he had seen her in the water, seen her stretch out her hands toward him. Now he would go to her.

When he passed the wooden buildings that marked the entrance to the swimming area, the film inside his head began speeding up. The onslaught of images felt like a knife slicing into his gut — so strong and sharp was the pain. He forced himself to look past it, to look forward.

He set one foot on the first step of the tower, and the wood gave a little under his shoe. Now he was breathing easier; there was no going back. He looked up as he climbed. The snow made the steps slippery, and he held on to the railing as he fixed his gaze on the top, which loomed against the black of the sky. No stars. He didn't deserve stars. Halfway up, he knew that she was behind him. He didn't turn around to look back, but he heard her footsteps following his. The same rhythm, the same resilient step. She was here now.

When he reached the platform at the top, he stuck his hand in his pocket and took out the rope that he'd brought from home. The rope that would bear the weight and pay for the blame. She waited on the stairs as he arranged everything. Tying and knotting the rope, fastening it to the railing. For a moment he felt uncertain. The tower was rickety and old and seemed terribly weather-beaten. What if it didn't hold? But her presence reassured him. She wouldn't allow him to fail. Not after she had waited so long, nourishing her hatred for so many years.

When he was done, he stood with his back

to the stairs and his eyes fixed on the outline of Fjällbacka across the water. Not until he heard her step right behind him did he turn around.

There was no joy in her eyes. Only the knowledge that he finally, after all that had happened, was prepared to atone for his crime. She was just as beautiful as he remembered her. Her hair was wet, and he was surprised that it wasn't frosty from the cold. But nothing about her was as expected. Nothing about a mermaid could ever be as expected.

The last thing he saw before he stepped out toward the sea was a blue dress fluttering in the summer wind.

"How are you feeling?" asked Erica when Patrik came downstairs, his hair tousled from sleep.

"Just a little tired, that's all," said Patrik, but his face was pale.

"Are you sure? You don't look well."

"Thanks a lot. Paula said the same thing. I wish you girls would stop telling me how awful I look. It's starting to get to me." He smiled, but he still didn't look like he was fully awake. He bent down to pick up Maja, who came running toward him.

"Hi, sweetie. You think Papa looks good,

don't you? Isn't Papa the most handsome guy in the world?" He tickled her tummy, making her giggle.

"Hmm," she said, nodding sagely.

"Thank goodness. Finally somebody with good taste." He turned to Erica and kissed her on the mouth. Maja grabbed his face and pursed her lips, as a sign that she wanted a kiss too.

"Sit down and snuggle with her while I make us some tea and sandwiches," said Erica, heading for the kitchen. "By the way, Paula left some things in a sack for you," she called, trying to sound as casual as possible. "It's in the front hall."

"Thanks!" Patrik called in reply, and then she heard him get up and come into the kitchen.

"Do you have to work tonight?" she asked, looking at him out of the corner of her eye as she poured boiling water into two mugs with teabags.

"No, I think I'll take it easy tonight and spend some time with my sweet wife, then go to bed early. I'm going to stay home tomorrow morning and go through the whole case in peace and quiet. Sometimes it's a real circus down at the station."

He sighed and came over to stand behind Erica, putting his arms around her.

"I can't even get my arms all the way around you anymore," he murmured, burrowing his face into the back of her neck.

"I know. I feel like I'm about to burst."

"Are you worried?"

"I'd be lying if I said no."

"We'll help each other," he said, hugging her even harder.

"I know. And Anna says the same thing. I think it'll go better this time around, since I know what to expect. But there will be two of them."

"Twice the joy," said Patrik, smiling.

"Twice the work," said Erica, turning around so she could hug him from the front. Which wasn't exactly easy at this point.

Erica closed her eyes and pressed her cheek against Patrik's. She'd been wondering when would be the best time to tell him about her trip to Göteborg, and she'd decided it had to be tonight. But Patrik looked so tired, and since he was planning to work at home tomorrow morning, she could wait until then. Besides, then she'd be able to do what she had in mind after listening to the cassette tape. So it was decided. If she managed to find out anything important for the investigation, Patrik was bound to be less upset that she'd interfered.

It didn't really bother him so much not to have any friends. Because he had books. But the older he got, the more he yearned for what he saw everyone else had. A sense of community, of belonging, of being part of a group. He was always alone. The only person who wanted to be with him was Alice.

Sometimes they used to chase him home from the school bus. Erik, Kenneth, and Magnus. They would roar with laughter as they raced after him, moving slower than they were actually capable of running. The only purpose was to make him run.

"Hey, fatso, get moving!"

And he ran, even though he despised himself for complying. In his heart he kept wishing for a miracle, that one day they would simply stop, that they would see him and understand that he was somebody. But he knew this was only a dream. No one saw him. Alice didn't count. She was a retard. That was what the boys called her, especially Erik. He used to roll the word around on his tongue whenever he saw her. "Reeetard. . . ."

Alice was often waiting for him when the bus stopped. He hated it when she did that. She looked perfectly normal as she stood inside the bus shelter with her long dark hair tied back in a ponytail, her cheerful blue eyes eagerly looking for him as the kids from the high school in Tanumshede got off the bus. Sometimes he actually felt a bit proud when the bus pulled up at the stop and he saw her through the window. That long-legged, dark-haired beauty was his sister.

But then came the moment when he stepped out of the bus and she saw him. She would come toward him with that awkward gait of hers, as if she had invisible strings attached to her arms and legs that someone was randomly tugging on. Then she would call his name in her thick voice, and the boys would howl with laughter. "Reeetard!"

Alice didn't understand at all, and that was actually what embarrassed him most. She merely smiled happily, and sometimes she even waved to them. Then he would take off running, not because anyone was chasing him but in order to escape from Erik's bellowing taunts that echoed all over town. But he could never escape from Alice. She always thought it was a game. She would easily catch up with him, and sometimes, laughing, she would throw her arms around his neck with such force that he almost fell over.

At those moments he hated her just as much as when she had cried non-stop and taken Mother away from him. He wanted to punch her in the face so she would stop embarrassing him. He would never get to be part of the group as long as Alice stood there in the bus shelter waiting for him, calling his name and throwing her arms around his neck.

He wanted so desperately to be somebody. And not just for Alice.

22

When she woke up, Patrik was still sound asleep. It was seven thirty, but Maja was still asleep too, even though she was usually up before seven. Erica was feeling restless. She had awakened several times in the night, thinking about what she'd heard on the cassette tape. She was anxious for morning to arrive so she could do something about it.

Now she slipped out of bed, got dressed, and went downstairs to the kitchen to make herself some coffee. When the caffeine of the first cup of coffee had kicked in, she glanced with impatience at the clock. It was possible that they were already awake. With young children in the house, it was even likely.

She left a note for Patrik, explaining in vague terms that she had gone out to take care of an errand. He was going to wonder what she was up to, but she would give him a full report when she got back.

Ten minutes later, she drove into Hamburgsund. She had called Information to find out where Sanna's sister Agneta lived, and she found the place at once. It was a big house built of Mexitegel brick. She held her breath as she entered the long driveway, squeezing her car between two stone pillars positioned close together. It was going to be tricky backing the car out, but she would worry about that later.

Erica could see people moving around inside, and she was relieved to find that she'd guessed right: they were up. She rang the bell and soon she heard footsteps coming downstairs. A woman who had to be Sanna's sister opened the door.

"Hi," said Erica, introducing herself. "I was wondering if Sanna is up yet. I need to have a few words with her."

Agneta gave her a quizzical look, but didn't offer any objections.

"Sure, Sanna and the little monsters are awake. Come on in."

Erica stepped inside and hung up her jacket. She followed Sanna's sister up a steep flight of stairs to another hallway. Then they turned left and entered a big open space that served as kitchen, dining room, and living room.

Sanna and the boys were eating breakfast with the cousins, a boy and a girl who looked a few years older than both of Sanna's sons.

"I'm sorry for interrupting your breakfast," said Erica, looking at Christian's wife. "I just need to ask you about one thing."

At first, Sanna made no motion to get up. She was holding a spoon halfway to her mouth, looking as if thoughts were whirling through her head. But then she put down the spoon and stood up.

"Why don't you go downstairs and sit on the veranda so you can talk in peace," said Agneta.

Erica followed Sanna down the stairs, through a few more rooms, and into a glass-enclosed veranda that looked out on the lawn and the small center of Hamburgsund.

"How are you and the boys doing?" Erica asked as they sat down.

"All right, I suppose." Sanna looked pale and haggard, as if she hadn't had much sleep. "The boys keep asking about their father, and I don't know what to tell them. I also don't know whether I should try to get them to talk about what happened or not. I was thinking of phoning Child Psychiatric Services today, to ask for advice."

"That sounds like a good idea," said Erica.

"But kids are tough. They can handle more than we think."

"You may be right." Sanna stared into space, her expression blank. Then she turned to Erica and said:

"What was it you wanted to talk about?"

Like so many times before, Erica wasn't sure how to begin. She had no authority to be here, no mandate to ask questions. All she had was her curiosity. And her concern. For a moment she pondered what to say. Then she leaned down and took the drawings out of her purse.

Sven-Olov Rönn was up at dawn. That was something he was enormously proud of, and he seized every opportunity to mention it. "There's no use lying in bed, practicing for the nursing home," he liked to say with satisfaction, and then he'd explain that he was always up by six at the latest. His daughter-in-law sometimes teased him about the fact that every night he went to bed by nine. "And you don't call that practicing for the nursing home?" she'd ask with a smile. But he chose to ignore those kinds of remarks. He always made good use of his daytime hours.

After a solid breakfast of oatmeal, Sven-Olov sat down in his favorite armchair and took his time reading the newspaper as the dark slowly faded outside the window. By the time he finished, it was usually light enough for him to make his morning survey. It had become a ritual over the years.

He got up, fetched the binoculars hanging on a hook, and sat down in front of the window. His house stood on the slope across from the boathouses, with the church behind him, and he had an excellent view of Fjällbacka's harbor approach. He raised the binoculars to his eyes and began his inspection, moving from left to right. First the neighbors. Yes, they were up too. These days not many people lived here in the wintertime, but he was lucky enough to have one of the few permanent residents in the area as his neighbor. And as a bonus, the man's wife liked to walk around in nothing but her underwear in the morning. She was about fifty, but had a damned nice figure, he noted as he moved the binoculars to continue his survey.

Empty houses, one empty house after another. Some were completely dark, others had lights with timers, so here and there he saw lights on. He sighed as he always did. It was terrible how things had changed. He could still remember when all the houses were occupied and filled with activity year-round. By now, the summer visitors had bought up almost everything, and they didn't bother to spend more than three months a year in Fjällbacka. Then they would return to the cities with a flattering suntan, which they enjoyed talking about at parties and dinners well into the autumn: "Oh, yes, we were at our house in Fjällbacka all summer. Just imagine living there all year round. What peace and quiet that would be. We could really unwind." But of course they didn't mean a word of it. They wouldn't last twenty-four hours out here in the winter, when everything was closed up and quiet and it was way too cold to be lying on the rocks trying to bask in the sun.

The binoculars moved on, crossing Ingrid Bergman Square, which was deserted. Sven-Olov had heard that the people in charge of Fjällbacka's website had installed a camera so it was possible to log on to the computer and see what was happening in town. Anybody who does that must not have enough to do, he thought. Because there certainly wasn't much to see.

He swung the binoculars onward, letting them glide over Södra Hamngatan, past Järnboden, and over toward Brandparken. For a moment he paused at the Coast Guard boat, admiring it as he always did.

Simply magnificent. He'd loved boats all his life, and the *MinLouis* always gleamed so beautifully when she was in dock. Then he followed the path toward Badholmen. Memories from his youth always came back to him whenever he saw the wooden buildings with the high fence, which was where people changed their clothes. Men on one side, women on the other. When he was a boy, he and his pals were always trying to find a way to peek in at the ladies. Though rarely with any success.

Now he could see the rocks and the trampoline that the kids used so much in the summer. Then the tower, looking a bit worn these days. He hoped they would fix it up and not just tear it down. In a way, it was an essential part of Fjällbacka.

Sven-Olov moved past the tower to look out over the water toward Valön. Then he gave a start, and moved the binoculars back a bit. What on earth? He adjusted the focus and then squinted his eyes in an attempt to see more clearly. If he wasn't mistaken, something was hanging from the tower. Something dark, swaying slightly in the wind. Again he squinted his eyes. Maybe some kids had been up to no good and decided to hang a doll or something from

516

the tower. He couldn't really see what it was.

His curiosity got the better of him. He put on his coat and stuck his feet in a pair of shoes, attaching snow cleats to the soles. Then he went outside. He'd forgotten to put sand on the top step, and he held on tight to the railing so he wouldn't land on his backside. Down on the road it was easier, and he headed off as fast as he dared in the direction of Badholmen.

The whole town seemed asleep as he passed Ingrid Bergman Square. He wondered whether he should flag down a car if he saw one drive by, but decided not to. It was silly to cause a commotion if it turned out to be nothing.

As Sven-Olov came closer, he slowed down even more. He usually tried to take a long walk at least a couple of times a week, so he was still in fairly good condition. Even so, he was breathing hard by the time he reached the buildings at Badholmen.

He stopped for a moment to catch his breath. At least he pretended that was the reason for stopping. The truth was that he'd had a bad feeling ever since he saw that dark silhouette in his binoculars. He hesitated, but then took a deep breath and stepped through the entrance to the swimming area.

He couldn't bring himself to look up at the diving tower yet. Instead, he stared at his feet, setting them down carefully on the rocks so he wouldn't fall and then not be able to get up. But when there were only a few yards left to the tower, he raised his head and slowly let his eyes move upwards.

Patrik sat up with a jolt. Something was buzzing. He looked around and at first couldn't tell where he was or identify where the sound was coming from. Finally he woke up enough to reach for his mobile. He'd turned off the ringer, but the VIBRATE function was on, and the phone was frantically hopping around on the bedside table, with the display glowing in the dim light of the room.

"Hello?"

He was instantly wide awake and started getting dressed as he listened and asked follow-up questions. A few minutes later he was fully dressed and on his way out the door when he saw the note that Erica had left, and he realized that she hadn't been lying in bed next to him. He swore and ran back upstairs. Maja was in her room, but she had climbed out of bed and was sitting on the floor, playing quietly. What the hell was he going to do? He couldn't leave her home alone. Annoyed, he tried Erica's mobile, but it just kept ringing until her voicemail took over. Where could she be this early in the morning?

He ended the call and instead punched in Anna and Dan's number. Anna answered, and he sighed with relief as he quickly explained his dilemma. Then he stood in the front hall, impatiently shifting from one foot to the other during the ten minutes it took Anna to jump in her car and drive over.

"I can't believe all the emergency calls I've been getting from the two of you lately. First Erica needing to make a trip to Göteborg yesterday, and now you call, sounding as if there's a fire somewhere." Anna laughed as she swept past Patrik and came into the house.

He quickly thanked her and then ran for his car. Not until he was behind the wheel did Anna's remarks sink in. A trip to Göteborg? Yesterday? He didn't understand. But it would just have to wait. Right now he had other things to think about.

The whole police force was on site by the time he reached Badholmen. He parked his car in front of the Coast Guard boat and jogged out to the island. Torbjörn Ruud and the other techs were already at work.

"When did the call come in?" Patrik asked

Gösta, who had come over to meet him. Torbjörn and his team must have driven over from Uddevalla, and shouldn't have been able to get here faster than he had. Gösta and Martin either, since they had to come from Tanumshede. Why hadn't anyone phoned him sooner?

"Annika tried to reach you several times. Apparently last night too, but you didn't answer."

Patrik pulled his mobile out of his pocket, prepared to show Gösta that he must be mistaken. But when he looked at the display, he saw that there were five missed calls. Three from yesterday and two from this morning.

"Do you know why she phoned me yesterday?" said Patrik, cursing himself for turning off the ringer, even for just one evening. Of course something had to happen the minute he allowed himself not to think about work, for the first time in ages.

"I have no idea. But this morning it's because of this." He motioned toward the diving tower, and Patrik gave a start. There was something so primeval and dramatic about the sight of a man swinging in the wind with a rope around his neck.

"Damn it to hell," he said, and he really meant it. He thought about Sanna and the children. And about Erica. "Who found him?" Patrik tried to step into his professional role, to lose himself in the work that needed to get done and push aside any thought of all the repercussions. Right now he couldn't think of Christian as someone who had a wife and children, friends, and a life. At the moment he was just a victim, a mystery that had to be solved. The only thing Patrik could allow himself to think about was that something had happened here, and it was his job to find out what and why.

"The old man over there. Sven-Olov Rönn. He lives in the white house." Gösta pointed toward one of the houses on the slope across from the row of boathouses. "Apparently he's in the habit of surveying the area through his binoculars every morning. And that's when he caught sight of something hanging from the diving tower. At first he thought it was some sort of kids' prank, but when he made his way over here, he saw that it was for real."

"Is he okay?"

"A bit shaken up, of course, but he seems to be made of stern stuff."

"Don't let him leave until I have a chance to talk to him," said Patrik. Then he went over to Torbjörn, who was cordoning off the

521

area around the tower.

"You're certainly keeping us busy, and that's an understatement," said Torbjörn.

"Believe me, we'd prefer a little peace and quiet." Patrik prepared himself to take another look at Christian, and then turned his gaze upward. The body's eyes were open and the head had fallen forward a bit when the neck was broken. It looked as if he were staring down at the water.

Patrik shuddered.

"How long do we have to leave him hanging there?"

"Not much longer. We just need to take our photographs before we cut him down."

"What about transport?"

"On the way," said Torbjörn tersely. He looked keen to get to work.

"Do whatever you have to do," said Patrik, and Torbjörn immediately began issuing orders to his team.

Patrik went over to join Gösta and the elderly man, who looked like he was freezing.

"Patrik Hedström, Tanum police force," he said, holding out his hand.

"Sven-Olov Rönn," said the man, shaking hands as he practically stood to attention.

"How are you feeling?" asked Patrik, studying the man's face for signs of shock.

Rönn was a little pale around the gills, but otherwise he looked quite composed.

"Well, this wasn't exactly pleasant," he said, "but I'm going to have myself a small fortifying drink when I get home, and then I'll be fine."

"Would you like to talk to a doctor?" asked Patrik, prompting a horrified expression to appear on the face of the man standing in front of him. Apparently he was the type of old man who would rather amputate his own arm than consult a doctor.

"No, no," said Rönn, "that's not necessary."

"All right, then," said Patrik. "I know that you've already talked to my colleague here," and he nodded toward Gösta, "but I'd like to hear for myself how you happened to find . . . the man in the tower."

"Well, you see, I'm always up at the crack of dawn," Rönn began, and then he went on to tell the same story that Gösta had reported to Patrik a few minutes earlier, although with a few more details added. After asking several follow-up questions, Patrik decided to send the old man home so he could get warmed up.

"So, Gösta. What do you think this means?" he asked after Rönn had left.

"The first thing we need to find out is

whether it was suicide. Or whether it was the same. . . ." He didn't finish the sentence, but Patrik knew what he was thinking.

"Have you seen anything to indicate a struggle, or any type of resistance?" Patrik called to Torbjörn, who had stopped halfway up the steps to the diving tower.

"Not so far. But we're just getting started," he said. "We'll take the photographs first." And he waved the big camera he was holding in his hand. "Then we'll see what else we can find. I'll let you know as soon as I can."

"Good. Thanks," said Patrik. He realized that there wasn't much more he could do right now. And there was another task that required his attention.

Martin Molin came over to join them, his face as pale as it always was whenever he had to be near a dead body.

"Mellberg and Paula are on the way too."

"How nice," said Patrik without enthusiasm. Both Gösta and Martin knew that it wasn't Paula who had prompted that tone of voice.

"What do you want us to do?" asked Martin.

Patrik took a deep breath as he tried to form a plan in his mind. He was tempted to delegate the task that he was dreading, but his sense of responsibility took over, and after another deep breath he said:

"Martin, you wait here for Mellberg and Paula. We won't count on Mellberg for any sort of help; he'll just wander around and get in the way of the crime techs. But take Paula with you and start knocking on the doors of all the houses near the entrance to Badholmen. Most of them are empty this time of the year, so it shouldn't take long. Gösta, I'd like you to come with me when I talk to Sanna."

Gösta's expression darkened, but he said "Fine. When do you want to go?"

"Right now," said Patrik. He just wanted to get it over with. For a moment he considered ringing Annika to find out why she'd been trying to reach him the day before. But that would have to wait until later. He didn't have time for it now.

As they left Badholmen, both Patrik and Gösta made an effort not to turn around to look at the figure still swaying in the wind.

"But I don't understand. Who could have sent these to Christian?" Sanna was staring in bewilderment at the drawings that lay on the table in front of her. She reached out her hand to pick up one of them, and Erica was glad that she'd had the presence of mind to put each drawing in a separate plastic bag so they could be handled without destroying any potential evidence.

"I don't know. I was hoping that you might be able to come up with some sort of explanation."

Sanna shook her head. "I have no idea. Where did you find them?"

Erica told her about her visit to Christian's old apartment in Göteborg, and about Janos Kovács, who had saved the letters all these years.

"Why are you so interested in Christian's life?" Sanna gave her an inquiring look.

For a moment Erica pondered how to explain her actions. Even she was hard-pressed to understand why she had become so involved.

"Ever since I heard about the threatening letters, I've been worried about him. And since I'm the kind of person that I am, I couldn't let it go. Christian wouldn't tell me anything, so I started digging around a bit on my own."

"Have you shown these to Christian?" asked Sanna, picking up another drawing to study it more closely.

"No. I wanted to talk to you first." She paused for a moment and then said, "What do you know about Christian's background?

About his family and childhood."

Sanna smiled sadly.

"Almost nothing. You have no idea. I've never met anyone who is so unwilling to talk about himself. There's so much I've wanted to know about his parents, how they lived, what he did when he was a kid, what sort of friends he had . . . all those questions people ask when they're getting to know someone. But Christian has never been willing to discuss his past. He told me that his parents are dead, that he has no brothers or sisters, and that his childhood was just like everyone else's, so it's not really worth talking about." Sanna swallowed hard.

"Didn't that seem strange to you?" asked Erica, and she couldn't help letting a trace of sympathy slip into her tone of voice. She could see how hard Sanna was fighting to hold back the tears.

"I love him. And he always got annoyed if I pestered him with those kinds of questions, so I stopped. All I wanted . . . all I ever wanted was for him to stay with me." She whispered the words, her eyes fixed on her lap.

Erica had an urge to sit down next to Sanna and put her arms around her. She suddenly looked so young and vulnerable.

It couldn't be easy to live in that kind of relationship, always feeling at a disadvantage. Because Erica understood what Sanna was hinting at: the fact that she loved Christian, but he had never loved her.

"So you don't know who that small figure standing next to Christian might be?" asked Erica gently.

"I have no idea, but a child must have made these drawings. Maybe he has kids that I don't know about." She attempted to laugh, but the laugh lodged in her throat.

"Now don't go jumping to conclusions." Erica was suddenly worried that she might be making things even worse for Sanna, who was clearly on the verge of a breakdown.

"I won't, but I have to admit that I've been wondering too. I've asked him a thousand times since the letters started arriving, and he just says that he doesn't know who sent them. But I'm not sure I believe him." She bit her lip.

"So he has never mentioned any old girlfriends or anything like that? Nothing about a woman who might have been part of his life before?" Erica realized that she was being a bit pushy, but maybe Christian had said something once, something that might be buried deep in Sanna's subconscious.

Sanna shook her head and laughed bitterly. "Believe me, I would remember if he'd ever mentioned another woman. I even thought —" she stopped herself, looking as if she regretted starting the sentence.

"What did you think?" asked Erica, but Sanna retreated.

"It's nothing. Just foolishness on my part. I have problems with jealousy, you might say."

And no wonder, thought Erica. Living with a stranger for so many years, and loving someone without being loved in return. It was no wonder that Sanna was jealous. But she didn't say anything. Instead, she chose to steer the conversation toward what had been on her mind since the day before.

"You talked to one of Patrik's colleagues yesterday, didn't you? Paula Morales?"

Sanna nodded. "She was really nice. And I liked Gösta too. He helped me get the children washed up. Tell Patrik to thank him for me. I don't think I remembered to do that yesterday."

"I will," said Erica, and then paused for a moment before going on. "There was one thing in your conversation that I don't think Paula caught."

"How would you know that?" asked Sanna in surprise.

"Paula taped your conversation, and Patrik was listening to it at home last night. I couldn't help overhearing."

"Oh," said Sanna, seeming to accept the white lie. "What was it you. . . ."

"Well, you said something to Paula about Christian not having an easy time of it. And it sounded like you were thinking about something specific."

Sanna's expression froze. She avoided looking Erica in the eye and started plucking at the fringe of the tablecloth.

"I don't know what —"

"Sanna," Erica pleaded. "This isn't the time for secrets or keeping quiet in order to protect someone, to protect Christian. Your whole family is in danger, and others too, but maybe we can prevent anyone else from sharing Magnus's terrible fate. I don't know what you're not saying, or why. It might not even have anything to do with this, and maybe that's what you're thinking. Otherwise I'm sure that you would have mentioned it. Especially after what happened to your children yesterday. But can you be absolutely sure about that?"

Sanna looked out of the window, staring at a spot far away, beyond the buildings, out toward the frozen water and the islands. She didn't speak for a long time, and Erica didn't either, allowing Sanna to fight the battle with herself.

"I found a dress up in the attic. A blue dress," said Sanna at last. Then she proceeded to tell Erica everything. About how she had confronted Christian, about her anger and her uncertainty. About what he had finally told her. The whole horrible story.

When Sanna was finished, she seemed to shrink, looking utterly drained. Erica sat motionless, trying to digest what she'd just heard, but it was impossible. There were certain things that the human brain just couldn't fathom. All she could do was reach out her hand and place it on top of Sanna's.

For the first time, Erik felt panic overwhelm him. Christian was dead. He was swaying in the wind like a rag doll, hanging from the diving tower at Badholmen.

A female police officer had phoned to tell him the news. She told him to be cautious, and not to hesitate to call the police. He had thanked her, saying he didn't think that would be necessary. For the life of him, he couldn't understand who could be after them. But he had no intention of just sitting around, waiting for his turn. This time he was determined to take control, to hold on to his power.

Patches of sweat appeared on his shirt, proving that he wasn't as calm as he tried to pretend. He still held the phone in his hand, and with fumbling fingers he punched in Kenneth's mobile number. After five rings, his voicemail answered. Angrily Erik ended the call and tossed the mobile on his desk. He tried to force himself to act rationally and think through everything he now needed to do.

The phone rang. He jumped and then looked at the display. Kenneth.

"Hello?"

"I can't pick up the phone on my own," Kenneth explained. "I have to have help to put on the Bluetooth. I can't hold the phone," he said, without any self-pity in his voice.

For a moment Erik thought he should have taken the trouble to visit Kenneth in the hospital. Or at least sent him flowers. Oh, well, he couldn't think of everything, and somebody had to be at the office. He was sure Kenneth would understand.

"How are you doing?" he asked now, trying to sound as if he were actually interested.

"Fine," said Kenneth curtly. He knew Erik too well to think that he had asked about his health because he cared.

"I have some unpleasant news." Might as well get right to the point. Kenneth didn't reply as he waited for him to go on. "Christian is dead." Erik tugged at the collar of his shirt. He was still sweating heavily, and he could feel that the hand holding the phone was damp. "I just heard about it. The police called. He's hanging from the diving tower at Badholmen."

Still no answer.

"Hello? Did you hear what I said? Christian is dead. The officer I talked to refused to tell me more, but any idiot can see that it's the same nutcase who's been doing everything else."

"Yes, it's her," said Kenneth at last. His voice was icy and calm.

"What do you mean? Do you know who it is?" Erik practically screamed. Kenneth knew who it was, and yet he hadn't told anyone? If nothing else happened to Kenneth first, he was going to kill the man himself.

"She'll be coming after us next."

The eerie calm in his voice made the little hairs on Erik's arms stand on end. For a moment he wondered whether Kenneth might have suffered a blow to the head.

"Would you please let me in on what you know?"

"She'll probably save you for last."

Erik had to restrain himself from slamming his mobile against the desk out of sheer frustration. "Who is it?"

"You mean you really don't know? Have you hurt and injured so many people that you can't pick her out of the crowd? For me it was easy. She's the only person that I ever harmed. I don't know whether Magnus ever realized that she was after him. But I do know that he suffered. That's not something you've ever done, have you, Erik? You've never suffered or lain awake at night because of what you've done." Kenneth didn't sound upset or accusatory. He was still calm and composed.

"What are you talking about?" snarled Erik, as thoughts raced through his head. A vague memory, an image, a face. Something began stirring. Something that had been buried so deep that it was never supposed to resurface again.

He gripped the phone hard. Could it be . . . ?

Kenneth was silent, and Erik didn't need to say out loud that he now knew too. His own silence spoke volumes. Without saying good-bye, he ended the conversation with

Kenneth, trying to push away the certainty that had been forced upon him.

After that, he opened his email and swiftly began doing what had to be done. It was urgent.

As soon as he saw Erica's car parked in the drive in front of Agneta's house, Patrik got an uneasy feeling in his stomach. Erica had a tendency to get involved in matters that didn't concern her. And even though he had many times admired his wife for her sense of curiosity and the way she used it to produce results, he didn't like her to interfere with police business. He would have preferred to protect Erica, Maja, and the unborn twins from all the evil in the world. But that was a tough job when it came to his wife. Time after time, she had landed in the center of the action, and he realized that without his knowing it she had probably landed herself up to her ears in this investigation too.

"Isn't that Erica's car?" asked Gösta laconically as they drove up and parked next to the beige Volvo.

"Yes, it is," replied Patrik. Gösta didn't ask any more questions, simply raised one eyebrow.

They didn't have to ring the bell. Sanna's

sister had already opened the front door and was waiting for them, a worried look on her face.

"Has something happened?" she asked tensely.

"We'd like to talk to Sanna," said Patrik, without answering her question. He wished that he'd brought Lena the pastor along this time too, but she had been out when he phoned, and he didn't want to delay delivering the news.

The expression on Agneta's face was even more concerned as she stepped aside to let them in.

"She's on the veranda," she said, pointing.

"Thanks," said Patrik. "Could you make sure that the children are kept busy for a while?"

Agneta swallowed hard. "Yes, I'll do that."

Patrik and Gösta made their way out to the veranda. Sanna and Erica looked up when they heard them come in. Erica had a guilty expression on her face, but Patrik motioned to her, indicating that they would talk later. He sat down next to Sanna.

"I'm afraid I have some very bad news to tell you," he said, keeping his voice calm. "Christian was found dead early this morning."

Sanna gasped for breath and her eyes

filled with tears.

"We don't know very much at the moment. But we're doing everything we can to find out what happened," he added.

"How . . . ?" Sanna's whole body began shaking uncontrollably.

Patrik hesitated, unsure how to tell her.

"He was found hanged. From the tower at Badholmen."

"Hanged?" Her breathing was fast and shallow. Patrik put his hand on her arm to calm her.

"That's all we know right now."

She nodded, her eyes glassy. Patrik turned to Erica and said, in a low voice:

"Could you trade places with her sister? Ask Agneta to come down here while you take care of the kids?"

Erica got up at once, casting a glance at Sanna before she left the veranda. A moment later, they heard her heading upstairs. Then, as soon as they could tell that someone was on the way down, Gösta went out to the hall to speak to Sanna's sister. Patrik was grateful to his colleague for wanting to report what had happened out of earshot so Sanna wouldn't have to hear it twice.

Agneta came in, sat down next to Sanna, and put her arms around her. And that was how the two women stayed as Patrik asked if they'd like him to call anyone, and whether they wanted to speak to a pastor. All the usual questions that he clung to in order not to fall apart at the thought of the two little boys upstairs who had lost their father.

But he really needed to be on his way. He had a job to do, a job that entailed doing something for this family. First and foremost for them. It was the victim and the victim's family members that he always pictured in his mind as he sat in his office at the station and spent so many long hours trying to find a solution to cases he was investigating — some of them more complicated than others.

Sanna was sobbing uncontrollably as Patrik met her sister's gaze. Agneta gave an almost imperceptible nod in answer to his unvoiced question, so he stood up.

"Are you sure there isn't someone you'd like me to phone?"

"I'll call Mama and Papa as soon as I can," said Agneta. Even though she was very pale, she had a calm air about her that made Patrik feel okay about leaving them.

"Call us any time, Sanna," he said, pausing in the doorway. "And we. . . ." He was uncertain how much he dared say. Because the worst thing that could happen to a police officer in the middle of an investigation had now happened to him. He was about to lose hope. The hope that they'd ever find out who was behind all of these horrible events.

"Don't forget the drawings," said Sanna, sniffling as she pointed to some papers lying on the table.

"What drawings?"

"Erica brought them. Someone sent them to Christian's old address in Göteborg."

Patrik stared at the pictures and then carefully gathered them up. What had Erica been up to now? He needed to have a talk with his wife as soon as possible; this demanded a proper explanation. At the same time, he couldn't deny that he felt a certain sense of anticipation when he saw the drawings. If they turned out to be important, it wouldn't be the first time Erica had stumbled upon some crucial information.

"You're certainly doing a lot of babysitting lately," said Dan as he came into Erica and Patrik's house. He had called Anna on her mobile, and when she explained where she was, he had driven over to Sälvik.

"Uh-huh. I don't really know what Erica is mixed up in, and I'm not sure I want to know, either," said Anna, as she sauntered over to Dan and turned her face up for a kiss.

"So they won't mind if I crash the party?" said Dan. In the next second he was almost bowled over by Maja, who threw herself into his arms. "Hi, cutie! How's my girl? You're still my girl, right? You haven't found some other guy, have you?" said Dan, looking stern. Maja laughed so hard that she started hiccupping, and she rubbed her nose against his, which he took to mean that he hadn't lost his high-ranking status.

"Did you hear what happened?" asked Anna, her expression suddenly turning serious.

"No, what?" asked Dan, hoisting Maja up and then dropping her down. Considering how tall he was, Maja was getting quite a ride, much to her delight.

"I don't know where Erica is, but Patrik had to go off to Badholmen. Somebody found Christian Thydell there this morning — hanged."

Dan stopped instantly, which left Maja upside down. She thought it was all part of the game and laughed even louder.

"Are you kidding me?" Dan slowly put Maja down on the rug.

"No, but that's all Patrik told me before

he raced off. Christian is dead." Anna didn't know Sanna Thydell very well, but occasionally she would run into her, which was inevitable since so few people lived in Fjällbacka. Now she was thinking about those two little boys.

Dan dropped onto a chair at the kitchen table, and Anna tried to chase away the images that kept cropping up in her mind.

"Bloody hell," he said, staring out of the window. "First Magnus Kjellner, and now Christian. Not to mention Kenneth Bengtsson, who's in the hospital. Patrik must be up to his ears with this investigation."

"I'm sure you're right," said Anna, pouring some juice for Maja. "But let's talk about something else, okay?" She always got very upset thinking about other people's troubles, and her pregnancy had made her a hundred times more sensitive. She couldn't stand to hear about anyone having difficulties.

Dan understood the signals and pulled her close. He closed his eyes and placed his hand on her stomach, spreading out his fingers.

"Soon, sweetheart. Soon he'll be here."

Anna's face lit up. Every time she thought about the child, it felt as if nothing bad could reach her. She loved Dan so much, and she practically burst with joy whenever she thought about how the small creature inside her was uniting the two of them. She stroked Dan's hair, murmuring:

"You need to stop saying 'he.' Because I think we've got a little princess inside here. I think this baby kicks like a ballet dancer," she teased him.

After having three daughters, Dan was longing for a boy. At the same time, Anna knew that he would be overjoyed with the baby, no matter whether it was a girl or a boy. Because it was their child.

Patrik dropped Gösta off at Badholmen. After thinking for a moment, he decided to drive home. He needed to talk to Erica and find out what she knew.

As soon as he stepped inside, he paused to take a deep breath. Anna was still there, and he didn't want to drag her into any dispute that he had with Erica. Anna had the annoying habit of always siding with her sister, and he didn't need two people facing him in the opposite corner of the ring. But after thanking Anna — as well as Dan, who had turned up as an extra babysitter — Patrik tried to make it as clear as possible that they should leave him and Erica in peace. Anna picked up on what he wanted and took Dan with her, although he had a bit of a struggle before Maja would let him go.

"I assume Maja isn't going to the day-care center today," said Erica cheerfully, glancing at the clock.

"Why were you at Agneta's house talking to Sanna? And what were you doing in Göteborg yesterday?" asked Patrik in a sharp tone of voice.

"Er, well, I. . . ." Erica tilted her head, trying to look as sweetly innocent as she could. When that brought no response, she sighed and realized that she might as well confess. She had intended all along to tell Patrik everything; he had just beaten her to it.

They sat down at the kitchen table. Patrik clasped his hands in front of himself and stared her straight in the eye. Erica took her time as she decided where to begin.

Then she explained how she couldn't stop wondering why Christian had always been so secretive about his past. So she had decided to work backwards and drive to Göteborg, to the address where he had lived before moving to Fjällbacka. She told Patrik about the kindly Hungarian man and about the letters that had arrived for Christian. But he had never received them because he hadn't left any forwarding address. Erica took a deep breath and then explained how she had surreptitiously read through the case material and hadn't been able to resist listening to the cassette tape. And how she had heard something that had stuck in her mind, until she realized that she needed to get to the bottom of it. That was the reason for her visit to Sanna earlier that morning. She also told Patrik what Sanna had said. About the blue dress and what was almost too awful to comprehend. When Erica was finished, she was out of breath and hardly dared look at Patrik, who hadn't moved a muscle since she began her report.

He was silent for a long time, and she swallowed hard, prepared for the worst lecture she'd ever received in her life.

"I just wanted to help you," she added. "You've been looking so tired lately."

Patrik stood up. "We'll talk more about this later. I need to go back to the station. I'm taking the drawings with me."

Erica sat staring into space for a long time after he was gone. This was the first time since they'd known each other that he'd left the house without giving her a kiss.

It wasn't like Patrik not to call back. Annika had phoned him several times since yesterday, leaving him a message that she needed to speak to him, but not explaining why. She wanted to tell him in person what she had found.

When he finally arrived at the station and she saw his exhausted expression, she was even more worried. Paula had told her that she'd ordered Patrik to stay home and take it easy, and Annika had silently applauded the decision. Lately she'd been thinking of doing the very same thing.

"You were looking for me?" said Patrik as he entered her office behind the glass separating it from the reception area. She spun around in her chair.

"Yes, and it hasn't been easy to reach you by phone," she said, peering at him over the rims of her computer glasses. The tone of her voice wasn't reproachful, just concerned.

"I know," said Patrik, sitting down on the visitor's chair next to the wall. "I've had a lot on my mind."

"You need to take better care of yourself. I have a friend who hit the wall a few years ago, and her health still isn't a hundred percent. It's a long way back up, once you let yourself hit bottom."

"I know, I know," said Patrik. "But things aren't that bad. I've just had a lot of work to do." He ran a hand through his hair and leaned forward, resting his elbows on his knees. "So what did you need to talk to me about?"

"I finished looking into Christian's background." She fell silent. Only now did she remember where Patrik had been all morning. "How did it go, by the way?" she asked quietly. "How did Sanna take it?"

"How would anyone take it?" said Patrik. He nodded for her to go on, indicating that he didn't want to discuss the news he had just been forced to deliver.

Annika cleared her throat. "Okay. First of all, Christian is not listed in our own police records. He has never been charged with a crime or even suspected of anything. Before he came to Fjällbacka, he lived for several years in Göteborg. He was studying at the university there, and then online to get his library degree. The library school is in Borås, you know."

"Uh-huh . . . ," said Patrik, a bit impatiently.

"Furthermore, he has never been previously married, nor does he have any children other than the two sons with Sanna."

Annika fell silent.

"Is that all?" Patrik couldn't hide his disappointment.

"No. I haven't told you the interesting part yet. I discovered very quickly that Christian was orphaned when he was only three years old. He was born in Trollhättan, by the way, and that was also where he was living when his mother died. The father was never in the picture. I decided to dig a bit deeper into the past."

She picked up a paper and began reading. Patrik was now listening intently. Annika could see that thoughts were swirling around in his mind, attempting to link this new information with the little they already knew.

"So it was his mother's last name that he took back when he turned eighteen," said Patrik. "Thydell."

"That's right. I also found out quite a bit about her." She handed a paper to Patrik, who quickly read through it, eager to learn more.

"It looks like we're getting closer to untangling a few threads," said Annika when she saw Patrik's reaction. She loved digging up information, combing through the public records and researching small details that could be later connected to form a whole picture. Especially when her work turned up a lead that could move the investigation forward.

"Yes, and now I know where to start," said Patrik, getting to his feet. "I'm going to begin with the blue dress."

Annika looked at him in astonishment as he left her office. What in the world was he talking about?

Cecilia was not surprised to see who was standing outside when she opened the door. She had actually been expecting this. Fjällbacka was a small town, and secrets could never be kept for long.

"Come in, Louise," she said, stepping aside. She had to resist an impulse to place her hand over her stomach, which was something she'd started doing often, now that her pregnancy had been confirmed.

"I hope Erik's not here," said Louise. Cecilia could hear how she was slurring her words, and for a moment she felt a pang of sympathy. Now that the love affair was over, she realized what a hell it must be to live with Erik. In Louise's place, she probably would have taken to drink as well.

"No, he's not here. Come in," she repeated, leading the way to the kitchen. Louise followed. She was elegantly dressed, as usual, wearing an expensive outfit classically tailored, along with discreet gold jewelry. Cecilia felt slovenly in her casual attire. The first customer wasn't due at the salon until one o'clock, so she was allowing herself a relaxing morning at home. Besides, she was also suffering from morning sickness and couldn't keep up her usual pace.

"There have been so many women in his life that I'm finally feeling worn out."

Cecilia turned to look at Louise in surprise. This was not the opening that she'd been expecting. Instead, she was prepared for anger and accusations. But Louise merely looked sad. And when Cecilia sat down across from her, she noticed some cracks in the elegant façade. Louise's hair was dull-looking, and the polish was chipping off her fingernails. She had buttoned her blouse wrong and one end was sticking out of the waistband of her trousers.

"I told him to go to hell," said Cecilia, noticing how wonderful it felt to say the words out loud.

"Why?" asked Louise, listlessly.

"I got what I wanted from him."

"What do you mean?" Louise was staring at her with a vacant, distracted expression.

Cecilia suddenly felt such a tremendous sense of gratitude that she had to gasp for breath. She would never be like Louise; she was a much stronger person. But maybe Louise had also been strong at one time.

Maybe she had been filled with expectations and a will to make things good. Those hopes were now gone. All that remained were the years of lies and the wine.

For a moment Cecilia considered lying to Louise, or at least holding back the truth for a while. It would come out soon enough. But then she realized that she had to tell her. She couldn't lie to someone who had lost everything she had ever held dear.

"I'm pregnant. It's Erik's child," she said. For a moment neither woman spoke. Then Cecilia went on: "I made it very clear that the only thing I want from him is financial support. And I threatened to tell you everything."

Louise snorted. Then she started to laugh. Her laughter got louder and shriller. Tears began running down her face, and Cecilia looked at her in fascination. This was not the reaction she had expected either. Louise was certainly full of surprises.

"Thank you," said Louise after her laughter subsided.

"Why are you thanking me?" wondered Cecilia. She had always liked Louise. She just hadn't liked her enough to stop fucking her husband.

"For giving me a good kick up the backside. This is exactly what I needed. Good

Lord, just look at me." She glanced down at her mis-buttoned blouse and almost tore off the buttons in her eagerness to fix it. Her fingers were trembling.

"You're welcome," said Cecilia, and she couldn't help laughing a bit at the situation. "What are you planning to do?"

"What you've already done. I'm going to tell him to go to hell," said Louise firmly, and she no longer had a vacant look in her eyes. The feeling that she still had power over her own life had triumphed over her former mood of resignation.

"Make sure you have your finances in order first," said Cecilia drily. "I have to admit that I was infatuated with Erik for a while, but I know what kind of man he is. He'll strip you of everything if you leave him. Men like Erik refuse to be dumped."

"Don't worry. I'll make sure to get the most out of him that I can," said Louise as she tucked her blouse, now properly buttoned, inside the waistband of her trousers. "How do I look? Is my makeup running?"

"A little. Wait a minute and I'll fix it." Cecilia got up, held a piece of paper towel under the tap, and then came back to stand in front of Louise. Carefully she wiped off the mascara from under her eyes. She stopped abruptly when she felt Louise's hand on her stomach. At first neither of them spoke. Then Louise whispered:

"I hope it's a boy. The girls have always wanted a little brother."

"My God," said Paula. "That's one of the most horrifying stories I've ever heard."

Patrik had told her what Erica had found out from Sanna. Paula now gave her colleague a surreptitious look as he sat next to her in the passenger seat. After the near-death experience on the road the day before, she wasn't planning to let him get behind the wheel again until he started looking more rested.

"But what does it have to do with the investigation? That happened so many years ago."

"Thirty-seven years ago, to be exact. And I don't know whether it has anything to do with the case, but everything seems to be linked to Christian. I think the answer has to lie in his past; it's there that we'll find some sort of connection with the other events. If there is a connection, that is," he added. "Maybe they were just innocent bystanders and were targeted because they were close to Christian. But that's what we need to find out, and we might as well start from the beginning."

Paula overtook a truck at high speed, almost missing the exit to Trollhättan.

"Are you sure you don't want me to drive?" asked Patrik anxiously, gripping the door handle.

"Now you see how it feels," laughed Paula. "After yesterday, you're no longer reliable. Did you get any rest, by the way?" She glanced at him as she accelerated through a traffic circle.

"Actually, I did," said Patrik. "I slept for a couple of hours, and then I had a nice, relaxing evening with Erica. It was great."

"You need to take better care of yourself."

"That's exactly what Annika told me. The two of you need to stop being such mother hens," said Patrik.

Paula shifted her gaze to the map that they'd printed out from the Internet. Then she looked at the street signs along the road, almost hitting a cyclist who suddenly appeared on the right.

"Let me read the map. Apparently it's not true that girls are good at multi-tasking," said Patrik with a grin.

"Watch what you say," said Paula, although she didn't really seem insulted.

"Turn right here. We're getting close," said Patrik. "This is going to be interesting. Apparently the documents still exist, and the

553

woman I talked to on the phone knew instantly what case I was talking about. But then, it's not the sort of thing that would be easy to forget."

"It's great that everything went so smoothly with the prosecutor. Otherwise it would have been difficult to get access to these kinds of documents."

"You're right," said Patrik, focusing his attention on the map.

"There it is," said Paula, pointing at the building that housed the social welfare offices in Trollhättan.

A few minutes later they introduced themselves to Eva-Lena Skog, the woman that Patrik had spoken to on the phone.

"There are plenty of people here who remember the story," she told them, taking out of her desk a folder containing papers that had turned yellow with age. "It was a long time ago, but that kind of thing stays with you," she said, pushing back a lock of gray hair. She looked like the stereotypical schoolteacher, with her long hair pulled back in a neat bun.

"Did anyone suspect that the situation was as bad as it was?" asked Paula.

"Yes and no. We'd received some reports, and we'd made . . ." she opened the folder and ran her finger over the page on top.

"We'd made two home visits."

"And there was nothing to indicate that some sort of intervention might be necessary?" asked Patrik.

"It's hard to explain, but those were different times," said Skog with a sigh. "Today we would have stepped in at a much earlier stage, but back then . . . well, we simply didn't know any better. Apparently things improved during certain periods, and most likely our visits took place during those times when she was doing better."

"And there weren't any relatives or friends who reacted?" asked Paula. It was difficult for her to understand how something like this could have happened without anyone noticing.

"There were no other family members. I don't think there were any friends either. They lived a very isolated life, and that's why things happened the way they did. If it hadn't been for the smell. . . ." She swallowed hard and looked down. "We've made a lot of progress since then. It would never happen today."

"Let's hope not," said Patrik.

"As I understand it, you need this information in connection with a murder case," said Skog, pushing the folder across her desk toward them. "But you'll be careful how you handle the material, won't you? It's only under special circumstances that we allow access to this sort of file."

"We'll be extremely discreet, I promise," said Patrik. "And I'm positive that these documents are going to help us move forward with our investigation."

Skog looked at him with ill-concealed curiosity.

"What could your case possibly have to do with this? It all happened so many years ago."

"I'm afraid I can't discuss that," said Patrik. The truth was that he had no idea whatsoever. But they had to start somewhere.

"Mama?" He tried again to shake her, but she didn't move. He didn't know how long she'd been lying there like that. He was only three and didn't know how to tell time yet. But it had turned dark twice. He didn't like the dark, and his mama didn't either. They always left the lamp on when they went to bed, and he'd turned it on all by himself when it started getting too dark in the apartment to see. Then he had crept close to her. That was how they usually slept. Close to each other, very close. He pressed his face against her soft body. There was nothing angular about his mama, nothing that poked out or felt hard. Nothing but softness, warmth, and security.

But last night she had no longer felt warm. He had nudged her and pressed closer, but she didn't stir. Then he got an extra blanket out of the wardrobe, even though he was afraid to set his feet on the floor when it was dark. He was afraid of the monster under the bed. But he didn't want Mama to freeze. He didn't want to freeze either. Carefully he tucked around her the striped blanket that smelled so strange. She still didn't get warm. He didn't either. Shivering, he had lain next to her all night, waiting to wake up so this odd dream would be over.

When it started to get light, he climbed out of bed. Then he pulled the blanket over her again, since it had shifted during the night. Why was she sleeping so long? She never slept this long. Occasionally she might spend all day in bed, but she would wake up now and then. She would talk to him and ask him to get her a glass of water or something else. On those days when she stayed in bed, she sometimes said strange things. Things that scared him. She even shouted at him once in a while. But he would have preferred that to this, when she lay in bed so quiet and so cold.

He could feel hunger tearing at his stomach. Maybe Mama would think he was clever if she woke up to find that he'd made breakfast. The idea made him more cheerful, and he headed for the kitchen. But halfway there, he thought of something and turned back. He wanted Teddy to come too. He didn't want to be alone. With his teddy bear dragging along the floor, he again headed for the kitchen. Sandwiches. That's what Mama used to make for him. Jam sandwiches.

He opened the refrigerator. There was the jar of jam, with a red lid and strawberries on the label. And there was the butter. Carefully he took them out of the fridge and lifted them up onto the counter. Then he fetched a chair and set it in front of the counter so he could climb up onto the seat. This was starting to feel like an adventure. He reached for the bread box and took out two slices of bread. He pulled out a kitchen drawer and found a wooden butter knife. Mama didn't let him use the real knives. Slowly he spread butter on one of the pieces of bread, and jam on the other. Then he slapped them together. All right. The sandwich was ready.

He got down from the chair and again opened the fridge. He found a container of juice on a shelf in the door. With an effort he lifted the juice out and placed it on the kitchen table. He knew where the glasses were: in the cupboard above the bread box. Up on the chair again, then he opened the cupboard and took out a glass. He didn't want to drop it. Mama would be mad if he broke a glass.

He set the glass on the table, placed the sandwich next to it, and pushed the chair back into place. He climbed onto the chair, kneeling so that he could pour the juice. The container was heavy, and he struggled to hold it over the glass. But just as much juice ended up on the table as in the glass. He had to lean down and slurp up what had spilled onto the oilcloth.

The sandwich tasted wonderful. It was the first sandwich he had ever made all by himself, and he ate the whole thing in a few greedy mouthfuls. Then he noticed that his stomach had room for more, and this time he knew what to do. Mama was going to be so proud of him when she woke up and discovered that he could make his own sandwiches.

23

"Did anyone see anything?" Patrik was talking to Martin on the phone. "No? Okay, I wasn't really expecting it. But keep knocking on doors. You never know."

He ended the conversation and bit into his Big Mac. They had stopped at McDonald's to eat lunch and to discuss how they should proceed.

"Nothing?" asked Paula, who had been listening to Patrik while she poked at her fries.

"Nothing so far. There aren't many people living in the area now that it's winter. So it's not surprising that they haven't had much luck."

"How's it going at Badholmen?"

"They've taken the body away," said Patrik as he took another bite. "That means Torbjörn and his men will probably be done soon. He promised to call if they found anything."

"So what should we do now?"

Before getting their food, they had glanced through the copies of the documents that they'd been given at the social welfare office. Everything seemed to match with what Sanna had told Erica.

"We keep moving forward. We know that Christian was placed with a couple named Lissander shortly afterward. Here in Trollhättan."

"I wonder if they still live here," said Paula.

Patrik carefully wiped off his hands before looking through the file to find the right page. Then he memorized the information and phoned directory assistance.

"Hi, I wonder if you have a listing for Ragnar and Iréne Lissander in Trollhättan. Okay, thanks." His face lit up, and he nodded to Paula that he was in luck. "Could you text me the address?"

"They still live here?" Paula stuffed a few more fries into her mouth.

"It seems so. What do you say we go over there and have a little chat with them?" Patrik stood up, looking at Paula impatiently.

"Shouldn't we phone them first?"

"No, I want to see what happens if we turn up unannounced. There must be some reason why Christian changed his last name back to the name of his biological mother and never mentioned their existence to anyone, not even his wife."

"Maybe he didn't live with them for very long."

"That's possible, but I don't think so." Patrik tried to formulate why he had such a strong feeling that this was a lead worth following. "Because he didn't change his name until he turned eighteen. Why wait? Why keep the name at all if he didn't live with them for very long?"

"I suppose you're right about that," said Paula, though she still didn't sound convinced.

But they would soon find out. In a very short time one of the missing puzzle pieces about Christian Thydell would fall into place. Or rather, Christian Lissander.

Erica hesitated, her hand on the phone. Should she or shouldn't she? Finally she decided that it would soon be public knowledge anyway. Gaby might as well hear the news from her.

"Hi, it's Erica."

She closed her eyes as Gaby showered her with the usual effusive greetings. But she cut off the publishing director in the middle of the torrent of words.

"Christian is dead, Gaby."

There was silence on the phone. Then she heard Gaby take a deep breath.

"What? How?" she stammered. "Is it the same person who . . . ?"

"I don't know." Erica closed her eyes again. The words sounded so terrible and final when she said them out loud: "He was found hanged this morning. The police aren't saying anything more at the moment. We don't know whether it was suicide or whether. . . ." She couldn't finish the sentence.

"Hanged?" Gaby gasped. "That can't be true!"

Erica didn't reply at once. She knew that the news had to sink in slowly before it became real. She'd been through the same experience herself when Patrik told her.

"I'll let you know if I hear anything else," said Erica. "But I'd appreciate it if the media could be kept as much out of this as possible. It's hard enough for his family right now."

"Of course, of course," said Gaby, sounding as if she actually meant it. "But keep me posted about what happens, okay?"

"I will," said Erica, putting down the phone. She knew that even if Gaby could resist calling the press, it wouldn't be long before Christian's death would be on all the front pages. He had become an overnight star, and the papers had quickly realized that he was newsworthy material. His mysterious death would undoubtedly dominate the news placards in the days ahead. Poor Sanna, and those poor boys.

Erica had hardly been able to look at the boys when she was supposed to be taking care of them at Agneta's house. They were sitting on the floor, playing with a big pile of Lego blocks. Carefree and happy, just squabbling a bit now and then, as siblings do. The terrifying experience with the red paint from the day before seemed to have rolled right off them. But maybe they were just keeping it all in. Maybe they were hurting inside, even though it didn't show on the outside. And now their father was gone. How was that going to affect their lives?

She had sat on the sofa without saying a word until she finally forced herself to look at them. With their heads close together, the two little boys were discussing where to put the siren on the toy ambulance. They looked so much like both Christian and Sanna. And now they were the only thing left of him. Aside from his book, of course. *The Mermaid.*

Erica suddenly had a strong urge to read the story again. Read it as a form of memorial for Christian. First she looked in on Maja, who was sleeping soundly in her cot. Maja had been allowed to stay home from the day-care center today, since the morning had been filled with so much commotion. Gently Erica stroked Maja's blond head lying on the pillow. Then she went to get the book, settled herself comfortably, and opened the novel to the first page.

They were going to bury Magnus in two days. In two days he would be put in the ground. Into a hole in the ground.

Cia hadn't left the house since receiving the news that they'd found him. She couldn't stand the thought of people staring at her, couldn't bear to see their eyes filled with sympathy as they wondered what Magnus could have done to deserve such a death. Everyone was probably speculating about what he might have done to bring this misfortune down on himself.

She knew that people were talking; over the years she'd participated in the gossiping too. Not contributing much, she was glad to say, but all the same she had listened without offering any protests.

"There's no smoke without fire."

"I wonder how they could afford a trip to Thailand. He must be getting paid under the table."

"You wouldn't believe the plunging necklines she's suddenly taken to wearing. I wonder who she's trying to impress."

Scattered rumors taken out of context and then patiently piled up to form a mixture of fact and fiction. Until finally it became the truth.

She could just imagine what stories were circulating through town. But as long as she could stay at home, it didn't matter. She could hardly bear to think about the video that Ludvig had shown the police yesterday. She hadn't lied when she said that she didn't know about it. At the same time, it had gotten her thinking. She had occasionally sensed that there was something Magnus wasn't telling her. Or had she just made that up after the fact, now that her whole life had been turned upside down in such a bewildering way? But she thought she could recall sometimes wondering what was behind the strange melancholy that occasionally came over her husband, who was otherwise such a happy person. It would fall over him like a shadow, a solar eclipse. A few times she had actually asked him about it. Yes, now she remembered. She had patted his cheek and asked him what he was thinking about. And it was always as if he switched on the light again, chasing away the shadow before she could see any more of it.

"I'm thinking about you, of course, sweetheart," Magnus had answered, leaning forward to give her a kiss.

Sometimes Cia had noticed the shadow even when there was no outward sign of it. Each time, she had quickly dismissed the whole thing, since it occurred so seldom, and she had nothing more to go on.

But ever since yesterday, she hadn't been able to get it out of her mind. The shadow. Was that the reason Magnus was no longer alive? Where had it come from? Why hadn't he ever said anything to her? She had thought they told each other everything, that she knew everything about him, just as he knew everything about her. What if she was mistaken? What if she actually knew nothing about her husband?

In her mind the shadow kept getting bigger. She pictured his face. Not the happy, warm, and loving man that she'd been lucky enough to wake up next to each morning for the past twenty years. Instead, she saw his face as it had looked in the video. Desperate and contorted.

Cia covered her face with her hands and wept. She wasn't sure about anything anymore. It felt as if Magnus had died a second time, and she didn't think she could survive losing him again.

Patrik rang the bell, and after a moment the door opened. A short, skinny old man peered out.

"Yes?"

"Patrik Hedström. From the Tanum police force. And this is my colleague, Paula Morales."

The man studied their faces.

"That's a long way to come. How can I be of service?" he said lightly, although there was a guarded edge to his voice.

"Are you Ragnar Lissander?"

"Yes, that's right."

"We'd like to come inside and have a few words with you. Preferably with your wife as well, if she's at home," said Patrik. Even though he spoke politely, it was clear that he wasn't prepared to take no for an answer.

The man seemed to hesitate for a moment. Then he stepped aside and let them in.

"My wife is a bit under the weather, so she's resting. I'll go and find out if she can come downstairs for a moment."

"That would be good," said Patrik, uncertain whether Ragnar Lissander expected them to stand in the front hall while he went upstairs.

"Go in and sit down. I'll be right back," he said then, as if in answer to Patrik's unspoken question.

Patrik and Paula looked in the direction the man was pointing and then entered a living room on the left. They took a look around as they listened to Mr. Lissander climbing the stairs.

"Not exactly a cozy place, is it?" whispered Paula.

Patrik had to agree. The living room looked more like a display in a furniture store than a room that was actually used. Everything gleamed with polish, and the occupants seemed to have a certain fondness for decorative items. The sofa was brown leather, and in front of it stood the obligatory glass coffee table. Not a fingerprint was visible on the glass, and Patrik shuddered at the thought of how it would look if the table was in his own home, with Maja's sticky fingers nearby.

The most striking thing was that there were no personal possessions in the room. No photographs, no drawings from grandchildren, no postcards with greetings from family members or friends.

He cautiously sat down on the sofa, and Paula sat down next to him. They could hear voices upstairs, a heated exchange, although they weren't able to make out any of the words. After a few more minutes they heard footsteps on the stairs, this time from two people.

Ragnar Lissander appeared in the doorway. He truly personifies the term "little old man," thought Patrik. Gray, stooped, and invisible. The woman behind him was a whole different story. She didn't merely walk toward them — she strode forward, wearing a dressing gown that seemed to consist of a plethora of apricot-colored flounces. She emitted a deep sigh as she shook hands with Patrik.

"I certainly hope this is important, since you're interrupting my nap."

Patrik felt as if he'd landed in a silent film from the nineteen twenties.

"We just have a few questions," he said, sitting down again.

Iréne Lissander took a seat on the armchair across from him. She hadn't bothered to say hello to Paula.

"So, Ragnar says that you're from . . ." she turned to her husband. "Was it Tanumshede, you said?"

He mumbled affirmatively, sitting down at the far end of the sofa. His hands hung between his knees, and he fixed his eyes on the shiny glass table.

"I don't understand what you could possibly want with us," the woman said haughtily.

Patrik couldn't help casting a glance in Paula's direction. She discreetly rolled her eyes.

"We're investigating a murder," he said. "And we've found some information that points back in time, to an event that occurred here in Trollhättan thirty-seven years ago."

Out of the corner of his eye, Patrik saw Ragnar give a start.

"You took in a foster child at that time, is that right?"

"Christian," said Iréne, bobbing one foot up and down. She was wearing high-heeled slippers with open toes. Her toenails were exquisitely painted a fiery red that clashed with the color of her dressing gown.

"Exactly. Christian Thydell, who was then given your surname. Lissander."

"He changed his name back later on," said Ragnar quietly, receiving a murderous look from his wife. He fell silent, his whole body slumping forward again.

"Did you adopt him?" asked Paula.

"No, absolutely not." Iréne pushed a lock of her dark hair, obviously dyed, out of her face. "He just lived with us. He was allowed to use our last name for . . . the sake of convenience."

Patrik was dumbfounded. How many years had Christian spent in this home, treated like some lowly lodger, judging by the coldness with which his foster mother spoke of him?

"I see. And precisely how long did Christian live with you?" He could hear the disapproval in his own voice, but Iréne Lissander didn't seem to notice.

"Hmm, how long was it, Ragnar? How long was the boy here?" Her husband didn't reply, so she turned back to Patrik. She still hadn't deigned to give Paula a single glance. Patrik had the feeling that other women didn't exist in Iréne's world.

"It should be easy to work out. He was about three when he came to us. And how old was he when he left, Ragnar? He must have been eighteen." She smiled apologetically. "He wanted to seek his fortune elsewhere. And since then we've never heard a word from him. Isn't that right, Ragnar?"

"Yes, that's right," said Ragnar Lissander quietly. "He simply . . . disappeared."

Patrik felt sorry for the little man. Had he always been like this? Browbeaten and cowed? Or was it the years that he'd spent with Iréne that had stripped him of all virility?

"So you don't know where he went?"

"No idea. We have absolutely no idea." Iréne's foot was bobbing up and down again.

"Why are you asking us these questions?" said Ragnar. "How is Christian involved in a murder investigation?"

Patrik hesitated. "Unfortunately, I have to tell you that he was found dead this morning."

Ragnar couldn't hide his shock. He at least had cared about Christian and hadn't just thought of him as a lodger.

"How did he die?" Ragnar asked, his voice unsteady.

"He was found hanged. That's all we know at the moment."

"Did he have a family?"

"Yes, two fine sons and a wife named Sanna. He's been living in Fjällbacka, working as a librarian. Last week his first novel was published. It's called *The Mermaid.* And it's been getting great reviews."

"So that was him," said Ragnar. "I read about the book in the newspaper because the title caught my attention. But the picture of him was nothing like the Christian who used to live with us."

"Who would have thought it possible? That a boy like that could make something of himself," said Iréne, her expression as hard as stone.

Patrik bit his tongue so as not to say something negative to her. He needed to be professional and keep his eye on the objective. He could feel that he had started to sweat again, and he tugged at his shirt to get some air.

"Christian had a rough start. Was that something you could see in his behavior?"

"He was so young. Children forget those sorts of things very quickly," said Iréne, waving her hand dismissively.

"Sometimes he had nightmares," said Ragnar.

"But all children do. No, we didn't notice anything. He was rather an odd child, but with his background, well. . . ."

"What do you know about his biological mother?"

"A slut. Lower class. And not quite right in the head." Iréne tapped her finger against her temple and sighed. "But I really don't understand what you think we might be able to tell you. So if there's nothing more, I'd like to go back upstairs and lie down. I'm not feeling well."

"Just a few more questions," said Patrik. "Is there anything else about his childhood that you'd like to mention? We're looking for a person, most likely a woman, who issued threats toward Christian, and others."

"Well, back then the girls weren't exactly swarming around him," said Iréne, indifferently.

"I'm not just thinking of love affairs. Were there any other women who were close to him?"

"No. Who would that be? We were all he had."

Patrik was just about to end the conversation when Paula interjected a question:

"One last thing. Another man was found dead in Fjällbacka. Magnus Kjellner, one of Christian's friends. And two other friends seem to have been subjected to the same sort of threats that Christian had received. Erik Lind and Kenneth Bengtsson. Do you recognize those names?"

"As I said, we haven't heard a peep from him since he moved," said Iréne, abruptly getting to her feet. "And now you really must excuse me. I have a weak heart, and this has been such a shock that I simply must go and lie down." She left the room, and they heard her climbing the stairs.

"Do you have any idea who it could be?" asked Ragnar, with a glance toward the doorway where his wife had just left.

"No, not at the moment," said Patrik. "But I think that Christian is the central figure in this whole thing. And I have no intention of giving up until I know how and why. Earlier today it was my job to deliver the bad news to his wife."

"I understand," said Ragnar softly. He opened his mouth again, as if to say something more, but then pressed his lips together. He stood up and looked at Paula and Patrik. "I'll see you out."

When they reached the front door, Patrik had a feeling that he shouldn't leave. He wanted to stay and give the man a good shake until he told them what he had been on the verge of saying. Instead, Patrik merely pressed his business card into Ragnar's hand, and then he and Paula left.

A week later, the food ran out. He'd eaten all the bread a couple of days earlier, and then resorted to cornflakes out of the big package. Without milk. Both the milk and the juice were gone, but there was water, and he had pushed a chair over to the sink so he could drink straight from the tap.

But now there was nothing more to eat. There hadn't been much in the fridge to start with, and in the pantry he found only canned goods, which he couldn't open. He'd thought of going out to shop for groceries himself. He knew where Mama kept her money, in the purse that was always in the front hall. But he couldn't open the door. It was impossible for him to turn the lock, no matter how hard he tried. Otherwise Mama would have been even prouder of him. He could have shown her that not only could he make his own sandwiches, but he could also do the shopping all by himself while she slept.

The past few days he'd started to wonder if she might be sick. But he knew that when a person was sick, they got a fever and felt hot. Mama was very cold. And she smelled strange. He had to hold his nose at night when he crept into bed to sleep close to her. There was also something sticky about her. He didn't know what it was, but if she'd gotten sticky, then she must have been out of bed when he wasn't watching. Maybe she would wake up soon.

He spent every day playing by himself. He would sit in his room with his toys spread out around him. He also knew how to turn on the TV by touching the big button. Sometimes a children's program would be on, and it was fun to watch them after he'd been playing alone all day.

But Mama would probably be angry when she saw how dirty things were in the apartment. He needed to clean up. But he was so hungry. So incredibly hungry.

A few times he'd glanced at the telephone and even picked up the receiver, listening to the signal say "beep, beep, beep." But who should he call? He didn't know anyone's number. And nobody ever phoned the apartment.

And Mama would be waking up soon. She would get out of bed and take a bath and make the bad smell go away, the smell that made him feel sick. Then she would smell like Mama again.

His stomach was screaming with hunger as he crawled into bed and moved close to her. He didn't like the smell in his nose, but he always slept next to Mama. Otherwise he couldn't fall asleep.

He pulled the covers over them. Outside the window, darkness fell.

24

Gösta got up as soon as he heard Patrik and Paula come in. An oppressive mood had settled over the police station. Everyone was feeling frustrated. They needed some sort of concrete lead in order to move forward with the investigation.

"Let's meet in the kitchen in five minutes," said Patrik, and then he disappeared into his office.

Gösta went into the kitchen and sat down in his favorite place next to the window. Five minutes later the others showed up, one after the other. Patrik was the last to arrive. He took up his position in front of the counter, leaning his back against it with his arms crossed.

"As you all know, Christian Thydell was found dead this morning. At the present time, we can't say whether his death was murder or suicide. We'll have to wait for the results from the postmortem. I've talked to

Torbjörn, and unfortunately he had very little to add. But based on the preliminary examination, there doesn't seem to be any sign of a struggle at the site."

Martin raised his hand. "What about footprints? Anything to indicate that Christian wasn't alone when he died? If there was snow on the steps, maybe they could be lifted for analysis."

"I asked Torbjörn about that," said Patrik. "But it would be impossible to say when any shoe prints were actually made, and besides, all of the snow had blown off the steps. But the techs did manage to lift a number of fingerprints, mostly from the railing, and they'll be carefully analyzed, of course. It'll be a few days before we have a report." He turned around to fill a glass with water from the tap and took a few sips. "Any new developments from knocking on doors?"

"No," said Martin. "We've pretty much knocked on every door in the lower part of town. But no one seems to have seen anything."

"Okay. We need to go over to Christian's house and carry out a proper search. See if we can find anything that shows he might have met the murderer there first."

"Murderer?" said Gösta. "So you think it

was murder and not suicide?"

"I don't know what I think at the moment," replied Patrik, wearily rubbing his forehead. "But I suggest that we assume Christian was also murdered, until we find out more." He turned to Mellberg. "What do you think, Bertil?"

It was always wise at least to pretend to involve the boss.

"I agree," said Mellberg.

"We're also going to have to wrestle with the press. As soon as they get wind of what happened, there's going to be huge interest from the media. I recommend that nobody talk to any reporters; just refer them all to me."

"On that point I have to object," said Mellberg. "As the police chief here, I should be the one to handle such an important task as liaison with the media."

Patrik weighed his options. It would be a nightmare to give Mellberg free rein to talk with journalists. On the other hand, it might take too much energy to try to dissuade him.

"Okay, let's say that you'll be the one to keep in contact with the media. But if I might offer a word of advice, it would be best if we say as little as possible, under the circumstances."

"Don't worry. Considering my extensive

experience, I'll be able to twist them around my little finger," said Mellberg, leaning back in his chair.

"Paula and I have been out to Trollhättan, as all of you probably already know."

"Did you find out anything?" asked Annika eagerly.

"I'm not sure yet. But I think we're on the right track, so we'll keep digging." Patrik took another sip of water. It was time to tell his colleagues what they'd discovered and what he was having such a hard time digesting.

"As Annika found out, Christian was orphaned at a very young age. He lived alone with his mother, Anita Thydell. There's no record of who his father was. According to information from the social welfare office, the boy and his mother were terribly isolated, and at times Anita had difficulty caring for Christian because of a mental illness she suffered, combined with drug abuse. The authorities kept a watchful eye on Anita and her son after receiving several calls from the neighbors. But apparently the only home visits were made during the periods when Anita had the situation more or less under control. At least that was the explanation we were given for why no one intervened. And the fact that 'times were different' back then," Patrik added without concealing the sarcasm in his voice.

"One day when Christian was three years old, another tenant reported to the welfare office that he'd noticed a stench coming from Anita's apartment. The authorities obtained a master key, and when they went in they discovered Christian alone with his dead mother. Presumably she'd been dead about a week, and Christian had survived by eating whatever he could find in the kitchen, and drinking water from the tap. But the food had apparently run out after a few days, because when the police and medics arrived, the boy was starving and weak. They found him huddled close to his mother's body, only semiconscious."

"Good Lord," said Annika, and her eyes filled with tears. Gösta was also blinking away tears, and Martin's face had turned green. He looked like he was fighting hard not to be sick.

"Unfortunately, Christian's troubles didn't end there. He was placed very quickly with a foster family, a couple by the name of Lissander. Paula and I paid them a visit today."

"Christian couldn't have had an easy childhood with them," said Paula quietly. "To be honest, I got the impression that something wasn't quite right with Mrs. Lissander."

Gösta felt something flash through his mind. Lissander. Where had he heard that name before? He somehow associated it with Ernst Lundgren, their former colleague who had been fired from the police force. Gösta tried to think what the connection could be. He considered telling everyone that the name sounded familiar, but then decided to wait until the explanation came to him on its own.

Patrik went on: "The Lissanders say that they've had no contact with Christian since he turned eighteen. That was when he apparently broke off the relationship with them and left."

"Do you think they're telling the truth?" asked Annika.

Patrik looked at Paula, who nodded.

"Yes," he said. "Unless they're very good liars."

"And they didn't know of any woman who might bear some sort of grudge against Christian?" Gösta asked.

"They said they didn't. But on that point I'm not sure they were being completely truthful."

"Did he have any brothers or sisters?"

"They didn't mention any, but maybe you

could find out, Annika. That ought to be easy enough to research. I'll give you all the names and information you need. Could you work on it right away?"

"I can do it now, if you like," said Annika. "It won't take long."

"Okay, great. There's a yellow Post-it note with everything you need on the folder that's lying on my desk."

"I'll be back," said Annika, getting to her feet.

"What about having a chat with Kenneth? Now that Christian is dead, he might decide to start talking," said Martin.

"Good idea. So that means we have the following items on our to-do list: talk with Kenneth, and conduct a thorough search of Christian's house. We also need to find out all the details of Christian's life before he came to Fjällbacka. Gösta and Martin, I'd like you to talk with Kenneth, okay?" They both nodded, and Patrik turned to Paula. "You and I will drive over to Christian's house. If we find anything of interest, we'll call in the tech team."

"That sounds good," she said.

"Mellberg, you'll stay here at the station to answer any questions from the media," Patrik went on. "And Annika will keep digging into Christian's past. At the moment we have a few facts to go on, at least."

"More than you thought," said Annika, appearing in the doorway.

"Did you find out anything?" asked Patrik.

"Yes, I did," she said, giving her colleagues an excited look. "The Lissanders had a daughter two years after they took in Christian as a foster child. So he has a sister. Alice Lissander."

"Louise?" Erik called, standing in the front hall. Could he be so lucky that she wasn't at home? In that case, he wouldn't have to think up some excuse to get her to leave for a while. Because he needed to pack his suitcase. He felt as if he had a fever, as if his whole body was screaming at him to get out of town.

He'd taken care of all the practical matters. He'd made a reservation under his own name for a plane departing tomorrow. He hadn't bothered to set up a false identity. That would take far too much time, and to be honest, he really had no idea how to go about it. But there was no reason to believe that anyone would try to stop him from leaving. And after he reached his destination, it would be too late.

Erik hesitated outside the upstairs rooms belonging to his daughters. He wished he could go in and have a look around, as his way of saying good-bye. At the same time, he couldn't get himself to do it. It was easier just to focus only on what he needed to get done.

He put the big suitcase on top of the bed. It was always stored downstairs in the basement, so by the time Louise noticed it was missing, he would be far away. He planned to leave tonight. What he'd learned from talking to Kenneth had shaken him badly, and he didn't want to stay here even a minute longer. He'd write a note to Louise saying that he had to leave on an urgent business trip. Then he'd drive to Landvetter Airport in Göteborg and get a room at a nearby hotel. Tomorrow afternoon he'd be sitting in a plane, heading for southern climes. Unreachable.

Erik tossed one item of clothing after another into the suitcase. He couldn't take much. If the chest of drawers and wardrobe were noticeably empty when Louise came home, she'd know what he was up to. But he took as much as he could. Later he could buy new clothes. Money was not going to be a problem.

While he packed, he was on the alert for Louise's arrival, not wanting her to surprise him. If she came home now, he'd have to shove the suitcase under the bed and pretend to be packing the small carry-on bag that he kept in the bedroom. That was the one he always took on business trips.

For a moment he paused. The memory that had surfaced now refused to sink back into oblivion. He couldn't say that it particularly upset him. Everybody made mistakes; that was only human. But he was fascinated by the fact that someone could be driven by such a single-minded purpose. After all, it had happened so long ago.

Then he shook himself. It would do no good to brood over things. The day after tomorrow he would be safe.

The ducks came rushing toward him. By now they were old friends. He always stopped here, bringing a sack of stale bread. Now they flocked around his feet, eager for what he had to offer.

Ragnar thought about the conversation with the two police officers, and about Christian. He should have done more. He should have known, even back then. All his life he had been little more than a bystander, weak and silent, watching without intervening. Her bystander. That's how it had been between them from the very beginning. Neither of them had been able to break the pattern they'd created.

Iréne had always been preoccupied with her own beauty. She had loved the good things in life: parties, drinks, and men who admired her. He knew all about them. Just because he'd hidden behind his inadequacies didn't mean he was unaware of the affairs she'd had with other men.

And that poor boy had never had a chance. Christian could never measure up, never give her what she wanted. The boy had probably thought Iréne loved Alice, but he was wrong. Iréne was incapable of loving anyone. She had merely seen her own reflection in her daughter's beauty. Ragnar wished that he had spoken to the boy before they chased him away like a dog. He wasn't sure what had really happened, or what was the truth. He wasn't like Iréne, who had accused and condemned him all in one breath.

Doubt had been gnawing at Ragnar, and it still was. But over the years the memories had faded. They had gone on living their lives. He stayed in the background while Iréne continued to believe that she was still beautiful. No one had dared tell her that her looks were gone, so she kept on behaving as if she could again be the life of the party at any moment. The woman who was both beautiful and desirable.

But it had to end. At that moment Ragnar understood why the police had come, and he realized that he'd made a mistake. A huge, fateful mistake. And now it was time to put things right.

Ragnar took Patrik's business card out of his pocket. Then he got out his mobile phone and punched in the number from the card.

"Seems like we keep driving this same road over and over," said Gösta as he accelerated past Munkedal.

"And we do," said Martin. He cast a quizzical look at his colleague, who had been unusually quiet ever since they left Tanumshede. Gösta wasn't a big talker at the best of times, but right now he seemed more taciturn than ever.

"Is something wrong?" Martin asked after a while when he could no longer stand the lack of at least sporadic conversation.

"What? No, it's nothing," said Gösta.

Martin didn't press the issue. He knew that it would do no good to try forcing something out of Gösta if he didn't want to share what was on his mind. He'd reveal whatever it was in his own time.

"What a bloody awful story. Talk about getting a rough start in life," said Martin.

He was thinking about his little daughter and what might happen if she was subjected to such a terrible experience. It was true what everyone said about becoming a parent. It made a person a thousand times more sensitive to everything concerning children in difficult circumstances.

"That poor little boy," said Gösta, and all of a sudden he looked less distracted.

"Don't you think we should wait to talk to Kenneth until we find out more about the sister, Alice?"

"I'm sure Annika will double-check and triple-check everything while we're away from the station. The first thing we need to know is where to find Alice."

"Couldn't we just ask the Lissanders?" said Martin.

"Since they never even mentioned her existence when Patrik and Paula were there, I assume that Patrik thinks there's something fishy about the whole situation. And it won't hurt to find out as many facts about the family as possible."

Martin knew that his colleague was right. He felt foolish for even asking the question.

"Do you think she's the one behind it all?"

"I have no idea. It's too early to speculate about that."

They drove the rest of the way to the

hospital in silence. After parking the car, they went straight to the ward where Kenneth was a patient.

"We're back," said Gösta as they entered his room.

Kenneth didn't reply, just looked at them as if he didn't care who came in.

"How do you feel? Are your wounds starting to heal?" asked Gösta, sitting down on the same chair as before.

"It's going to take a lot more time for that," said Kenneth, moving his bandaged arms. "They're giving me painkillers. So it doesn't really hurt much."

"You heard about Christian?"

Kenneth nodded. "Yes."

"You don't seem particularly upset about it," said Gösta, without sounding unfriendly.

"Not everything is visible on the outside."

Gösta gave him a puzzled look.

"How's Sanna?" asked Kenneth, and for the first time they could see a glint of something in his eyes. Sympathy. He knew what it felt like to lose someone.

"Not so good," said Gösta, shaking his head. "We were over there this morning. It's very sad for the boys too."

"Yes, it is," Kenneth agreed, his face clouding over.

Martin was starting to feel superfluous.

He was still standing, but now he pulled a chair over to the other side of the bed, across from Gösta. Then he glanced at his colleague, who nodded, encouraging him to ask his own questions.

"We think that everything that has happened lately is connected to Christian, and so we've been delving into his background. One thing we found out is that he had a different last name when he was growing up. Christian Lissander. He also has a stepsister named Alice Lissander. Did you ever hear him talk about any of this?"

Kenneth paused before answering.

"No. It doesn't sound familiar."

Gösta fixed his eyes on the man, looking as if he'd like to climb into Kenneth's head to see if he was telling the truth or not.

"I said this before, and I'll say it again: If you know something that you're not telling us, you're putting not only your own life in danger, but Erik's too. Now that Christian is dead, you must realize how serious this is."

"I don't know anything," said Kenneth calmly.

"If you're withholding information, we're going to dig it up sooner or later."

"I'm sure you'll make a very thorough job of it," said Kenneth. He looked small and fragile as he lay there with his bandaged arms resting on top of the blue hospital blanket.

Gösta and Martin exchanged glances. They realized that they weren't going to get any more out of Kenneth, but neither of them believed that he was telling the truth.

Erica closed the book. She'd spent the last few hours curled up in an armchair reading, interrupted only by Maja, who came over once in a while to ask for something. On such occasions, Erica was grateful for her daughter's ability to play by herself.

The novel was even better the second time. It was truly amazing. It wasn't an uplifting kind of book; instead, it had filled her mind with dark musings. But somehow, that didn't seem unpleasant. It dealt with issues that a person needed to think about, issues that required the reader to take a stand and in that way find out what sort of person he or she was.

In Erica's opinion, the story was about guilt, about how it could eat up a person from the inside. For the first time she wondered what it was that Christian had wanted to convey through his book, what message he wanted his story to present.

She placed the book on her lap with a feeling that she'd missed something that was actually right in front of her eyes. Something she was too dense or blind to see. She turned to the back of the book to look at the inside flap of the dust jacket. There was a photo of Christian, in black and white. A classic author pose, and he was wearing wire-rimmed glasses. He'd been handsome in a rather reserved way. There was a loneliness evident in his eyes that made it impossible to know whether he was ever really present. He always seemed to be alone, never in the company of anyone else. As if he were inside a bubble. Paradoxically enough, it was this sense of distance that had exerted such an attraction on others. People always wanted to have what they couldn't get. And that was exactly how it had been with Christian.

Erica hauled herself out of the armchair. She was feeling a bit guilty because she'd been so engrossed in the book that she'd ignored her daughter. With great effort she now managed to lower herself to the floor to sit next to Maja, who was overjoyed that her mother was going to join in her games.

But still hovering in the back of Erica's mind was the Mermaid. She wanted to say something. Christian wanted to say something. Erica was sure about that. She just wished she knew what it was.

Patrik couldn't resist taking his mobile out of his pocket again to look at the display.

"Stop that," said Paula, laughing. "Annika isn't going to call any sooner just because you keep checking your phone all the time. I promise you'll hear it when it rings."

"I know," said Patrik, smiling with embarrassment. "I just feel like we're so close now." He went back to pulling out drawers and opening cupboards in the kitchen of the house belonging to Christian and Sanna. It hadn't taken them long to obtain a warrant to search the premises. The problem was that he didn't know what they were looking for.

"It should be easy enough to find out where Alice Lissander lives," Paula consoled him. "Annika will probably call any minute to give us the address."

"Right," said Patrik, looking inside the dishwasher. There was no sign that Christian had received any visitors the day before. Nor had they found any indications of a forced entry or that he might have left the house against his will. "But why didn't the Lissanders mention anything about their daughter?"

"We'll find out soon enough. But I think

it's wise for us to make our own inquiries about Alice before we talk with her parents again."

"I agree. But they're going to have to answer a lot of questions."

Patrik and Paula went upstairs. Here, too, everything looked the same as it had on the previous day — except in the children's room. There the text on the wall, the blood-red words, had been replaced by a swath of thick black paint.

They stopped in the doorway.

"Christian must have painted over the words yesterday," said Paula.

"I can understand it. I probably would have done the same thing."

"So what do you really think?" asked Paula, going into the bedroom next door. She put her hands on her hips as she surveyed the room before starting a meticulous search.

"About what?" said Patrik as he joined her, going over to the wardrobe and opening the doors.

"Was Christian murdered? Or did he take his own life?"

"I know what I said at the meeting back at the station, but I'm not ruling anything out. Christian was an odd person. The few times we talked to him, I had the feeling that things were going on in his head that simply defied comprehension. But apparently there's no suicide note, at any rate."

"People don't always leave a note. You know that as well as I do." Paula carefully pulled out the bureau drawers, putting her hand inside to go through the contents.

"You're right, but if we'd found one, we wouldn't have to speculate about what happened." Patrik straightened up, pausing to catch his breath. His heart was pounding, and he wiped the sweat from his forehead.

"I don't think there's anything here that's worth a closer look," said Paula, closing the last drawer. "Shall we go?"

Patrik hesitated. He didn't want to give up, but Paula was right.

"Let's go back to the station and wait for Annika to find something. Maybe Gösta and Martin have had better luck with Kenneth."

"We can always hope so," said Paula, sounding skeptical.

They were just on their way out the door when Patrik's mobile rang. He yanked it out of his pocket, but he was disappointed to see it wasn't the station calling. In fact, he didn't recognize the number.

"Patrik Hedström, Tanum police," he said, hoping to keep the conversation brief so that the line wouldn't be busy if Annika tried to call. Suddenly he froze.

"Hello, Ragnar." He motioned to Paula, who stopped halfway to the car.

"Yes? I see. Well, we've also found out a few things. . . . Of course. We can discuss that when we meet. We could drive out there now. Should we come to your house? Oh, all right. We'll find it. Right. See you soon."

He ended the call and looked at Paula. "That was Ragnar Lissander. He says he has something to tell us. And something to show us too."

All the way back from Uddevalla, the name had kept whirling through his mind. Lissander. Why was it so hard to remember where he'd heard that name before? And his former colleague Ernst Lundgren kept turning up in his thoughts too. Somehow the name was linked to him. Approaching the exit to Fjällbacka, Gösta finally came to a decision. He deliberately turned the wheel to the right and got off the highway.

"What are you doing?" asked Martin. "I thought we were heading back to the station."

"We just need to make a brief stop at someone's house first."

"At someone's house? Whose house?"

"Ernst Lundgren's." Gösta shifted down and turned left.

"Why are we going to see Ernst?"

Gösta told Martin what he'd been thinking about.

"But you have no idea where you've heard that name before?"

"If I did, I would have told you," snapped Gösta. He suspected that Martin thought his age was making him forgetful.

"Take it easy," said Martin. "We'll go over to Ernst's house and ask him, to see if he can spark your memory. It's great that he might actually be able to make a positive contribution for a change."

"That would be a new development, wouldn't it?" Gösta couldn't help smiling. Like his colleagues, he didn't have a very high opinion of Ernst's competence or his personality. At the same time, he didn't detest him as wholeheartedly as he knew the others did, with the possible exception of Mellberg. After working with Ernst for so long, Gösta had grown used to him. Nor could he ignore the fact that over the years they had shared a good many laughs together. On the other hand, Ernst certainly had a tendency to make a mess of things. Especially the last time he had been part of the investigative team, before he was fired.

But maybe he'd actually be of some help this time.

"Looks like he's home, anyway," said Martin as they pulled up in front of the house.

"Yes, it does," said Gösta, parking the police vehicle next to Ernst's car.

Ernst opened the door before they even rang the bell. He must have seen them from the kitchen window.

"How about that? I wasn't expecting such important visitors," he said, letting his former colleagues come in.

Martin looked around. Unlike Gösta, he'd never been to Ernst's house before, but he was not impressed. Even though he hadn't kept his own apartment very neat when he was a bachelor himself, it had never approached the chaos he saw here. Dishes were piled high in the sink, clothes were scattered everywhere, and the kitchen table looked like it had never been wiped clean.

"I haven't got much to offer," said Ernst. "But I can always come up with a wee dram." He reached for a bottle standing on the counter.

"I'm driving," said Gösta.

"What about you? Looks like you could use a pick-me-up," said Ernst, holding out the bottle toward Martin, but he declined.

"Okay, okay. I can see you're a couple of

teetotallers." He poured a healthy shot for himself and gulped it down.

"All right. Why are you here?" He sat down on a chair at the table, and his former colleagues followed suit.

"I've been wondering about something that I think you might know about," said Gösta.

"Aha. So that's it."

"It has to do with a name. It sounds familiar to me, and for some reason I keep associating it with you."

"Well, we worked together for a lot of years, you and I," said Ernst, and he almost sounded on the verge of tears. This was probably not his first drink of the day.

"Yes, we did," said Gösta, nodding. "And now I need your help. Are you willing to keep this to yourself, or not?"

Ernst thought for a moment. Then he sighed and waved his empty glass.

"Okay. Shoot."

"Do I have your word of honor that whatever I say stays here?" Gösta stared hard at Ernst, who nodded reluctantly.

"Okay, okay. Go ahead and ask your question."

"We're investigating the murder of Magnus Kjellner, which I'm sure you've heard about. In the process we've come across the name Lissander. I don't know why, but it sounds familiar. And for some reason the name makes me think of you. Do you recognize it?"

Ernst swayed a bit on his chair. There wasn't a sound in the room as Ernst considered the question while Martin and Gösta both stared at him expectantly.

Suddenly Ernst broke into a smile.

"Lissander. Of course I recognize that name. Bloody hell!"

They had agreed to meet at the one place that Patrik and Paula were sure they could find in Trollhättan: the McDonald's right near the bridge. That's where they'd had lunch only a few hours earlier.

Ragnar Lissander was waiting inside, and Paula sat down next to him as Patrik bought coffee for all of them. Ragnar seemed even more invisible than he had at home. A small, balding man in a beige coat. His hand shook slightly as he accepted the coffee cup, and he was having a hard time looking them in the eye.

"You wanted to talk to us?" said Patrik.

"We . . . we didn't really tell you everything."

Patrik didn't speak. He was curious to find out how the man was going to explain that they hadn't mentioned having a daughter.

"It hasn't always been easy, you know. We had a daughter. Alice. Christian was about five when she was born, and it wasn't easy for him. I should have. . . ." His voice faded, and he took a sip of coffee before continuing. "I think he was damaged for life after what he'd been through. I don't know how much you know about it, but Christian was alone for more than a week with his dead mother. She was mentally ill and couldn't always take care of him — or herself either. Finally she died in their apartment, and Christian wasn't able to tell anyone. He thought she was just asleep."

"Yes, we know about that. We talked to the social welfare authorities and got copies of all the documents relating to the case." Patrik heard how formal it sounded when he said "the documents." But that was the only way for him to maintain the necessary distance from the horrible event.

"Did she die from an overdose?" asked Paula. They hadn't had time to read through all the details yet.

"No, she wasn't a junkie. She went through bad periods when she drank too much, and she was on prescription drugs, of course. But it was her heart that finally gave out."

"Why was that?" Patrik really didn't understand.

"She didn't take care of herself, and the alcohol and drugs came into the picture too. She was also tremendously obese. She weighed over three hundred pounds."

Something began stirring in Patrik's subconscious. Something that didn't make sense. But he'd have to think about that later.

"And then Christian came to live with you?" said Paula.

"Yes, then he came to live with us. Iréne was the one who decided we should adopt him. We didn't seem able to have any children of our own."

"But you never did adopt him, right?" asked Patrik.

"We probably would have if Iréne hadn't gotten pregnant soon afterwards."

"That actually happens quite often," said Paula.

"That's what the doctor said too. And after our daughter was born, Iréne didn't seem interested in Christian anymore." Ragnar Lissander looked out of the window, holding his coffee cup in a tight grip. "Maybe it would have been better for the boy if she'd gotten her wish."

"And what was that?" asked Patrik.

607

"To give him back. She didn't think we needed to keep him since we had our own child." He gave them an embarrassed smile. "I know how that sounds. Iréne can be difficult at times, and sometimes it gets a bit crazy. But she's not always as mean as it sounds."

A bit crazy? Patrik was about to choke in disgust. They were talking about a woman who wanted to give back her foster child after she had a child of her own. And the old man was actually defending her.

"But you didn't take him back, did you?" Patrik asked coldly.

"No. It was one of the few occasions when I put my foot down. At first she refused to listen, but when I told her that it would look bad, she agreed to let him stay. I probably shouldn't have, though. . . ." Again his voice faded, and they could see how hard it was for him to be talking about this topic.

"How did Christian and Alice get along with each other when they were growing up?" asked Paula, but Ragnar didn't seem to hear. He seemed to be far away in his own thoughts. Quietly he said:

"I should have taken better care of her. That poor boy. He didn't understand a thing."

"What didn't he understand?" asked

Patrik, leaning forward.

Ragnar gave a start and woke up from his reverie. He looked at Patrik.

"Would you like to meet Alice? I think you need to meet her in order to understand."

"Yes, we'd like to meet Alice." Patrik couldn't hide how agitated he felt. "When can we do that? Where is she?"

"We can go there now," said Ragnar, getting to his feet.

Patrik and Paula exchanged glances as they walked to the car. Was Alice the woman they were looking for? Were they finally going to put an end to this case?

She was sitting with her back to them when they came in. Her long hair reached past her waist. Dark and gleaming.

"Hi, Alice. It's Papa." Ragnar's voice echoed in the very plain room. Someone had made a half-hearted attempt to add some cozy touches, but without entirely succeeding. A drooping potted plant stood on the windowsill, and a poster for the film *The Big Blue* hung on the wall above a narrow bed with a worn coverlet. There was also a small desk with a chair placed in front of it. That was where she was sitting. Her hands were moving, but Patrik couldn't see what she was doing. She didn't react when her father spoke to her.

"Alice," he repeated, and this time she slowly turned around.

Patrick looked at her in surprise. The woman in front of him was stunningly beautiful. He quickly calculated that she must be about thirty-five, but she looked at least ten years younger. There wasn't a wrinkle on her oval face. Her eyes were enormous and very blue, with thick black lashes. He found himself staring at her.

"She's a beautiful girl, our Alice," said Ragnar, going over to her. He placed his hand on her shoulder, and she leaned her head against him. Like a kitten pressing close to its master or mistress. Her hands lay limply on her lap.

"We have visitors, Alice. This is Patrik and Paula." He hesitated. "They're friends of Christian's."

A glint appeared in her eyes when she heard her brother's name. Ragnar gently stroked her hair.

"So now you know. Now you've met Alice."

"How long?" Patrik couldn't stop staring at her face. The resemblance to her mother was striking. Yet there was something very different about the way Alice looked. All the malevolence that had become etched into her mother's face was absent from this . . . magical creature. He realized that was a strange way to describe her, but he couldn't think of anything better.

"A long time. She hasn't lived at home since the summer she turned thirteen. This is the fourth place she's lived. I didn't much care for the others, but this one is quite nice." He leaned forward and kissed his daughter on the top of the head. There was no reaction in her face, but she pressed closer to him.

"What . . . ?" Paula didn't know how to formulate her question.

"What's wrong with her?" said Ragnar. "If you ask me, there's nothing at all wrong with her. She's perfect. But I know what you mean. And I'll tell you in a minute."

He squatted down in front of Alice and spoke to her gently. Here, with his daughter, he was no longer invisible. His posture was more erect and his eyes were clear. Here he was somebody. He was Alice's papa.

"Sweetheart, Papa can't stay very long today. I just wanted you to meet Christian's friends."

She looked at him. Then she turned around and took something from the desk. A drawing. She held it up for him to see.

"Is that for me?"

She shook her head, and Ragnar's shoulders sagged a bit. "Is it for Christian?" he asked in a low voice.

She nodded and held it out again.

"I'll send it to him. I promise."

The shadow of a smile. Then she turned back to the desk, and her hands began moving again. She had started on a new drawing.

Patrik cast a glance at the paper in Ragnar Lissander's hand. He recognized the drawing style.

"And you've always kept your promise, haven't you? You sent her drawings to Christian," he said after they'd left Alice's room.

"Not all of them. She makes so many. But occasionally, so that he'd know she was thinking about him. In spite of everything."

"How did you know where to send the drawings? From what I understood, Christian had broken off all contact with you and your wife when he turned eighteen," said Paula.

"Yes, he did. But Alice really wanted Christian to have her drawings, so I tried to find an address for him. I suppose I was a bit curious too. At first I searched for him under our surname, but without success. Then I tried with his mother's last name and found an address in Göteborg. For a while I lost track of him because he moved and the letters came back, but then I found him again. Living on Rosenhillsgatan. But I didn't know that he had moved to Fjäll-backa. I thought he was still in Göteborg, since the letters weren't returned."

Ragnar went back into Alice's room to say good-bye, and then led the way along the corridor as Patrik told him about the man who had taken care of the letters for Christian. Then the three of them sat down in a big, bright room that functioned as both a dining room and cafeteria. It had an impersonal air, with big palm plants that were clearly lacking both water and attention, just like the plant in Alice's room. They had the whole place to themselves.

"She cried a lot," said Ragnar, stroking the pastel-colored tablecloth. "Presumably due to colic. During her pregnancy, Iréne had already lost interest in Christian, so when Alice was born and became so demanding, my wife had no time for the boy. And he was already in a fragile state because of what had happened to him before."

"What about you?" said Patrik. When he saw Ragnar's expression, he realized that he'd hit on a sensitive point.

"Me?" Ragnar stopped moving his hand on the table. "I closed my eyes and refused to see. Iréne has always been the one who makes the decisions. And I've let her do it. It's just been easier that way."

"Didn't Christian like his little sister?" asked Patrik.

"He used to stand next to her cot and stare at her. I saw the dark expression on his face, but I never thought that . . . I just had to leave the room to open the door when the bell rang." Ragnar sounded distracted, and he was staring at a spot somewhere behind them. "I was only gone a few minutes."

Paula opened her mouth to ask a question, but decided not to interrupt. He should be allowed to tell the story at his own pace. It was obvious that Ragnar was having a hard time formulating his words. His whole body was tensed, his shoulders hunched.

"Iréne had gone upstairs to take a nap, and for once I was put in charge of Alice. Otherwise Iréne never let anyone else take care of her. She was such a sweet baby, even though she cried all the time. It was as if Iréne suddenly had a new doll to play with. A doll that she refused to share with anyone else."

Another pause, and Patrik had to make a real effort not to coax the man to get on with his story.

"I was only gone a few minutes . . . ," Ragnar repeated. It was almost as if he'd gotten stuck. As if it was impossible for him to put the rest into words.

"Where was Christian?" asked Patrik calmly, wanting to help the man along a bit.

"In the bathroom. With Alice. I was giving her a bath. We had one of those contraptions that you could put the baby in, and that way you'd have both hands free to wash her. I filled the tub with water and then put her in the baby seat. And that's where Alice was sitting."

Paula nodded. They had a similar device for her son Leo.

"When I came back to the bathroom . . . Alice was. . . . She wasn't moving. Her head was all the way under the water. Her eyes were . . . open, wide open."

Ragnar swayed a bit in his chair. It was obvious that he had to force himself to go on, to confront those awful memories and images.

"Christian was just sitting there, leaning against the bathtub and looking down at her." Ragnar fixed his eyes on Paula and Patrik, as if he'd suddenly returned to the present. "He was sitting very still, and he was smiling."

"But you saved her, right?" Patrik could feel the goose bumps on his arms.

"Yes, I saved her. I got her breathing again. And then I saw. . . ." He cleared his throat. "I saw the disappointment in Christian's eyes."

"Did you tell Iréne what had happened?"

"No, that would never . . . no!"

"Christian tried to drown his little sister, and you didn't tell your wife?" Paula looked at him in disbelief.

"I felt like I owed him something, after everything he'd been through. If I had told Iréne, she would have sent him away at once. And he wouldn't have survived that. Besides, the damage was already done." He sounded as if he were pleading with them. "I didn't know how serious it was at the time. But it didn't really matter, because there was nothing I could do to change things. Sending Christian away wouldn't have made it any better."

"So you pretended that nothing had happened?" said Patrik.

Ragnar sighed, slumping forward even more. "Yes, I pretended that nothing had happened. But I never allowed him to be alone with her again. Never."

"Did he try anything else?" Paula's face was pale.

"No, I don't think so. Somehow he seemed satisfied. Alice stopped crying so much. She mostly just lay still and was not at all demanding."

"When did you and your wife notice that something was wrong?" asked Patrik.

"It gradually became obvious. She didn't learn things at the same pace as other kids. When I finally got Iréne to admit to it, and we had Alice examined . . . well, the doctors concluded that she was suffering from some sort of brain damage, which would most likely keep her at a child's level, mentally speaking, for the rest of her life."

"Did Iréne suspect anything?" asked Paula.

"No. The doctor even said that Alice had probably been that way since birth. It just wasn't noticeable until after she started to develop."

"How did things go as the two children grew up?"

"How much time do you have?" said Ragnar, smiling. But it was a sad smile. "Iréne cared only about Alice. She was the prettiest child I've ever seen, and I'm not just saying that because she's mine. Well, you've seen what she looks like."

Patrik thought about those enormous blue eyes.

"Iréne has always loved anything beautiful. She herself was very beautiful as a young woman, and I think that she saw Alice as an affirmation of her own beauty. She devoted all her attention to our daughter."

"And what about Christian?" said Patrik.

"Christian? It was as if he didn't exist."

"That must have been terrible for him," said Paula.

"Yes," said Ragnar. "But he staged his own little revolt. He loved to eat, and he put on weight very easily. He probably inherited that tendency from his mother. When he noticed that his eating habits annoyed Iréne, he started eating even more and got even fatter, just to spite her. And it worked. The two of them waged a constant battle over food, but for once Christian was able to defeat her."

"So Christian was always overweight when he was growing up?" asked Patrik. He tried to picture the slim, adult Christian that he knew as a plump little boy, but he couldn't do it.

"He wasn't just chubby, he was fat. Really fat."

"How did Alice feel about Christian?" asked Paula.

Ragnar smiled, and this time the smile was also evident in his eyes. "Alice loved Christian. She adored him. She was always following him around like a little puppy dog."

"And how did Christian react to that?" Patrik asked.

Ragnar paused to think. "I don't think he really minded. He mostly left her alone. But occasionally he looked a bit surprised by the love she showered on him. As if he didn't understand why."

"Maybe he didn't," said Paula. "Then what happened? How did Alice react when he moved away?"

A curtain seemed to fall over Ragnar's face. "A lot happened all at once. Christian disappeared, and we couldn't take care of Alice anymore — not the way she needed."

"Why not? Why couldn't she live at home any longer?"

"She was practically grown up, and she needed more support and assistance than we could give her."

Ragnar Lissander's mood had suddenly changed, but Patrik didn't know why.

"Has she never learned to talk?" he interjected. Alice hadn't spoken a word while they were in her room.

"She can talk, but she doesn't want to," said Ragnar with the same closed expression on his face.

"Is there any reason why she might hold a

grudge against Christian? Would she be capable of harming him? Or anyone else close to him?" In his mind Patrik again pictured her — the girl with the long dark hair, her hands moving over the white piece of paper, drawing pictures that might have been done by a five-year-old.

"No, Alice wouldn't hurt a fly," said Ragnar. "That's why I wanted to bring you here, so you could meet her. She could never hurt anybody. And she loves . . . loved Christian."

He took out the drawing that she'd given him and placed it on the table in front of them. A big sun at the top, green grass with flowers at the bottom. Two figures: one big and one small, happily holding hands.

"She loved Christian," he repeated.

"Does she even remember him? It was so many years ago that they last saw each other," Paula pointed out.

Ragnar didn't reply. He just motioned toward the drawing. The two figures. Alice and Christian.

"Go ahead and ask the staff here if you don't believe me. But Alice is not the woman you're looking for. I don't know who would want to harm Christian. He disappeared out of our lives when he was eighteen. A lot must have happened since then, but Alice was the one who loved him. She still does."

Patrik looked at the little old man. He knew that he would have to do as Ragnar had suggested. He needed to question the staff here. Yet he was convinced that Alice's father had spoken the truth. She was not the woman they were looking for. They were back to square one.

"I have something important to report," Mellberg interrupted Patrik just as he was about to present the new information. "I'm going to cut back my work hours to part-time for a while. I've realized that my leadership has been so successful here at the station that I can now entrust all of you with certain tasks. My knowledge and experience can be put to better use else-where."

Everyone stared at him in surprise.

"It's time for me to devote myself to the most important resource in our society: the next generation. The ones who will carry us into the future," said Mellberg, hooking his thumbs under his suspenders.

"Is he going to be working at the youth center?" Martin whispered to Gösta, who merely shrugged in reply.

"Besides, it's also important to give the

women a chance. As well as the immigrant minorities." He glanced at Paula. "I know that you and Johanna are having a hard time working out how to juggle the maternity leave you're both entitled to so you can care for Leo. And the boy needs a strong male role model right from the start. So I'm going to be working here part-time; it's already been approved by the top brass. The rest of the time I'll be spending with the boy."

Mellberg looked around at his colleagues, apparently expecting them to applaud. But an astonished silence had fallen over the room. Most surprised of all was Paula. This was news to her, but the more she thought about the idea, the better she liked it. It meant that Johanna could start working again, while she could combine her work schedule with hours of maternity leave. And she couldn't deny that Mellberg took good care of Leo. So far he'd proven to be an excellent babysitter, except maybe for the incident with the taped diaper.

After the initial surprise had worn off, Patrik could only agree with the plan. From a practical standpoint, it meant that Mellberg's hours at the station would be reduced by at least half. And that might not be such a bad thing.

"I commend your initiative, Mellberg. I

wish more people shared your point of view," Patrik said. "And now I think we'd better get back to the investigation. A lot has happened today."

He reported on the second trip to Trollhättan that he and Paula had made, about their conversation with Ragnar Lissander and their visit with Alice.

"So you have no doubt in your mind that she's innocent?" asked Gösta.

"I'm positive she's not the one. I talked to the staff, and her mental capabilities are at the level of a child."

"I can't imagine how Christian could live with the knowledge of what he'd done to his sister," said Annika.

"And the fact that she adored him couldn't have made it any easier," added Paula. "It must have been a heavy burden for him to bear. Provided that he knew what he'd done."

"We also have something to report." Gösta cleared his throat and cast a glance at Martin. "I thought I recognized the name Lissander, but I couldn't recall where I'd heard it before. And I wasn't one hundred percent positive. The old gray matter isn't as reliable as it once was," he said, pointing at his head.

"And?" said Patrik impatiently.

Gösta again glanced at Martin. "Well, first we had a talk with Kenneth Bengtsson, but he claims to know nothing. He also says that he never heard the name Lissander. But I kept wondering why our former colleague Ernst kept popping into my head every time I thought about that name. So we went to see him."

"You drove over to Ernst's house?" said Patrik. "But why?"

"Just listen to what Gösta has to say," Martin said, and Patrik fell silent.

"Okay, well, I told Ernst about what I'd been thinking. And he worked it out."

"What did he work out?" Patrik leaned forward.

"He was able to tell me where I'd heard the name Lissander before," said Gösta. "It was because they lived here in Fjällbacka for a while."

"Who?" Patrik asked in bewilderment.

"Mr. and Mrs. Lissander, Iréne and Ragnar. With their children Christian and Alice."

"But that's impossible," said Patrik, shaking his head. "If that was true, why didn't anyone ever recognize Christian? Ernst must be mistaken."

"No, it's true," said Martin. "Evidently Christian took after his biological mother,

624

and he was terribly overweight when he was growing up. Take away a hundred and twenty-five pounds and add on twenty years and a pair of specs, and it would be hard to believe he was the same person."

"How did Ernst happen to know the family? And you too?" asked Patrik.

"Ernst was infatuated with Iréne. Apparently they got to know each other at some party, and after that Ernst always wanted to drive past their house as often as we could. So we took a lot of drives past the Lissander home."

"Where did they live?" asked Paula.

"In one of the houses right near the Coast Guard dock."

"You mean near Badholmen?" asked Patrik.

"Yes, very close. It was Iréne's mother who originally owned the house. She was a real bitch, from what I heard. For many years she and her daughter had no contact whatsoever, but when the old lady died, Iréne inherited the place, so the Lissanders moved here from Trollhättan."

"Did Ernst know why they moved away from Fjällbacka?" asked Paula.

"No, he had no idea. But apparently it was quite sudden."

"So it seems that Ragnar didn't tell us

everything," said Patrik. He was really getting sick and tired of all the people who apparently had secrets that they refused to divulge. If everyone had been willing to cooperate, they probably would have solved this case long ago.

"Good work," he said, nodding to Gösta and Martin. "I'm going to have another talk with Ragnar Lissander. There must be some reason why he never mentioned that they had once lived in Fjällbacka. He ought to have realized that it was just a matter of time before we found out anyway."

"But that still doesn't tell us who the woman is who we're looking for. It seems she should be someone Christian knew when he was living in Göteborg. After he moved away from home and before he came back to Fjällbacka with Sanna." Martin was thinking out loud.

"I wonder why he came back here," Annika interjected.

"We need to find out more about the years that Christian spent in Göteborg," said Patrik. "So far we know of only three women who have figured in Christian's life: Iréne, Alice, and his biological mother."

"Could it be Iréne? She would have a motive for seeking revenge, considering what Christian did to Alice," said Martin.

Patrik paused to think for a moment, but then shook his head.

"I've also been thinking about her, and we can't rule her out. But I don't think so. According to Ragnar, she never found out what had happened. And even if she did know, why would she also target Magnus and the others?"

In his mind he pictured the disagreeable woman they had encountered at the house in Trollhättan. He heard again her contemptuous remarks about Christian and his mother. And suddenly a thought occurred to him. It was something that had been hovering in the back of his mind ever since they'd met with Ragnar for the second time. It was the one thing that didn't seem to fit. Patrik picked up his mobile and quickly tapped in a number. Everyone sitting at the table looked at him in surprise, but he held up one finger as a sign that they shouldn't speak.

"Hi, this is Patrik Hedström. I actually wanted to talk to Sanna. Okay, I understand. But could you go and ask her a question for me? It's important. Ask her if the blue dress she found was her size. Yes, I know it's an odd question. But it would be a big help if you could ask her. Thanks."

Patrik waited, and after about a minute

Sanna's sister, Agneta, was back on the line. "Oh, really? Okay. Good. Thanks a lot. And say hi to Sanna." Patrik ended the conversation with a pensive look on his face.

"The blue dress was Sanna's size."

"And?" said Martin. He seemed to be speaking for everyone.

"That's a little odd, considering that Christian's mother weighed around three hundred pounds. So the dress must have belonged to someone else. Christian lied to Sanna when he told her it was his mother's."

"Could it have belonged to Alice?" said Paula.

"That's possible. But I don't think so. There must have been another woman in Christian's life."

Erica glanced at the clock. It was turning out to be a long workday for Patrik. She hadn't heard from him since he'd left the house that morning, but she hadn't wanted to bother him by phoning. Christian's death must have caused utter chaos at the station. Patrik would come home when he could.

She hoped that he wasn't still mad at her. He'd never been truly angry with her before, and the last thing she wanted was to disappoint or upset him.

Erica ran her hand over her belly. It

seemed to be growing uncontrollably, and sometimes she felt such a dread of what was to come that she could hardly breathe. At the same time she was longing for it. Such ambiguous emotions: joy and concern; panic and anticipation. Everything blissfully mixed together.

Anna must be feeling the same way. Erica felt guilty that she hadn't been very receptive to listening to her sister talk about her own pregnancy. She had been so caught up in her personal situation. Yet after everything that had happened with Lucas — Anna's former husband and the father of her two children — plenty of emotions had probably been stirred up now that she was pregnant. And with a new man in her life. Erica was ashamed by how selfish she'd been, talking only about her own feelings and worries. She would phone Anna tomorrow morning and suggest having coffee together, or maybe taking a walk. Then they'd have time for a proper chat.

Maja came over and crawled onto her lap. She looked tired, even though it was only six o'clock, which was two hours before her bedtime.

"Papa?" said Maja, pressing her cheek against Erica's stomach.

"Papa will be home soon," said Erica.

"But you and I are both hungry, so I think we should make ourselves some dinner. What do you say to that, sweetie? Shall we have a girls' dinner tonight?"

Maja nodded.

"How about Falu sausage and macaroni? With lots of ketchup."

Maja nodded again. Her mama knew just what to serve for a girls' dinner.

"So how should we do this?" said Patrik, pulling up a chair to sit next to Annika.

It was pitch-dark outside, and everybody should have left for home long ago, but no one was even thinking of leaving the station. Except for Mellberg, that is, who had gone out the door about fifteen minutes earlier, whistling to himself.

"Let's start with the public records, even though I doubt we'll find anything. I went through them before, when I was checking on his background, and I really can't believe that I missed anything." Annika sounded apologetic, and Patrik patted her on the shoulder.

"I know that you're a perfectionist when it comes to doing research, but oversights can happen to anyone. If we look through the files together, maybe we'll see something that you missed the first time. I think Christian must have lived with a woman when he was in Göteborg — or at least had a relationship with someone. Maybe we can find something that will help us find out who that might have been."

"Let's hope so," said Annika, turning the computer screen so that Patrik could see it too. "But as I said, he had no previous marriages."

"What about children?"

Annika typed something on the keyboard and then pointed at the screen.

"No, he's not listed as the father of any children other than Melker and Nils."

"Shit," said Patrik, running his hand through his hair. "Maybe it's a stupid theory. I don't know why I have such a strong feeling that we've missed something. The answer has to be somewhere in these files."

He got up and went into his own office. He sat there for a long time, staring at the wall. The ringing of his phone abruptly interrupted his brooding.

"Patrik Hedström." He could hear how discouraged his voice sounded. But when the man on the phone introduced himself and then explained why he was calling, Patrik sat up straighter in his chair. Twenty minutes later, he rushed into Annika's office.

"Maria Sjöström!"

"Maria Sjöström?"

"Christian was living with a woman in Göteborg. Her name is Maria Sjöström."

"How did you . . . ?" asked Annika, but Patrik went on without answering her question.

"There's also a child. Emil Sjöström. Or rather, there was a child."

"What do you mean?"

"They're dead. Both Maria and Emil are dead. And there's an unsolved homicide investigation."

"What's going on?" Martin came rushing in after hearing Patrik shouting in Annika's office. Even Gösta moved faster than usual to appear in the doorway, crowding inside with the others.

"I've just talked to a man named Sture Bogh. He's a retired police detective in Göteborg." Patrik paused for effect before he continued. "He read in the paper about Christian and the threats he'd received, and he recognized the name from one of his investigations. He thought he might have information that could prove useful to us."

Patrik told his colleagues about his conversation with the former detective. In spite of all the years that had passed, Sture Bogh had never been able to forget those tragic deaths, and he gave Patrik a precise summary of the important facts in the case.

Everyone was left gaping when they heard Patrik recount what the detective had told him.

"Can we get ahold of the case documents?" asked Martin eagerly.

"It's a little late for that now. I think it would be difficult," said Patrik.

"No harm in trying," said Annika. "I have the number for the Göteborg police right here."

Patrik sighed. "My wife is going to think that I ran off to Rio with some buxom blonde if I don't get home soon."

"Phone Erica first, and then we'll try to get ahold of someone in Göteborg."

Patrik gave in. None of them looked as though they wanted to leave, and he didn't want to either — not until they'd done as much as they could.

"Okay, but the rest of you need to go do something else while I make the calls. I don't want you leaning over my shoulder."

He went into his own office, closed the door, and phoned home first. Erica was very understanding. She and Maja had already eaten dinner together. Suddenly Patrik had such a longing to be home with his two girls that he almost felt on the verge of tears. He couldn't remember ever feeling so tired. But he took a deep breath and tapped in the number Annika had given him.

At first Patrik didn't notice that someone had answered. "Hello?" said a voice on the line, and he jumped, realizing that he was supposed to say something. He introduced himself and explained what he needed. To Patrik's surprise, his colleague in Göteborg was remarkably friendly and accommodating, offering to try to locate the investigative materials.

Patrik hung up, crossing his fingers. After waiting only about fifteen minutes, the phone rang.

"Really? You did?" Patrik could hardly believe his ears when his colleague said that they'd located the file. Patrik thanked him profusely, asking him to put the file aside. He'd make arrangements to collect the materials the next day. In the worst-case scenario, he'd drive to Göteborg himself, or maybe he could get the station to pay for a courier delivery.

Patrik remained sitting at his desk after putting down the phone. He knew that the others were in their offices, waiting to hear whether it was possible to get the investigative files. But first he needed to collect his thoughts. All the details, all the puzzle pieces were whirling through his head. He knew they fit together somehow. It was just a matter of working out how.

Erik felt strangely sad as he was preparing to leave. Of course it was hard to say good-bye to his two daughters. He gave them both a hug, pretending that he'd be back in a few days. But he was surprised to find that it was also difficult to say good-bye to the house and to Louise, who stood in the front hall, looking at him with an inscrutable expression.

His original plan had been to slip away, just leaving a note behind. But then he suddenly felt a need to say a proper farewell. In order not to provoke suspicion, he had already placed the big suitcase in the trunk of the car. He wanted Louise to think that this was just another business trip, requiring only a small carry-on bag.

Even though it was unexpectedly hard to say good-bye, Erik knew that he would soon settle into his new life. All he had to do was think about that Swedish lawyer named Joachim Posener who had fled the country back in 1997, suspected of embezzlement. He'd managed to stay away without suffering any pangs of conscience at leaving a child behind. Besides, his own daughters were teenagers now. They didn't really need him anymore.

"What kind of business trip is it?" Louise asked him.

Something in her tone of voice caught Erik's attention. She didn't know, did she? He dismissed the thought. Even if she had her suspicions, there was nothing she could do about it.

"Meeting with a new supplier," he said, fiddling with the car keys in his hand. He was actually being quite decent, now that he thought about it. He was planning to take the smaller car and leave the Mercedes for Louise. And the money that he'd left in the bank account was enough to pay expenses for his wife and children for at least a year, including the mortgage on the house. So she'd have plenty of time to work out the situation.

Erik stood up straighter. There was really no reason for him to feel like an asshole. If anyone ended up suffering because of his actions, that wasn't his problem. It was his life that was in danger, and he couldn't just sit here waiting for the past to catch up with him.

"I'll be back the day after tomorrow," he

said lightly, giving Louise a nod. It had been years since he'd given her a hug or a kiss when he left for a trip.

"Come back whenever you want," she said with a shrug.

Again he thought he noticed something odd about her, but it was probably just his imagination. And in two days' time, when she would be expecting him to return home, he'd already be in a safe place.

" 'Bye," he said, turning his back to her.

" 'Bye," said Louise.

He got into the car, and as he drove off, he took one last glance in the rear-view mirror. Then he switched on the radio and began humming along. He was on his way.

Erica looked at Patrik with concern when he came in the door. Maja had been in bed for quite a while, and she was sitting on the sofa, having a cup of tea.

"Tough day?" she asked cautiously, getting up to put her arms around him.

Patrik buried his face in her neck, and for a moment he didn't move.

"I need a glass of wine," he said then.

He went into the kitchen while Erica went back to her place on the sofa. She could hear sounds of a glass clinking and a cork being removed from a bottle. She remembered how nice it was to have a glass of wine, but right now she had to make do with her tea. That was one of the big disadvantages of being pregnant and then nursing a baby — not being able to have a glass of red wine once in a while. Every now and then she would take a tiny sip from Patrik's glass, and she had to be satisfied with that.

"It feels great to be home," said Patrik with an audible sigh as he sat down next to Erica. He put his arm around her shoulders and propped his feet up on the coffee table.

"And I'm so happy to have you home," said Erica, snuggling closer to him. For several minutes, neither of them spoke as Patrik sipped his wine.

"Christian has a sister," he said at last.

Erica gave a start. "A sister? I never heard that before. He always said that he didn't have any family."

"That wasn't really true. I know I'll probably regret telling you about all this, but I'm just so damn tired. Everything that I've heard today keeps buzzing around in my head, and I really need to talk to somebody. But this has to stay between the two of us. Okay?" He gave her a stern look.

"I promise. Go ahead and tell me."

So Patrik told her about everything that he'd found out. They sat in the dark living room, the only light coming from the TV screen. Erica didn't say a word, just listened carefully. Although she couldn't help shuddering when Patrik told her how Alice had ended up brain-damaged and how Christian had lived with that secret all those years while Ragnar both protected him and kept an eye on him. Erica shook her head after Patrik finished telling her everything about Alice and about the emotionally callous childhood Christian had been forced to endure until he left the Lissander family.

"Poor Christian."

"But that's not the end of the story."

"What do you mean?" asked Erica, and then gasped as one of the babies gave her a hard kick in the lungs. The twins were especially lively tonight.

"Christian met a woman during the time he was studying in Göteborg. Her name was Maria. She had an infant son, almost a newborn when they met. She had no contact with the father. Maria and Christian soon moved in together, in an apartment in Partille. The boy, Emil, became Christian's own son. The three of them seemed to have been very happy."

"So what happened?" Erica wasn't sure that she really wanted to know. It might be easier to put her hands over her ears and shut out what she suspected was going to be a dreadful and difficult end to this story. But she couldn't help asking Patrik what had happened.

"One Wednesday in April, Christian came home from the university." Patrik kept his voice carefully neutral, and Erica took his hand. "The door was unlocked, which immediately made him uneasy. He called for Maria and Emil, but there was no answer. He walked through the apartment, looking for them. Everything looked the same as always. Their coats were hanging up in the hall, so he didn't think they'd gone out. And Emil's stroller was in the stairwell."

"I don't know if I want to hear any more," whispered Erica, but Patrik was staring straight ahead and didn't seem to hear her.

"He found them at last. In the bathroom. Both of them had drowned."

"Dear God." Erica put her hand over her mouth.

"The boy was lying on his back in the tub. His mother's head was submerged in the water, but the rest of her body was outside the bathtub. The postmortem found bruises left by fingertips on the back of her neck. Someone had forcibly held her head underwater."

"Who . . . ?"

"I don't know. The police never managed to find the murderer. Strangely enough, Christian was never considered a suspect, even though he was the closest to the victims. That's why we never found out about the case when we looked for his name in the police records."

"How is that possible?"

"I'm not really sure. Everyone who knew them testified that they were an exceptionally happy couple. Even Maria's mother defended Christian. And besides, a neighbor saw a woman enter the apartment about the time the deaths occurred, as established by the medical examiner."

"A woman?" said Erica. "The same one who . . . ?"

"I don't really know what to think anymore. This case is driving me mad. Somehow it all fits together — everything that has happened to Christian. Someone hated him so intensely that not even the passage of time was able to dull those emotions."

"And you have no idea who it might be?" Erica could feel an idea taking shape in her mind, but she couldn't really grasp what it was. The image was blurry. But there was one thing she knew for sure: Patrik was right. Somehow all of the events were connected.

"Would you mind if I went to bed?" said Patrik, putting his hand on her knee.

"Not at all. You do that, sweetheart," she said absentmindedly. "I'm going to stay up for a little while. Then I'll come to bed too."

"Okay." He gave her a kiss and then headed upstairs to their bedroom.

She stayed where she was, sitting on the sofa in the dark. The TV news program was on, but she left the sound off so she could listen to her own thoughts. Alice. Maria and Emil. There was something she ought to be seeing, something she ought to understand. She shifted her gaze to the book lying on the coffee table. Slowly she picked it up and placed it in her lap so she could look at the cover and the title. *The Mermaid.* She thought about depression and guilt. About what Christian had wanted to convey in his novel. She knew that the answer was there, in the words and the sentences he had left behind. And she was going to find out what it was.

The nightmares started haunting him every night, as if they had been waiting for his conscience to awake. It was actually strange that it took so long. He had always known what happened, after all. He had pictured the way he had removed the baby bath seat and let Alice sink down into the water. And how her little body had kicked and flailed as she tried to breathe, and then how she grew so still. He had always seen her eyes, those blue eyes looking at him, unseeing, from under the water. He had always known, but he had never understood.

It was just a small thing, a tiny detail, that made him comprehend at last. It happened one day during that last summer. By then, he already knew that he couldn't stay. There had never been a place for him, but that insight came to him only gradually. Finally he knew that he had to leave the family.

The voices told him the same thing. One

day, they too had appeared, not unpleasant or nasty, but more like friends and confidants whispering to him.

The only time he doubted his decision was when he thought about Alice. But that feeling of hesitation never lasted long — because it made the voices grow stronger. So he decided to stay only until the summer was over. Then he would leave and never look back. And everything having to do with Mother and Father would be left behind.

On that particular day, Alice wanted some ice cream. She always wanted ice cream, and if he felt like it, he would go with her to the kiosk near the square. She always asked for the same thing: a cone with three scoops of strawberry ice cream. Sometimes he would purposely pretend to misunderstand and order chocolate ice cream for her instead. Then she would shake her head vigorously and tug at his arm, struggling to say the word "strawberry."

Alice was always in seventh heaven when she got her ice cream. Her face lit up with delight, and with the greatest satisfaction she would begin methodically licking at the ice cream. Round and round so that it wouldn't start dripping. The same thing happened on that day. She got her cone first and slowly began walking away as he waited for his and then paid for both of them. When he turned around to follow Alice, he stopped in mid-stride. Erik, Kenneth, and Magnus. All three of them were sitting there, looking at him. Erik grinned.

He could feel the ice cream dripping from the cone onto his hand, but he had to walk past them. He tried looking straight ahead, out at the water. Tried to ignore their eyes and ignore the way his heart was pounding faster and faster. He took one step forward, then another. Suddenly he felt himself falling headlong. Erik had stuck out his foot just as he was passing. At the last second, he managed to put out his hands to break his fall. The weight of his body made his wrists twinge. The ice cream flew out of his hand, landing on the dirty pavement.

"Whoops," said Erik.

Kenneth laughed nervously, but Magnus gave Erik a reproachful look.

"Did you really have to do that?" he asked.

Erik didn't seem to notice what Magnus said. His eyes were shining. "You didn't need any more ice cream."

With an effort he got to his feet. His arms hurt, and tiny pieces of gravel were stuck to the palms of his hands. He brushed himself off and limped away, moving as fast as he could, while Erik's laughter rang in his ears.

A short distance ahead, Alice was waiting for him. He ignored her and just kept on going. Out of the corner of his eye he saw her come trotting after him, but not until they had almost reached home did he stop to catch his breath. Alice stopped too. At first she merely stood there, listening to him wheeze as he tried to get enough air. Then she held out her cone to him.

"Here, Christian. Take my ice cream. It's strawberry."

He looked at her outstretched hand and at the ice cream. Strawberry ice cream, which Alice loved with such passion. At that moment, he realized the full extent of what he'd done to her. And then the voices began to scream. They were about to make his head explode. He fell to his knees, holding his hands over his ears. They had to stop, he had to make them stop. Then he felt Alice's arms around him, and everything went quiet.

25

Patrik had slept like a log all night. Yet he still didn't feel rested.

"Sweetheart?" No answer. He glanced at the clock and swore to himself. Eight thirty. He really needed to get going; they had a lot to do today.

"Erica?" He went downstairs but didn't hear a sound from either his wife or daughter. In the kitchen he found a pot of fresh coffee waiting for him, and a note in Erica's handwriting was lying on the table.

Sweetheart, I took Maja to the day care center. I've been thinking about what you told me yesterday, and there's something I need to check out. I'll call as soon as I know more. Could you find out two things for me? 1. Did Christian have a nickname for Alice? 2. What sort of mental illness did Christian's mother suffer from? Hugs and kisses, Erica. P.S. Don't be mad at me.

What on earth was she up to now? He should have known that she wouldn't be able to leave well enough alone. He picked up the phone on the table and called Erica's mobile. After a few rings, he was transferred to her voicemail. He told himself to calm down, since he realized there was nothing more he could do at the moment. He needed to get to the station, and he had no idea where she was.

Besides, the questions Erica had included in her note had piqued his interest. Had she come up with some sort of theory? Erica was smart — there was no denying that. And she often saw things that he'd missed. He just wished that she wouldn't keep going off on her own this way.

He drank a cup of coffee as he stood at the counter. After a moment's hesitation, he filled a special travel mug that Erica had given him as a Christmas present. Today he was going to need some extra caffeine.

The first thing he did upon arriving at the police station was to go into the kitchen to have a third cup.

"So, what's on the agenda for today?" asked Martin when they almost collided in the corridor.

"We need to go through all the material about the murder of Christian's girlfriend

Maria and her child. I'll phone Göteborg and see if we can have the files delivered. I'll probably have them sent by courier, which means I'll have to hide the expense somehow so Mellberg won't notice. Then we need to check with Torbjörn to find out if he's heard anything from the forensics lab about the rag and the can of paint in Christian's basement. The report probably isn't ready yet, but we might as well put a little pressure on them. Could you start with that?"

"Sure, I'll take care of it. Anything else?"

"Not at the moment," said Patrik. "I need to check on something with Ragnar Lissander. I'll tell you about it after I find out a bit more."

"Okay. Just let me know if there's anything else you need me to do," said Martin.

Patrik went into his office. It was so odd, how tired he felt. Even all the caffeine was having no effect on him today. He took a deep breath in an attempt to rally himself and then phoned Christian's foster father.

"I can't really talk right now," said Ragnar, and Patrik understood that Iréne must be nearby.

"I just have two questions," he said, finding himself lowering his voice, even though that wasn't necessary on his end of the line.

He considered asking Ragnar why he hadn't said anything about the time the family had lived in Fjällbacka. But he decided to let that wait until they could speak more openly. Besides, he had a feeling that the questions Erica wanted answered were more important.

"Okay," said Ragnar. "But make it quick."

Patrik asked him the questions from Erica's note and was surprised by what he learned. What did all of this mean?

He thanked Ragnar, ended the conversation, and then tried Erica again. But he still got her voicemail. So he left a message for her and then leaned back in his chair. How did this new information fit into the picture? And where was Erica?

"Erica!" Thorvald Hamre leaned down and wrapped his arms around her. Even though Erica was almost five feet seven inches tall and had put on a lot of extra pounds, she felt like a dwarf compared to him.

"Hi, Thorvald! Thanks for seeing me on such short notice," she said, hugging him back.

"You're always welcome. You know that." There was just a touch of Norwegian intonation in his speech. He'd lived in Sweden for close to thirty years now, and over time he'd become more of a Göteborg fan than people who were born there. A gigantic IFK football flag on the wall attested to his loyalties.

"How can I help you this time? What sort of exciting project are you working on now?" He tugged on his enormous gray moustache, his eyes shining.

They'd become friends when Erica was looking for someone who could help her with the psychological aspects of the true-crime books she wrote. Thorvald was a therapist with a successful private practice, but he devoted all his free time to studying the dark side of human nature. He had even taken a course with the FBI. Erica didn't really want to speculate on what might have prompted him to take an interest in this particular topic. The important thing was that he was a tremendously skilled psychiatrist who was willing to share his knowledge with her.

"I need answers to several questions. I hope you'll be able to help me."

"Of course. I'm always at your service."

Erica gave him a grateful look and then wondered how to begin. She hadn't really managed to put all the pieces together yet. The pattern kept shifting, like the colors and shapes in a kaleidoscope. But somewhere there had to be a structure, and maybe Thorvald could help her find it. Before she reached Göteborg, she'd listened to the message that Patrik had left her, but chose not to call him back. She didn't want to answer his questions at the moment. The information he'd left on her voicemail didn't surprise her; it merely confirmed what she had already suspected.

After pausing to gather her thoughts, Erica started telling the story to Thorvald. In one long account, without stopping, she told him everything she knew. Thorvald listened intently, resting his elbows on his desk and making a tent with his fingertips. Every once in a while, Erica felt her stomach clench into knots, as she heard for herself just what a horrible story it was.

When she finished, Thorvald at first didn't say a word. Erica almost felt out of breath, like she'd been running a race. One of the babies kicked her hard in the diaphragm, as if to remind her that there was something good and loving in the world.

"What's your own opinion?" asked Thorvald at last.

After a moment's hesitation, Erica presented her theory. It had emerged during the night as she lay in bed, staring at the ceiling while Patrik slept soundly at her side.

It had further taken shape as she drove along the E6 toward Göteborg. She had quickly realized that she needed to talk to Thorvald about it. He'd be able to say whether the theory was as absurd as it seemed. He would tell her if she'd allowed her imagination to run wild.

But that's not what he said. Instead, he looked at her and said: "It's entirely possible. What you're suggesting is entirely possible."

His words made the air escape from her lungs in a mixture of alarm and relief. Now she was positive that her idea was right. But the consequences were almost beyond comprehension.

They talked for nearly an hour. Erica asked Thorvald questions and tried to absorb everything he told her. If she was going to take this theory further, she needed to have all the facts in place. Otherwise it could go terribly wrong, and she was still missing a few pieces of the puzzle. She had enough to see the motive, but there were still gaps; before she could present her theory, she needed to fill them in.

When she got back in the car, she leaned her forehead on the steering wheel. It felt cool against her skin. She wasn't looking forward to her next visit and the questions she needed to ask — or what she might hear. There was one puzzle piece that she wasn't sure she wanted to find. But she had no choice.

She started up the car and headed for Uddevalla. A glance at her mobile showed her that she'd missed two calls from Patrik. He would just have to wait.

Louise phoned the bank as soon as it opened. Erik had always underestimated her. She was good at cajoling people and finding out what she wanted to know. Besides, she had all the information she needed to ask the right questions — the account numbers and the company taxpayer ID. She also had such an efficient and commanding voice that the banker didn't even consider doubting her right to obtain the information.

After Louise hung up the phone, she remained sitting at the kitchen table to think. It was all gone. Well, not really all. He'd been generous enough to leave her a little so they could get by for a while. But he had largely emptied their bank accounts, both the personal and business ones.

Anger rushed through her like a primeval force. She had no intention of letting him get away with this. He was so fucking stupid that he thought she was equally dumb. He'd booked a plane ticket under his own name, and it didn't take her many phone calls to find out exactly which flight he was taking and what his destination would be.

Louise got up and took a glass out of the cupboard. She held it under the tap of the wine box, which she twisted and then watched as the marvelous red liquid came gushing out. Today she needed the wine more than ever. She raised the glass to her lips — but stopped when the smell of the wine filled her nostrils. This was not the right moment. She was surprised to find that thought occurring to her, because over the past few years it had always been the right moment for a glass of wine. But not today. Right now she needed to be clear-headed and strong. Right now she had to be decisive.

She had all the necessary information. She could point her magic wand and make everything disappear with a "poof," just like Magica De Spell. She giggled and then began whooping with laughter. She laughed as she set the glass on the kitchen counter, and she kept on laughing as she looked at her own reflection in the shiny surface of the refrigerator door. She had taken back control of her life. And soon it was going to go "poof."

Everything was arranged. The courier bringing the documents from Göteborg was on his way. Patrik knew he ought to feel pleased, but he couldn't muster any real joy. He still hadn't gotten ahold of Erica, and it made him uneasy to think of her running around in her advanced stage of pregnancy and getting involved in who knew what. He realized that if anybody could take care of herself, she could. That was one of the many reasons why he loved her. But he still couldn't help feeling worried.

"They'll be here in half an hour!" shouted Annika, who had put in the order for the courier delivery.

"Great!" he shouted back. Then he stood up and grabbed his jacket. He mumbled something incomprehensible to Annika as he passed her on his way out and then jogged through the biting wind over to Hedemyr's. Patrik was annoyed with himself. He should have done this earlier, but it just wasn't part of the way he usually handled an investigation. To be honest, the idea hadn't even occurred to him. Not until he heard the nickname that Christian had given to his sister. The Mermaid.

The book section was located on the

ground floor of the department store, and he quickly found his way there. Books by local authors were prominently displayed, and he smiled when he saw the big stack of Erica's books, along with a life-sized cardboard cutout of her.

"How awful that it should end like that," said the clerk as he paid for the book. He merely nodded, since he wasn't in the mood for small talk. He slipped the book inside his jacket and ran back to the police station. Annika glanced at Patrik when he came in but didn't say anything.

He went into his office and closed the door, then sat down at his desk, trying to make himself as comfortable as possible. He opened Christian's novel and began to read. There were actually lots of other things that Patrik should have been doing, both practical chores and police tasks. But something told him that this was important. So for the first time in his career, Patrik Hedström sat at his desk reading a novel during work hours.

Kenneth wasn't sure when he would be discharged from the hospital, but it really didn't matter. He could stay here or he could go home. She would find him wherever he was.

Maybe it would be better if she found him at home, where Lisbet's presence was still palpable. And there were a few things he wanted to take care of first. Including Lisbet's funeral. The service would be only for her family and closest friends. No black clothing, no mournful music. And she would be wearing her yellow scarf. She'd been adamant about that.

A cautious knock on the door roused him from his reverie. He turned his head. Erica Falck. What did she want? he wondered, though it didn't really interest him.

"May I come in?" she asked. Like everyone else, she couldn't help looking at his bandaged arms. He motioned with one hand, an ambiguous gesture that could mean come in or get lost. Even he wasn't sure which he intended.

But Erica came into the room, pulled up a chair, and sat down at his bedside, close to his head. She gave him a friendly look.

"You know who Christian was, don't you? Not Christian Thydell, but Christian Lissander."

At first he considered lying to her, the same way he'd lied to the police officers who had come to see him. But her tone of voice was different. Her expression was too. She knew. She already had the answer, or at least part of it.

"Yes, I know that," said Kenneth. "I know who he was."

"Tell me about him," she said. He felt as if she were nailing him to his bed with her questions.

"There's not much to tell. He was the one everybody picked on at school. And we . . . we were the worst of the lot. With Erik taking the lead."

"You bullied him?"

"We wouldn't have called it that back then. But we made his life miserable as often as we could."

"Why?" she asked, and the word seemed to hover in the air for a moment.

"Why? Who knows? He was different, and he wasn't from here. He was also fat. People always have to have someone to kick around, someone to look down on."

"I can understand Erik doing that sort of thing. But why you? And Magnus?"

She didn't sound reproachful, but it still upset Kenneth. He'd asked himself that very same question so many times before. There was something lacking in Erik's character. It was hard to pinpoint, but it might be an inability to feel empathy. That was no excuse, but it did explain Erik's behavior. But he and Magnus knew better. Did that make their sins bigger or smaller? Kenneth couldn't answer that question.

"We were young and stupid," he said, but he could hear how false that sounded. He had continued to follow Erik, to be governed by him. He had even admired him. It was a matter of ordinary human stupidity. Fear and cowardice.

"So you didn't recognize Christian when he moved here as an adult?" Erica asked.

"No, never. Believe it or not, I never made that connection. None of the others did either. Christian was a completely different person. It wasn't just his appearance, it was . . . he wasn't the same person. Even now, when I know. . . ." Kenneth shook his head.

"What about Alice? Tell me about Alice."

He grimaced. He didn't want to do that. Talking about Alice was the same thing as sticking his hand in a fire. Over the years, he'd buried all thought of her so deep in his subconscious that it was as if she'd never existed. But that time was now gone. He would simply have to endure the fire, if need be. Because he had to talk about her.

"She was so beautiful that it took your breath away just to look at her. But as soon as she moved or started talking, you could tell that something wasn't quite right with her. She was always hanging on Christian. We couldn't really work out whether he liked it or not. Sometimes he seemed annoyed, but other times he seemed almost happy to see her."

"Did any of you ever talk to Alice?"

"No, except for the taunts that we shouted at her." He felt so ashamed. He remembered it all so clearly now, everything they had done. It could have been yesterday; it *was* yesterday. No, it was a long time ago. He was starting to feel confused. The memories he had suppressed seemed now to be pouring out with such force that they swept everything along in their path.

"When Alice was thirteen, the Lissanders moved away from Fjällbacka, and Christian left the family. Something happened, and I think you know what it was." Erica's voice was calm, non-judgmental, and for that reason he decided to tell her. She'd find out eventually anyway. And soon he'd be joining Lisbet.

"It was in July," he said, closing his eyes.

Christian could feel the agitation taking over his body. It was getting worse and worse, making it impossible for him to sleep at night. And causing him to see eyes under the water.

He had to leave — he knew that. If he was ever going to find a place for himself, he needed to go away. Far away from Father and Mother, and from Alice. Oddly enough, that hurt the most. Having to part with Alice.

"Hello! Hey, you!"

He turned around in surprise. As usual, he was on his way over to Badholmen. He liked to sit there, staring out across the water at Fjällbacka.

"Over here!"

Christian didn't know what to think. Over near the men's changing booths he saw Erik, Magnus, and Kenneth. And Erik was calling to him. Christian gave them a suspicious look. Whatever it was they wanted, he knew it wouldn't be good. But the temptation was too strong, and with feigned nonchalance he stuck his hands in his pockets and sauntered over to the three boys.

"Want a smoke?" asked Erik, holding out a cigarette. Christian shook his head. He was still waiting for the hammer to fall, when all three would attack him. Anything but this . . . show of goodwill.

"Sit down," said Erik, patting the ground next to him.

As if in a dream, Christian sat down. The whole situation seemed unreal. He had imagined just such a scene so many times, hoped and longed for it. And now it was actually happening. He was sitting here, one of the group.

"What are you doing tonight?" asked Erik, exchanging glances with Kenneth and Magnus.

"Nothing special. Why?"

"We're planning to have a party here. A private gathering, so to speak." Erik laughed.

"Really?" said Christian. He shifted his position a bit to get more comfortable.

"Want to come?"

"Me?" said Christian. He wasn't sure he'd heard right.

"Yes, you. But everyone has to bring something to get in," said Erik, again exchanging glances with Magnus and Kenneth.

So there was a catch, just as he'd thought.

What sort of humiliating task had they planned for him?

"What do I have to bring?" he asked, even though he knew he shouldn't.

The three boys whispered to each other. Finally Erik looked at him again and said defiantly:

"A bottle of whiskey."

Was that all? Relief washed over him. He could easily sneak one out of the house.

"Okay. No problem. What time should I be here?"

Erik took a couple of puffs on his cigarette. He looked so worldly wise, holding that cigarette in his hand. Grown up.

"We have to make sure that nobody bothers us. So after midnight. Shall we say twelve thirty?"

Christian felt himself nodding a bit too eagerly. "Okay. Twelve thirty. I'll be here."

"Good," said Erik.

Christian hurried away. His feet felt lighter than they had in a long time. Maybe his luck would now change and he'd finally belong.

The rest of the day passed very slowly. At last it was time for bed, but he didn't dare close his eyes for fear of oversleeping. So he lay there, wide awake, staring at the hands of the clock as they slowly moved toward midnight. At twelve fifteen he climbed out of bed and got dressed, careful not to make any noise. He slipped downstairs and went over to the drinks cabinet. There were several whiskey bottles inside. He took the one that was nearly full. The bottle clinked as he took it out, and for a moment he didn't move. But no one seemed to have heard the sound.

When he got close to Badholmen, he could hear the other boys. It sounded like they had already been there a while, like the party had started without him. For a second he considered turning around. He could just walk back to the house, slip inside, put the bottle back in the cabinet, and crawl into bed. But then he heard Erik laughing, and he wanted to join in that laughter; he wanted to be one of the boys that Erik exchanged glances with. So he kept on going, carrying the whiskey bottle firmly under his arm.

"Hey, take a look," said Erik, slurring his words and pointing at Christian. "Here comes the king of the party." He sniggered, and Kenneth and Magnus followed suit. Magnus looked like he'd had the most to drink. He was swaying as he sat there, and he was having a hard time focusing.

"Did you bring the admission ticket?" asked Erik, motioning him forward.

Feeling wary, Christian handed him the bottle. Were they going to humiliate him now?

Were they going to chase him away, since he'd brought what they wanted?

But nothing happened. Erik simply opened the bottle, took a big slug of the whiskey, and then handed it back to Christian. He just stared. He wanted to take a drink, but he didn't know if he dared. Erik urged him to try it, and Christian realized that he would have to do as Erik said if he wanted to be part of the group. He sat down with the bottle in his hand, and then raised it to his lips. And just about choked when he swallowed too much of the whiskey, which ran down his throat.

"So how was that, lad?" Laughing, Erik pounded him on the back.

"Good," said Christian, taking another gulp just to prove it.

The bottle passed from hand to hand a few times, and he began to feel a pleasant warmth spreading through his body. His anxiety vanished. The whiskey pushed away everything that had been keeping him awake at night lately. The eyes. The smell of rotting flesh. He took another swallow.

Magnus was lying on his back, staring up at the stars in the sky. Kenneth didn't say much. He just agreed with everything Erik said. But Christian was enjoying being in their company. He was somebody. Part of a group.

"Christian?" a voice said from nearby. He

turned to look. What was she doing here? Why did she have to turn up and ruin everything? His old anger awoke.

"Get lost," he snarled, and then he saw her face contort in disappointment.

"Christian?" she repeated, her voice thick with tears.

He got up to chase her away, but Erik put his hand on Christian's arm.

"Let her stay," he said, and Christian looked at him in surprise. But he complied and sat down again.

"Come here!" Erik waved for Alice to come closer.

She gave Christian an inquiring glance, but he merely shrugged.

"Sit down," said Erik. "We're having a party."

"Party!" said Alice, her face lighting up.

"What luck that you happened to stop by. We need some pretty girls here too." Erik put his arm around Alice and touched a lock of her dark hair. Alice laughed. She liked being called pretty.

"Here. If you want to come to our party, you have to drink." He took the bottle away from Kenneth, who was just about to take a swig, and handed it to Alice.

Again she looked at Christian, but he didn't care what she did. If she was going to keep following him, she'd just have to play along.

She started to cough, and Erik stroked her back. "There, there, what a good girl. Don't worry, you'll get used to it. You just have to try again."

Hesitantly she raised the bottle and took another swallow. This time it went better.

"Good. That's the kind of girl I like. Someone who's pretty and knows how to drink whiskey," said Erik with a smile that made Christian's stomach start to churn. He wanted to take Alice by the hand and lead her home. But then Kenneth sat down next to him, put an arm around his shoulder, and mumbled:

"Shit, Christian, just think — here we are with you and your sister. I bet you never thought that would happen, did you? But we knew there was a bloody decent lad under all that flab." Kenneth pointed at Christian's stomach, and Christian didn't know whether to take his remark as a compliment or not.

"She's really cute, your sister," said Erik, moving even closer to Alice. He helped her raise the bottle again, pouring more whiskey down her throat. Her eyes were shining, and she had a big smile on her face.

Christian suddenly felt everything start to spin. All of Badholmen was spinning. Around and around, like the globe. He giggled and lay down on his back next to Magnus, looking up at the stars that seemed to be whirling through the sky.

A sound from Alice made him sit up. He was having a hard time focusing, but he could see Erik and Alice. And he thought Erik had his hand inside Alice's shirt. But he wasn't sure, with everything spinning around him. He lay down again.

"Shh. . . ." Erik's voice and the same whimpering sound from Alice. Christian rolled onto his side and rested his head on his outstretched arm. He looked at Erik and his sister. Her shirt was gone. She had small, perfect breasts. That was the first thought that occurred to him. That she had perfect breasts. He'd never seen them before.

"Don't worry. I'm just going to feel them a little. . . ." Erik kneaded her breasts with his hands as he started breathing harder. Kenneth was staring at Alice's bare torso.

"Come and feel," said Erik, nodding to Kenneth.

Christian saw that Alice was scared, that she was trying to cover her breasts with her arms. But his head felt so heavy that he couldn't lift it.

Kenneth sat down next to Alice. After waiting for a signal from Erik, he lifted his hand and began touching her left breast. He squeezed it cautiously at first, then harder, and Christian could see the bulge in his shorts grow.

"I wonder if the rest is just as nice?" murmured Erik. "What do you say, Alice? Is your pussy just as nice as your tits?"

Her eyes were big and frightened. But she didn't seem to know how to defend herself. Without resistance, she allowed Erik to slip her panties off. He let her keep her skirt on, just lifting it up to show Kenneth.

"What do you think? I doubt anyone's been here before." He pushed her knees apart, and Alice numbly let him do it, incapable of protesting.

"Shit, check this out. Magnus, wake up! You're missing something here."

Magnus merely groaned. A faint drunken muttering.

Christian could feel the lump in his stomach growing. This was wrong. He could see Alice staring at him, wordlessly pleading for help. But her eyes looked just like they had when she'd looked up at him from underwater, and he couldn't make himself move, couldn't help her. All he could do was lie on his side and let the world keep spinning.

"I get first dibs," said Erik, unbuttoning his shorts. "Hold her down if she starts fighting."

Kenneth nodded. His face was pale, but he couldn't take his eyes off Alice's breasts gleaming white in the moonlight. Erik forced her down onto her back, forced her to lie still and stare up at the sky. At first Christian felt relieved that her eyes had disappeared. They were staring at the stars instead of at him. Then the lump inside him grew, and with an effort he hauled himself into a sitting position. The voices were screaming at him, and he knew that he should do something, but he didn't know what. Alice didn't say a word. She just lay there and let Erik separate her legs, let him lie down on top of her, push inside her.

He began sobbing. Why did she have to ruin everything? Take what was his, follow him everywhere, love him? He had never asked her to love him. He hated her. And she just lay there.

Erik suddenly stopped moving, then groaned. He pulled out and buttoned his fly. He lit a cigarette, cupping his hand around the match, and then looked at Kenneth.

"Your turn."

"You mean me?" stammered Kenneth.

"Yes, now it's your turn," said Erik, and his tone of voice demanded obedience.

Kenneth hesitated. Then he looked at Alice's breasts again, those firm breasts with the pink nipples that had turned hard in the summer breeze. Slowly he began unbuttoning his shorts, then he started moving faster until he practically threw himself on top of Alice and began thrusting at her. It didn't take long before he too groaned, his body rippling with spasms.

"Impressive," said Erik, puffing on his cigarette. "Now it's Magnus's turn." He pointed at Magnus, who had fallen asleep, drooling saliva out of the corner of his mouth.

"Magnus? He'll never be able to do it. He's too sloshed." Kenneth laughed. He wasn't looking at Alice anymore.

"Then we'll have to help him out," said Erik, lifting Magnus up. "Come on, give me a hand," he said to Kenneth, who rushed to his side. Together they dragged Magnus over to Alice, and Erik began unbuttoning his trousers.

"Pull down his underpants," he ordered Kenneth, who, with an expression of distaste, did as he was told.

Magnus wasn't ready to do anything, and for a moment Erik looked annoyed. He gave Magnus a few kicks, which woke him up a bit.

"Let's just put him down on top of her. But he's going to fuck her too."

The voices were quieter now, echoing inside his head. Christian felt like he was watching a film, not something that was actually happening, or something he was participating in. He saw how they dropped Magnus down on top of Alice, how he woke up enough to start making disgusting animal-like sounds. He never got as far as the others; just passed out halfway through, his body heavy on top of Alice.

But Erik was satisfied. He dragged Magnus off because he was ready again. The sight of Alice lying there, so beautiful and remote, seemed to excite him. Harder and harder he thrust into her, holding her long hair wrapped around his hand and pulling so hard that he pulled out big tufts of it.

Then she started to scream. The sound was sudden and unexpected, piercing the night, and Erik abruptly stopped. He looked down at her. Began to panic. He needed to make her stop screaming.

Christian heard the screams forcing their way into his silence. He put his hands over his ears, but that didn't help. It was the same screaming as it had been when she was a baby, when she took everything away from him. He saw how Erik was sitting astride her, saw him raise his hand and then hit her, how he too was trying to make the screams stop. Alice's head thumped against the wooden deck with each blow, bouncing up as it struck. And then came the sound of something crunching as Erik's fist struck the bones of her face. He saw how Kenneth, very pale, was staring at Erik. And Magnus had been awakened by the screaming. He sat up groggily, looking at Erik and Alice and his own unbuttoned trousers.

Then the screams stopped. It was very quiet. And Christian fled. He got up and ran — away from Alice, away from Badholmen. He ran home, in through the front door, and upstairs to his room, where he got into bed and pulled the blanket over his head, over the voices.

Slowly the world stopped spinning.

26

"We left her there." Kenneth couldn't make himself look at Erica. "We just left her there."

"Then what happened?" asked Erica. She still didn't sound reproachful, which made him feel even worse.

"I was terrified. In the morning when I woke up, I thought at first that it was all a bad dream, but when I realized that it really did happen, that we really had. . . ." His voice broke. "All day I waited for the police to knock on the door."

"But they didn't?"

"No. A couple of days later, we heard that the Lissanders had moved away."

"What about the three of you? Did you talk about it?"

"No, never. It wasn't that we agreed not to talk about it, we just never did. Until that Midsummer party when Magnus had a little too much to drink and he brought up the topic."

"That was the first time?" asked Erica in disbelief.

"Yes, that was the first time. But I knew that he was suffering. He was the one who had the hardest time living with what we'd done. I somehow managed to suppress it. I focused on Lisbet and my life. Chose to forget. And Erik . . . well, he didn't even need to forget. I don't think it bothered him at all."

"And yet the three of you remained friends all these years."

"Yes, and I don't really know why. But we . . . deserved this." He motioned with his bandaged arms. "I deserve even worse, but Lisbet didn't. She was completely innocent. The worst thing is that she must have learned what happened. I think that was the last thing she heard before she died. I wasn't the person she thought I was. Our life together was a sham." He was trying to hold back the tears.

"What the three of you did was horrible," said Erica. "There's no other way to describe it. But the life you had with Lisbet was not a sham, and I think she knew that. No matter what she was told."

"I'm going to try to explain it to her," he

said. "I know that it's my turn next. She's going to come for me too, and then I'll have a chance to explain. I have to believe that's possible, or else. . . ." He turned his face away.

"What do you mean? Who's coming for you?"

"Alice, of course." Hadn't Erica heard anything he'd said? "She's the one who's been doing all this."

At first Erica didn't reply. She just looked at him with pity.

"It's not Alice," she said then. "It's not Alice."

Patrik closed up the book. He didn't understand everything — it was a little too deep for his taste, and the language was somewhat convoluted in places — but he'd been able to follow the basic story line. And he realized that he should have read the book earlier, because certain things were now becoming clear.

A memory surfaced in his mind. A fleeting image of the bedroom belonging to Cia and Magnus. Something he'd noticed but hadn't thought important at the time. There was really no reason why it should have caught his attention, but he still couldn't help reproaching himself.

He tapped in the number on his mobile.

"Hi, Ludvig. Is your mother home?" He stayed on the line as he listened to Ludvig's footsteps and the faint murmur of voices. Then Cia picked up the phone.

"Hi, it's Patrik Hedström. I'm sorry to bother you, but I've been wondering about one thing. What did Magnus do on the night before he disappeared? No, I don't mean the whole evening, just after you'd gone to bed. He did? All night? Okay, thanks."

He ended the conversation. It fit. Everything fit. But he knew he wouldn't get far on theory alone. He needed concrete proof. And he wasn't about to tell his colleagues his idea until he had that proof, because otherwise they might not believe him. But there was one person he could talk to, one person who should be able to help. He reached for his phone again.

"Sweetheart, I know you're not picking up because you think that I'm mad at you or that I'll try to persuade you to stop what you're doing. But I just finished reading *The Mermaid,* and I think we're both on the same track. I need your help, so call me back as soon as you can. Hugs and kisses. I love you."

"The documents from Göteborg are here," said a voice from the doorway, making Patrik jump.

"Oi, did I scare you?" asked Annika. "I knocked, but I guess you didn't hear me."

"No, I was thinking about something else," he said, giving himself a shake.

"I think you should go over to the clinic for a checkup," Annika told him. "You're not looking well."

"I'm just a bit tired," he murmured. "But that's great news about the documents. I've got to go home for a while, so I'll take them with me."

"They're on my desk in the reception area." She was still looking worried.

Ten minutes later, Patrik stepped out into the corridor, carrying the papers that Annika had given him.

"Patrik!" called Gösta behind him.

"Yes?" he said, sounding more annoyed than he had intended. But he was in a hurry to get going.

"I've just talked to Erik Lind's wife. Louise."

"And?" said Patrik, still without any show of enthusiasm.

"According to her, Erik is about to leave the country. He emptied all their bank accounts, both their personal accounts and the ones belonging to the company. He's booked on a plane leaving from Landvetter at five o'clock."

"Really?" said Patrik. His interest was now definitely aroused.

"Yes, I've checked it out. What do you want us to do?"

"Take Martin and leave for Göteborg immediately. I'll make a call to make the necessary arrangements and ask our colleagues to meet you at the airport."

"That'll be a real pleasure for me!"

Patrik couldn't help smiling as he headed for his car. Gösta was right. It would be a pleasure to throw a monkey wrench into Erik's plans. Then Patrik thought about the book he'd just read, and his smile disappeared. He hoped Erica would be at home when he got there. He needed her help to put an end to this case.

Patrik had come to the same conclusion. Erica understood that, as soon as she heard his message on her voicemail. But he didn't know everything. He hadn't heard the story that Kenneth had told her.

She'd been forced to make a detour to Hamburgsund to take care of something. But when she was back out on the highway, she stomped on the accelerator. There really wasn't any reason to hurry, but she was feeling impatient. It was time for all the secrets to be revealed.

As she turned into the driveway at their house, she saw Patrik's car parked in front. She had phoned him to say that she was on her way and to ask if she should meet him at the police station. But by that time he was already at home, waiting for her. And for her piece of the puzzle.

"Hi, sweetheart." Erica went into the kitchen and gave her husband a kiss.

"I've read the book," he said.

She nodded. "I should have worked it out sooner. But I had read an unfinished manuscript. And in stages — not all in one sitting. I still don't know how I could have missed it, though."

"I should have read the book earlier," said Patrik. "Magnus read it the night before he disappeared. Which was also most likely the night before he died. Christian had given him the manuscript. I just talked to Cia, and she said that Magnus started reading it in the evening and surprised her by staying up all night to finish it. She asked him about it in the morning, wanting to know whether it was a good book. But he told her that he didn't want to discuss it until after he'd talked to Christian. The worst part is that if we go back and look through our notes, I'm sure we'll find that Cia mentioned this before. We just didn't think it was important and never gave it a second thought."

"Magnus must have understood everything after he read the manuscript," said Erica quietly. "And realized who Christian was."

"And Christian must have intended for him to find out. Otherwise he never would have given Magnus the manuscript."

"But why Magnus? Why not Kenneth or Erik?"

"I think Christian was drawn back here to Fjällbacka, and to all three of the men," said Erica, thinking about what the psychiatrist Thorvald had said. "It may seem strange, and he probably couldn't explain it himself. Then I think he may have actually grown to like Magnus. From everything I've heard about him, Magnus seems to have been a very nice person. He was also the one who participated against his will."

"How do you know that?" asked Patrik, giving a start. "In the novel, it just says that three boys were involved. But there aren't a lot of details."

"I had a talk with Kenneth," said Erica calmly. "He told me everything about what happened on that night." Then she recounted Kenneth's story, as Patrik's face grew paler and paler.

"Bloody hell. And they got away with it. Why didn't the Lissanders ever report the rape? Why did they just leave Fjällbacka and then send Alice away?"

"I don't know. But I'm sure that Christian's foster parents could answer those questions."

"So Erik, Kenneth, and Magnus raped Alice while Christian watched. Why didn't he try to stop them? Why didn't he help her? Is that why he got those threatening letters, even though he didn't participate in the assault?"

Some of the color had returned to Patrik's face, and he took a deep breath before he went on:

"Alice is the only one who had any reason to seek revenge, but she can't be the one who did it. We also don't know who's to blame for this." He shoved a stack of papers over to Erica. "Here's all the documentation from the investigation into the murders of Maria and Emil. They were drowned in their own bathtub. Someone held a one-year-old boy under the water until he stopped breathing, and then did the same thing with his mother. The only clue the police had was that a neighbor saw a woman with long dark hair leaving the apartment. But as I said, it couldn't have been Alice, and I don't think it was Iréne either, even though she would also have a motive for doing such a thing. So who the hell was that woman?" He pounded his fist on the table out of sheer frustration.

Erica waited for him to calm down. Then she said quietly:

"I think I know. And I think I can prove it to you."

Erik carefully brushed his teeth, put on his suit, and meticulously knotted his tie. Then he combed his hair and finished by ruffling it a bit with his fingers. He looked at himself in the mirror with satisfaction. He was a handsome and successful man who had his life under control.

He picked up his suitcase in one hand and his carry-on bag in the other. The plane ticket had been left for him at the front desk and was now securely stowed in his jacket pocket, along with his passport. He took one last look in the mirror and then left the hotel room. He'd have time for a beer at the airport before boarding the plane. He could sit there in peace and quiet, watching all the Swedes rushing about, knowing that soon he would no longer have to deal with them. He'd never been especially fond of the Swedish temperament. Too much group

thinking, too much talk about how everything had to be fair. Life wasn't fair. Some
people had better qualities than others. And
in another country, he would have a good
chance of taking advantage of those qualities.

He would soon be on his way. His fear of
her was something that he pushed aside,
burying it deep in his subconscious. Soon it
wouldn't matter. She would never be able
to find him.

"How do we get inside?" asked Patrik as
they stood at the door of the boathouse.
Erica hadn't wanted to say anything more
about what she knew or suspected. She just
insisted that he come with her.

"I picked up the keys from Sanna," said
Erica, taking a big key ring out of her purse.

Patrik smiled. Erica was nothing if not
resourceful.

"What are we looking for?" he asked as he
followed his wife into the small building.

She didn't answer his question directly,
but said, "This is the only place I could
think of that Christian had all to himself."

"Doesn't the boathouse belong to Sanna?"
Patrik asked, blinking his eyes to get used
to the dim lighting.

"On paper, yes. But this was where Christian always retreated in order to be alone and to write. I think he must have considered it his private refuge."

"And?" said Patrik, sitting down on the narrow sofa next to the wall. He was so tired that his legs couldn't really hold him up any longer.

"I don't know." Erica looked around uncertainly. "I just thought that. . . ."

"What did you think?" said Patrik. The boathouse wasn't much of a hiding place, no matter what they were looking for. It consisted of two minuscule rooms, and the ceiling was so low that Patrik had to stoop. The place was filled with old fishing gear, and over by the window stood a worn drop-leaf table. Anyone who sat there would have a magnificent view of the Fjällbacka archipelago. And of Badholmen.

"I hope we find out soon," said Patrik as he stared at the diving tower, a looming black shape against the sky.

"Find out what?" Erica was aimlessly roaming about in the cramped space.

"Whether it was murder or suicide."

"You mean Christian?" said Erica, but she didn't wait for his answer. "If only I could find . . . damn it, I thought . . . then we'd be able to. . . ." She was muttering incoher-

686

ently, and Patrik couldn't help laughing at her.

"You look like you're really confused," he said. "Can't you at least tell me what we're looking for? Then maybe I could help."

"I think Magnus was murdered here. And I was hoping I could find something. . . ." She scrutinized the rough, blue-painted wooden walls.

"Here?" Patrik got up and began studying the walls too. Then he looked at the floor and, after a moment, he said:

"The rug."

"What do you mean? It's perfectly clean."

"Exactly. It's too clean. In fact, it looks brand-new. Here, help me lift it up." He grabbed ahold of one end of the heavy rag rug. With an effort, Erica picked up the other end.

"Oh, sorry, sweetheart. It might be too heavy for you. Don't strain yourself," said Patrik with concern as he heard his very pregnant wife puffing.

"It's okay," she said. "Come on, let's do it instead of standing here chattering."

They moved the rug aside and looked at the wooden floorboards underneath. They looked very clean.

"Maybe in the other room?" said Erica. But when they glanced inside, they saw a floor that was equally clean, and without any rug on top.

"I wonder if. . . ."

"What?" asked Erica, but Patrik didn't answer. Instead, he knelt down on the floor and began examining the cracks between the floorboards. After a moment, he stood up.

"We need to get the tech guys over here and then wait for their results. But I think you're right. The place has been meticulously cleaned, but it looks like blood ran down between the planks."

"If that's true, shouldn't the planks have soaked up some of the blood too?" said Erica.

"Yes, but that would be hard to see with the naked eye if someone scrubbed the floor afterwards." Patrik squinted at the old planks, which were discolored with age in numerous places.

"So he died here?" Even though Erica had been sure of her theory, she could still feel her heart beating faster.

"Yes, I think so. And this place is close to the water, where the body could be dumped. So now will you tell me what's going on?"

"Let's take another look around first," she said, ignoring the look of frustration on Patrik's face. "Go and check up there." She pointed to the attic above them. The only access was by means of a rope ladder.

"Are you kidding?"

"It's either you or me." And Erica demonstratively placed her hands on her huge stomach.

"Okay," he said with a sigh. "I suppose it's easy enough to climb up there. And I assume you're still not going to tell me what I'm looking for, right?"

"I'm not really sure," said Erica truthfully. "I just have a feeling that. . . ."

"A feeling? I'm supposed to climb up a rope ladder because of a feeling?"

"Just do it."

Patrik went up the ladder and crawled inside the attic.

"Do you see anything?" Erica called, craning her neck.

"Of course I see something. But it's mostly old blankets, rags, and a few comic books. It looks like the kids' cubbyhole."

"Nothing else?" said Erica, feeling discouraged.

"No, it doesn't look like it."

Patrik began coming back down the rope ladder but then stopped midway.

"What's in there?"

"Where?"

"In there." He was pointing to a hatch

door right next to the opening to the attic.

"That's usually where people store their junk in boathouses, but let's check."

"Okay, take it easy. I'll do it." He tried to balance on the ladder as he used one hand to jiggle the hasp loose. He could see that it was possible to lift away the entire hatch door, so he gripped one side of it, pulled it off, and handed it to Erica below. Then he turned to look inside.

"What the hell?" he said in surprise.

Suddenly the hooks that attached the ladder to the ceiling gave way, and with a crash Patrik fell to the floor.

Louise filled a wine glass with mineral water, then raised it to drink a toast. It would soon be all over for him. The police officer she'd spoken to had understood immediately what was going on. And he'd told her that they would be taking prompt action. He had also thanked her for calling. "You're very welcome," she had replied. "It was my pleasure."

I wonder what they'll do with him, she mused. The idea hadn't really occurred to Louise until now. Her only thought was to stop him, prevent him from fleeing like a cowardly brute with his tail between his legs. But what would happen if Erik was sent to prison? Would she still get all the money back? She started feeling anxious but then calmed down. Of course she'd get the money back. And she planned to thoroughly enjoy spending every öre of it. He would sit there in his prison cell, knowing that she was using up all of his — and her — money. And he wouldn't be able to do shit about it.

Suddenly she made up her mind. She wanted to see his expression. She wanted to see how he looked when he realized it was all over.

"I've seen a lot in my day, but this . . . this takes the cake," said Torbjörn. He was standing on the ladder that they'd borrowed from the boathouse next door.

"It really does beat all," said Patrik, rubbing the small of his back, which he'd hit hard when he fell. His chest was aching a bit too.

"There's no doubt that it's blood, at any rate. And a lot of it." Torbjörn pointed at the floor, which now had an odd sheen to it. The luminol revealed all traces of blood, no matter how much the surface had been scrubbed. "We've taken a few samples that the lab should be able to match with the victim's blood."

"Good. Thanks."

"So these things belong to Christian Thydell?" said Torbjörn. "The man we cut down from the diving tower?" He crawled into the small space, and Patrik cautiously climbed up the ladder to join him.

"That's what it looks like."

"But why . . . ?" Torbjörn began but then stopped himself. This wasn't his case. His task was to secure the technical evidence, and with time he'd have all the answers. He pointed.

"Is this the letter you were talking about?"

"Yes. At least it proves that his death was definitely a suicide."

"Indeed," said Torbjörn, although he still didn't seem to believe his eyes. The whole space was filled with female belongings. Clothes, makeup, jewelry, shoes. And a wig with long, dark hair.

"We're going to bring everything in. It'll take a while to collect it all." Torbjörn carefully backed up until he reached the edge of the hatch and could lower his feet onto the ladder. "I've seen a lot of things in my day . . . ," he muttered again.

"I'm going back to the station. There are a number of matters I need to review before I can present my report to everyone," said Patrik. "Give me a ring later, after you've finished here." He turned to Paula, who was intently watching the crime techs as they worked.

"Are you staying here?"

"Absolutely," she said.

Patrik left the boathouse and took a deep breath of the fresh sea air outdoors. After they found Christian's hiding place, Erica had told him more of the story. Combined with the letter they'd found, the pieces of the puzzle were now falling into place, one by one. It was incomprehensible, but he knew that it was true. He understood everything now. And when Gösta and Martin came back from Göteborg, he'd be able to explain the whole sad tale to his colleagues.

"It's almost two hours until the plane takes off. We didn't really need to get here so early." Martin glanced at his watch as they approached Landvetter Airport.

"I don't think we need to just sit on our tails and wait for him," said Gösta as he turned in to the car park outside the international terminal. "Let's go in and take a look around, and if we find him, we nab the son-of-a-bitch."

"Shouldn't we wait for backup from Göteborg?" asked Martin. It always made him anxious if things weren't done by the book.

"You and I can easily handle this guy," said Gösta.

"Okay," said Martin doubtfully.

They climbed out of the car and went inside the airport.

"So, how should we do this?" Martin glanced around the terminal.

"How about a cup of coffee? We can survey the scene at the same time."

"But shouldn't we walk around and look for Erik?"

"What did I just say?" said Gösta. "We can keep an eye out for him at the same time. If we sit over there," and he pointed to a coffee stand in the middle of the departure hall, "we'll have an excellent view in both directions. He'll have to walk past us when he gets here."

"Okay, you're right about that," Martin relented. He knew there was no use arguing once Gösta had set his mind on having a cup of coffee.

They each bought coffee and an almond cake. Then they sat down at a table. Gösta beamed as he took his first bite.

"This is food for the soul."

Martin didn't bother to point out that an almond cake didn't really count as food. But he couldn't deny that it was delicious. He had just stuffed the last piece in his mouth when he caught sight of someone out of the corner of his eye.

"Look, isn't that him?"

Gösta quickly turned around.

"Yup. You're right. Come on, let's bring him in." He stood up with unusual speed, and Martin jumped up to follow. Erik was walking away at a good clip, with a carry-on bag in one hand and a big suitcase in the other. He was impeccably dressed in a suit and tie with a white shirt.

Gösta and Martin had to jog to catch up with him. Since Gösta had been the first to get up from the table, he reached Erik first, clapping a hand on the man's shoulder.

"Erik Lind? We're going to have to ask you to come with us."

Erik turned around with a look of surprise on his face. For a second, he seemed to consider running, but he settled for shaking off Gösta's hand.

"There must be some sort of misunderstanding. I'm leaving on a business trip," he said. "I don't know what this is about, but I have a plane to catch. I'm going to an important meeting." Beads of sweat had appeared on his forehead.

"I'm afraid you'll still have to come with us. You'll have a chance to present your own explanations a little later," said Gösta, ushering Erik toward the exit. Everyone nearby had stopped to stare.

"I'm telling you that I have to get on that plane!"

"I understand," said Gösta calmly. Then he turned to Martin. "Would you mind taking his baggage?"

Martin nodded but swore inwardly. He never got to do the fun stuff.

"So it was Christian?" Anna's mouth fell open in surprise.

"Yes — and no," said Erica. "I talked to Thorvald about it, and we'll never know for sure. But by all indications, that's what happened."

"Christian had a split personality? And his two selves didn't know about each other?" Anna sounded skeptical. She'd come right over when Erica phoned after returning from the boathouse. Patrik had to go back to the station, and Erica didn't want to be alone. Her sister Anna was the only one she wanted to confide in about everything she'd found out.

"Apparently. Thorvald suspected that Christian must have been schizophrenic. His disease also showed aspects of what's called dissociative identity disorder. That was what caused the split in his personality.

It can stem from an enormous amount of stress, as a way of dealing with reality. And Christian definitely had some terribly traumatic events in his baggage. First his mother's death and the week that he spent with her body. Then what, in my opinion, was outright child abuse, if not psychotic behavior, at the hands of Iréne Lissander. The way that Christian's foster parents decided to ignore him after Alice was born must have felt like being abandoned all over again. And so he blamed the baby — he blamed Alice."

"And he tried to drown her?" Anna placed a protective hand on her stomach.

"Yes. Alice's father saved her, but she suffered serious brain damage from oxygen deprivation. Mr. Lissander decided to protect Christian by never speaking of what happened. He probably thought he was doing the boy a service, but I'm not sure he made the right decision. Imagine growing up knowing that you'd done something like that. And with the guilt. The older Christian got, the more aware he became of what he'd done. And his feelings of guilt were probably even greater because Alice loved him."

"In spite of what he'd done to her."

"She never knew. Nobody knew, except

for Ragnar Lissander and Christian."

"And then the rape."

"Yes. Then the rape," said Erica, and she felt her throat close up. She counted up everything that had happened in Christian's life, as if it were a mathematical problem that was finally solved. But in reality, it was a tragedy.

The phone rang and she answered.

"Erica Falck. Yes? No. No, I have no comment. Don't call me again." And she angrily slammed down the phone.

"What was that all about?" asked Anna.

"A newspaper reporter. They wanted me to say something about Christian's death. The vultures are circling again. And they don't even know the whole story yet." She sighed. "Poor, poor Sanna."

"But when did Christian get sick?" Anna was still looking confused, and Erica could understand why. She had asked tons of follow-up questions when she talked to Thorvald, and he had patiently tried to answer all of them.

"His mother was schizophrenic, and it's an inherited condition. It often surfaces during the teenage years, and that's when Christian may have started to notice something was wrong without fully understanding it. A sense of anxiety, dreams, voices, visions — there are many different symptoms. Mr. and Mrs. Lissander probably never noticed, because he left home right about that time. Or rather, he was chased away."

"Chased away?"

"Yes, that's what it said in the letter that Christian left in the boathouse. The Lissanders assumed, without even investigating, that Christian was the one who had raped Alice. And he didn't defend himself. Presumably he felt so guilty because he hadn't intervened and protected her, that he thought he might as well have done it himself. But that's just my own speculation," said Erica.

"So they threw him out?"

"Yes, and at the moment I can't say how that might have affected his disease. But Patrik should look for some sort of medical case files. If Christian received any type of care or treatment when he arrived in Göteborg, there should be a record somewhere. It's just a matter of finding it."

Erica paused. It was so hard for her to comprehend everything that Christian must have gone through. And everything he had done.

"Patrik thinks that the police will reopen the investigation into the murders of the woman that Christian was living with, and her little boy," she went on. "Considering everything that has now come to light."

"Do they think that Christian killed them too? But why?"

"It's highly likely that we'll never know for sure whether he did it," said Erica. "Or why. If the other part of his personality — the Mermaid, or Alice, whatever you want to call her — was mad at the Christian part, maybe she couldn't stand to see him happy. That's Thorvald's theory, anyway, and he may be right. Perhaps Christian's happiness unleashed something. But as I said, I don't think we'll ever really know the answer."

In reality she had nothing against either the child or the woman. She didn't really mean them any harm. Yet she couldn't allow them to continue to live. They did something that no one had ever done before: they made Christian happy.

He laughed often now. A carefree, hearty laugh that came from his stomach and bubbled upward. She hated that laugh. For her part, she was no longer able to laugh; she was empty and cold inside, dead. He had been dead too, but thanks to the woman and the child, he was now alive.

Sometimes he would watch them in secret. The woman carrying the child in her arms. They would dance, and he would smile when the child laughed. He was happy, but he didn't deserve it. He'd taken everything from her, lowered her down into the water until her lungs felt like they would burst, until her brain took in no oxygen, and it was as if she were slowly being extinguished while the water rose up to cover her face.

Yet in spite of it all, she had loved him. He was everything for her. She didn't care about the others, didn't care about how they looked at him. For her, he was the nicest and handsomest person on earth. Her hero.

But he had betrayed her. Allowed them to take her, violate her, and hit her until the bones in her face were broken. He had allowed her to lie there, staring up at the starry sky with her legs apart. And then he had fled.

Now she no longer loved him, and no one else would be allowed to love him either. Just as he would not be allowed to love anyone. Not the way he loved the woman in the blue dress, and the child, who wasn't even his.

He wasn't at home right now. As usual, the door wasn't locked. The woman was careless. He was always scolding her about it, telling her that she should lock the door, that they never knew who might try to get in.

Cautiously she pressed down on the handle and opened the door. She heard the woman humming in the kitchen. A splashing sound came from the bathroom. The child was sitting in the tub, which meant the woman would be going into the bathroom at any minute. She was careful about such things. Never leaving the child alone in the bath for very long.

She went into the bathroom. The boy's face lit up like a sun when he saw her.

"Shhh," she said, opening her eyes wide as if it were a game. The child laughed. As she listened for approaching footsteps, she went over to the tub and stared down at the naked child. It wasn't the boy's fault, but he made Christian happy. And that was something she couldn't allow.

She took the child by the arms and lifted him up a bit so she could lay him down on his back in the tub. The boy was still laughing. Happy and secure in the belief that nothing bad could happen in the world. When the water closed over his face, he stopped laughing and started flailing his arms and legs about. But it wasn't difficult to hold the child down. She simply put one hand on his chest and pressed lightly. The child flailed harder and harder until his movements began to taper off, and then he lay still.

Now she heard the woman's footsteps. She looked down at the child. He looked so calm and peaceful lying there. She stood up with her back against the wall, just to the right of the door opening. The woman came into the bathroom. When she saw the child, she stopped abruptly. Then she screamed and rushed forward.

It was almost as easy as it had been with

the child. Silently she slipped forward and grabbed the neck of the woman, who was leaning over the edge of the tub. She used her own weight to hold the woman's head underwater. It took less time than expected.

She didn't look back as she left. Merely felt a sense of satisfaction spreading through her body. Christian was not going to be happy anymore.

27

Patrik was looking at the drawings. And all of a sudden he understood. The big figure and the small one — Christian and Alice. And in one of the drawings the black figures that were so much darker than the rest.

Christian had taken the guilt onto his own shoulders. Patrik had just talked with Ragnar, who had confirmed it. When Alice came home that night, he and his wife assumed that it was Christian who had raped her. They had been awakened by a scream, and when they got out of bed to find out what was going on, they found Alice lying on the floor in the front hall. She was wearing only a skirt, and her face was bloody and swollen. When they rushed over to her, she said only one word.

"Christian," she whispered.

Iréne rushed upstairs to his room and yanked him out of bed. She smelled the booze on him and immediately drew her own conclusions. To be fair, Ragnar had thought the same thing, although he did have some doubt. Maybe that was why he kept sending Alice's drawings to Christian. Because he'd never been certain about what actually happened.

Gösta and Martin had managed to nab Erik before he got on the plane. Patrik had just received a report, telling him that they were on their way back from Landvetter. That was something. Later they would have to see what was legally possible, so many years after the fact. At least Kenneth was not going to keep silent any more; Erica was convinced of that. And if nothing else, Erik had a lot of explaining to do with regard to his financial dealings. He'd probably end up behind bars, at least for a while. But considering the circumstances, that seemed like small comfort.

"The newspapers have started calling!" Mellberg came rushing in, beaming like a sun. "It's about to get very lively around here. Great publicity for the station."

"I suppose so," said Patrik, still looking at the drawings.

"We did a really good job on this case, Hedström! I have to admit it. It took us a while, but once we picked up the pace and did some good old-fashioned police work, the path was clear."

"Right," said Patrik. Today he didn't even have the energy to feel annoyed by Mellberg. He rubbed his hand over his chest. It still hurt. He must have banged himself harder than he thought when the ladder collapsed.

"It's probably best that I go back to my office," said Mellberg. "A reporter from *Aftonbladet* just phoned, and it's only a matter of time before somebody from *Expressen* calls too."

"Hmm," said Patrik as he kept rubbing his chest. Damn, it hurt. Maybe the pain would ease up if he moved a bit. He got up and went into the kitchen. How typical. Whenever he wanted a cup of coffee, the pot was empty.

Paula came in. "We've finished over there. I'm completely speechless. I would never have suspected any of this."

"I guess not," said Patrik. He realized how unkind that sounded, but he was so tired. He didn't feel like talking about the case, didn't want to think about Alice and Christian, or about a little boy who kept vigil over his dead mother's body as it rotted in the summer heat.

Keeping his eyes fixed on the coffee machine, he put in several scoops. How many was that? Two or three? He couldn't remember. He tried to concentrate, but the next scoopful landed outside the machine. He put the scoop in the package of ground coffee to take out some more, but a sharp pain in his chest made him gasp for air.

"Patrik, what's the matter? Patrik?" He heard Paula's voice, but it was coming from far, far away. He ignored it, wanting to finish putting more coffee in the machine, but his hand refused to obey. He saw a flash of light before his eyes, and the pain in his chest was suddenly a thousand times worse. He managed to think that something was wrong, that something was about to happen.

Then everything went black.

"Did he send the threatening letters to himself?" Anna asked, shifting her position a little. The baby was pressing on her bladder, and she actually needed to pee, but she couldn't tear herself away.

"Yes, and to the others too," said Erica. "We don't know whether Magnus got any. Most likely not."

"Why did the letters start coming when he began working on the book?"

"Again, we only have theories to go on. But according to Thorvald, it might have been difficult for Christian to keep taking the medication for schizophrenia at the same time as he was writing the book. The medicine can have significant side effects, such as fatigue and lethargy, and maybe it made it hard for him to focus on the writing. My guess is that he stopped taking the medicine, and that's when the illness flared up, after being kept in check for so many years. And then the identity disorder also manifested itself. The foremost object of Christian's hatred was himself, and I presume that he couldn't cope with the guilt that had been getting worse and worse. So he split himself in two: Christian, who tried to forget and live a normal life; and the Mermaid, or Alice, who hated Christian and wanted him to bear the guilt."

Erica continued patiently trying to explain. It wasn't easy to understand; in fact, it was really an impossible task. Thorvald had been careful to emphasize that the disease rarely took such an extreme form. This was by no means an ordinary case. But Christian had not had an ordinary life. He'd had to endure things that would have broken even the strongest person.

"That was also why he took his own life," said Erica. "In the letter he left behind, he said that he was forced to save his sons from her. And the only way to do that was to give her what she wanted. Himself."

"But he was the one who painted the words on the children's wall. *He* was the threat to their safety."

"Yes, exactly. When he realized that he loved his sons, he understood that the only way to protect them was to kill the person who wanted to hurt them. Meaning himself. In his world, the Mermaid was real, not a figment of his imagination. She really existed, and she wanted to kill his family. Just as she had killed Maria and her son Emil. So he saved his boys by taking his own life."

Anna wiped away a tear. "The whole thing is just so awful."

"I agree," said Erica. "It's horrible."

Erica's mobile began ringing shrilly. Annoyed, she picked it up. "If that's some bloody reporter, I'm going to. . . . Hello, this is Erica Falck." Erica's face lit up. "Hi, Annika!" Then her expression changed again, and she gasped. "What did you say? Where did they take him? He is? In Uddevalla?"

Anna looked at Erica with concern. Her big sister's hand had started to shake as she held the phone.

"What is it?" asked Anna when Erica ended the conversation.

Erica swallowed hard. Her eyes were filled with tears.

"Patrik collapsed at work," she whispered. "They think it might be a heart attack. They're taking him in an ambulance to Uddevalla."

For a moment Anna was so shocked she couldn't move. Then she rallied her efficient side, quickly got up, and headed for the front door. The car keys were on the hall bureau, and she went over and grabbed them.

"We're going to Uddevalla. Come on. I'm driving."

Erica followed mutely after her sister. She felt like the whole world was about to fall apart around her.

Louise sped out of the driveway so fast that gravel sprayed up from the tires. She had to hurry. Erik's plane was due to leave in two hours, and she wanted to be there when the police caught him.

She drove fast. It was necessary if she was going to get to the airport in time. But when she reached the filling station, she realized that she'd forgotten her wallet at home. And she didn't have enough gas to make it all the way to Göteborg. She swore loudly and made a U-turn at the intersection. She was going to lose time by driving back to get her wallet, but she had no choice.

Yet it was a magnificent feeling to have taken control. That was what she was thinking as she raced through Fjällbacka. She felt like a new person. Her whole body was pleasantly relaxed; the sense of power made her feel beautiful and strong. Life was splendid, and for the first time in many years, the world was hers.

Erik was going to be surprised. He had probably never thought that she would figure out what he was up to, let alone call the police. She laughed as the car zoomed over the crest of Galärbacken. She was free now. She was going to escape from their humiliating dance. Escape from all the lies and degrading remarks, escape from him. Louise pressed her foot down on the accelerator even harder, really floored it. The car flew forward like a spear, heading toward her new life. She owned the speed, she owned everything. She owned her life.

She didn't see it until it was too late. For just a second she had glanced away to look out toward the sea, marveling at how beautiful the ice was. She only looked away for an instant, but that was enough. She suddenly realized that she had veered into the oncoming lane, and she had time to see two women sitting in the car coming toward her, two women with mouths open wide, screaming.

Then she heard the sound of metal against metal, echoing off the massive rock wall. After that, there was only silence.

ABOUT THE AUTHOR

Camilla Läckberg's novels have all been #1 bestsellers in Sweden, and she is the most successful native author in Swedish history. Her previous novels include *The Ice Princess, The Stonecutter, The Stranger,* and *The Hidden Child.*

The employees of Thorndike Press hope you have enjoyed this Large Print book. All our Thorndike, Wheeler, and Kennebec Large Print titles are designed for easy reading, and all our books are made to last. Other Thorndike Press Large Print books are available at your library, through selected bookstores, or directly from us.

For information about titles, please call:
  (800) 223-1244

or visit our Web site at:
  http://gale.cengage.com/thorndike

To share your comments, please write:
  Publisher
  Thorndike Press
  10 Water St., Suite 310
  Waterville, ME 04901